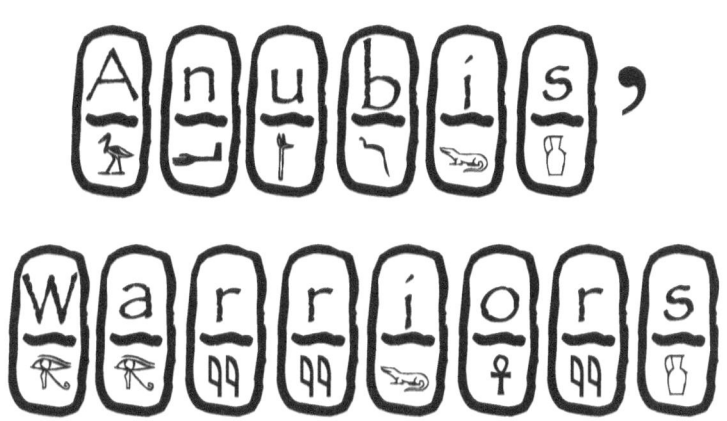

Anubis, Warriors

MARISA CHENERY

CONTENTS

EMBRACED BY A WARRIOR

As a warrior of Anubis, Darius always believed he was destined to be alone. Never to come into contact with others like him, or experience passion in the arms of a woman for more than just one night. After eight hundred years alone, he begins to question what he has always known. He finds a woman who stirs not only his desire, but his heart as well.

Brisa's not blind, so she's very much aware of the hot man who frequents the bar where she works. But he's always been aloof. Throwing caution to the wind, she approaches the sexy stranger and finds herself completely swept away. But a shocking secret and an unsavory demon stand between them. Brisa must decide if she can love a man like Darius...for eternity.

CHAPTER ONE

Darius headed in the direction of the bar he inevitably arrived at once his night was just about over. This habit of getting a drink before he returned to his home had started six months before. Out of the last five years he'd lived in Miami, not once had he'd been drawn to a place as he was to the White Sands Bar.

He knew exactly why he went there night after night. It had nothing to do with the bar's atmosphere. To be honest, Darius really didn't pay much attention to the mortals who sat around him. No, the other patrons would never hold his interest as one mortal in particular would. The image of the woman bartender rose in his mind.

Before Darius let his thoughts wander down a path they shouldn't, he felt a familiar pull on his senses. It was something he couldn't ignore. Something that had him out walking Miami's streets once the sun went down each night.

Changing direction, he followed the invisible trail that tugged him closer to its source. His nose picked up the scent of evil, something only he could smell because of what he was. Ducking down a dark alley, Darius prepared himself for what would play out when he arrived. Even though he'd been through it thousands of times, it still wasn't pleasant to experience.

He reached the end of the alley and turned the corner into a shorter one that dead-ended. And there was the source of the pull. A man had a woman up against the brick wall, a knife held to her throat while he groped her, tearing at her clothes. The woman's whimpers of fear reached Darius' ears.

He walked closer, the man oblivious to Darius' presence. As he did so, Darius felt the change start to take him over. His eyesight was keener, heralding the shift. It happened quickly, but it didn't mean it was any less painful. He growled as his bones realigned themselves, growing larger. He grew taller to stand at almost seven feet. His body shifted to his half-human and half-jackal form, his muscles becoming bigger. Black fur sprouted from his skin until he was completely covered from head to toe. Gold armbands appeared around each of his thick biceps, and last, a snow-white Egyptian-styled kilt formed around his hips to fall to the middle of his thighs.

Having finally caught sight of him, the woman let out a scream. Darius' pointed ears on top of his head twitched, but he ignored her and focused his sights on the man assaulting her. The scent of evil seemed to ooze out of every one of the man's pores. He was Darius' prey. The man didn't know it yet, but he was about to finally get his comeuppance for every evil deed he'd ever done.

With one furred hand, Darius grabbed the man by the back of his shirt collar and threw him. A loud growl rumbled out of him as the man sailed across the narrow alley and slammed into the opposite wall before he slumped to the ground. Darius only took the few seconds needed to snag the frightened woman's gaze and to wipe her memory of him before he sent her on her way.

He turned to the man to find him slowly regaining his feet. Darius moved in to subdue him. His prey slashed out with the knife he still held. Darius blocked it with a sweep of his arm and knocked it from the man's hand. With a snarl, he took hold of his prey by his throat and lifted him off the ground with one hand, the man's feet dangling in the air.

"What the fuck are you?" the man gasped as he struggled for breath.

"The one who sends you to be judged," Darius said, his voice deeper and gruffer in that form.

He pushed into the man's mind, not caring the pain he caused. Scenes of each crime and assault his prey had ever committed flashed through Darius' mind. The screams of the man's victims echoed inside it. Darius lived each one as if he'd been the one on the receiving end. He felt their pain, their terror.

Seeing all he could, Darius definitely knew this one was for Anubis. He willed a gold dagger into his hand. The blade had hieroglyphs carved on it—the spell Anubis had infused into it to send evildoers to the underworld. All it took was one cut to do its job. He sliced it across the man's chest, cutting through his shirt to his skin. His prey gasped some more, clawing at Darius' hand.

It was already too late. The dagger had already done its magic. The man's body lost its solidity, then he was gone. Sent on his way to face the god of the underworld. There, Anubis would weigh the man's heart on the Scales of Justice. If he was evil, his heart would be fed to Ammit to be consumed.

Lowering his arm, Darius willed the dagger away. The shift took hold of him. He growled as the familiar pain tore through him once again. After it was over, he stood in human form, wearing his black jeans and T-shirt. He'd become one of Anubis' warriors back in 1218, as a dying

German soldier lying on the banks of the river Nile, having fought in the fifth crusade to Egypt. Only Anubis had answered his call, not the god Darius had worshipped.

He pushed the thoughts of that fateful day aside. His work done, he headed out of the alley. Once he hit the sidewalk, he backtracked to where he'd been. This time he reached the bar with no interruptions.

Inside, Darius scanned the place with his gaze as he "felt" it out. If there happened to be prey there, he'd have no choice but to act quickly to get that individual outside before Darius shifted. As long as the person wasn't in the middle of an evil deed, the change could be held at bay for a short period of time.

Not feeling a pull, Darius walked farther into the bar and sat at a table at the back corner of the room. He'd learned long ago if he wanted to be around mortals without being set off, he had to choose places where evil did not go. The White Sands Bar was such an establishment.

After a waitress took his order for a beer, he ignored the mortals who sat nearby and focused his gaze across the room at the bar. She was there, working. Darius followed her movements, able to see her face clearly even from that distance with his sharper-than-normal eyesight. His gaze touched on her long, black hair, which hung to the middle of her back. Her hazel eyes crinkled as she smiled at his waitress when she came up to the bar to place his drink order.

Darius could stare at her beautiful face all day. And her slim, curvy body heated his blood, making his cock hard with thoughts of how good she'd feel under him as he took her. Even now he was getting an erection. He let out a deep breath, sighing silently. He wanted her, but he wouldn't approach her. She wasn't the type of woman he'd be able to have a one-night stand with and just walk away. He'd become too obsessed with her. One taste and he'd crave more, which wasn't something he could do. What he was, what he did, left no room for a woman in his life. Besides, he doubted one would be able to accept his being a warrior of Anubis, and what it entailed. No, he was better off alone, only finding a willing woman to slake his lust when his need became too great, then leaving her behind.

*

Brisa took the cap off the bottle of beer she held, knowing it would go to him. She snuck a quick look across the room at the large man who sat at the back corner of it, alone. He was always alone.

When he'd first started coming to the bar, she'd noticed him right away. What hot-blooded woman wouldn't have? The man was sinfully gorgeous. Besides being at least six-feet-five and having a build of a bodybuilder, he had the sexiest longish, light-brown hair with blond highlights. It was the type she wanted to run her fingers through. Having never gotten close enough to see his eyes, she'd found out from the waitresses who had served him that they were a piercing blue. And his face, God, the man would make any woman wet just from looking at him.

"Are you done staring, so I can give him his beer?" Janey, her friend and his waitress, asked.

Brisa knew exactly which "him" Janey referred to. They'd talked about him enough. "Hey, you were staring at him as he came in."

"Yeah, true, but I'm not the one who practically has her tongue hanging out."

She tore her gaze off the hottie and scowled at her friend. "I am not that bad."

Janey shook her head. "Oh yes, you are. I'm surprised you haven't set the bar on fire with your erotic thoughts. The ones starring him."

Brisa lifted a brow. "And how exactly would you know I'm having erotic thoughts, hmm? Are you a mind reader now?"

Her friend laughed. "No, but I know you have your mind in the gutter as much as I do."

She chuckled. "So true. We do have sex on the brain."

"Yeah, but at least I have a boyfriend to get me some. You, on the other hand, do not."

"So I'm not seeing anyone right now. It's not the end of the world, you know. I've just decided I need to be pickier in my choice of men."

"I have to agree with you on that. The last one was a loser with a capital 'L'. He wanted you to be his mother more than a girlfriend. I don't know how you stuck it out for a month."

Brisa groaned. "Don't remind me. I'd hoped he'd get over it. He wasn't that bad of a guy."

Janey gave her a look that said who was Brisa kidding. "Maybe, but he wasn't that good either." She glanced over her shoulder, then turned back to Brisa. "I think the hunk over there would be perfect for you. Why don't you go over and talk to him?"

"No way." Brisa shook her head. "I'm waiting to see if he'll talk to me first. I've caught him watching me a few times."

"Brisa, you'll be waiting a long time if you leave it up to him. He's been coming in here for six months and hasn't even said hello to you. There is nothing wrong with a woman making the first move."

She nibbled her bottom lip. "I know. I just can't."

"Why not?"

"Well, look at him. I'm sure he has women throwing themselves at him all the time. I doubt he'd appreciate it if I were to do the same thing."

Janey rolled her eyes. "I'm not suggesting you jump his bones or anything. Just go up to him and start off by saying hi and introducing yourself."

"I don't know. I have to be at the bar," Brisa hedged.

She'd love nothing more than to talk to the hottie, but every time she thought about it, she found herself not getting up enough nerve. Brisa had a sick feeling she'd make an ass of herself in front of him by saying something really stupid. As she'd said to Janey, he was so good-looking he probably had women going after him all the time. Brisa felt she'd have to make a good impression if she wanted to stand out in the crowd. And coming across as an airhead wouldn't cut it.

"Stop thinking up excuses," Janey said. "And that's what it is. I've seen you handle guys who have tried to hit on you here with no problem. This should be much easier than warding off those dumbasses."

"Maybe, but—"

"But nothing. Tonight's your night. I'll watch the bar while you serve the hunk his beer. I'll even let you keep the tip."

Brisa shook her head. "You're not going to let up, are you?"

"Nope."

"All right. You win. I'll take him his beer, but I'm giving you the tip."

She walked out from around the bar and went to where Janey stood. After picking up the beer bottle, Brisa turned and headed for the hottie's table. As she came closer, his gaze landed on her and stayed. Her body instantly stood at attention. Her nipples grew taut beneath her white cotton blouse. With each step, she felt more nervous. The hand holding the beer shook ever so slightly. *Get a grip*, she berated herself. She was a mature woman of twenty-nine. She'd talked with enough men that she shouldn't be feeling this way. Finally reaching the table, her mouth suddenly went dry when she looked into his blue, blue eyes. With his tanned skin, they seemed to pop.

Brisa quietly cleared her throat. "Here's your beer," she said as she placed the bottle in front of him. "I'm Brisa, the bartender, by the way."

Now didn't she sound really intelligent with that one? Duh, he had to already know she was the bartender. Any idiot would know that, considering that's where she spent all her time when working her shift.

His gaze met hers. "I'm Darius."

His deep, slightly accented voice washed over Brisa. A shiver of delight shot through her. God, she could have an orgasm just from listening to him talk. As if her pussy agreed wholeheartedly, an ache built inside it and she grew wet.

Darius' chest rose as he took a deep breath. And for a second there, Brisa swore she saw hunger lurking in the blueness of his eyes. She became tongue-tied, only able to stare back at him, wishing she could strip him out of the black T-shirt that seemed molded to his broad shoulders and wide chest. Better yet, she wished she could plop down on his lap, take a good grip of his hair, and have her way with his mouth.

He shifted, reaching into the front pocket of his jeans, and Brisa snapped her thoughts back to reality. He took out some bills to pay for his beer. She reached for them when he held them out. As their fingers touched, and she took the money, his hand wrapped around hers before she could pull away. His was warm and seemed to envelop all of hers. At the simple contact, her heart beat faster, her breath speeding up as well. It wouldn't take much to have her melt into a pile of goo at his feet.

"Keep the change," he said. Still holding her hand, he continued. "Have a drink with me, Brisa."

"Ah, I can't. I'm not allowed to drink while I'm working." Where they touched, a current of pleasure rode through her bloodstream all the way to her pussy.

"Then once you're finished your shift."

"That'll be closing time."

"I'll wait and walk you to your car."

Brisa was about to tell him that he didn't have to when Janey breezed by, and said, "She'd love for you to walk her to her car."

She figured her friend had to have been somewhere close enough to eavesdrop on her conversation with Darius, even though she was supposed to be watching the bar. Brisa shook her head as the other woman went to another table to take orders.

Brisa turned her attention back to Darius. He still hadn't let go of her hand. "I guess my answer is yes."

"Until then."

Darius released her. Brisa instantly missed the warmth of his hand surrounding hers. She smiled and slowly backed up, clutching the money. She spun around and beat a hasty retreat.

She wasn't too surprised to find Janey approaching the bar a short time after Brisa had gone behind it. The knowing smile her friend wore said everything.

"Aren't you glad I made you go talk to him?" Janey asked.

"Yes." Brisa rang in the sale of Darius' beer in the cash register, then took out the change and handed it to Janey.

The other woman pocketed the money. "And don't worry. I won't stick around to see what happens when he walks you to your car." She winked. "Maybe you'll get lucky tonight."

Brisa doubted it. For one thing, she wasn't the type of woman to hop into the sack with a man she'd just met. Considering how late it would be when the bar closed, it wasn't as if she and Darius would have a lot of time to get to know each other enough for sex to be part of the picture. If he asked her out on a real date, that would be another matter.

"Oh yeah, I'm going to have some hot sex with Darius

in the back of my car in the parking lot," Brisa said. "And given how small it is, I doubt the man would manage to fit inside it."

Janey laughed. "Okay, I just got the mental picture of him sitting in the backseat with his legs hanging out the car door as he does the nasty with you."

Brisa smacked her friend in the arm with the towel she'd used to dry some glasses. "You really do have a gutter mind."

"Takes one to know one."

"Yeah, well, yours is worse than mine."

After Brisa mixed the drinks Janey needed for one of her orders, and Janey left to serve them, Brisa turned her gaze in Darius' direction. He seemed to stare at her with a slight smile on his lips. The expression made him even better-looking. She sighed. She'd have to wait and see what happened when the bar closed.

CHAPTER TWO

Darius spent the last couple of hours that the bar remained open slowly sipping on beer. He only had two, not wanting Brisa to think he'd had too much to drink. Not that two, or much less six of them, would affect him. Since becoming immortal, he'd lost the ability to become drunk. He figured it had to do with the way his body now metabolized anything he put into it. He could eat as much as he wanted, whatever he wanted, and remain the same as the day he'd vowed to serve Anubis. The perks of being one of the god's warriors.

He drank the last swallow of beer and turned his gaze on Brisa. It was almost closing time, and she was cleaning up the bar. He still didn't know what had come over him, causing him to ask to walk her to her car at the end of the night. He'd told himself repeatedly she wasn't one he could have anything to do with, that admiring her from afar was all he was allowed.

When she'd served him his beer instead of the waitress, then introduced herself, he'd been unable to resist her.

Especially when their fingers had touched. Something had zapped through him straight to his cock, making it strain even more against the zipper of his jeans. He'd smelled the scent of her arousal and his good intentions had flown out the window.

Seeing Brisa's waitress friend wave to her before she headed out the door, Darius took that as his cue to go up to the bar. He grabbed the empty bottle from the table and stood. He was the last customer in the room.

Darius wove his way around the tables. Once he stood in front of the bar, he placed the bottle on top of it. "Are you just about ready to leave?" he asked.

She grabbed the empty beer and placed it in a case behind her. She straightened and turned back to him. "Just about. I have to bring the money from the register to the manager, then I can go."

He watched her push a couple of buttons on the till, which caused the cash drawer to open. She took out the tray and covered it with a piece of metal before she walked out from behind the bar and headed to the offices at the opposite end of the room. It didn't take her very long to come back. He noticed she now carried a purse.

Brisa stopped in front of him. "All right. I can go now."

As they walked toward the bar's entrance, she fished her keys out of her purse. Once outside, as they headed to the parking lot at the side of the building, Darius did his sweep of the area with his gaze. It was late enough that there was hardly anyone else around. Neither he nor Brisa said anything. Out of the corner of his eye, he saw her look at him a few times.

After they reached a silver, compact car, she said, "Well, this is me." She looked at him shyly as she played with her key ring.

He shifted closer, crowding her against the car's door, forcing her to crane her neck to look up at him. Darius shifted even closer until they were toe-to-toe. Her breath caught, and the scent of her growing arousal drifted on the breeze that swirled around them.

Even though he damned himself for being a fool, Darius couldn't stop himself from bending his head and brushing his lips against Brisa's. She was just too tempting. And when she made an almost inaudible sigh, he had to have more of her.

Angling his lips for a tighter fit, he claimed her mouth fully. He increased the pressure before he swept his tongue along the crease of her lips, seeking entrance. She opened for him, and he pushed inside. He moaned at the taste of her. Kissing her was better than he'd imagined.

As her tongue twined with his, she lifted her arms and wrapped them around his neck. Darius dropped his hands to her hips, spread his legs slightly, and pulled her between them. His hard cock twitched when she rubbed against him. Need pounded through him, causing his dick to throb in time with his rapidly beating heart.

He sucked her tongue into his mouth, and she swept the inside, tasting him as he'd tasted her. His libido increased. Darius ground his erection into her. He ached for her, but this was neither the time nor the place.

Darius lifted his head, knowing the little he'd taken from Brisa wouldn't be enough. He'd had his taste and craved more. He may well damn himself, but he wasn't ready to end what they'd started.

"When can I see you again?" he asked, his voice gruff with the arousal still pounding through him.

She blinked a few times, seeming to come out of a daze. Her lips were swollen from his kisses. She licked them, making him want to claim them once more, but he did nothing of the sort.

"Tomorrow," she said in a quiet voice. "During the day, if you want. I have to work at night again."

"That'll be good for me. Give me your phone number and I'll call you sometime after lunch."

"Sure. Let me write it down for you." Brisa reached inside her purse and took out what looked like an old receipt along with a pen. She scribbled her number on the back of the piece of paper before she handed it to him. "That's my cell. I don't have a landline."

Darius shoved it into his jeans front pocket. "I'll look forward to seeing you tomorrow."

He turned before he weakened and pulled Brisa back into his arms. His body still thrumming with desire, Darius walked away. On the sidewalk, he headed in the direction where he'd left his car a few blocks up, having chosen the section of the city near the bar as his hunting grounds for that particular night.

Once at his sports car, he started the engine before he pulled away from the curb. As he drove to his home, he relived every taste and feel of having Brisa in his arms. Even the small sounds of pleasure she'd made while he kissed her. Having lived eight hundred and twenty-two years, for the first time, he'd found a woman he thought he wanted to spend his life with. It was too bad he'd never be able to keep Brisa as his own.

* * * *

Brisa watched Darius walk away until he disappeared down the sidewalk. Her body had yet to cool, and she still felt as if her brain was only functioning at half capacity. The man had kissed her senseless. She'd completely forgotten where they were and had let the desire building inside her take over. All that had mattered was having his arms around her and his lips taking hers.

She felt her face flush with renewed arousal when she remembered how big and hard his cock had felt pressed against her. It had made her want to undo his pants and see just how large he actually was. Her pussy had ached to be filled by him.

Giving her head a shake over her heated thoughts, Brisa turned to unlock the driver's side door of her car. If she didn't stop it, she'd have to go home and take a cold shower. Or take care of what Darius had started herself. She shook her head again. Janey was right. Brisa was just as bad as her when it came to having a gutter mind.

Once she was inside her car and had pulled out of the parking lot, she drove to her apartment. She really didn't know what to expect when Darius called the next day. They hadn't had a whole lot of conversation to get much beyond learning each other's names. No, she'd been too busy sticking her tongue down his throat to get to know him better. A small smile played along her lips. He hadn't seemed to mind, though.

Brisa gave herself a mental kick. She had to stop thinking about sex with Darius. Tomorrow, she'd keep herself under control long enough to find out more about the man who'd asked her out. Rushing into intimacy didn't necessarily mean a relationship would work out. Oh, who was she kidding? If he put the moves on her again as he'd done back in the parking lot, she wouldn't be able to resist. He was just too gorgeous and made her want to jump his bones every time she looked at him.

* * * *

The following morning, Darius awoke, looking forward to what the day would bring for the first time in a long while. Being immortal, he'd started to lose interest in the people and places around him. He did his job each night as one of Anubis' warriors, but he had long since stopped associating with mortals. Their lifespans seemed too short. Eighty years was nothing to him. And what family he'd had before he'd gone on crusade, he'd never kept track of. Having never married or had children, he'd thought it best to stay away from the land of his birth.

After eating a late breakfast, he took a shower. That done, Darius stood in front of the steamed mirror with a towel wrapped around his hips. He used a small hand towel to clear some of the glass in front of him so he could shave. His gaze landed on the mark the god of the underworld had placed on him once Darius had taken his vow to become one of his warriors. It was situated on his chest, over his heart. It was a picture of Anubis with a jackal's head. In one hand he held an ankh while in the other was a flail. The whole thing was inside a cartouche, colored black.

Darius picked up his razor and proceeded to shave off the stubble that was a shade darker than the hair on his head. He combed his hair and left it to dry by itself. After stepping into his bedroom, he headed for his closet. He frowned when he found nothing but jeans and jackets that were leather and denim. Without having to look, he knew the rest of his wardrobe would consist of T-shirts and long-sleeved ones. He didn't have anything that would be considered "dressy."

Figuring there wasn't much he could do about it now, Darius pulled out a pair of blue jeans from the closet before he picked a light gray T-shirt from the dresser. Once clothed, he sat on the bed and put on his shoes. As he did so, he thought of what he wanted to do with Brisa that day, besides thinking about getting her into bed. He'd never "dated" anyone before. When he'd been mortal, there had been no such thing. There'd been more arranged marriages than not. At least that was the case in his station. His father had been a knight, as had Darius. He still had his armor, sword, and spurs to prove it.

Before leaving his bedroom, Darius picked up the piece of paper he'd taken out of his pants pocket when he'd changed out of his clothes the night before. He stared at Brisa's handwriting. It was small and neat, unlike his hen scratching. He'd had a minimal amount of education when growing up. Learning how to read and write hadn't been part of it. He'd had to learn in the years after becoming immortal.

He headed down the stairs and then into his living room. His cell phone sat on an end table, charging. Like Brisa, he didn't have a landline. He liked to keep a minimal paper trail, since every thirty years or so he had to change his identity. The only pain in the ass side effect of never aging in this day and age. It wasn't like the old days where he could just move to another city or country and be done with it, keeping his same name.

Darius unplugged his cell and pocketed it, then went to the room that was meant to be a den. Inside, there was a mini-temple he'd created for Anubis with religious pieces to the god of the underworld that Darius had picked up in Egypt shortly after he'd taken his vow. Through worshipping Anubis, Darius kept the link between them strong. That way he could call upon the god whenever he needed him.

After going through his morning ritual and placing a bit of beer and bread on the altar in offering for Anubis, Darius left the room and then closed the door behind him. Back in the living room, he sat on the black leather couch. He took out his cell and the piece of paper with Brisa's number on it. It was already after twelve.

He added the number to his list of contacts first before he called. Brisa picked up after the third ring.

"Hi, Brisa. It's Darius."

"Hi," she said in return.

"Are we still on for today?"

"Yes. I just have to be at work by seven, since I work until closing."

"How about I pick you up and take you to my place, then we can go out for an early dinner before you head into work?"

"Sure, I'd love to. What time will you get here?"

"Whenever you think you'll be ready."

"In that case, depending on how far you live from my apartment, give or take a half hour?"

"Sounds good. What's your address?"

Brisa gave it to him, then ended the call by saying she was looking forward to seeing him again. Darius added her address where her cell number was stored on his phone. He still had a little time to wait before he could leave to pick her up. It wouldn't take the full half hour to reach her apartment from his house.

Once he'd let enough time elapse, Darius walked through the door that connected the three-car garage to the house. With a push of a button on the remote clipped to the driver's side visor, the large door quietly lifted, and Darius backed his car out onto the drive.

It only took him about fifteen minutes or so to reach Brisa's apartment building. It was situated right downtown, no more than five minutes away from the bar she worked at. Darius parked in the visitors parking out front, then went inside.

He found Brisa's apartment number and hit the code on the panel inside the vestibule to call up to her place. After telling her he was there, she buzzed him through the secured entrance door. A short elevator ride up, and he was at her door, knocking.

Brisa opened it wide. "Come on in for a minute. I just have to grab my purse."

As she walked farther into the apartment, Darius stepped inside. He looked around, following Brisa with his gaze. She disappeared into what he assumed was the bedroom. The place was light and airy looking. She'd gone for colors that were closer to pastels, whereas he was more into the darker tones.

She returned with purse in hand. "Just to forewarn you, I have to be back here to get ready for work by six thirty at the latest."

He nodded. "That'll be no problem."

Brisa walked by him to put on her shoes, and Darius took a deep breath. The scent of her perfume, and one that was uniquely hers, filled his nose. His cock twitched with interest. Just being in the same room with her brought his libido to life.

Once she was ready, he guided her out of the apartment, then outside to his car. So used to not associating with others, Darius had a hard time trying to come up with conversation starters. He glanced at Brisa and found her looking out the passenger window. The only women he'd let into his life were the ones who were interested in sex, then walking away when it was over.

"So," he said. "Have you worked at the bar long?"

Out of the corner of his eye, he saw Brisa turned her head in his direction. "For a couple of years now. I know most people wouldn't think being a bartender was that great of a job, but I enjoy it. What about you? What do you do?"

"I guess you could say I work for myself."

"Doing what?"

"I'm a, ah, bounty hunter."

In a way, that was what he did. He hunted down the bad guys, only he wasn't after the ones who had run out on their bail. He sent them to face their final judgment.

"That has to be an interesting job. You must come across all kinds of people."

He grinned, "Yes, you could say I do."

"And you must be pretty good at it," Brisa said as she looked out the passenger window again.

"Why do you say that?"

She turned back to him. "Well, for one thing, we're now in Miami Shores. Where some of the most expensive homes can be found in the city. I take it this is where you live, right? And your car isn't exactly what the average Joe could afford."

"Yes. I bought a place here five years ago when I came to Miami."

"I've only ever driven by the houses here. With a bartender's salary, there is no way I'd ever be able to afford one, let alone rent it."

"Well, today you can say you've been inside one of them."

Money had never been a problem for him since he'd become one of Anubis' warriors. The god had made sure of that. Over the years, Anubis had given him more than enough precious jewels and gold to make Darius a very rich man. The god looked after his own.

As he pulled onto his long, curving drive, Brisa let out a low whistle. "Wow. Your place is gorgeous. You live here by yourself? It's huge."

Parking his car outside the garage, Darius turned off the engine and then turned to Brisa. "Thanks, and yes, I do live alone. I like to have my space."

"I guess so. You'd probably be able to fit three of my apartments in there."

He chuckled and got out of the car. Brisa followed suit and walked around the back end to meet him at his side. Once at his front door, Darius unlocked it and then moved aside for her to enter first. She let out another whistle as he stepped in behind her and closed them inside.

"It's beautiful, Darius. I especially like the banister. It's the type I would have spent hours riding down when I was a kid."

He looked at the wide, mahogany staircase that started near the center of the cathedral-ceilinged foyer, rising to the upper level. He focused back on Brisa. "Go ahead."

She gave him a questioning look. "Go ahead what?"

"Go ride down the banister."

Brisa laughed. "You really want me to do it? I didn't mean I should slide down it now. I'm too old for things like that."

"Why not?" he asked. "I know you want to. And I won't think you're any less mature for doing it." He gave her smile. "I have to admit I've tried it out a time or two. If it can hold me, it'll definitely hold you."

She gnawed her bottom lip as she appeared to think over what he'd said. Seeing her doing it made Darius want to lean in and claim her mouth, do some nibbling of his own.

"I don't know," she said. "It's a long banister, and there isn't much of a newel post at the bottom of the staircase. It's nothing but a small square piece of wood. If I can't stop in time, I could fly off at the end."

"I'll be here to catch you just in case."

Brisa chuckled and shook her head. "I can't believe I'm going to do this, but who am I to turn down a chance to go banister riding inside a mansion."

She put her purse on the floor and then ran up the stairs. Once she reached the top, Darius shifted into position at the end of the railing. Brisa swung her leg over it with her back facing toward him.

"All right," she called down. "Are you ready?"

"I'm all set."

She let go and started a controlled ride down. She giggled as she went. Darius followed her progress with his gaze. It landed on her bottom and didn't shift away. Her jeans were pulled tight across it, molded to it perfectly. He had to bite back a moan at the sight of it. Unlucky for him, Brisa managed to stop herself before she reached the newel post. He would have liked the excuse to fondle that rear end.

Brisa got off the banister and smiled. "One more time."

He nodded, then watched her hurry back up. This time she went a little faster and it looked as if she wouldn't be able to stop in time. Darius stepped onto the bottom stair, snagged Brisa around the waist and lifted her off. He pulled her tight against his chest and swung around so they faced the other way.

She relaxed into him and laughed. "I guess I went a little too fast that time. Thanks for catching me."

"No problem," he said, his voice sounding husky to his ears.

Where he held her to him, her nicely rounded bottom rested against the front of his jeans. His cock was hard, liking where it was. Brisa must have felt it, because her laughter slowly died. She turned her head to look at him and licked her lips.

Darius knew he couldn't let the opportunity pass. He took her mouth, groaning as she kissed him back. He made no move to put her down or turn her in his arms. He pushed his tongue past her lips and licked and sucked. His cock throbbed, and he rubbed it against Brisa, aching to have it buried deep inside her.

She curved one of her arms up, her hand coming to rest on the back of his head. She moaned into his mouth and pressed her bottom tighter along him. The intoxicating scent of her arousal filled the air around them, making him harder. Their kisses became hotter, more carnal. Darius felt as if his body had been set on fire. Need and lust pounded in his veins. God, how he wanted the woman he held in his arms.

CHAPTER THREE

Brisa was so turned-on she couldn't think beyond the pounding pleasure that surged through her body. What had started off as some immature antics had turned into something way more adult. And quickly at that. Whenever Darius touched her, she seemed to go up in instant flames.

She squirmed in Darius' arms, tying to let him know she wanted to face toward him without having to break contact with his lips. He must have gotten the message. Brisa let go of his head as he turned her as if she weighed nothing at all.

Since he hadn't put her down on her feet, she lifted her legs and wrapped them around his waist. They moaned as her pussy came to rest atop his erection. A shiver of delight swept through her at the feel of him. She wanted more. So much more.

Darius turned and walked in a direction away from the stairs. As his steps slowed, she cracked open her eyes to see he carried her into a spacious living room. His lips trailed from her mouth to the side of her neck. Brisa leaned her head to the side, turning it slightly to give him better access and saw the black leather couch with a chaise attached at one end. He headed right for it, then slowly lowered her onto it. He followed her down, still nuzzling her throat.

"Please don't tell me I'm going too fast for you," he said against her skin.

She sank her fingers into the sides of his hair and lifted his head. She nibbled his bottom lip before she swept her tongue along it. "No, you're definitely not going too fast."

"So, you won't mind if I take your top off?"

Brisa tilted Darius' head back and licked the hollow of his throat. "God, no. Do it."

He moaned, then shifted to lie half off her, holding his upper body up on a bent arm as he used his other hand to take hold of the bottom of her T-shirt. He pushed it up, baring first her belly, then her satin bra, to his view. His heated gaze landed on it, causing her nipples to tighten even more. Darius reached out with a finger and circled each one through the material that covered them.

With a couple of tugs, he pulled her shirt up and over her head. He tossed it to the floor. A large hand covered one of her breasts, and a thumb stroked back and forth over the taut peak that tipped it. Brisa pressed closer when Darius pulled her bra cup aside and bent his head to sweep her nipple with his tongue.

He made short work of unhooking her bra and dragging it off her. Once he had her free of it, he took the tight bud into his mouth, sucking on it. Each pull on her breast, Brisa felt deep inside her pussy. She grew wetter, her juices leaking into her panties. She shifted beneath him, and Darius placed a hard thigh between her legs. She rubbed against it, becoming more excited.

Darius switched to her other nipple, lavishing the same attention on it as he'd done the first. Brisa's pants and moans filled the room. He breathed just as heavily as she. She ran her hands over his broad shoulders and onto his back. Bunching the material of his T-shirt in her hands, she yanked it up. He let her nipple go with a quiet pop and reached behind his neck to pull off his shirt.

Brisa ran her gaze over his well-defined chest and abs. She focused on the Egyptian-styled tattoo over his heart. She didn't get to look at it too closely before Darius reclaimed her mouth for a breath-stealing kiss. She promised herself she'd check it out later.

He ran caressing strokes down her side and across her stomach, leaving goosebumps in his wake. Going lower, he deftly undid the button and zipper on her jeans before he shoved a hand inside. He cupped her pussy, the heel of his hand pressing against her pubic bone.

Darius released her mouth and trailed kisses to her ear. He whispered, "I can feel how wet you are through your panties."

Brisa ran her hands up and down his muscular back. "Then what are you going to do about it?" she asked with a breathy moan as he brushed a finger against her clit.

He gave a husky chuckle. "I know exactly what I want to do."

Darius tugged at her pants until he had them down her legs and off. Her pussy clenched with anticipation as he ran a finger just under the waistband of her panties. He teased her for a bit longer before he took them off as well.

She tried to pull him on top of her, but he resisted and shifted farther down the chaise. He licked the underside of her breast, then worked his way lower on her body, kissing and licking as he went. As his tongue circled her bellybutton, dipping inside, her stomach quivered.

He delved his fingers between her legs while he nuzzled her belly. The digits trailed in the dampness found there before one pushed inside her pussy. Darius pumped it in and out, his thumb brushing her clit as he did so. Brisa opened her legs wider, her body coiling tighter.

A second joined the first, and Brisa could no longer keep her hips still. She rode Darius' fingers, squeezing around the plunging digits, matching his strokes. At the rate her arousal built, it wouldn't take much for her to come.

As if he'd sensed how close she was to reaching release, Darius pulled out of her pussy. Brisa whimpered at the loss, but soon found herself gasping his name when he wedged his shoulders between her thighs and took her with his mouth.

He lapped at the wetness, circling her clit with his tongue as he went. He cupped her bottom in his hands and angled her hips up. He licked and sucked, driving her orgasm ever closer. Brisa shoved her fingers into his hair, holding him to her as she rocked against his mouth.

"Yes," she panted. "Just like that. A little more."

She moaned, riding the waves of pleasure that shot through her as her climax took her over. Her pussy rhythmically clenched in release. Once it was over, Brisa relaxed against the couch, trying to catch her breath. She had to give Darius an A-plus for his oral-sex skills. He knew his way around a woman's anatomy.

Darius rose along her body. He licked his lips clean of her juices, seeming to savor the taste of her. A jolt of desire shot through her. Feeling his hard cock pressed against her thigh, she pushed on his shoulder to get him to change places so she was on top.

She smiled down at him once he'd complied. "I get to play now."

Brisa undid Darius' jeans and yanked them past his hips. He lifted them from the couch to help when she dragged the pants farther down his legs and off. She tossed them to the floor without looking, her gaze centered on what she'd revealed.

It appeared that Darius was the type of man who shunned underwear. He'd been commando under his pants. His cock was out in the open, jutting up from his body. A shiver of longing ran down her spine. He was perfectly thick and long. She'd never slept with a man quite as large as him. Brisa couldn't wait to have that part of him inside her, but first she wanted to learn his body as he'd learned hers. See what would make him groan louder, push him to the greatest arousal.

Darius put his hands behind his head and gave her a grin that was sexy as all hell. "You want to play? Then go right ahead."

She bent her head and took his bottom lip between her teeth and gave it a tug, then nipped his chin before continuing downward. She explored the contours of his defined chest, taking the time to lave each of his flat nipples with her tongue. They tightened into tiny buds. Next, she went on to nibble her way down his six-pack abs. The man had a body she could get lost in for days.

At his cock, Brisa wrapped her fingers around him, marveling at the fact they didn't quite meet. She pumped up and down, enjoying the hot, thick length of him in her hand. She stroked a few more times, and a bead of pre-cum leaked out of the head of his erection. The urge to taste it was too hard to resist. She bent her head and captured it on the tip of her tongue. Darius moaned, his hips lifting off the couch. He obviously wanted more.

She had no problem doing that. Brisa opened her mouth and took his cock inside. She sucked him almost to the back of her throat, but she still couldn't manage all his length. What she couldn't, she stroked with her hand as she slid him in and out. Darius' moans increased in volume.

Brisa continued to suck, loving the way his erection grew harder. She planned to push him to the brink but would stop before he reached the point of no return. She wanted his big cock deep inside her pussy, filling her all the way up when he came, preferably after she'd come at least once more. Twice would be even better.

She'd thought he was at that peak when his whole body seemed to clench. It took her a few seconds to realize his moans of pleasure had suddenly changed to groans that sounded as if he were in pain.

Brisa had just let him slip from her mouth, about ready to ask if anything was wrong, when Darius shoved her away and scrambled off the couch. Totally naked, he rushed from the room, leaving her wondering what had happened.

When he didn't return after a few seconds, Brisa sat up. She hadn't thought her blowjobs were *that* bad. At least she'd had no complaints from the other men she'd done it to. Really at a loss as to what had come over Darius, she wondered if she'd inadvertently done something wrong to put an end to their date.

*

Darius gritted his teeth to keep his groans stifled as he rushed to the main-floor powder room. Once inside, he closed and then locked the door behind him. He held on to his head as blinding pain shot through it. It was so intense he was surprised he hadn't blacked out. He'd never felt anything like it. He looked in the mirror above the sink and noticed his eyes had shifted to a jackal's.

The pain moved to the rest of his body. His bones shifted, heralding the beginnings of a change in forms, but only to stop and return to normal. Holding up his hands, he watched claws break through the tips of his fingers only to recede a second later. Black fur sprouted on his arms, then it too disappeared beneath his skin. What the hell was happening to him?

He'd experienced nothing like that before. Once a shift

started, it didn't stop until it was complete. And the other thing that didn't make sense was the fact he didn't feel the pull of evil—the one thing needed to bring on the change. He'd been lost in the pleasure Brisa had given him, then wham, the pain had slammed into him.

Slowly it faded, leaving him breathing hard, his body sheened with sweat. A quick look in the mirror showed his eyes had returned to normal. Whatever it was, it seemed to be over. At least he hoped it was. There was no way he could have Brisa see any of that. She'd run from his house, screaming. Not how he wanted his time with her to end.

His erection long gone, he waited a few extra minutes just to be on the safe side. Nothing else happened. No pain, no unwarranted shifting. Breathing a sigh of relief, Darius rinsed his face in the sink before he unlocked the door and left the powder room. He'd just have to keep a close watch on himself. At the first sign of pain, he'd have to make a mad dash once again. He just hoped Brisa wouldn't think he'd lost his marbles.

Darius walked into the living room thinking he and Brisa would start up where they'd left off. Having her in his arms, naked and willing, had felt good. Real good. His cock stirred to life, but it soon deflated when he saw her sitting on the couch fully dressed. *Shit.*

Brisa gave him a small smile as he approached. "I, ah, thought since you ran out in the middle of things, then didn't come back right away, that you'd changed your mind."

He pulled her to her feet and dragged her close. He did the quickest thing he could think of that would show her how wrong she was. Darius claimed her lips in a heated kiss, pouring all the desire that quickly rose inside him into it. He didn't stop until he had her clutching him.

He lifted his head. "Does that feel as if I changed my mind about you?" For good measure, he pressed his renewed erection against her belly.

Brisa stood there for a few seconds with her eyes closed. Her cheeks were flushed. Her eyelids fluttered, then opened all the way. She met his gaze. "No, not really." Her voice sounded breathy.

"Good." He went to kiss her once more, but she turned her head.

"Then why did you run out of the room so fast? Are you okay?" She grinned. "I've never had a guy bolt like that in the middle of a blowjob. You could give me a complex doing that. Make me think I messed it up."

He dropped his hands to her backside and rocked his cock into her. "Believe me when I say it didn't have anything to do with you. Or what you were doing. It was me, though it ended up being nothing."

She eyed him. "I don't know about that. You sounded as if you were in pain."

"I'm fine. I...ah, had a cramp in my leg. So I had to walk it off before it got worse."

Brisa didn't look as if she totally believed him. "A cramp? While we were...I've never heard of that happening, especially in the leg." She gave him a saucy wink. "Maybe in other places, but not there. You weren't exactly using it at the time. And you needn't have left the room to walk it off. I would have helped you with it."

"Well, it was a little embarrassing. Having to put an abrupt end to things because of a cramp isn't exactly sexy, now is it? I thought it best to take it out of the room, then come back and continue." Darius squeezed Brisa's bottom.

She put her hands on his chest and used a finger to draw an invisible circle around Anubis' mark. "Okay, I'll let you have that one, but try not to let it happen again. Especially when we've gotten to the good part."

"I promise. How about I show you the upstairs? Specifically, my bedroom. I'm sure you'll like it."

Brisa glanced at the couch. "I suppose there would be more room up there."

"Definitely. I have a king-sized bed."

She broke his hold by stepping back. "All right. Show me." Brisa walked toward the living room's entrance, then paused to look over her shoulder. "Don't forget to bring your clothes."

Darius quickly gathered them up and then followed her out of the room. They'd just reached the bottom of the staircase in the foyer when the sound of a cell phone ringing could be heard.

Brisa walked to her purse and picked it up off the floor where she'd left it. "That's me." She reached inside and took out the phone, then grimaced. "It's my boss. I'd better take this."

He listened to her answer, then after a few seconds heard her ask, "Are you sure there is no one else except for me?" Seeing a look of disappointment flash across her face, he figured the answer wasn't something Brisa wanted to hear.

"All right," she said into her cell. "The next time someone else has to cover it." She ended the call and then put her phone back into her purse with a sigh. "I'm sorry to do this to you, Darius, but I'm going to have to get a rain check on seeing your bedroom. The dayshift bartender took sick at the bar and couldn't finish his shift. My boss is covering now, but he has a family commitment at five and can't get out of it to hang around until my shift starts. And the two guys who cover the weekends have other full-time jobs they work during the day. So that leaves me. And since I have to go in two hours earlier, I'm going to have to have an even earlier dinner. You'll probably want to drop me off at my place. Sorry."

He stepped closer and cupped the side of her face, angling it up so she looked at him. "No need to apologize. It's your job. How about I take you for something to eat now, then afterward I'll drop you off at your apartment. I don't mind eating as well. I plan on meeting up with you at work at the end of the night, anyway."

She smiled. "You do?"

He nodded. "I hoped I'd be able to convince you to come back here and spend the night with me."

"Sounds good to me. And since tomorrow is the start of the weekend, I have the next two nights off. So I don't have to worry about going into work the following day."

"Can I take that to mean you'd be willing to spend Saturday and Sunday with me?" he asked.

Darius figured if he'd broken the promise he'd made to himself when it came to Brisa, he might as well jump in with both feet. As the saying went, in for a penny, in for a pound. The damage was already done. What he and Brisa had shared in the living room had pretty much sealed his fate. There would be no walking away. He craved her touch. Where he expected all of this to go, he had no idea. For now, he intended to enjoy her while he could.

Brisa nodded. "I think me spending the weekend with you can be arranged. If you'll be able to put up with me that long. You never know. I might drive you nuts after a while."

He chuckled. Darius hadn't found much humor in his life for ages, but with Brisa around, she had him laughing when he least expected it. "I doubt that will happen, considering I will probably keep you in my bed for the majority of it."

She put her purse on the floor and then stepped closer. With a playful grin, she reached behind him and grabbed his ass. "You really shouldn't say things like that while standing buck naked. As my friend Janey tells me all the time, I have a gutter mind. Now all night at work I'll be thinking about sex, with you. And I'll have hours to wait until I get to see you at the end of my shift. Just be prepared to be pounced on later."

He smiled. "I think I'll enjoy that."

Darius gave Brisa a quick kiss, then dropped his clothes

to the floor, giving her a good view of what her saucy talk had done to his cock. Her gaze seemed to eat him up as he grabbed his jeans and then pulled them on. He shoved his erection inside before he reached for the zipper.

"Careful," Brisa said. "Maybe I should help you with that. We wouldn't want you getting yourself caught in it. I intend to make use of that appendage tonight."

"You do, and we'll never get out of here to eat. And the likelihood of you making it to work won't be very good. I doubt your boss would understand."

She laughed. "All right, I'll behave. Getting fired tonight isn't on my to-do list."

Darius finished dressing, then guided Brisa outside to his car. They ate at a Chinese place, spending a lot of the time talking. Once the meal was over, he wished he didn't have to take her to her apartment. Brisa was actually the first woman he'd really enjoyed being with, learning about her. Even when he'd been mortal, he hadn't found a woman who hadn't bored him to death after a while.

Parked in a visitor's spot at her apartment building, Darius reached across to the passenger seat and pulled Brisa into his arms. He kissed her thoroughly, already wishing he could take her to his place.

Releasing her, he said, "I'll see you tonight. And if you want to bring enough clothes with you for the weekend, go right ahead."

"I'll do that," she said before she gave him a quick peck on the lips and then got out of the car.

Darius watched Brisa cross the parking lot to the front entrance of the building. He'd make love to her tonight. Whatever had come over him earlier hadn't happened again, making him think it was just some weird instance. Not worried about it anymore, he figured there would be nothing to get in his way of having Brisa.

CHAPTER FOUR

Once darkness took over the city, Darius was out on the hunt. He picked a section where he knew he'd run across at least one evildoer in the act that would cause him to shift quickly. Even though he had no worries about what had happened back at his place repeating again, a small part of him wanted to make sure nothing else had been screwed up by it.

Darius walked down a couple of streets, then along another. He was in the middle of an industrial park with large buildings looming on either side of him. Some of them were closed while others were open, running a shift through the entire night. That didn't stop unsavory types from lurking around.

Rounding a bend in the road, he felt the pulling sensation he'd anticipated. Darius followed it to the back of one of the smaller buildings in the sector to what looked to be a storage facility for a retail business. The stench of evil filled the air.

Two men stood in front of a docking bay, having a

heated argument. Darius closed in on his prey with silent feet. Not that they would have noticed him, since they were too busy verbally abusing each other. That didn't last long when one of them pulled a knife and stuck it into the other's belly.

The pain of shifting tore through Darius, making his breath catch as the wounded man dropped to the ground. His attacker stood over him, looking as if he were ready to strike again. With a loud growl, Darius drew the attention of the knife wielder.

The man spun around, his eyes widening as his gaze landed on Darius in his half-human and half-jackal form. He brought the knife up and brandished it in front of him. "I don't know what the fuck you are, but you have no business here."

Darius snorted inside. The guy was scared shitless. The scent of his fear was heavy in the breeze around them. So this particular prey wouldn't go down easy, in fact, would put on the tough act, maybe even try to fight Darius. Not that the man would win. In this form, Darius was almost twice his size, and twice as strong. He was all predator.

Stalking closer, Darius curled his upper lip and growled once more. The man's bravado seemed to slip a bit, but he quickly recovered. The hand holding the knife shot out as soon as Darius came within range. He blocked it easily and knocked the weapon from his prey's grasp. Still the man didn't give up, resorting to his fists.

Darius let him swing a few punches, though he avoided each one before he decided it was time to end it. Catching the man's fist in his hand, Darius squeezed hard enough to break bones. His prey yelled in agony.

Darius released him and grabbed him by his throat. He brought his muzzle close to the man's face, snaring his gaze as Darius tore into his mind. All his evil deeds filled Darius' head, forcing him to live through them all. Stabbing someone in the gut was petty compared to what his prey had gotten away with.

With a single thought, Darius willed his gold dagger into his hand. He struck fast and sure, slicing across the man's stomach in the same spot where his prey had stabbed the other male. The evildoer faded out of existence, sent on his way to meet Anubis.

Darius turned to look at the wounded man who had fallen to his knees, his hands pressed to his abdomen. Darius closed the short distance between them and tilted the other man's head up.

"Don't," the man whimpered. "Please don't make me disappear like you did Jimmy."

"Why shouldn't I?" Darius asked. "Your friend was here to steal from this place. I saw it in his memories before I sent him to meet his judgment. You were here with him."

"I wasn't here to help Jimmy. I only tried to stop him. I'll admit at first, I was going to help him, only because I owed him a lot of money, but I couldn't do it. I have a problem when it comes to gambling. I'm no thief."

"I'll be able to see if you tell the truth." Darius met the man's gaze and pushed into his mind. He met with no resistance. After a few seconds, he released the wounded man's chin. "You didn't lie." He willed his dagger away.

This man, Sam, had been coerced into helping Jimmy break into the building, and at the last minute had backed out. Sam just had a weakness with gambling, would accept any bet someone made him. There was no evil in him.

Snagging Sam's gaze once more, Darius erased himself and what had happened to Jimmy from the man's memory. In its place he planted a new one, of how Jimmy and Sam had argued. Jimmy had then pulled a knife and stabbed Sam before he took off, taking the weapon with him. While in that entranced state, Darius told Sam to wait until he'd left before dialing 9-1-1 to get himself help.

Darius growled, pain tearing through his body as he

shifted back to his human form. Once it was complete, he looked at Sam one final time to make sure he was still in a trance before Darius turned and took off at a run. He didn't go far, but kept hidden to make sure an ambulance showed up for Sam. If the other man hadn't managed to call for help, Darius would get him some.

It didn't take long before the sound of sirens heading toward the industrial park could be heard. Darius stepped deeper into the shadows of his hiding spot as a police cruiser sped up to the building where he'd left Sam. Shortly after, an ambulance arrived with lights flashing and sirens wailing.

Darius remained where he was until all the vehicles left, taking Sam with them. Once everything was quiet again, he stepped from his hiding place and continued to make his circuit of the industrial park.

He'd just turned to head back to his car so he could meet up with Brisa at the bar when the same pain he'd experienced at his house earlier slammed into him, only this time worse. It drove Darius to his knees, his vision fading in and out. He lifted his hands to cradle his head, the center of all his agony, and watched claws burst through his fingertips before receding again.

"I see you," said a disembodied male voice that seemed to come from all directions. "I see you, warrior of Anubis." An evil-sounding laugh followed.

"Show yourself," Darius bellowed as he painfully rose to his feet, his body shifting in and out of his human form.

"All in good time," said the voice. "I get to have my fun first. I've waited a long time to find one of you."

"Who the fuck are you?"

"Someone who now gets to hunt you. Because of your kind and the stupid god Anubis you serve, we who live in the other part of the underworld aren't getting the souls meant to join us. Now that I've found you, I get to make you pay. As I said before, I get to have some fun time first."

Darius let out a bellow of pain as the change to his half-human and half-jackal form tore through him faster than it ever had. The sound of his bones reshaping was loud in the night air. Once it was over, he stood on legs that barely held him up.

It took a few seconds for him to feel steady. Darius looked down at himself, seeing he was fully shifted, wearing a snow-white kilt instead of his jeans. After a couple of minutes with him not changing back, and not feeling the pull of evil, he wondered if whatever had accosted him had been the one to make him shift. At that moment, Darius hated the fact that he had no control over his shifting ability. He had a sneaky suspicion that he was stuck in that form.

Knowing he couldn't stay out in the open in the state he was in, that the risk of being spotted was too great, Darius took off at a run toward his car. He kept to the darkest spots along the road, hoping like hell he didn't hear someone shouting in alarm behind him. He had to go to his place and talk with Anubis. The god was the only person he thought of who could fix him.

At his sports car, he pulled on the door handle on the driver's side. It didn't open. *Shit.* He carried his keys in his jeans pocket, which were now gone wherever they went when he shifted. Darius tried to will them back the same way he did the number of weapons he had at his disposal, but that accomplished nothing.

"Ah, fuck," he said under his breath.

He was going to have to smash the window. The longer he stood there, the greater the chances of him being seen. Thinking this was going to hurt, but not in the physical sense, Darius pulled back his arm, then punched his fist through the car window. He quickly unlocked the door, sweeping the broken glass off the seat and onto the road before he got inside. He instantly felt cramped with the steering wheel too close to his furred chest. Of course he was much bigger in that form, and he'd never driven while in it either. Darius adjusted the seat to accommodate his larger size.

With no keys, he had no choice but to hotwire his car. Luckily, it was something he already knew how to do, having gone through a period where he'd wanted to learn just for the hell of it. In a matter of a minute, the engine roared to life. Darius took the longer route to get home, to avoid as many main streets as possible. It being so late, there weren't that many people around to see him drive by.

At his place, he had to break one of the small windows that lined either side of the front door to get in. The amount of glass repairs he'd have to have done were racking up.

Darius headed straight to the small temple just off the living room. Standing before the altar, he closed his eyes to concentrate and sent out a call to the god he served. "Anubis, I have need of you."

What troubles you, Darius? Anubis' deep voice filled his head.

"Something happened while I was out on the hunt tonight. I'm stuck shifted."

Show me.

Darius played the whole conversation with the disembodied male voice in his mind as Anubis watched the scenes play out. When the god didn't say anything right away, Darius asked, "Do you have any clue who the voice belonged to?"

It was a demon. Normally, his kind wouldn't have the power to force you to shift, especially while in the underworld. I have a feeling this one has found a way out of it and into the mortal realm.

"A demon? That doesn't sound good." Out of all his years of serving Anubis, not once had Darius come across one.

It isn't. Let loose on mortals, there is no telling what a demon will do. It seems for now he's set his sights on you.

"Is there anything you can try to get me to shift back to my human form?"

Let me see what I can do.

Darius felt the god's presence move inside him. He gritted his teeth as Anubis tried to bring on the shift, only to have it stop, keeping Darius trapped in his present form. Anubis brought it on several more times before he pulled out of Darius' body.

I can't get you to shift.

"So, I'm stuck like this?" Darius did not like the sound of that.

I do not think it is something permanent. It has the feel of a spell. Dark magic, to be exact. It is not a very strong one. If it were, I never would have been able to start the change at all. I have a feeling it will wear off.

"Wear off? How long will that take? I could be trapped in this form for days. I won't be able to leave the house. If mortals were to see me like this, they'd freak." Then Darius remembered about Brisa. "Oh shit."

What?

"I was supposed to meet someone tonight. As of right now I'm late. She's not going to be too happy with me if I don't show up."

Your date will have to wait. I think by morning the spell will have weakened enough to let the change come on naturally. If it does not, I should be able to push past it enough to do it. For now, try to get some sleep.

Darius felt Anubis' presence completely disappear. That had not turned out as he'd planned. Now he wouldn't be able to see Brisa. And thinking about it, he had no way of phoning her, either. His cell phone disappeared along with his clothes and keys. He was going to have to stand her up. Terrific. The night wasn't going to end the way he'd wanted it. Not only that, but he'd have Brisa pissed-off at him. She was going to think he was an asshole.

* * * *

"Still no sign of him?"

Brisa put down the glass she'd been drying and shook her head at Janey. "No, and the bar closes in two minutes."

"Did you try calling him?"

"Yeah. About five times. It goes straight to his voice mail. I've left a message, but either Darius didn't get it or he's ignoring me. So much for the weekend he wanted to spend with me. And it looks as if I packed that bag for nothing."

"Maybe something came up. You told me he was a bounty hunter or something. Maybe he had to chase down a bad guy."

"I think that's just wishful thinking on your part, Janey. I figure Darius would have called if it were something like that."

Her friend shrugged. "I like to give people the benefit of the doubt. Plus, you seem really in to Darius. The way you've talked about him, I know you like him a lot."

Brisa sighed. "The man is perfect. He has good looks, a great body, I actually enjoy being around him, and he has money. That's the thing. He's too perfect. I knew it had to be too good to be true. I'm not lucky enough to land a guy like Darius and actually get to keep him. Maybe he decided I'm not his type, after all."

"Would you stop being so down on yourself? I think Darius is the one who is lucky to have you, not the other way around. I have a feeling he'll call you tomorrow with an explanation as to why he didn't show up tonight." Janey winked. "Maybe you'll get some apology sex out of him too."

Brisa laughed. "Apology sex? I take it that's like make-up sex?"

"Of course. Just wait and see. Darius won't give up on you." Janey looked at her watch. "Well, it's closing time, which means I'm out of here. Try to have a good weekend, Brisa. And I want all the juicy details on Monday."

Brisa shook her head as her friend walked away. Janey was always the optimist. Brisa, on the other hand, wasn't much of one. In her eyes, Darius not showing up without calling wasn't a good sign, especially after the afternoon they'd spent together. She'd thought for sure he was as in to her as she was in to him.

Finished doing the last-minute tasks of cleaning up behind the bar, Brisa went back to the room where she'd put her purse and the bag she'd packed for the night and weekend. The one she now didn't need.

She left the bar and headed to the parking lot and her car. Usually, when a guy stood her up, that meant she didn't give him a second chance. If he did it once, he was liable to do it again. If Darius called her tomorrow and had a legitimate excuse, she didn't think she'd be able to tell him she didn't want to see him. As she'd said to Janey, he was perfect in every way. He was the type of guy she'd hoped to meet, fall in love with, and end up married to.

She gave herself a mental kick as she started her car, then pulled out of the lot. She was getting way ahead of herself. There was no guarantee Darius would even call her tomorrow. And she sure as shit wouldn't call him. Coming across as desperate was not something she wanted to do. No, if he really wanted to see her again, Darius would have to be the one doing the calling. And he'd better have a good excuse. He might be the ideal man she was looking for, but that didn't mean she'd be his doormat.

* * * *

Darius came awake as pain tore through him. Once it was over, he held his hand up in front of his face and breathed a sigh of relief. He was back in his human form. The spell must have worn off as Anubis had said it would.

Sitting up, Darius stretched, feeling as if he really hadn't slept at all. He'd probably spent the majority of what had been left of the night pacing, only to finally fall into bed shortly after dawn. He'd been too worried to sleep. About being stuck shifted, and about what Brisa's reaction had been when he hadn't shown up at the bar. Even though he didn't think he could have a permanent relationship with her, that didn't mean he was ready to let her go.

Darius stood and shoved his hand into the front pockets of his jeans, then took out his keys and cell phone. He threw the first onto the bed and looked at the latter to make sure the battery wasn't dead. He still had a couple of bars left.

It was just after nine a.m. It was a bit too early to call Brisa, considering she'd worked a night shift. Darius decided to shower first before he called her. If she refused to talk to him, he had every intention of going over to her apartment to try to convince her to see him.

By the time he finished all that, it was going on quarter to ten. It was still fairly early, but Darius couldn't wait any longer. He picked up his cell phone and called Brisa's number. She picked up after the fourth ring.

"Hello?"

"Hi, Brisa."

"Hi, Darius. I wasn't sure if I'd hear from you today."

He swore to himself. She sounded a bit ticked with him, which he totally understood. "I'm so sorry about last night. I planned to show up right until the last minute."

"You could have called, you know. Actually, it would have been nice if you had instead of leaving me to wonder if you just forgot about me."

"I would have if I could. I'd forgotten to take my phone with me, and by the time I got home it was so late I knew you would be asleep. That's why I'm calling now. I still want to spend the weekend with you, Brisa. Can I come and pick you up? We can go out for some breakfast, then I'll bring you here. Please don't be angry at me."

She sighed. "If I say yes, you have to promise never to stand me up again. I won't give you another chance if you do."

"You have my word." At least Darius hoped nothing like that happened again.

"All right. As I said, this is the last time I'll overlook you standing me up."

"I'll make it up to you. I just have to take care of one thing here, then I'll come to your apartment."

"Okay. See you then."

Darius hung up, then headed to the garage. He found a piece of plywood he had lying around and roughly cut it to the shape of the window he'd had to break the night before. With a few nails to tack it in place until he had it repaired, Darius figured it would be good enough. His car wouldn't be quite so easy to jerry-rig. He'd have to take it in to get it repaired, but not today, which left only his motorcycle. He hoped Brisa wouldn't mind riding on the back of it.

CHAPTER FIVE

Brisa opened her apartment door and stepped back for Darius to come inside. It was a half-hour since he'd called and asked to see her. As she'd predicted, hearing his voice, she hadn't been able to tell him no. And it hadn't helped that she'd awoken that morning after having an erotic dream that starred him. She'd been so turned-on her pussy had been wet, aching to be filled.

"Do you want to go out for some breakfast?" Darius asked once she shut the door behind him.

"Actually, I'm not much of a breakfast eater. Give me a cup of tea and I'm fine until lunch. Thanks for the offer, anyway."

Darius met her gaze. "You're mad at me."

She shook her head. "Not really. I'd say it's more like annoyed. I don't like being left in the lurch like that."

He wrapped his arms around her and pulled her up against his chest. "I'm sorry. I tried everything in my power to make it, but it didn't happen. I wasn't happy about it, believe me. I'd looked forward to being with you again. I missed not showing you my bed."

Brisa put her hands on Darius' chest and smiled. "Yeah, you were going to do that."

He bent his head and brushed his lips across hers. "Do you think you can forgive me enough to see it now?"

Her heart rate increased at the thought of what they'd do in his bed. It looked as if she'd get some apology sex, after all. "Hmm, I think I can be persuaded."

"Maybe this will help."

Darius took her mouth fully. He held her tighter as he pushed his tongue past her lips, twining it with hers. Pressed against him from chest to knees, Brisa felt how hard his cock was. Her pussy clenched in reaction as a surge of arousal shot through her. She wanted him, there was no denying that.

After another minute, Darius lifted his head. "Well?"

It took Brisa a few seconds to understand what he'd asked. "Oh, I'd say that definitely helped."

"Good, because if I have to do more persuading we'll never get out of here."

A shiver of anticipation ran down Brisa's back. "Should I pack an overnight bag?"

"Make it for two nights."

Brisa left Darius at the door and rushed to her bedroom. She made short work of throwing what she needed into the athletic bag she'd used the night before. She stopped at the bathroom to get her toothbrush before she returned to him.

"All set," she said.

He took the bag from her and then opened the door. Darius waited in the hallway as Brisa locked it behind her. He took her hand, linking their fingers, as he guided her to the elevators.

Once they were outside, he led her to the visitors parking lot. Not seeing Darius' car, but noticing he walked toward a motorcycle, Brisa had to force herself to keep following him.

She swallowed when Darius unlocked a helmet from the side of the bike and handed it to her. She gave him a weak smile. "You aren't driving your car," she said, stating the obvious.

"With the craziness of last night, the driver's side window was smashed. I have to take it in to get repaired."

"Maybe I should drive my car and follow you."

Darius gave her a crooked smile. "Don't tell me you're afraid to ride on a motorcycle."

"Well, maybe a little. They can be dangerous."

"Only if you don't know what you're doing. You have nothing to worry about. I'm a good driver."

"What about my bag?"

He took it from her and put the strap over his head so it lay diagonally across his chest. "It can sit on my lap."

"Darius, I really don't know."

He kissed the tip of her nose as he took the helmet she still held. He placed it on her head and then did the strap up under her chin. "You'll be fine, Brisa. Just put your arms around my waist and hold on tight."

He put on the second helmet. He climbed onto the bike and then adjusted her bag so it was in front of him. Darius patted the seat behind him. Taking a deep breath for courage, hoping he was as good a driver as he'd said, Brisa sat at his back. She put her arms around his waist, locking her hands together. He put up the kickstand, and with a press of a button, started the bike's engine. As he drove out of the lot, she held on for dear life.

After they'd driven down a few streets, Brisa forced herself to watch the scenery go by. Being on the back of the motorcycle wasn't as scary as she'd thought it would be. Mostly because Darius wasn't driving like a speed demon.

She soon changed her opinion about that when he sped up and took a corner too fast for her liking. She clutched Darius even tighter, sure she was cutting off some of his circulation to his waist. Brisa didn't care. She heard him chuckle over the roar of the motorcycle and realized he'd done it on purpose. In case he did it again, she put her face to the center of his back and closed her eyes. Eventually, the bike came to a stop, but Brisa didn't open her eyes to see if they'd reached their destination, or if they were only stopped at a red light.

Darius patted her linked hands. "You can let go now, Brisa. We're at my place." The bike's engine cut off after he'd said the last word.

She turned her head and opened her eyes. They sat in front of Darius' large house on the drive by the front door. It took a few seconds for her to unlock her hands, then she swung her leg over the back of the motorcycle and got off. As she removed her helmet, he put down the kickstand before he joined her. He took the helmet from her and then locked it to the bike as he'd done with his.

The first thing Brisa noticed when they walked closer to the door was the piece of plywood where a glass window had been next to it. She turned her gaze on Darius. "Did this happen last night as well?"

He gave her a half smile. "Yeah. I kind of locked myself out, so I punched out the window to get in. Let's just say last night wasn't my night."

"I guess not."

Darius let them inside the house. Brisa's gaze landed on the banister and a small smile played on her lips as she remembered her wild rides down it the day before. She turned to say something along those lines to him but found all the words left her mind when she looked at him. He stared at her as if he wanted to gobble her up. Arousal spiked through her, making her insides melt. She wanted the gorgeous man who stood in front of her right here, right now.

Without a word, Brisa stepped into Darius' arms and met his lips halfway when he lowered his head to kiss her.

The passion that had flared to life at her apartment grew ten times hotter. He buried his hand in the hair at the back of her head as he angled his mouth for a tighter fit, nipping and sucking her lips.

She fisted her hands in the front of Darius' T-shirt, trying to drag him even closer when they were already as close as they could get. Her pussy throbbed and wetness pooled between her thighs. She moaned into his mouth, loving the taste of him on her tongue.

Darius shifted his hands to her waist and released her mouth. "I think we'll be more comfortable upstairs."

"My thoughts exactly," she said, a bit breathless.

He took her hand and tugged her up the staircase. At the top, Darius guided her down the hallway to the end where they stepped into his large bedroom. Brisa took in the high ceiling, small sitting area at one side, and the king-sized, four-poster bed, which was the focal point of the room.

She turned back to Darius at the sound of her bag hitting the hardwood floor. His heated gaze ran over her body. Brisa shivered as if he'd touched her physically. He closed the distance between them and took her into his arms. His cock, thick and hard, nestled against her belly, making her ache even more.

"I think you should strip me naked and have your way with me," Brisa said in a husky voice.

Darius groaned. "Have to love a woman who knows what she wants."

He lifted the bottom of her shirt. Brisa held up her arms as he yanked it all the way off. Her bra quickly followed, leaving her naked from the waist up. Darius circled a taut nipple with the tip of his finger before he moved to the top of her jeans. She toed off her shoes and kicked them to the side. He undid the button and zipper, shoving the material past her hips until it fell down her legs to pool around her ankles. She stepped out of her jeans and then shoved them out of the way.

Her panties were hooked with a finger and stripped from her as Darius bent his head and sucked a nipple past his lips. Brisa held on to him for balance, pleasure shooting through her with each tug of his mouth. He paid the same amount of attention to the second before running his gaze over her entire body.

"You're beautiful," Darius said in a strained voice. "I can't wait to be inside you."

Brisa cupped the front of his jeans, squeezing his cock. "I want you, Darius. Don't make me wait any longer."

With a noise that sounded partway to a growl, Darius tore his shirt over his head and then tossed it away. His pants were jerked down and kicked aside. Brisa watched as each inch of male flesh was uncovered. He was all hard muscle without an inch of fat anywhere.

Brisa dropped her gaze to his cock. Fully engorged, it stuck out straight from his body. She licked her lips as she remembered what it had been like to have it in her mouth. She wrapped her hand around his thick length and pumped, loving the sensation of him in her grasp. Her pussy clenched. It would feel so good having him fill her, sliding in and out.

Darius picked her up and gently placed her on the center of the bed before he followed her down. He took her mouth in a demanding kiss while he delved a hand between her legs. She spread them wider, aching for his touch. He caressed along her pussy, a finger dipping inside. A second soon joined it as he stroked them in and out. Brisa clenched her inner walls around the digits working her, pleasure surging through her with each pass of his thumb over her clit.

Brisa broke the contact with his mouth. "Darius." She moaned. "Now. I'm more than ready for you."

"Then no more waiting," he replied huskily.

Darius shifted so he lay on top of her with his hips

wedged between her thighs. The head of his cock pushed against her pussy. Brisa bent her legs and matched each of his strokes as he slowly worked his erection inside her. His thickness stretched her, filling her up, feeling as good as she'd imagined it would. Once he was sheathed to the hilt, they were breathing heavy.

Canting back his hips, Darius almost pulled all the way out before he slid back home. In and out he pumped, driving her ever closer to her climax. It wasn't going to take much to send her flying, not this first time. His thrusts became faster, harder. The sound of their combined moans filled the room.

Darius lifted his upper body onto his hands, his hips continuing to thrust between her spread thighs. He angled his inward strokes so he hit just the right spot that gave her the most pleasure. Brisa clutched his arms, matching his pace. His cock grew even harder deep inside her. She was so close. It would only take a few more thrusts and she'd come.

Once, twice he pistoned into her, then she whimpered his name as her body shattered with an intense orgasm. Her inner walls clutched and released his erection, milking it in a tight fist. Darius continued to move until her climax ended.

Having not come when she had, he pulled out and urged her onto her stomach. Hands on her hips, he lifted her onto her knees. Brisa held her upper body on her bent arms as Darius shifted behind her. He ran his fingers down her back in a caress and plunged back into her pussy.

He set a fast pace, sinking in deeper than he had in the other position. Again, her body coiled tighter and another orgasm built. Brisa pushed back to match Darius' strokes. He held on to her hips as he took her in hard thrusts.

Her second climax snuck up on her and crashed over her in a torrent. Darius pumped into her once, then a second time, before he leaned down, blanketing her with his body. Brisa felt the scrape of sharp teeth at her back where her shoulder and neck met but was too lost in the sensations tearing through her body to care. His cock pulsed deep inside her pussy while he moaned and groaned, holding her tightly to him.

Once it was over, he brought them down to their sides, her head tucked under his chin. She felt completely surrounded by him, his body heat sinking into her skin. She snuggled closer, content just to lie in his arms.

*

Darius' breathing slowly returned to normal, as did Brisa's. He was sated, but he had a feeling that wouldn't last long. He'd want her again shortly. Deep down inside, he didn't think he'd ever get enough of her. Sex with her didn't compare with the one-night stands he'd only allowed himself since becoming one of Anubis' warriors. The pleasure he found in her arms was more intense, more fulfilling.

The only thing that marred what was otherwise the best sex of his life was what had happened just before he'd come. He'd had an almost overpowering urge to mark Brisa, to sink his teeth into her, then keep them there as he filled her with his cum. As if in response, he'd felt the burning in his gums as his eyeteeth had become longer, sharper, what they were like when he was in his shifted form. Unlike the last time he'd had an unexpected shift, only his teeth had changed, nothing else. And the instant his orgasm had ended they'd gone back to normal.

Darius kissed the top of Brisa's head as she pressed against him. His cock twitched in renewed interest, but he did nothing about it. He wanted to give her enough time to recover before he took her again.

"You're awfully quiet back there," she said, a smile sounding in her voice.

"I'm just enjoying having you in my arms."

Brisa rolled to her other side so she faced him. "I have to admit I like being in yours as well."

"Have I made it up to you for last night?"

She kissed his chin. "I'd say that was a good start."

"A start?"

"Yes. You didn't think I'd let you off that easy, did you? I have to make you work for it a little."

"I hope this doesn't mean you're going to be a hard woman to please," Darius said with a grin.

"I'm not hard, but I'm hoping you will be again very soon." She pointedly glanced down at his cock.

Darius laughed as he rolled to his back, taking Brisa with him so she ended up sprawled atop him. He shoved his fingers into her hair and brought their lips together. He kissed her long and thorough until his cock was well on its way to being hard.

"Is this what you want?" he asked, voice rough with renewed arousal.

Brisa rocked against him. "Mmm, very much so."

"Then I suggest you use it."

"Oh, I will."

She took his mouth this time, all teeth, lips, and tongue. Brisa shifted a bit to the side and trailed her hand down his front until she reached his cock. She wrapped her fingers around it and pumped. Darius lifted his hips, pushing himself tighter into her grip. He grew harder, wanting to sink back inside the warm wetness between her legs, but he let her keep the control.

After letting go of her hair, he reached between them and covered her breast. The taut nipple pressed against his palm. He squeezed and plucked at the tight peak. Brisa moaned softly. The sound seemed to wrap around his cock, stroking him along with her hand.

Brisa sucked on his tongue before she released his mouth and straddled him. She lifted onto her knees, still holding on to the base of his shaft. She impaled herself on his erection, taking him all the way inside her pussy. Darius had to fist his hands in the sheets beneath him to stop himself from taking hold of her hips and ramming up into her.

Up and down she rode him, her inner walls squeezing around his cock, driving him mad with desire. Unable to lie still any longer, Darius surged up until he sat upright. He cupped one of Brisa's breasts and dragged his tongue across her nipple before he sucked on it. She dug her nails into the tops of his shoulders, giving a little bit of pain to go along with his pleasure.

Brisa set a faster pace, her moans filling his head, as she rocked against him. Darius released her nipple and left a trail of wet kisses over her chest as he reached between them and found her clit. He rubbed the little bundle of nerves with the tip of a finger. She threw back her head and let out a whimpered moan as her pussy rhythmically clutched and released his cock while she came.

Feeling the point of no return rushing up to meet him, Darius took hold of Brisa's hips and moved her on and off him. He looked down and watched his shaft sliding in and out of her pussy. Just as he started to come, he felt the burning in his gums, the telltale sign that his eyeteeth had become longer, sharper. The urge to bite her surged through him. He viciously fought it, clenching his teeth so hard his jaw ached. He pushed up into her one final time, lifting her knees off the bed, his orgasm taking him over.

Spent, Darius nuzzled the hollow of Brisa's throat and wrapped his arms around her. She embraced him, stroking his back. That was the second time his teeth had changed, both instances when he'd been about to come. At least he'd been able to keep it from Brisa, but it was something he'd have to tell Anubis about.

CHAPTER SIX

"Come on, Brisa. Nobody is going to see you."

She gave Darius a stare that said she wasn't totally convinced. They were outside in his backyard in the late-afternoon sun. After they'd scrounged up some lunch in his kitchen that consisted of sandwiches, he'd suggested they come out there to take a dip in his hot tub. The first thing Brisa had said was that she didn't have a bathing suit with her. His reply had been she didn't need one.

So now there she stood only wearing one of Darius' T-shirts, which was miles too big, as he stood at the edge of the hot tub with just a towel around his waist to hide his nakedness.

"Are you sure your neighbors can't see into your backyard?" she asked.

"Brisa, I have over an acre of land, and privacy fences surround the whole thing."

Darius turned away and dropped the towel to the concrete at the edge of the hot tub before climbing in. The man had no shame, but with a body like his, she figured he had no reason to have any. She didn't have issues with hers, but that didn't mean she liked to go running around outside butt naked.

"Come on, Brisa," Darius urged. "Just do it." When she didn't move so much as an inch to do as he suggested, he said, "Do you want me to strip you out of my shirt and throw you in?"

Brisa sighed. She had a feeling he'd do that if she didn't get in by herself. She walked closer to the hot tub. "Fine, I'll do it, even though I'll feel uncomfortable as all hell." Before she could talk herself out of it, she whipped off the large T-shirt and quickly clambered into the hot tub next to Darius. "Happy now?" she asked.

"Yes," he said with a sexy smile. He pulled her down so she sat on his lap. "Now isn't this nice?"

Actually, it was. "All right, this was a good idea." She wrapped her arms around Darius' shoulders. "Just don't expect me to go into the pool. It'll be freezing after being in here."

"It just makes it refreshing."

"No, it makes it damn cold."

"You win. No pool, at least not for you."

With that said, Darius pushed her off his lap before he pulled himself up onto the side of the hot tub. In long strides, he reached the pool and then dove into the deep end. His head broke the surface of the water.

"Cold?" she asked.

He shook his hair out of his eyes. "No. It's perfect." Darius swam to the end, then did laps.

Brisa followed him with her gaze. His muscular shoulders and arms flexed with each stroke he made. She sighed to herself. She was falling for Darius, and it was something she never expected to happen so fast. She'd had her share of infatuations, been in lust with more than a couple of men, but not like what she felt right now for the man in the pool.

She wasn't doing herself any favors by letting her feelings get too involved in a start of a relationship, but knowing and doing were two different things. And she wouldn't be telling Darius how she felt about him either. Not right now, at least. She didn't know him well enough yet to know if he was the type of guy who wouldn't run for the hills when a woman told him how she truly felt about him.

No, she was better off keeping that knowledge to herself. Brisa would just have to watch that she didn't get her heart broken if she and Darius didn't work out. For now, she'd enjoy just being with him.

Darius hauled himself out of the pool and then jumped into the hot tub. Before she knew what he intended, he scooped her up into his arms and got out of the warm water. Brisa struggled when he headed back to the pool.

"Don't you dare," she said in her sternest tone.

"You mean this?"

He took a few running steps and jumped into the pool. Brisa held her breath as they went under, then kicked away from Darius. She came up screaming like a banshee.

"That's fricking cold," she yelled.

Darius bellowed with laughter. "You look pretty hot when you're angry."

Using her palm, Brisa sent a wave of water into his face. He sent an even bigger one, making her sputter when she ended up with a mouthful. That started a water fight, which ended with her surrendering and feeling as if she'd swallowed half the water in the pool.

Back in the warmer water, Darius climb in beside her. He pulled her close and kissed her slow and tender. Goosebumps rose on her skin, and not from being cold.

Once he lifted his head, he said, "Thanks."

"For what?"

"For giving me a chance to let loose and have some fun. My life hasn't given me that opportunity in a very long time. I'd almost forgotten what it was like to not be so serious."

Brisa put her arms around Darius. "I'm glad I can give it to you, even though it was at my expense. You do realize that now I'll have to think of something to get you back for dumping me in the pool."

"I guess that means I should keep an eye on you then."

He gave her a grin that did warm things to her body. Yup, she was in trouble. It wouldn't take much for Darius to worm his way into her heart, and once there, she'd want to keep him forever.

* * * *

Darius sat across from Brisa at the restaurant they'd picked to have dinner. He couldn't remember the last time he'd had such an enjoyable day. Most of it stemmed from the woman who was coming to mean more to him than she should.

Since pledging himself to the god of the underworld, he'd only thought about the job he did for Anubis. Darius had never thought about doing anything beyond that. He realized now he'd basically been living half a life. He might be immortal, but that didn't mean he had to keep himself distanced from mortals. Brisa had shown him that.

"So, what do you want to do for the rest of the weekend?" Brisa asked. Their waitress had already taken their orders, and they waited for the food to arrive.

Darius reached across the table and captured her hand in his. "Get you naked in my bed and not let you out until Monday."

Brisa licked her lips, reminding him of what it felt like to have them wrapped around his cock. It jerked, pressing against the zipper of his jeans.

"I'm sure that can be arranged," she said, her voice tinged with a seductive huskiness.

He sucked in a big gulp of air and smelled the scent of Brisa's arousal. His cock went hard. One sniff and he was raring to go. She enticed him like no other. The longer he spent with her, making love to her or just talking, he felt as if he never wanted to let her go. Even though they'd only known each other for a couple of days, he felt as if she had been a part of his life for much longer.

"Does that mean you'd be willing to get our food for takeout instead?" he asked.

Brisa shook her head. "No way. I'm starving. You promised a meal out at a nice restaurant, and I'm holding you to it."

As if on cue, the waitress returned with their orders. Wearing a smile, Brisa picked up her fork and then dug into her food with gusto. Darius settled for watching her eat. Even though she wasn't doing anything overtly sexy, she was still turning him on. His gaze followed her tongue as she licked the melted butter off her fingers after dipping the crab she'd ordered into it. He got so caught up in her, he ate without really tasting anything. The throbbing in his cock — and the person who caused it to be in that condition — demanded too much of his attention.

Brisa held out a bit of her food. "Would you like some crab? It's really good."

Drawn to her like a moth to a flame, Darius leaned forward over the table. He opened his mouth for the morsel she offered. She placed it on his tongue. He closed his lips around Brisa's fingers before she could pull away and licked each one thoroughly clean, then released her.

He didn't miss how much faster she breathed. Her cheeks had a splash of color on them that hadn't been there a few seconds ago. And her scent had become more potent, telling him he'd gotten to her.

"Feed me something off your plate," Brisa said.

Darius selected a plump shrimp, using his fingers instead of his fork. It had been cooked in lemon butter, so he ran it through the extra sauce before he picked it up. Brisa leaned forward as he'd done and opened her mouth. Instead of waiting for him to give it to her, she took it from him, closing her lips around his digits.

He had to hold back the moan of pleasure that threatened to break free when she pushed the shrimp to the side of her mouth, then sucked and licked his skin. She pulled back, scraping her teeth along his fingers. Too much more of that and he'd be making a mess in his jeans. Something he hadn't done since he was a young teenager.

"Give me another one," Brisa said after finishing the mouthful, her eyes taking on a slumberous look.

He shook his head and cleared his throat. "If I do, you'll find yourself dragged outside, put up against the nearest wall away from prying eyes, and have me between your thighs before you know what hit you."

"Oh my," she breathed and waved a hand in front of her face. "Did it just suddenly get very hot in here?"

It had, at least between him and Brisa. Darius was surprised not to see waves of heat rolling off them. Passion had flared to life in an instant, growing more intense by the second. He needed to get her out of the restaurant. His hunger for her was outdoing his need for food.

"I suggest we hurry up and finish our meals," Darius said. "Then we can have our own dessert back at my place, which doesn't necessarily have food involved."

"Then what are you waiting for? Stop talking and eat." Brisa attacked her plate, eating at a faster pace than she had before.

The bill paid and the waitressed tipped, Darius walked Brisa out of the restaurant. It was now evening, the sky just starting to darken. They were halfway to his car—he'd managed to have the window fixed on the way to the restaurant, since Brisa refused to ride on his motorcycle—when he felt it, the familiar pull on him. Given how he wasn't on the verge of a shift coming on, he figured the evil he sensed wasn't in the middle of a criminal act, but that didn't mean he could just drive away with Brisa and ignore it. Once an evildoer had been sensed, he physically couldn't walk away until he'd dealt with the individual.

"What's the matter?" Brisa asked as he slowed their steps.

Fighting to not follow where the pulling would take him, Darius racked his brain to come up with a reasonable excuse as to why he had to leave her for a little while. Something that wouldn't have her wanting to go with him. He'd never told a mortal about what he was and hadn't made up his mind if he wanted Brisa to know. For now, it had to remain his secret.

"Nothing," he said. "I just have to make a quick stop in the restaurant's men's room. Sorry. I'll be fast." They reached his vehicle. "I'll let you in the car first."

Darius unlocked the passenger door and held it open as Brisa sat on the seat. The pulling sensation became stronger and would the longer he ignored it. Once she brought her legs in, he shut her inside, then turned to head back to the restaurant.

At the door, he looked behind him to see Brisa had turned her head to watch him through the window. He ducked inside the entrance, then waited until she looked away. Darius slipped outside and ran in the direction of the rear of the restaurant, where he was being led.

*

After Darius disappeared through the restaurant's door, Brisa glanced down as she adjusted her purse on her lap. She looked in the direction Darius had gone again and could have sworn she saw him running around the corner of the building, heading toward the rear of it. Only having glimpsed the back of a male figure before it was out of sight, she wasn't all that sure it had been him.

When a couple of minutes ticked by and there was no sign of Darius walking out to the parking lot, her curiosity got the better of her. Maybe that *had* been him running to the back of the building. More than likely wrong, that didn't stop her from getting out of the car and then heading in the direction she'd seen the man going.

Brisa gave the entrance doors a quick look as she came closer just to make sure Darius still wasn't there. Not seeing him, she continued on. It was getting darker, and the alleyway she entered after rounding a corner was mostly in shadows. She was probably wasting her time, trudging around in the dark. She wouldn't find anything and would end up going back to the car to find Darius waiting, wondering where she'd gone.

She heard what sounded like a bit of a scuffle at the opposite end of where she walked, a place where the light over the back entrance of the restaurant didn't quite reach. Brisa squinted, trying to see into the darkness. She went closer, and figured she had to be seeing things. A very tall figure that looked half human and some kind of animal stood in front of a man.

"Hello? Is anyone there?" she called.

After blinking a couple of times, still not really having a clear picture of what she thought she saw, the beast thing disappeared, along with the man she thought she'd seen.

Okay, she definitely was seeing things that weren't there. Deciding Darius had to be at the car already, and that he hadn't come back here, Brisa turned on her heel and walked the way she'd come. At the car, Darius still wasn't there. She got inside. She'd give him another minute or so, then go look for him in the restaurant. He took too long for just having to use the toilet.

A minute almost up, that's when Darius finally walked through the entrance doors and then out into the parking lot. He hurried across it before he got into the car once he reached it.

"Sorry," he said. "I had to wait my turn. I guess more than a few people needed to use the facilities at the same time I did."

"I was beginning to wonder what had happened to you. So you only went to use the men's room and didn't run outside to the back of the building?"

He gave her a confused look. "No. Why?"

Brisa shook her head. "Nothing. I just thought I saw something, but obviously I was mistaken." She leaned across her seat and gave Darius a hard kiss. "Now didn't you say something about getting some kind of dessert at your house?"

He returned her kiss before he pulled away and then put the key into the ignition. "You're right. I did." He started the car, then drove out of the parking lot.

*

Darius snuck glances at Brisa from the corner of his eye as he drove toward his home. That had been too close for comfort. Not in a million years had he expected her to end up in that alley behind the restaurant. He'd just about shit bricks when he'd heard her calling to see if anyone else was there. Only being well-practiced at hiding in the shadows had saved his ass from being caught. It hadn't been hard to keep his prey quiet.

Once Brisa had left, he'd quickly dispatched the evildoer, a rapist, to Anubis. Then he'd had to sneak his way into the restaurant through the back door. There had been no way he could risk going around to the front from the outside. Brisa would have seen him for sure.

After that close call, Darius decided he and Brisa would stay at his house for the rest of the weekend. While she was with him, he couldn't run the risk of sensing evil. As long as he didn't feel the pull, he was safe. Taking the weekend off would be a nice change, anyway. Especially considering he hadn't taken any time off from his duty to Anubis, not once in the close to eight hundred years since becoming a warrior. He figured he'd earned it.

Arriving home, Darius pulled the car into the garage. He let Brisa inside the house through the connecting entrance. He'd just clicked the lock into place and had turned around when he found himself pushed up against the door with her all over him.

She nuzzled the front of his chest as she worked the fasteners on his jeans. "I've been dying to do this for most of the time we were out."

Brisa yanked his pants down past his waist, springing his cock. It went instantly hard. She went down onto her knees, took hold of him in a firm grip, and sucked him into her mouth. Darius banged the back of his head against the door as waves of pleasure went through him, centering on his dick and what she did to him.

He moaned and dropped his keys. He looked down to watch Brisa taking his cock in and out of her mouth. The sight had him hardening even more. No longer able to hold still, he pumped his hips, matching the rhythm she'd set. Besides sucking on him, each time he slid almost out, she swirled her tongue around the head of his shaft, then stroked the sensitive underside. She brought him to the verge of coming, but Darius didn't want that. He wanted to be buried in her pussy when he reached his release. Wanted her to come when he did.

He pulled Brisa to her feet and switched positions so she was the one with the door at her back. He undid her jeans, yanked them down her legs, and off, taking her panties with them. Her weight felt like nothing as he lifted her. She put her legs around his waist, her pussy coming up against his cock. He groaned as her wetness bathed his erection.

Keeping her pressed against the door, Darius pulled back slightly, then pushed inside Brisa, sheathing himself to the hilt with one thrust. He pulled back again before pushing all the way home. She locked her ankles at the small of his back, using her heels to urge him on as he pumped in and out. This would be hard and fast. He couldn't take it slow. He wanted her too much.

"Yes, Darius," Brisa moaned. "Just like that."

"I want you to come for me," he said as he continued to thrust into her. "I'm too close."

"So am I. Only a little bit more."

Brisa cried out his name, arching her hips as her pussy milked his cock with her release. Darius followed her, holding himself tight to her as he filled her with his cum. This time the need to bite her didn't surface, nor did his teeth change. It made Darius think the two times it had happened had been a fluke. Or their lovemaking had been over too quickly.

Totally out of breath, his legs shaking since he'd come so hard, Darius pulled Brisa away from the door. She put her arms around his neck and held on. After pulling his pants up near his hips, high enough for him to walk without having to worry about falling, or dropping her, he turned and headed for the foyer. He went up the stairs.

Inside his room, he placed Brisa on the center of his bed. She stripped out of the rest of her clothes while he shed his. Naked, he climbed in beside her and tugged her into his arms with her positioned along his side with her head pillowed on his chest.

Darius kissed the top of her head when she relaxed, and her breathing evened out. The nap would do her good. Considering he couldn't get enough of her, he pretty much assumed he'd keep her up most of the night.

Brisa sighed, blowing a puff of air across his chest. Sated for now, Darius closed his eyes. The last thing he thought about before he followed her into slumber was how good it felt to have her in his arms as he slept.

#

arius turned his head and looked at Brisa who lay on her back, fast asleep. It was almost dawn, and as predicted, he'd kept her up for most of the hours of darkness. She didn't stir as he carefully slipped out of bed. He picked up his jeans before he silently walked out of the bedroom. Outside in the hall, he pulled them on.

He headed down the stairs. He needed to talk to Anubis again, without Brisa being around. After the quickie they'd had once they'd arrived back from the restaurant, they had made love three more times. Each of those had been longer and felt more intense. And each time his eyeteeth had dropped. One bout he'd come so close to biting her. He'd nipped her hard enough to almost break the skin.

Inside the mini-temple, Darius closed the door behind him, then approached the altar. As before, after he called out to the god of the underworld, Anubis was quick to reply.

Darius.

"I don't know if that demon's spell completely wore off.

I'm still having shifting problems."

In what way?

Darius paused. Even though Anubis was male, Darius still disliked talking about his sex life with anyone. He figured that was his private business. He never bragged about his sexual conquests.

"It happens while I'm in bed with a woman. Well, one in particular. Brisa. When I reach...completion, my eyeteeth become longer, and I have the almost overwhelming urge to bite her where her shoulder and neck meet. I haven't yet, bitten her that is, but I came pretty damn close once. That's never happened to me before, which has me thinking the demon's spell must be having an influence over me still."

Anubis chuckled in Darius' mind. *Let me assure you that the spell is completely gone. That is not the reason behind this new change in you. It is the woman.*

"I don't understand."

It's Brisa who brings on your urge to bite her. She's your mate, Darius.

"My mate?" Darius asked, feeling very confused. "How is that possible? I pledged to serve you. There is no room in my life for a woman."

Yes, you did, but I never expected you to be alone forever. I do not expect it for any of my warriors, though those of you who were the first to pledge will take longer to find the woman meant for you. You are the first.

"Brisa is mortal. It can't work."

Yes, it can. I gave you all the ability to bind your mate to you. One bite and her life force will be tied to yours.

"That'll give Brisa immortality, but won't it mean that if I die so does she? If I literally lose my head, it's all over for me."

True, but I have made you strong enough, so the chance of any prey being capable of doing that is next to nil.

"Then why not make her an immortal yourself as you did me?"

For me to do that, she would have to be near death and call out to me the same way you did, asking to be saved. That is the only way I am allowed to grant immortality. Would you like to put your mate through that?

"No." Feeling death slowly closing in, desperate to cling to life, was not a pleasant experience. "No, I wouldn't want that for Brisa."

Then you must bite her, but give her the choice first. Tell her exactly what you are. You cannot force her into it. That I will not allow.

"I'd never do that to her."

And he wouldn't. Choosing immortality was a decision that couldn't be made lightly. As for his feelings about Brisa being his mate, it felt right. He'd already started to lose his heart to her. Now knowing what she meant to him, Darius didn't want to let her go. Ever. He just hoped she could accept him and the world he lived in. Having to let her go would be beyond hard.

* * * *

Brisa rolled to her side and reached for Darius. Feeling the spot next to her on the bed empty, and finding the sheets cool, she came awake. A quick look around the room showed he wasn't there.

She sat up and stretched. It was still very early in the morning. Weak light shone through the crack in the curtains, chasing away some of the darkness in the room. In need of something to drink, Brisa pushed out of bed, deciding to go in search of some water and Darius.

Finding his T-shirt on the floor where he'd thrown it the evening before, she slipped it on. Out in the hallway, Brisa walked to the top of the stairs. She looked down but didn't see any lights on. Not letting that stop her, she took the steps to the main floor.

It was easy enough for her to find the kitchen. Her eyes

adjusted to the near dark, so she didn't bother with the lights and headed for the large stainless-steel fridge. Brisa opened it, happy to see some bottled water inside. She grabbed one and then twisted off the cap, closing the fridge with her hip as she took a big drink before she placed the bottle on the counter.

Her thirst taken care of, she went in search of Darius. He had to be around there somewhere. The living room was the first place she looked. Stepping inside the room, it appeared empty, but then she heard the muffled murmur of someone talking. The deep, slightly accented voice belonged to Darius.

Brisa looked around, at first not sure where he could be, then spotted the closed door. She stepped closer. Without knocking, she pulled it open. Her jaw dropped when she took in the smaller room.

The walls were painted stark white, whereas the living room's were dark beige. There were quite a few ancient Egyptian-looking pieces spaced throughout. Framed pictures looked like those found on the pharaohs' tombs in Egypt, painted in jewel tones and gold on real papyrus paper. There were small statues and other works of art. The majority of the items depicted the god of the dead, Anubis. And standing near the back of the room, in front of what suspiciously looked like an altar, was Darius.

"What are you doing in here?" she asked.

Darius whipped around, surprise showing on his face. "I couldn't sleep."

"So you came down here and closed yourself in a room that looks dedicated to the ancient Egyptian god Anubis?"

"I know you'll think this sounds crazy, but being in here helps me relax."

"And you talk to yourself too? I heard you."

"I was…ah…praying."

She gave Darius a quizzical look. "You pray to a god from an ancient race of people?"

He looked decidedly uncomfortable as he shifted in place. "It's just something I do sometimes, all right?"

Brisa gazed around the room again. "Well, this explains the tattoo on your chest. You must be in to the whole ancient Egyptian thing. At least now I know what I can get you for your birthdays and Christmas," she said with a smile.

Darius closed the distance between them and reached out to tuck some of her hair behind her ear. "Does that mean you'll stick around for both those things? Do you want to keep me, even though I have this strange hobby you might not understand?"

She chuckled. "It isn't too strange, except maybe for the praying part, but I can live with it." Brisa shyly met his gaze and put her arms around his waist. "Of course I do want to keep you. You have no idea how long I've lusted after you. You'd come to the bar, and I'd spend most of the time staring at you, thinking of all the things I'd like to do to you."

Darius smiled, making Brisa weak in the knees. "Well, I'm glad you decided to serve me the other night."

"You can thank Janey, your waitress, for that. She's a friend of mine, and she knew I liked you. She kind of coerced me into going to your table. She figured if it was left up to you, you'd never talk to me."

"Then I'll have to thank her on Monday night when I come in. I was a little slow on asking you out, but I did notice you. Why do you think I kept showing up at the bar night after night?"

Brisa lifted her arms and wound them around Darius' neck. She pressed herself against him. "Janey will like that. She thinks you're hot too, but don't tell her boyfriend."

Darius dropped his hands to her bottom, gripping it under the hem of the shirt she wore. "You're completely naked under this." He squeezed each globe of flesh.

"Of course I am. It's too early to get dressed." The last

word was said through a large yawn. She gave Darius a sheepish smile. "Sorry."

He shook his head with a grin. "And it's obviously too early for you to be up. I think we could use some more sleep. Let's get you back into bed."

"As long as you join me."

"I will. I think I'll be able to sleep now." Darius picked her up and then carried her out of the room, shutting the door behind them.

"You don't want to do anything else besides that?" Brisa asked as she played with the back of his hair.

"For now. Then we'll get up in a couple of hours and I'll make you breakfast in bed. How does that sound?"

"Make it brunch instead and I'm game. Remember, I'm not a breakfast eater."

"Then brunch it is."

Brisa put her head on Darius' shoulder, liking the fact that he could pick her up and cart her around. It made her feel, well, womanly. Very feminine. And when he held her in his arms, she felt protected and cared for. Hearing how he wanted her to keep him did delicious things to her body. At the rate they were going, she just hoped it didn't suddenly crash and burn, leaving her devastated.

* * * *

Early that evening, Darius suggested they go for a walk on the beach. Brisa had been quick to agree. Since he had access to it from the back of his property, they only had to step through a gate he unlocked to reach the sand.

Hand in hand, they walked. Brisa enjoyed the colors of the sunset, breathing in the salty air. It looked as if she and Darius had the stretch of beach to themselves. Given that private residences lined it, she wasn't too surprised.

Not too far from Darius' property, Brisa stopped and took off her shoes. She couldn't resist running to the edge of the water and then walking in far enough for it to cover her feet. She could get used to that, having the beach right at her back door, able to enjoy the ocean without having to drive to it.

"How's the water?" Darius called.

Brisa turned to face him. "Not too bad for how deep I'm only going to go. Wetting my feet is enough."

She ran her gaze over him, noticing he'd taken off his shoes as well and now held them. Brisa didn't think she'd ever tire of looking at him. He was handsome and sexy as all hell. And unbelievably all hers.

Walking out of the water, she headed for the man who was becoming to mean so much to her. Darius held his hand out to her, and Brisa hurried her steps to get to his side.

She'd just reached out, not quite touching his fingers, when a disembodied male voice said, "I found you again, warrior of Anubis."

Darius stiffened, pulled back his hand, and let out a bellow of pain. He gripped his head as he dropped to his knees. Brisa found herself frozen in place as his body changed. In a matter of seconds, accompanied by the sound of his bones cracking as they realigned themselves, he'd taken on another form. He looked half human and half animal, his body completely covered in black fur. Whatever animal it was, it was sort of wolfish-looking, but she didn't think it was that. After gaining his feet, he stood a lot taller. He had to be no less than seven feet, his muscles even more thickly padded. She also took in the gold armbands around his wide biceps and the snow-white Egyptian-styled kilt he wore around the lower half of his body.

Looking this new Darius in his animal-like face, she took a step back. Her heart threatened to jump out of her chest. Fear beat at her, especially when she realized she'd seen him like that before. Her eyes hadn't been playing tricks on her last night. She'd really seen him in that form, confronting another man, who she never saw leaving the alley.

"Brisa," Darius said, his voice a lot gruffer and deeper than normal. "It's all right. It's still me in here."

She took another step back. "What are you? I don't understand? I saw you at the rear of the restaurant with another man. What happened to him? Did you kill him?"

"Just calm down. I can hear your heart racing. I'll explain everything, but right now, I have to get back to the house before someone sees me like this."

Brisa looked Darius in the eyes. They had changed as well, looking more animal-like, except they were the same shade of blue as they were when he was human. He pleaded with them. She knew he wanted her to not freak out, but she was already walking a fine line.

"Please, Brisa," he said. "I realize this is way beyond anything you expected. It's going to be all right. Just come with me."

Looking up and down the beach, Brisa saw how out in the open they were. One positive thing, it was better for her. She had more avenues of escape than she would at the house. Other than the shifting into a creature that shouldn't exist, Darius hadn't done anything to harm her. There was intelligence in those animal-like eyes, and he was still capable of speech. He might look like a beast that could kill her with one swipe of his claw-tipped hand, but he'd made no move to come any closer. He waited for her to come to him.

Getting a grip on some of the fear coursing through her, Brisa gave a slight nod. She took a tentative step toward Darius, then another, but she didn't take the hand he held out to her. She wasn't quite ready for that yet.

Darius bent and picked up his shoes that he'd dropped when the change had started. He silently walked beside her back up the beach to the gate to his property. Brisa kept some distance between them, half watching him and where she was going.

On his property, Darius paused at the gate to replace the padlock on the latch. He turned toward her once that task was done. He let loose with a growl that had Brisa ready to bolt, especially when a sword suddenly appeared in his hand.

"Brisa, get down!" he bellowed.

She instantly dropped to the ground, just as Darius closed the distance between them and swung the sword over her head. The sound of it meeting something equally metallic rang in her ears.

"You're quick, warrior. I have to give you that," said the same voice she'd heard on the beach. Only this time it didn't seem to come from all around. It came from directly behind her.

Brisa slowly turned her head and looked up. A man was at her back, holding a sword crossed with Darius'. He might appear human at first glance, but his glowing, red eyes told her otherwise. Her fear returning to its previous level, she crawled out of the way, then gained her feet and went to stand behind Darius, closer to the gate.

Darius growled. "I know what you are, demon. You're not supposed to be in the mortal realm."

The man—demon—laughed. "But here I am. And guess what, I didn't escape the underworld alone. Others are hunting down the rest of the warriors of Anubis. We're going to get rid of you all."

Brisa screamed as the demon went on the attack, his sword moving so fast she could barely track it. Miraculously, Darius countered with the same speed. She watched mesmerized, unable to move, as the fight began in earnest.

To her, Darius and the demon seemed evenly matched, but then Darius lost some ground, bringing the pair of them closer to Brisa. She walked backward until her back hit the gate and she stood in a bit of sand that had worked its way under it.

Growls continued to rumble out of Darius as he blocked each hit. He seemed to push the demon back a bit. She held her breath when a gold knife appeared in his other hand and he tried to slip it past the demon's guard. His opponent ran his sword across Darius' forearm before he kicked the smaller blade out of his grip. It landed close to Brisa's feet.

"Your dagger won't work on me, warrior. It was made only for the mortal evildoers you hunt. This, on the other hand," a dagger Brisa hadn't seen him holding was thrust into Darius' side, "was made specifically to take you out."

Darius grunted in pain as he looked down at the dagger sticking from between his ribs. He dropped to his knees, his sword slipping from his fingers. He blinked his eyes, as if he had a hard time seeing or staying conscious.

The demon laughed cruelly. "Right about now, you should be weakening. The blade is as spelled as your gold one. And from looking at you, I think it's doing its job. Now all I have to do is finish you off."

Brisa didn't think, she just acted. She bent and picked up Darius' gold dagger with one hand and a fistful of sand with the other. As the demon moved in to make his next strike, she threw the sand into his face, hitting him in the eyes. He cried out and staggered back a step, wiping at them. Only thinking to protect Darius while he was down, she shifted closer to the demon and cut him across the cheek. He swung at her, knocking her to the ground.

She lifted her head, tasting blood in her mouth where he'd struck her. Darius lurched to his feet with a loud growl. He went after the demon, all teeth and claws. Taking sword cuts to his belly and thigh didn't deter Darius from trying to beat down his opponent. At one point, Brisa thought Darius was about to take the demon out, but just before he could make the final strike, the demon disappeared.

His disembodied voice said, "I'll be back, warrior, to take out you and your mortal bitch."

Shaking all over, Brisa saw Darius sway on his feet. He let out a groan before he collapsed onto the ground. She let out a shout and ran to his side. What fear she'd felt for him was now gone. The demon scared her more. Darius had done everything he could to protect her.

She kneeled beside him and dropped the gold dagger. His eyes were closed. "Darius." When he didn't stir, she tried again, louder. "Darius! You have to wake up. I can't get you into the house by myself."

Thinking the worst when she still didn't get any kind of reaction, she held her hand out in front of his muzzle. A puff of warm air hit her palm with each breath he took. Brisa sighed with relief.

Needing to rouse Darius, she took hold of his shoulders and shook him. He groaned. "Come on, Darius. You have to wake up."

He finally opened his eyes. "Brisa?"

"Yeah, it's me. We have to get you into the house."

"The demon."

"He's gone. For now. Let's get you onto your feet."

She grabbed his hand and stood before she slowly pulled him up into a sitting position. Getting him to stand proved a little more difficult. He was so much bigger than her. By the time she managed it, with his arm around her shoulders and hers around his waist, she breathed hard and her muscles shook from the strain.

Taking the time to only retrieve the two weapons, she steered Darius toward the back of the house. They stepped through the door at the kitchen, which he had left unlocked. That was as far as he made it. He stumbled, then fell. Brisa was forced to let him go before he dragged her down with him.

CHAPTER EIGHT

Still huffing and puffing, Brisa sat on the floor next to
Darius. "We'll rest for a bit, then try to get you
upstairs."

"No. Too far," Darius said. "Take the dagger out. It's
making me weak. I should heal after that."

She swallowed. "You want me to pull it out?"

"It's the only way."

Brisa stood, then crossed to the light switch before she
flipped it on. While she was at it, she opened drawers until
she found the one that had clean tea towels. She snatched
up a few and then returned to Darius.

She kneeled, her gaze taking in the spots where the fur
on his body was matted with blood. She swallowed past
the large lump that formed in her throat. "If I pull out the
dagger, you're going to bleed, a lot."

"Do it. Won't heal unless you do." Darius' voice
sounded weaker. His eyes kept trying to close.

Taking a deep breath for courage, Brisa gently wrapped
her hand around the hilt of the dagger. She counted to

three, then gave it a hard yank. It made a wet, sucking sound as it came free of Darius' body. He growled. She dropped it to the floor and then quickly wadded up a tea towel and pressed it to his side as blood seemed to gush from the wound. She continued to apply pressure, waiting to see his wounds heal as he'd said they would.

She started to feel concerned when the first towel became totally blood soaked. The second she reapplied was quickly doing the same. "Darius, I don't think you're healing."

His head rolled toward her. "I'm not. Need help. Have to talk to Anubis. He can..." Darius passed out.

Brisa shook him several times, but she couldn't rouse him. "No, no, no," she said, a chill running down her spine. Darius continued to bleed profusely. At that rate, he'd bleed out.

Concentrating on what Darius had said before he'd lost consciousness, she remembered the small room off the living room that was dedicated to the Egyptian god, Anubis. Darius had said he had been praying to the god. Maybe he'd actually spoken with Anubis.

Desperate and ready to try anything, Brisa surged to her feet and ran to the living room. She whipped open the door to the other room inside it. Not sure if this would work, or that Anubis would actually hear her if he truly were real, she cleared her throat.

"Anubis, help me. Please. Darius needs you. I think he's going to die if you don't. There's so much blood."

Brisa held her breath and waited. Then just about jumped out of her skin when a voice filled her mind.

Tell me what happened, Brisa.

"You know my name," she squeaked. Brisa felt another presence in the room with her. Holy shit, she was actually talking to an Egyptian god.

Anubis chuckled. *Yes, I know your name. Darius told me about you. Now what has happened?*

"Darius and I were on the beach when he suddenly shifted into something half human and some kind of animal. Then a demon appeared, and they fought. Darius ended up stabbed in the side with a spelled dagger that is making him too weak to heal. I can't get him to stop bleeding. I'm afraid he's going to die if you don't help him." Brisa's breath hitched on the last words.

It will be all right. Darius is one of my warriors. He is immortal. He cannot die from major blood loss. It will only make him very weak and vulnerable. The two spells – the one used to force him to shift and the one embedded in the dagger – must be stopping him from healing. I take it he is still in his half-human and half-jackal form?

"Yes. He's on the kitchen floor passed out." A jackal. That made sense. Anubis was mostly portrayed as the jackal-headed god.

I cannot come to you, but I can be of assistance from the underworld. Stay here while I look Darius over.

Brisa impatiently waited for Anubis to speak again. The seconds seemed to drag on. She wanted to get back to Darius. The thought of leaving him alone, lying on the kitchen floor, bleeding all over it, made her anxious to return to him. Seeing him so wounded, looking as if he could be close to dying, all she could think of was that she didn't want to lose him. She loved him. She didn't give a crap what he was, she just wanted the man. Wanted to see him unhurt, be as he'd been. She had to swallow back the tears that threatened to flow. Only one escaped, running down her cheek. With a rough sweep of her hand she wiped it away. Now was not the time to break down. He needed her.

Brisa?

"Yes." The sound of Anubis' voice never sounded so good.

I have done all I can for Darius. I managed to stop the bleeding, but until the spells wear off, he will not be completely healed. The one used on the dagger is stronger than I have seen a demon capable of wielding.

"Maybe it has something to do with the fact that this demon, along with I don't know how many others, have escaped the underworld. The demon said they were hunting down the rest of the warriors of Anubis."

That could be the case. Usually, demons do not work together, though. This is something new. I will warn my other warriors.

"How long before the spells wear off?"

I would think by morning. The one used to force Darius to shift could be before that. It is relatively weak compared to the one used on the dagger. Can you handle seeing Darius in his half-jackal form, Brisa?

She nodded, not sure if Anubis could actually "see" her. "I can now. Right after he shifted, it scared the hell out of me. Now I'm more concerned about the demon coming back. I did manage to cut him with Darius' gold dagger before he disappeared."

Where is it?

"Somewhere in the kitchen where I dropped Darius' sword as well."

Anubis was silent for a few seconds before he spoke again. *The demon's blood was still on the blade. I used it to put a protection spell around the house. You do not have to worry about him getting in while Darius is still too weak to fight him.*

"The demon is going to come back, isn't he?"

I am afraid so. He will not stop until either he or Darius is dead.

"I thought as much. Thanks for helping Darius. I should go to him."

You love him, do you not?

A little caught off-guard, Brisa stammered, "Y-yes."

Then I suggest you keep an open mind when Darius tells you his story, and what it means to be one of my warriors. I have moved him to his bed for you. I look forward to talking to you again, Brisa.

She felt Anubis' presence leave the room. Brisa walked out to the living room and headed for the staircase. She took the steps two at a time. At the top, she hurried down the hallway to Darius' bedroom.

He lay under the covers, lying so still. Brisa switched on the light before she crossed the room and then climbed onto the bed next to him. She lifted the sheets to see Anubis had cleaned and wrapped Darius' wounds with what looked like unbleached, homespun linen. She put her hand on his furred chest. It rose and fell with his even breaths.

With nothing to do but wait, Brisa climbed under the covers and carefully snuggled up against Darius' side. She kept her hand on his chest. The fur that covered it was soft to the touch. She lifted her gaze to look at his face. The temptation to touch him there was too great to ignore. She trailed her fingers along the top of his muzzle, then stroked his forehead to one of the pointed ears on his head.

Feeling no fear of him in that form, curiosity had taken its place. She now knew Darius was a warrior of Anubis, but she had no idea what all that entailed. Or how he'd become one. Anubis had said Darius was immortal. It made her wonder just how old Darius actually was. She had so many questions and none of the answers.

Knowing what Darius was, did that make the budding love she had for him any less? Not really. The only thing she had to wonder about was what his feelings were for her. Yes, he'd said he wanted her to keep him, but she wasn't immortal. She'd grow old and die, while he stayed young forever. And given what he was, Brisa didn't even know if he'd have room in his life for her.

It grew later, and Darius hadn't awakened. Brisa finally got up and turned on the big LED television that hung on the wall across from the bed, needing a distraction. Every once in a while, she found herself putting her hand on his chest to make sure he was still breathing. She left his side only long enough to get something to drink, then use the bathroom.

Around three in the morning Darius stirred. He groaned before he blinked open his eyes. A sense of relief washed through Brisa, making her feel weak.

"Welcome back," she said as she leaned over Darius. He tried to sit up, but she pushed him down. "Take it easy. We don't want you to start bleeding again."

He turned his head toward her. "You're still here."

"Of course I am."

"I thought...I thought I frightened you too much in this form."

"I'm not going to lie. You did, but I got over it." To prove it, Brisa leaned farther down and kissed the top of his muzzle.

"I was going to tell you. I just hadn't figured on doing it so soon."

"Well, now I know."

Darius reached across for her, then let out a groan as he dropped his hand back at his side. "That hurt. I don't understand why I haven't healed."

Brisa stroked his brow. "Anubis said it's the combination of the two spells used on you that is preventing it. He thinks once they wear off you'll be fine."

Darius gave her a surprised look. "You spoke to Anubis?"

She nodded. "Before you passed out, you said Anubis would help. I figured since you're a warrior of Anubis, and that you had a room dedicated to him, that you used that spot to talk to him. Hearing you 'praying' early this morning helped me to put two and two together. I wasn't sure Anubis would answer me, but he did. He managed to stop your bleeding and got you up here to your bedroom."

He looked at her solemnly. "Thank you, Brisa. If not for you, I would have been left vulnerable to the demon. I'm surprised he hasn't come back to finish me off as he said."

"Thanks to Anubis, he put a protection spell over the house, using the demon's blood from your gold dagger. I managed to slice him with it. As long as we stay inside, he can't get at us. Anubis also said he'd warn his other warriors. Maybe all of you should band together until the demons are taken care of instead of staying alone."

"We can't. Anubis keeps us apart from each other. He even makes sure there aren't two of us in the same city. I've never met the others and have no idea who they are. And I've been a warrior for a very long time."

"Just how long is that, Darius? Tell me your story."

"I guess there's no longer any point in not telling it to you. First, help me sit up. I'm not doing it flat on my back."

Brisa grabbed the pillow from her side of the bed and placed it against the headboard at Darius' head along with his. She took hold of his arm when he tried to push himself up but tugging at him seemed to cause him more pain. Switching positions so she straddled his waist, she helped lift him by hooking her arms under his. Once he sat up against the pillows, she shifted to move away, but he put his hands on her hips and stopped her.

"You can stay there," he said.

"What about your thigh? You're wounded there as well."

"You're low enough that you're not sitting on it."

Brisa settled back down, careful not to jar him. "Just tell me if it hurts."

"I will." Darius took a deep breath. "I've been a warrior of Anubis for seven hundred and ninety-four years."

"That's almost eight hundred years," she said, finding it so hard to believe.

"I know. I told you I have been one of the god's warriors for a very long time."

"How did it happen? How did you become a warrior?"

"I was already a warrior, a knight, just not one of Anubis'. I'd joined the fifth crusade in 1217. I was originally from Germany."

"You were on crusade?" Brisa asked, feeling a bit in awe.

"Yes. The fifth crusade was the last one sanctioned by the church. It was decided that we'd try to take Egypt. The first thing we did was attack an important Egyptian settlement called Damietta. The sultan there, by the name of Al-Adil, wasn't expecting us, but somehow managed to put up a resistance. Though we finally did take the city, which took several months and thousands of lives to accomplish."

"You came out of that okay?"

Darius nodded. "After all the loot we found in the city, it was decided we'd attack Cairo next. Once that great city was taken, it was thought it would make Egypt powerless and give us an open road to Jerusalem. We met with a small resistance from the sultan from Damietta on the way, but we outnumbered his men. After that, we pushed on to Cairo. We marched alongside the Nile." He paused and shook his head. "Our leaders forgot the river flooded. We ended up trapped behind a canal. Retreat was called, but not all of us made it out."

Brisa picked up Darius' claw-tipped hand and held it. "That's where something happened."

"Yes. I lay on the bank of the Nile, bleeding from the numerous wounds I'd received, on the verge of death, not wanting to go out like that. I called to the Christian god I'd pledged to crusade for to save me but got no response. So I called to any god who listened."

"Anubis heard you."

"He did. He offered to give me back my life. In exchange, I had to become one of his warriors. I didn't think twice and gave Anubis my vow that I would serve him."

Brisa squeezed Darius' hand. She couldn't imagine what it would have been like for him, lying on a battlefield, dying, not wanting to give up the fight to stay alive.

"What exactly does it mean to be a warrior of Anubis?" she asked.

"I'm charged with hunting evil in the mortal realm. When I encounter an evildoer, I feel pulled to him or her. I automatically shift into this form. While in it, I can capture their gaze and see, and live through, every evil thing they have ever done in their lifetime. Then I send them to Anubis in the underworld to be judged. My gold dagger is spelled to do that. One cut and they leave the mortal realm."

"So you don't kill them."

"No. I'm not their final judge. Anubis is."

Darius groaned and pushed Brisa onto the bed. His body realigned itself, shifting back to his human form. The sound of his bones cracking got to her, as did the sounds of pain he made. Once complete, he breathed heavily.

"Are you okay?" she asked softly.

He looked at her and gave her a small smile. "I've gone through a shift thousands of times, but it never gets any less painful."

She pulled back the covers and saw Darius now wore the clothes he'd had on before. With gentle fingers she lifted his T-shirt. Anubis' bandage was still there around his middle. "Are your wounds any worse?" Her gaze landed on the black tattoo of Anubis that was inside a cartouche on his upper chest, over his heart. "Did you get this tattoo after becoming one Anubis' warriors?"

"No, they feel about the same. I guess I have to wait for the second spell to wear off. And that's not a tattoo. Anubis placed his mark on me once I'd taken my vow."

She nodded. "Let me help you take off your shirt so you'll feel more comfortable."

Brisa reached for it, but found herself tugged up against Darius' chest, his lips moving over hers in a passionate kiss. He had her well on her way to being aroused when he pulled away, but she knew it would go no further than that, not with him so badly wounded.

"Thanks for staying with me, Brisa," Darius said in a husky-sounding voice. "I didn't know how alone I actually was until I met you."

She reached up and stroked the side of his face. "Well, I'm not going anywhere." She noticed his eyes were becoming heavy lidded. "I think we should get some sleep. It's late. Hopefully by the morning you'll be healed."

"I am tired." He gave her back her pillow, then tugged his until it was on the mattress under his head. Darius held out his arm. "Come here."

Brisa hesitated. "I could hurt you in my sleep."

Darius pulled her against his uninjured side and held her close. "It'll be worth the pain. I want to feel you next to me. I'll sleep better."

Settling her head on his chest, she relented. A minute later, Darius relaxed and his breathing even out. She closed her eyes. Before sleep took her, she thought of all that had happened that night. Being in love with an immortal warrior would take some getting used to, but she was glad he was hers.

CHAPTER NINE

Darius opened his eyes to find the room bright with the light of day. He looked at the curtains to see they hadn't been closed. He tried moving and found he could do so without experiencing pain. His wounds had healed while he'd slept.

He turned his head. Brisa lay next to him, still lost in slumber. Darius slipped out of bed without disturbing her. Standing next to it, he stripped out of his clothes and then tore off the linen bandages. There weren't any marks on his skin to show where he'd been hurt. Naked, he climbed back in next to her.

Shifting so he lay on his side with his head supported on his hand, he stared down at her. Last night, after he'd first shifted, he'd thought for sure he was going to lose her. She'd been too fearful of him. Even though she'd agreed to let him explain, he'd still felt as if she wouldn't be able to accept what he was.

Then the demon had showed up and gone on the attack. Darius had had only one thing on his mind—

protect Brisa. In the end, it'd been she who'd saved his life. If she hadn't been there, he wouldn't have walked away from the fight only wounded, if he'd walked away at all. He would have lost his head.

He reached out and brushed a lock of hair away that had fallen over Brisa's forehead. A surge of love and protectiveness washed through him as he looked at her beautiful face. The face of his mate.

Even though he'd told her his story of how he'd become a warrior to Anubis, and what his duty was to the god, he hadn't told her about being his mate. She'd already had a lot to take in without him adding that to the mix. Now was the time to do so. He wanted to make love to her and had a feeling he wouldn't be able to hold back from biting her, making them mates. Anubis had told him that he had to let Brisa have the choice, not to take that away from her.

Darius leaned down and brushed his lips across Brisa's. "Wake up."

She mumbled something incoherent and tried to push him away.

He chuckled. "Come on. You can sleep later." He nibbled her lips and covered one of her breasts with his hand, giving it a squeeze.

Brisa kissed him back. "Mmm," she said against his lips. "What a way to wake up. I'd like your kisses to do that every morning."

He pulled back and smiled. "I think that can be arranged."

She turned her head and looked at him. "How are you feeling? Did the other spell wear off?"

He nodded. "I'm all better. The wounds have healed. You want to see?" Darius flipped back the covers.

Brisa's gaze ran down his body and stopped at his cock. He was already aroused, his shaft fully engorged.

She licked her lips. "I can see that you are."

She rolled to her side and reached for his cock. She

wrapped her fingers around it, stroking up and down. Darius gloried in the feel of Brisa touching him, but he had to get her to stop until they'd had a chat.

"That feels good. Too good. I have to tell you something before we go any further," he told Brisa as he tugged her hand off his erection.

"Tell me what?"

Darius sank fully onto his side so he was on Brisa's level. "The day you heard me talking to Anubis in the room I set up as a temple to him, he and I spoke about something that concerns you."

"Was it good or bad?"

He smiled. "I like to think it's good, but that's for you to decide." Darius ran the pad of his thumb along Brisa's kissable bottom lip. "I've never had feelings this strong for a woman as I do you. Even when I was mortal, I had no wife. Back then, I was only interested in finding the next battle to fight. That was part of the reason I joined the crusade, not because I had a strong religious conviction."

"So you were a knight who liked to play with his sword," she said coyly.

Darius understood her double meaning and shook his head with a laugh. "There you go with your mind in the gutter again."

"Hey, I can't help it. I have a sexy, naked man in bed next to me. One who also happens to be horny."

"I'm trying to be serious here."

"Sorry. I promise to behave."

"Anyway," he said with a sigh. "What I'm getting at is that I've fallen in love with you, Brisa. I want you to be a part of my life. I'll always be one of Anubis' warriors, but if you think you can accept that, and what I have to do, I promise I'll do everything in my power to keep you happy."

She gave him a sad look. "I love you as well, Darius. There's one thing, though. You're immortal and I'm not. I know I'll love you when I'm old and gray, but the big question is, will you? You'll stay looking as you do now forever."

He put his arm around her waist and tugged her close so their fronts pressed together. "This is where my talk with Anubis comes in. I thought something was wrong with me, because just about every time we've made love, right before I come, a change comes over me. My eyeteeth become longer and sharper, as they do when I shift. I had the urge to bite you."

Brisa swallowed. "Bite me? You must have hidden that well, because I didn't have a clue about any of it."

"I guess I did. Anubis told me there wasn't anything wrong. That it was something that would happen when I found the woman to be my mate." He paused. "You're that woman, Brisa."

"So you want to bite me since I'm your mate."

"Yes. I'm giving you the choice, though. Once I bite you, you'll become immortal like me. Your life force will be tied to mine."

Brisa cupped the back of his head and brought his lips to hers. Her kiss was hot and demanding. She pushed her tongue inside his mouth before she sucked on his, driving him crazy. Darius rolled them so she was on her back with him on top of her.

As he made a trail of wet kisses along the side of her neck, she said, "Do it, Darius. Bite me. I want to have forever with you. I know you've waited a long time to find me, but I've waited for you as well, even though I didn't know it. Make me your mate."

He nipped her skin where her shoulder and neck met. "Not yet, but I will if that is truly what you want."

Brisa pulled his head up and met his gaze. "It is. I know what I want, and I want you."

Capturing her mouth again, Darius kissed her hard and long. He molded one of her breasts with his hand and plucked the taut nipple under her shirt. Brisa squirmed beneath him, pulling at her clothes. He ended their kiss and quickly stripped her naked. He groaned at the feel of her curves pressing along his naked skin.

He suckled at her breast as he reached between her legs to see how ready she was for him. Darius moaned. Her pussy was wet, and his finger easily slipped inside it. He added a second, pumping in and out, loving the sounds of pleasure Brisa made as he worked her.

His cock aching, wanting to be buried deep inside her, he shifted up higher on her body and then pushed the head of his shaft into her pussy. Brisa wrapped her legs around his waist. She rocked with him, matching his strokes, as he pushed deeper until she'd taken his full length. Her warm wetness bathed his cock while he slid in and out.

"Harder, faster," Brisa moaned.

He set a quicker pace, giving her what she wanted. His cock grew harder. Already an orgasm built, his balls drawing up close to his body. Brisa's whimpers of passion drove him on. He strained against her, taking her in harder thrusts.

She called out his name when her pussy clamped down around his cock, clutching it, holding it in a tight fist. It had him racing to the point of no return. He felt that now-familiar burning in his gums as his eyeteeth dropped. There was no denying his urge to bite Brisa this time. He bit where her shoulder and neck met, his teeth sinking beneath the skin. She stiffened under him, then let out another loud moan when she was thrown into another climax. Darius followed her, groaning against her skin, his cock pulsing deep inside her pussy, filling her with his cum. Just before the last wave of pleasure receded, something snapped into place between them, like an invisible bond.

He released her neck and looked down at her. "Did you

feel that?"

She nodded and looked up at him with the love she had for him showing in her eyes. "I think it worked."

"It did." His gaze landed on the spot where he'd bitten her. The teeth marks he'd left behind healed and disappeared.

Brisa pulled his head down and kissed him. "I love you."

"I love you too."

"I hope you weren't planning on doing anything else but staying in bed today," she said with a smile. "Since we're now mates, and I guess technically married, this is our honeymoon. I'm not going to waste any of it." She rolled him to his back with her ending up on top. "Starting right now."

Darius surrendered himself to his mate, quite happy to give her all that she wanted.

* * * *

"I really don't like this," Brisa said as Darius picked up his sword off the kitchen table.

"I know, but it's best if I do it this way."

It was now night. She and Darius had indeed spent the day making love, only coming down to eat when hunger drove them out of the room. It had been during one of those breaks that he had told her his plan to draw the demon out, to fight him.

"What if he stabs you again with a spelled dagger? He got the drop on you the last time."

"He won't be able to do so again. I'll be ready for it. Last night I was distracted by you, worried you wouldn't accept me. I'm not anymore."

"You're still sure he'll come?"

Darius gave a harsh chuckle. "He'll come. He won't resist having me out from under Anubis' protection. He already thinks he'll be able to defeat me."

"Just promise me you won't do anything that will get you killed. I just got my immortality. I don't want to lose it on the same day."

He gave her a hard kiss. "We being mated just gives me another incentive to get rid of the bastard."

Brisa silently nodded. She had to trust that Darius knew what he was doing. He walked out of the door in the kitchen that led to the backyard. When he headed past the pool and hot tub to a long stretch of lawn, she raced to the dining room where there were a set of French doors that gave her a better view.

Darius stood with sword in hand and waited for the demon to put in an appearance. Seeing him like that, Brisa saw the ancient knight he'd been. All he was missing was chain mail and armor.

Not like the other time, the demon didn't give Darius any warning that he was nearby. The demon didn't taunt him with a disembodied voice, nor did he force a shift on Darius. One second the demon wasn't there and the next he was, his sword slashing toward the man she loved.

Brisa's heart jumped into her throat, but she breathed a sigh of relief when Darius easily blocked the hit with his sword. This fight, he did seem more focused. Unlike the last time, the demon didn't gain any ground. Watching Darius, she decided his movements were beautiful and deadly at the same time.

The demon must have sensed that he wasn't going to win. He disappeared. Brisa thought for sure he'd taken a coward's way out and run, but he reappeared behind Darius. Not thinking of her own safety, she ran out of the house toward them, screaming a warning at Darius. He blocked the hit that would have skewered him in the back.

"Brisa," he yelled, "get back in the house."

Too late she realized her mistake. The demon disappeared again only to appear in front of her. She didn't have time to turn and run before he had her held with her back to his chest, an arm around her middle, and a knife held to her throat.

Darius gave a bellow of rage and advanced on them. The demon held the blade tighter against her skin, making Brisa hiss with pain when it cut her. "Stop right there, warrior. You want your precious mortal to live, you'll put down your sword."

Seeing Darius start to lower his weapon, Brisa said, "Don't, Darius. He won't let either one of us live, you know that."

Darius took another step closer, and the knife cut a little deeper. Brisa felt they were at a standoff. She racked her brain to think of a way to get herself out of the spot she'd stupidly put herself in.

A low growl brought her out of her racing thoughts. While she'd looked away, Darius had shifted to his other form. This time she didn't think the demon had used a spell on him. Her mate didn't seem surprised by it. If anything, a look of determination came over his face.

Moving faster than she could keep track of, Darius ripped the demon's knife from her throat and shoved her aside. Brisa spun around, feeling blood dripping down her chest, but didn't pay it any heed. Her attention focused on the scene that played out before her.

Darius took hold of the demon and quickly seemed to catch his gaze with his own. The demon suddenly gave up the fight as he stared into Darius' eyes.

"Evil." Darius growled. "Time for you to face your judgment."

A dagger appeared in his hand, but it wasn't gold. This one looked to be some kind of black metal. Darius cut the demon across the chest with it, and the sound of sizzling skin followed. Darius released the demon as he seemed to fade out of sight, screaming with rage.

Once they were alone, Darius growled as the change

swept through him until he again stood as a man. He turned to her and opened his arms. Brisa ran into them, holding him tight.

"Is it over?" she asked.

"Yes. I sent him to Anubis to be judged."

She pulled away only far enough to look at Darius. "I thought you couldn't do that."

"While he held you, threatening to end your life, it brought on the change."

"And the dagger?"

"Something new, though I've always had the ability to will any weapon I need into my hand. I just thought of what I would need to send a demon back to the underworld to face Anubis."

Brisa tucked her head under his chin. "That's one demon down, but how many more are out there hunting the rest of the warriors like you?"

"I don't know, but I'm sure Anubis will warn them."

Darius let her go, then scooped her up into his arms. "Right now, I'm just happy I sent the one after me to a place where he can't ever hurt us again." He carried her toward the house. "That taken care of, I'm going to make love to you for the rest of the night."

Brisa wrapped her arms around her mate's neck and whispered all the dirty things she wanted to do to him into his ear. She soon found herself laughing as Darius put on a burst of speed no mortal could manage and had them up in the bedroom where he showed her how much he loved her over and over again.

The End

HER ETERNAL WARRIOR

Protecting mortals from the evil preying upon them is Tor's number-one job. His dying pledge to serve the Egyptian god Anubis gave him immortality and a life of solitude as a jackal shifter — for thousands of years. But all that changes when he saves a young woman from being attacked. The moment he sees her face his blood — and his cock — stirs. For the first time ever, he is reluctant to wipe himself from a victim's mind. She becomes the center of his existence, and nothing but total possession will do.

Kenna can't believe her luck when the sexy-as-hell stranger approaches the Luxor Hotel reception desk and asks her out. There's something familiar about him, but she just can't place it. She falls hard and fast, and scorching sex is just the icing on the cake. Tor's guarded secret could change everything, however. Sure, she was open to settling down, but life with Tor would put a whole new meaning on the word forever.

CHAPTER ONE

After a long night of hunting evildoers, Tor was more than happy to call it quits with the coming dawn. Las Vegas wasn't called Sin City for nothing. Most nights he found more than enough prey to keep him on his toes. There were so many tourists around. Evil liked to stalk them, to try to steal from or harm those who were weak or unaware of the danger that lurked around.

Tor now called Las Vegas his home, but that hadn't always been so. He'd been born in ancient Egypt. He was also the very first warrior of Anubis. He'd given his vow to the god of the underworld when mortally wounded during a military expedition to Sinai Peninsula in Egypt while serving his pharaoh, Djoser. Tor had been a soldier during his pharaoh's reign in the third dynasty in the Old Kingdom. He'd stayed in the land of his birth for thousands of years before moving on to the New World.

Tor spotted his sports car ahead and his steps lengthened. The vehicle was a flashy red, and a recent purchase of his. Since the invention of motorized transportation, he'd always had an automobile. Every couple of years he'd see a newer model and would have to have it.

Tor got into the car and then the engine roared to life with push of a button. He pulled away from the curb before he headed for the center of the city. It was stupid of him, but from time to time he liked to take a drive by the Luxor hotel to look at the pyramid-shaped building and the Sphinx outside it. The hotel was the closest thing to remind him of Egypt and the time he'd been born into.

As he drove closer to the Luxor, Tor felt the familiar pull of evil. He had to see where it led. Once felt, he couldn't ignore it, had to follow it to the evildoer and ultimately determine if he had to send the mortal to Anubis in the underworld to be judged. It was his duty, what he'd vowed to uphold to the Egyptian god, to protect mortals from those who would harm them.

Tor followed it to the hotel's parking lot. He parked his car and then exited, the pull of evil growing stronger. He headed for the darkest shadows, spotting the figures of two people—a man and a woman. The man said, "Give me all your money, bitch," as he threatened her with a knife. When she didn't hand over her purse, his prey tried to snatch it from her, breaking the strap, but the woman didn't let it go.

The change tore through him. He shifted into his half-human and half-jackal form. The pain of it washed over him, but Tor didn't even break stride, he was so used to it by now. Even after going through it for thousands of years, it still felt as if someone took a shredder to his skin and a knife to his insides—the sound of his bones shifting and realigning loud in his ears.

Reaching the pair, with a furred hand, Tor grabbed the man by the shoulder and yanked him away from the woman. He threw him against a nearby wall, stunning his prey. He barely glanced at the woman as he grabbed the man again and pulled him to his feet. At seven feet tall in that form, he towered over the evildoer. Tor forced the mortal to look into his eyes. He pushed into the man's mind, not caring if he caused him pain.

The man yelled, "My head, God, stop. Let me the fuck go!" He tried to throw a punch at Tor, but Tor easily deflected it with a brush of his arm.

Tor took hold of his prey by the throat, the scent of evil that only he could smell wafted around him as he finally succeeded in getting into the man's mind. All the crimes and assaults his prey had ever perpetrated flashed through Tor's head. The screams of the man's victims echoed inside it. Tor lived each one as if he'd been the one on the receiving end. He felt their pain, their terror.

"Guilty," Tor said in a voice that was much deeper and gruffer than his normal one. "Time for you to face your judgment."

He held up his free hand and willed a hardened gold dagger into it. The blade had hieroglyphs carved on it — the spell Anubis had infused to send evildoers to the underworld. All it took was one cut to do its job. Tor didn't hesitate. He sliced it across his prey's chest, cutting through to the skin.

The man gasped before he let out a scream. His body slowly lost solidity before he disappeared completely. He'd been sent on his way to face the god of the underworld. There, Anubis would weigh the man's heart on the Scales of Justice. If he was evil, it would be fed to Ammit to be consumed.

That done, Tor turned in the direction of the woman. He willed the dagger away as her gaze seem to land on it, her eyes widening. The sound of her rapid heartbeat was loud in his ears. She slowly backed up, as if she thought she could get away from him.

Tor caught her by the arm and took his first real look at her. He found her beautiful, and was instantly attracted to her, his cock going hard under the snow-white Egyptian-styled kilt he wore. He couldn't remember the last time a woman had stirred his body so quickly. Her hair was long and blonde and fell over her shoulders in a river of silk. Blue-green eyes stared at him with fear clearly showing in their depths. She was a small thing, only standing around five-feet-four. Dressed in a blue, short-sleeved blouse — matching the color of her eyes — and black dress pants, her figure was slim and curvy.

The sound of a soft whimper brought Tor's gaze back up to her face. Her fear was thick between them. By how fast she breathed, he could tell she was on the verge of hyperventilating. If he'd been in his human form, he would have calmed her down by kissing her senseless. He could almost feel her soft, pouty lips under his, the taste of her on his tongue, but he couldn't. He wouldn't shift again until he'd finished the job at hand — wiping himself from her memory and everything she'd seen associated with the evildoer.

Tor gently took hold of her chin and forced her to look him in the eyes. "Don't be afraid. I won't hurt you. Let me in."

He carefully pushed into her mind. Her name was Kenna and she worked at the Luxor at the reception desk. She'd just gotten off her shift when the evildoer had accosted her at her car before pulling her into the shadows. She was scared out of her wits of him.

For the first time in the long time since he'd been one of Anubis' warriors, Tor didn't want to wipe his memory from a mortal's mind. He wanted Kenna to remember him. Not necessarily in the form he was in now, since she was terrified, but some part of him, but it had to be done. Anubis didn't allow his warriors to let a mortal retain the knowledge of what they were.

Tor ran his fingers from her chin, then across her cheek in a caressing stroke. He sighed deeply. Reluctantly, he set to work wiping Kenna's mind. Once he finished, she stared off into space, deep in the daze he'd put her in. She'd stay that way until he left the parking lot.

Backing away, Tor hissed in a breath between clenched teeth as the change overtook him. Now back in his human form, he stopped his backward movement. His gaze remained riveted on Kenna. Why the hell did he find it so hard to walk away?

Tor shook his head and mentally kicked himself as he closed the distance between them once again. He cupped Kenna's face in his hands and placed a soft kiss on her lips. He groaned as that simple touch had his cock jerking.

He released her to back away again. He turned on his heel after giving her one last look, memorizing Kenna's face. Tor climbed into his car and then drove out of the parking lot before he did something stupid like bring her out of her daze and make her remember everything he'd erased from her mind.

* * * *

Kenna blinked and looked around. She found herself standing in the shadowed corner of the Luxor's parking lot. Hadn't she been at her car not a second ago? She had no memory of walking to where she now stood. She shook her head as she headed back to her silver sedan. She must be a lot sleepier than she'd thought. By the end of her shift, she'd caught herself falling asleep on her feet a few times. She guessed that was what she got for trading shifts with someone who worked nights. And the worst part of it all was she had to come into work in the morning, back on her regular hours. Never again.

At her car, Kenna climbed in and then started the engine. She yawned as she pulled out of the lot and headed in the direction of her apartment. Her bed was calling her. Once at her place, she parked in the underground parking garage before she took the elevator up to her floor.

With her purse clutched in her hand, she used her other to fish inside it for her keys. It was then she noticed the strap was broken. How had that happened? Kenna knew for a fact it had been in one piece when she'd left the hotel. She distinctly remembered putting it on over her shoulder. She really must be exhausted. First sleepwalking in the Luxor's parking lot and now not remembering how she wrecked her purse.

Kenna opened the door, then stepped inside before she locked it behind her. She threw her purse onto the coffee table, deciding she'd deal with it in the morning. Now that she was home, her tiredness seemed to weigh heavier on her.

She went through the routine of changing out of her work clothes and getting ready for bed. Kenna let out a contented sigh as she climbed under the sheets and then pulled them over her. The next time her coworker asked her to trade shifts, she was going to tell him to get lost. There was a reason she preferred days. A night person she was not.

Kenna closed her eyes. She was just on the verge of falling into a deep sleep when an image of a man with black hair appeared in her mind. He bent to kiss her softly on the lips. She shivered as their mouths met. She couldn't see his face, but she felt drawn to him, wanted him to kiss her deeper, but he pulled away and then disappeared. Readjusting her pillow, she hoped she'd dream of the faceless man. For some reason, she didn't want to let go of his image.

* * * *

"You look about ready to fall over."

Kenna turned toward the counter of the reception desk

and looked at her male friend, Nick, who worked as a blackjack dealer at the Luxor casino. Most people thought he was gay, since he came across as a bit on the effeminate side, but that was the furthest thing from the truth. He went after anything female. He loved women, and usually ended up getting laid more often than not.

"Thanks," she said with sarcasm. "Tell me something I don't already know."

"Wish you hadn't decided to trade shifts?"

"Big time. I didn't get enough sleep before I had to come back in here."

"Well, this should be a lesson learned. You want to go do something tonight?"

Kenna shook her head. "Naw. I wouldn't want to cramp your style. Plus, I'd probably end up falling asleep on you. I think my night will be spent taking a long soak in the tub, maybe watching a movie, then early to bed."

Nick gave her a look that said he found her plans boring. "That sounds like a perfect night. Not."

"Maybe I'm just getting old."

He snorted. "Yeah, right. You're just an old granny at age twenty-six. You just need to get laid."

Kenna laughed. "And you're the man to do it?"

"Hell no. We're better as friends than lovers. You know that. Besides, I'm not your type."

"Oh, really. And what exactly is mine then?"

"Tall, dark, handsome, and built like a brick shithouse. I'm none of those things."

Nick had her pegged. She did find herself attracted to men who had all those characteristics. Like the man she'd dreamed about last night. Even though she didn't know what he looked like, she bet he was handsome as sin. He was her dream man, after all. Her friend, on the other hand, was five-feet-eight, had a slim build, and spent more time on his dark blond hair to get it just right than she did on her own. After they'd first met, it hadn't taken them very long to decide they'd only be friends.

"Okay," she said. "You know what I like. And maybe it has been a while since I've gotten laid, but, unlike you, I don't sleep with anything that moves."

Nick put a hand on his chest and gasped dramatically. "Did you just refer to me as a slut?"

"Man whore, slut, all the same."

He chuckled. "And I wouldn't want it any other way. At least I don't have to go home night after night to an empty bed if I don't want to."

"Only because you never take any of your conquests to your place. You always manage to talk them into inviting you to stay the night at theirs."

"I prefer it that way. Then I can leave when I want. It would be much harder to convince them to leave my apartment. I wouldn't want to be rude after they gave me a night of pleasure."

That was Nick. He might whore around, but he respected all the women he slept with. "You're just a nice guy."

He smiled. "I know I am."

"And conceited too."

With a roll of his eyes, he asked, "Are you ready to go? I'm done with my shift and so are you."

Kenna nodded. "Just let me grab my purse." She reached under the counter and retrieved it before she walked out to stand next to Nick.

Her friend gave her a quizzical look. "Is that a new purse? I thought you'd just bought one the other week."

"This is an old one. And I did. Somehow I managed to break the strap on the new purse last night after my shift."

"You don't remember how you did it?"

"No. I guess I was pretty tired and wasn't paying much attention. I didn't realize until I got home that I'd damaged it."

"No more night shifts for you," Nick said as he shook

his head and got them walking toward the hotel's exit.

"My thoughts exactly. Do you have your car back yet?" Nick's was a beater, and he seemed to have it in the shop a lot for repairs.

"No. I should get it tomorrow. Do you mind giving me a ride home?"

"I can give you a lift. I was going to ask you, anyway."

"I appreciate it. I hate having to take the bus. It takes three times longer to get anywhere."

"You know it would probably be cheaper just to get a newer car rather than having to pay for all these repairs."

"True, but I'd only be able to afford another beater again. I'm going to hold on to this one for a little longer."

They reached the parking lot, and Kenna slowed her steps as a feeling of anxiousness washed over her. Her heart raced as a shiver of fear ran down her spine. She had no idea what was wrong with her. She'd never had that feeling before. And she didn't think she had it this morning when she'd arrived at the hotel. But then she'd been rushing since she'd dragged her ass getting to work.

Nick slowed and turned his head to look at her. "Kenna? Are you all right? Your face has gone white."

She nodded before she cleared her throat. "Yeah. I sort of feel a bit…weird."

"I hope you're not coming down with something. Working that night shift must have really hit you hard."

"I guess so."

"A night in is probably the best thing for you. Especially a soak in the tub. Just make sure you have some wine or something to kill all the germs."

Pushing back the nervousness, Kenna laughed as she picked up her pace again. "I don't think having something alcoholic will do much to prevent me from getting a cold."

"Maybe not, but it'll help you relax."

"All right, doctor. I'll have some wine, as you prescribed."

"Good girl."

After unlocking the passenger door for Nick, Kenna came around to the driver's side. She got into the car, then started the engine. She had to resist the urge to gun it and peel out of the parking lot. He didn't seem to notice her agitation, which she was sure had to show on her face. She'd suddenly broken out in a cold sweat. Her gaze shifted to the corner of the lot where she'd found herself the night before as she put the car into reverse. She had to bite her bottom lip to hold back a whimper that threatened to bubble out of her. It took everything in her to pull out of the space at a proper speed, then merge into traffic. That particular spot scared her for some unknown reason.

Once she was away from the parking lot, all the anxiety disappeared. It didn't make any sense. She wasn't the type of woman who was frightened easily. So this unfounded fear wasn't her norm. Maybe she *was* coming down with something. That could be the only explanation. And she'd do as Nick suggested and have some wine. Maybe a glass, or two, or three.

She dropped Nick off at the front of his apartment building, telling him she'd see him at work the next day. Kenna drove to her place, deciding she'd definitely have to call it an early night. Hopefully getting a full night's sleep would have her feeling more like herself.

CHAPTER TWO

or had managed to stay away for two whole days, but his luck ran out on the third. He seemed irresistibly drawn to the mortal, to Kenna. After wiping her memory a couple of nights ago, he hadn't been able to stop thinking about her. The last two mornings he'd woken up with his cock in his hand, stroking himself and on the verge of coming because he'd dreamed it was her touching him, pleasuring him. He couldn't get her out of his mind.

Today, he could no longer ignore his need to see her outside his dreams. He was driving himself crazy. He had to put himself out of his misery, even if he just looked at her once from a distance. Then he should be able to walk away. He hoped.

Knowing there was no point in trying to talk himself out of it, Tor slid into his car and then drove out of the MacDonald Highlands community where he lived and headed for the Strip and the Luxor hotel. It was late morning, and from reading her memories, he knew Kenna would be at work. That late shift hadn't been her normal one.

Tor parked his car and then headed into the hotel. He walked through the entrance and took a deep breath to see if he could filter Kenna's scent from the myriad ones around him. He'd memorized it from the other night. He didn't have any luck. There were too many mortals.

That didn't stop Tor from heading in the direction where the reception desk would be. He wasn't going to get too close. Just far enough to have an unobstructed view of Kenna, and maybe catch a whiff of her scent. He'd look his fill, then leave.

As Tor drew nearer to where Kenna worked, he slowed, staying in the midst of the mortals who went about their business. He stared in the direction of the reception desk and spotted Kenna, busy talking to a patron of the hotel. His whole body seemed to come to attention, including his cock. Being that close to her made him crave her even more than he already had.

He ran his gaze over Kenna, drinking her in. The sound of the man she spoke to raising his voice had Tor headed to the reception desk before he could stop himself. He didn't like the man's tone. He had no right to talk to her that way.

Tor stepped up beside the man in time to hear him say, "Since you're totally useless, I'd like to speak to your manager."

"I'm sorry, sir," Kenna responded. "It's the hotel's policy not to give out that kind of information about our guests."

"I don't give a shit if it is. Let me speak to someone who has more authority than you."

Tor turned to face the man. "I think you need to be a little more respectful. She already told you it's against the hotel's policy. Take that for your answer and leave."

The man rounded on him. "Who the hell do you think you are? You're obviously not hotel security."

"No, but I could be the man to throw you out of here on your ass." Tor leaned closer to the mortal and glared into his eyes. "Leave."

The man must have seen something in Tor's eyes. His demeanor swiftly changed from aggression to scared shitless. He mumbled what sounded like an apology to Kenna, then walked away at a fast clip. Tor followed him with his gaze until he disappeared from sight.

"Thanks," Kenna said. "I had a feeling he wasn't going to let it go."

Tor turned to face her. "You're welcome. I'm glad I was around to help."

*

Kenna couldn't tear her gaze off the man on the other side of the counter. He was totally gorgeous and looked as if he belonged in a fashion magazine. He was the type of man she was attracted to with his short, black hair, and standing at least six-feet-six in height with a well-muscled body. And it didn't help that his brown-eyed gaze seemed to eat her up as he stared at her. Of course her body reacted. An ache throbbed deep inside her pussy. Her nipples grew taut beneath her blouse. She had to resist the urge to cross her arms over her breasts to hide them.

"Is there anything I can help you with?" she asked.

His gaze met hers. "You can tell me your name."

His deep voice seemed to go right through her to her pussy. He had the tiniest of accents, but she couldn't place what it was. "I'm Kenna," she said, a little too breathy for her liking. She pointed at her name tag, which he obviously hadn't looked at.

"Hello, Kenna. I'm Tor." He reached across the counter with his hand open.

Kenna placed hers in his. A jolt of desire shot through her as he closed his fingers around hers and shook her hand. Her heart raced. Maybe Nick had been right. She did need to get laid, especially if she was that turned-on from a simple handshake.

"Hi," she said stupidly.

Tor brushed his thumb along the inside of her wrist as he released her. "Maybe once you get off work we can continue this conversation."

Kenna blinked. Had he just asked her out? "I don't get off until five."

"I'll come back then. We can have something to eat at one of the restaurants here."

"Sure. I'd love to."

"Until then, Kenna."

She sighed to herself when Tor turned around and walked away, getting her first look at his muscular ass in his tight-fitting jeans. It looked hard enough to bounce a quarter off it. She practically licked her lips, thinking how good it would feel to fondle his butt.

"I think you have some drool at the corner of your mouth."

Kenna reluctantly tore her gaze off Tor's retreating back and looked at Nick, who stood at the counter. "No, I don't."

"Well, you might as well have, given the way you were ogling that guy's backside."

"At least I might have a chance to see more of it. Tor just asked me out for dinner after work."

Nick gazed in the direction Tor had gone, then back at Kenna. "Holy crap, you worked fast. I said you needed a man, but I didn't think you'd actually taken me seriously."

She smiled. "It wasn't as if I'd planned it. A patron gave me a bit of a hard time, and Tor happened to show up to put the guy in his place. We then got to talking, and he asked me out. There was no way I would turn him down."

"That's my girl. Now just make sure you get laid tonight and you'll be all set."

Kenna rolled her eyes. "I never said I'd hop into the sack with him on the first date."

"Why the hell not? You're attracted to him. He obviously is to you as well or he wouldn't have asked you out. Have some fun."

"I'll see how the date goes first before I make a decision about sleeping with him. Who knows, Tor could be a jerk and I'll want to ditch him after the meal."

Nick shook his head. "That wouldn't stop me."

Kenna chuckled. "Of course not. You're a man whore, after all."

"Whatever. I'm on break. You want to go on yours?"

"Sure. Just let me get one of the girls from the office to cover for me."

After a quick phone call, Kenna was on her way to the Pyramid Café inside the hotel with Nick. As her friend talked, her thoughts drifted to Tor and their date later that day. She looked forward to getting to know him better.

* * * *

Tor returned home after he left the Luxor. He had no idea how it had gone from him just wanting to watch Kenna from a distance to asking her out for dinner that evening. He hadn't been able to stop himself. Just being near her again, he hadn't been able to think straight. Speaking to her had made him want more than only staring at her from afar.

In his very long life, Tor had never wanted a woman as much as he wanted Kenna. He wasn't celibate, by any means, but he usually slept with women who didn't want a serious relationship. Ones who were quite happy to fall into bed with him to scratch an itch, then not see him for a month or more, though recently that hadn't really satisfied him.

Inside the house, Tor headed to the upper floor and to

the room he'd set up as a small temple to Anubis. He worshipped the god of the underworld every day, leaving food and drink on an altar. That way it kept the bond between him and Anubis strong. Not that Tor had any problem with that since Anubis was part of the pantheon of gods Tor had already worshipped from the time he was a small boy in Egypt of old.

He pushed open the door to the room and then stepped inside. Tor had painted the walls in a shade of brown that reminded him of the stone used for the temples in Egypt. The artifacts placed throughout the space were just as ancient as he was, all dedicated to Anubis. Some, like the pieces of stone with hieroglyphs carved on them, hanging on the walls, were old, but were purchased in the 1920s when the British had come to Egypt to excavate tombs. Back then the pieces found had been sold instead of being given to the Egyptian people. He had purchased anything he'd found that referred to the god of the underworld. At least in his possession they'd remain in the same condition as the day he'd bought them. He respected the rich culture of the land of his birth. Even though he no longer lived there, and hadn't for many years, he still considered himself Egyptian.

Tor.

He stood straighter as Anubis' voice filled his mind. "Yes." Only inside that mini temple was Tor able to communicate with the god.

While you are out hunting evildoers, you need to stay extra vigilant. Another one of my warriors has tangled with a demon who has escaped the underworld. There are more out there, hunting you and the others.

"How did they escape the underworld? I've never had to worry about their kind in the mortal realm before."

I do not know. Nor do I know how many escaped. The one that my other warrior dispatched had a couple of spells in his arsenal. One locked my warrior in his half-human and half-jackal form. The other was a spelled dagger that prevented him from healing, causing him to remain weak and vulnerable. Just be prepared if a demon finds you.

"I'll be on my guard."

And one last thing before I go, if you find your mate, ease her into your world.

"Mate?" That was the first Tor had ever heard Anubis say his warriors would have one. "How will I know a woman is mine?"

You will know. During intimate moments, a change will come over you. An urge that will be hard to ignore will accompany it. You must resist until the one meant for you knows and accepts what you truly are.

With that, Anubis' presence left him. He shook his head. The god of the underworld could be cryptic at the best of times, and this must be one of them. A mate? The thousands of years Tor had lived as a warrior of Anubis, he'd thought he'd always remain alone. The idea of having a woman of his own hadn't been an option as far as he was concerned. He was immortal. What mortal woman would want to stay with him when she'd grow old and die while he remained the same? Obviously, that wouldn't be an issue if Anubis wanted Tor to bring his mate into his world. At least that was what Tor thought the god meant by all that. Was there a chance Kenna was his? His reaction to her made him think there was a possibility, but he'd have to wait and find out.

Leaving the temple, Tor shut the door behind him, his thoughts turning to the demons Anubis had warned him about. It did not bode well for mortals to have those creatures roaming free amongst them. Demons were cruel and vicious, took joy in the pain of others. If one was to actually find him, he'd be more than happy to send the demon to the underworld to face Anubis. The spells gave him pause, though. He had no magic available to him to counteract whatever the demon would use. The gifts Anubis had given him were immortality, the ability to shape-shift to take down evildoers and send them to the underworld, and to will any weapon he needed into his hand. Magic spells weren't part of the package.

With time to kill before he could go back to the Luxor to meet with Kenna, Tor decided some sword practice was what he needed to make the hours pass more quickly. He headed for his room to change into some other clothes. He'd have a strenuous workout, then take a shower before getting ready for his very first date. And if he was lucky, he'd get a chance to see if Kenna could actually be his.

* * * *

Kenna had to force herself to stop looking at the clock on the computer screen in front of her every few minutes. It wasn't going to make the end of her shift come any sooner, nor have Tor show up.

For the rest of the day, she'd only gone through the motions of what were her duties at work, her mind half the time a million miles away, focused on the man she looked forward to seeing again.

Twenty minutes before Kenna's shift was to end, her manager, Carol, came behind the reception desk to talk to her. Carol was part of the reason Kenna loved her job so much. The other woman was a dream to work with. Having started at the bottom and working her way up to her current management position, Carol didn't look down her nose at any of those under her since she'd been in their place at one time. She was about ten years older than Kenna.

"So I heard you had a bit of a run-in with someone who wanted to give you a hard time," Carol said.

Kenna knew exactly who Carol referred to—the man Tor had chased off. "How did you learn about that?"

Her manager chuckled. "I received an irate phone call from him. He wanted me to suspend you without pay, and to make sure guests like the one who was rude to him were never allowed in the Luxor. I'm interested to hear about this other man." Carol winked.

Kenna smiled and shook her head. "I can't believe the idiot called you, but I guess I shouldn't be surprised since he didn't want to take no for an answer, no matter how many times I told him it was against hotel policy. I'd thought for sure Tor would have shut him up."

"Tor, huh? I take it that is the guest he talked about?"

"Yeah, though Tor isn't a guest. At least I'm pretty sure he isn't. I'll find out once he takes me out for dinner at the end of my shift."

"In that case, I'd better hang around to see this knight in shining armor who saved you from the idiot. So, what does Tor look like?"

"Tall, dark, handsome, and as Nick would say, built like a brick shithouse."

"Oh, he sounds delicious. I can always go for some eye candy. You know old married ladies like me need to get some of that every now and then."

"As if you don't have any of that every day. I've met your husband, remember? Malcolm is gorgeous, and you know it."

Carol laughed. "True, but I can still appreciate other good-looking men."

"That's true," Kenna said with a laugh.

"And I think your tall, dark, and sexy just arrived," Carol said as she jerked her head to a spot behind Kenna. "Wow. With that tanned skin and dark looks, he really is exotic-looking."

Kenna turned around to see Tor headed toward the reception desk. "Yeah, he is. Plus, he has a slight accent I can't place."

Carol nudged her in the side. "Hon, whatever you do, don't let that one go. There aren't too many like him around, especially ones who aren't taken. If you're not careful, some other woman will snap him up."

She watched Tor come closer. "Don't worry. I plan to hold on to him. I just have to make it past this first date."

"You'll do fine. He's about five minutes early, but you can go. I don't mind covering until the next shift starts. Have fun."

"Thanks, Carol," Kenna said as she grabbed her purse. She walked around the counter to meet Tor.

He was dressed in a dark gray, button-down shirt tucked into black jeans. He looked sexy as hell. Kenna wanted to sink her hands into the sides of his thick, black hair and plunder his mouth as she rubbed against his sinfully hard body. Her pussy clenched just from thinking about it. Maybe sleeping with Tor on the first date wasn't such a bad idea, after all. It had been a while since a man had given her a good orgasm.

"Hey," she said as she closed the distance between them. "You made it."

Tor smiled, flashing straight, white teeth. "Of course. I wouldn't stand you up. Are you ready for our date?"

"Yes. My manager let me leave a little early. So, which restaurant do you want to eat at?"

"I'm not sure. I've never eaten here before. You must be the expert since you work here. Which one do you suggest?"

"How about Tender Steak & Seafood? The steaks are to die for. I also called and made a reservation just in case you wanted to go there."

"Okay. Sounds good. And nice thinking ahead to make a reservation. I never thought of doing it. Shall we go?"

Kenna nodded and fell into step beside Tor. He was so tall he made her feel short, even in the high heels she wore. Not that that was hard to do since she was on the short side anyway. When they reached a group of people who blocked their way, he took her hand and steered her around them. He kept hold of her even after they'd passed the obstacle. A thrill shot through her. God, she had to be hard up.

At the restaurant, Kenna gave her name for the reservation, and they were taken to their table. Once they were seated, they opened the menus in front of them. She already knew what she wanted, but the food there was on the pricey side. And she didn't want to order too much just in case Tor hadn't expected to come to a place like this.

As if he'd known what she'd thought, Tor said, "Order whatever you want. Don't worry about the prices. I have more than enough on me to cover the bill."

If he insisted, she'd be more than happy to oblige. "All right. Then I'm going to have the raw oysters to start, then the porterhouse steak."

Tor met her gaze across the table. "I guess I'd better have the oysters as well. Them supposedly being an aphrodisiac and all, I don't want to be left out if you're eating some."

He gave her a sexy look that had Kenna's toes trying to curl inside her shoes. She hadn't even thought about what oysters were known for. She just loved them and had them whenever the opportunity came up, which wasn't very often since they were expensive. She swallowed and licked her suddenly dry lips. Tor's gaze seemed to follow the movement of her tongue. A jolt of desire shot through her in response.

Their waiter came and took their orders, then left them alone again. Kenna was the first to break the silence that had fallen between them. "So, you never said if you were a guest here or not."

Tor shook his head. "I'm not. I live in Las Vegas."

"Do you come to the Luxor often? I don't remember seeing you before."

"No, I don't. Actually, today is the first time I've come inside the hotel. I've driven by it many times, though."

"Not into the casino scene?"

"No," he said with a chuckle. "I'm not into gambling. I

thought I'd finally see what the Luxor looked like from the inside."

"Well, I'm glad you did. I have to thank you again for getting rid of that guy. Though he did call later and complain to my manager. He wanted me suspended without pay, and you and others like you never allowed inside the Luxor."

Tor laughed. The deep baritone of it went straight through Kenna to her pussy. Seeing this date end with her and Tor in bed together looked better and better.

"He did?" Tor asked, still chuckling. "What did your manager say?"

"I'm sure she told him the exact same thing I did. She thought he was an idiot. I love my job, interacting with all the different people who come to the hotel, but there can be some who I wish wouldn't come around."

"I guess."

Tor and Kenna fell silent as the waiter brought them their appetizer of oysters. Kenna's mouth watered just looking at them. She loved seafood. She picked up the wedge of lemon on her plate and squeezed the juice over the oysters. That done, she lifted the first one to her mouth and sucked it down, tipping the shell to get all the liquid still on it. Once finished, she licked her lips and reached for the second. Before it met her lips, Kenna looked at Tor. He hadn't touched his first one yet. His gaze appeared glued on her.

"You're not eating your oysters," she said as she placed the one she held onto her plate. "Have you had them before?"

"Yes, I have, and I like them. I was just enjoying watching you savor yours."

Kenna's cheeks heated, and not from embarrassment at the thought of Tor watching her so intently. No, they warmed with arousal. The way he looked at her, appearing to focus solely on her, had her thinking about doing dirty things to him. Like run her tongue over every inch of his skin and taking his cock into her mouth to see just how far she could push him before he lost control. She squeezed her legs together, trying to alleviate some of the ache that built deep inside her pussy. Yup, she'd gone too long without sex.

Feeling a bit naughty, Kenna picked up the second oyster again and brought it to her mouth. She slowly parted her lips and tipped her head back and allowed gravity to slide it inside. She swallowed it down with the juice, then licked her lips with a satisfied sigh. Tor made a quiet sound that almost sounded like a groan. Kenna smiled to herself. If he was going to get to her, she was going to get to him. It was only fair.

Tor pounded back his oysters in no time flat while Kenna took her time, eating each one as she had the second. Once she'd finished all six, the waiter appeared with their main course.

Kenna and Tor talked about everyday things, learning more about each other. Though she found he didn't talk too much about himself and that she seemed to tell him more about her family and what her life had been like growing up than he did about his. What he said in regard to his childhood was very little and vague at best. One thing she did learn about Tor was that he was considered rich and worked most nights. At what, she wasn't entirely sure since he sort of sidestepped the whole question about his actual career. Not that she really cared. If he didn't want to talk about his work, that was his decision. It didn't make him any less attractive to her.

"I guess since you have to work tonight, you'll want to leave after we finish our meals," she said, hoping that wouldn't be the case.

"No." Tor reached across the table and captured Kenna's hand. "I don't have to work until it's dark. There is still time for me to get you alone somewhere and have you all to myself."

Kenna swallowed, riding out a wave of desire. "Then how about you come to my apartment?"

CHAPTER THREE

For grinned, more than pleased with Kenna's offer. He enjoyed being with her, and given the fact she'd turned him on while eating her oysters, he couldn't wait to get her alone and kiss her senseless. And he was pretty sure she'd known exactly what she'd done to him. He'd seen the hint of a knowing look on her face as she'd sucked back each one.

Now he sat with his napkin strategically placed over his lap to hide the raging hard-on he wasn't sure he'd be able to tame before they got up to leave. So far, everything he'd tried, picturing the most mundane of things, hadn't brought his wayward cock under control. He couldn't remember aching so badly for a woman as he did for Kenna.

Bringing his thoughts back to her question, he said, "Sure, I'd love to go to your place."

She gave him a smile that was downright sexy. "Good. I have some beer in the fridge. I'm not much of a wine drinker so I don't have any. I hope that's okay."

"Beer is fine. I prefer it." In ancient Egyptian times, Tor had drunk a lot of beer. It was a big part of his culture. And he was pleased Kenna preferred it as well. Something they had in common.

After they finished eating, Tor caught their waiter's attention and asked for the bill. He paid it, leaving a generous tip for their server, before he guided Kenna out of the restaurant. He walked them toward the hotel's exit.

"You can follow me to my place," Kenna said as they headed for the parking lot.

"All right."

Once they arrived, Tor couldn't help noticing how Kenna's steps had slowed and that she seemed to keep searching the area as if she expected someone to jump out at her.

"Is anything wrong?" he asked, not sure he would like the answer. He hadn't forgotten how he'd first seen Kenna in this parking lot being accosted by an evildoer wielding a knife, trying to rob her. She shouldn't remember anything from that night. He'd wiped it from her mind.

Kenna gave him a half smile. "I'm fine. For some reason, the past three days, I've had a weird feeling wash over me when I come here. And the strange thing is it only happens when it's at the end of my shift. I'm fine when I arrive in the morning. I haven't a clue why I feel so freaked out."

Tor wasn't sure if that was normal or not. He hadn't exactly sought out a mortal after he'd wiped their memory of him to find out if they had echoes of what he'd taken. He figured it could be possible, but it also could be just Kenna who experienced it. Could it be a sign she was his mate and that eventually she'd remember what he'd wiped from her mind? Until he knew for sure whether she was his or not, he'd have to watch her, though he wouldn't be able to wipe her in that form. He could only do that while in his half-human and half-jackal one. And with no evildoer around, he wouldn't be shifting any time soon.

"Hopefully it will pass," he said as he walked with her down a row of cars.

"I hope so. I don't like the feeling. I'm not usually the skittish type." Kenna stopped at a silver sedan. "Here I am."

"I'm just over there." He pointed to his red sports car at the end of the row.

"Nice car. Makes mine look like a rust bucket," Kenna said with a chuckle. "When we get to my apartment, you can park in the visitors parking, then get into my car. It will be easier if we take the elevator from the garage."

"Sounds like a plan."

Tor waited until Kenna had her car unlocked before he hurried to his. Once they were on the road, he easily kept up with her. Since Kenna's building was located close to the Strip, it didn't take them very long to arrive at her place. As she'd instructed, he parked in the visitors parking, then got into the passenger side of her sedan for the ride down to the garage.

They took the elevator there up to Kenna's floor. She led him to her apartment and then unlocked the door before she stepped inside. Tor followed her in, pushing it closed behind him. Her place was light and airy looking. The flooring was white slate tiles and the walls had been painted cream. There was a matching black suede couch and loveseat with an LED TV hanging on one wall.

"Make yourself at home," Kenna said as she led him into the living room. "If you don't mind, I'm going to get out of my work clothes and change into something more comfortable."

Tor would have loved nothing more than to ask her if he could come with her and help her take off her clothes, maybe even suggest she just stay naked, which would definitely be more comfortable. He said nothing of the sort. It was a little too soon for that. Maybe after they'd had a beer he could steer things in that direction.

"Go ahead," he replied. "I'll wait right here." Tor took a seat on the couch.

As Kenna disappeared down the short hallway off the living room, she said, "You can watch some TV while you wait. The remote is on the coffee table."

Tor reached for the remote and then switched on the television. He needed the distraction. Knowing Kenna was in her bedroom undressing, he could almost picture what she'd look like under each article of clothing she took off. His cock, which had settled down enough back in the restaurant to not embarrass him, went rock hard once more. If he didn't get to touch her soon, he was going to lose his mind. Her scent, the way she teased him, drove him crazy.

A few minutes later, Kenna came back wearing a pair of black yoga pants and a pink T-shirt. Her feet were bare. She went to the kitchen and took out two bottles of beer, then headed to the living room.

Tor accepted the one she held out to him. "If you want a glass, I can get you one," she said as she sat beside him. "I usually just drink mine out of the bottle."

A woman after his own heart. "So do I."

"So, what are you watching?" she asked, then took a sip of her beer.

He had no idea. He really hadn't paid too much attention to what had come up on the screen. "I was just flipping through the channels."

"I have The Movie Channel. Why don't we see if something good is playing?"

Tor nodded and passed Kenna the remote. Their fingers met, and a shot of awareness surged through him. He took a swallow of his beer, hoping it would calm him down a bit. Having her next to him, her scent filling his nose with each move she made, made him hunger for Kenna even more.

He forced himself to focus on the TV. Kenna turned it to an action flick, one he'd seen before. It was one he'd enjoyed. Tor actually watched a fair amount of television, mostly movies. Being alone with no others to associate with, there really weren't a whole lot of things he could do to entertain himself. He could only work out so much, and the Internet wasn't really his thing.

"I think we just missed the beginning of the movie," Kenna said. "Is that okay? Or do you want me to find one that's just starting?"

"No, this is fine. I've seen this one before. It's good."

Kenna put the remote on the coffee table, then settled back on the couch. She sat so close she was right up against Tor. They silently drank their beer. All the while, he couldn't ignore her presence. No longer able to take it, he lifted his arm and put it around Kenna's shoulders. She shifted, snuggling closer to his side and rested the back of her head on his chest. She perfectly fit against him as if she'd been made for him.

Tor bent his head and smelled Kenna's hair. The scent of some exotic-smelling fruit filled his nose. He closed his eyes and breathed deeper, dragging it farther into his lungs. She pressed closer and placed a hand on his thigh. His cock jerked when she used her fingers to draw circles on his leg. If he got any harder, his shaft would bust the zipper on his jeans.

His heartrate sped up even more as Kenna changed from drawing circles to running her hand up and down his thigh. With each pass up, she came closer and closer to his dick. Tor found it hard to just sit there and let her do what she did to him, but he liked it at the same time. He wanted her to touch him. Wanted her hands all over him, touching and stroking.

His breath punched out of him and he stiffened in anticipation as Kenna's fingers came within a hairsbreadth from touching the tip of his cock. Then she made contact.

Tor heard a quiet, breathy sigh escape her, and she used the tip of one to run over the full length of him.

That small sound along with her light touch pushed him to the point where he couldn't sit there any longer without acting on his arousal. Tor turned his head to see Kenna looking at him. With a groan, he lowered his lips to hers. He kept it gentle at first, but when she kissed him back and nipped his lower lip, he claimed her mouth fully.

Somehow, he managed to put his beer on the table, then hers, all the while kissing Kenna as if his life depended on it. With both hands now free, Tor angled her toward him and shifted them so they lay stretched out on the couch with him on top of her.

She opened her thighs wide to cradle his hips. Tor's cock came in direct contact with her pussy. Even through their pants she felt good. He ground against her as he fed from her mouth, pushing his tongue between her lips, thoroughly tasting her. Kenna lifted her hands and threaded her fingers through the sides of his hair. She seemed to hold him exactly where she wanted him, kissing him with a fervor that ramped up his libido.

Tor reached between them and palmed her breast. Her taut nipple brushed against his palm. Kenna moaned and arched her back, pressing herself tighter into his grip. He wanted to suck on the tight bud.

He lifted his head and stared into Kenna's blue-green eyes. "If you want me to stop, tell me now, because I want more of you and might not be able to do so later."

"Don't stop," she said in a breathy voice. "I want this. I want you."

His cock throbbed at her words. All the blood in his body seemed to be centered there. Tor took hold of the bottom of Kenna's T-shirt and dragged it up and over her head. He tossed it away as he stared down at her pink-lace-covered breasts. The twin mounds were more than a handful, her rosy nipples barely visible through the almost sheer material. They were gorgeous, and he couldn't wait to have them in his mouth.

He pushed his hands under her and found the clasp on her bra. He undid it and then pulled his hands out so he could push the straps down her arms. Once they were free, he tossed the undergarment in the same direction as her T-shirt had gone. Tor bent his head and laved a nipple with the flat of his tongue. Kenna moaned, her fingers sinking into his hair again.

Tor brushed his lips across the tight bud before he sucked it into his mouth. Kenna's nails dug into his scalp as she held him to her, her hips lifting to rock her pussy against his erection. He ached to free himself, but he wanted to explore her body first.

He switched to her other breast and paid it the same attention as he had to the first. Kenna's moans grew louder, her breath coming in gasps. As he continued to suck on her nipple, he trailed a hand down to the waistband of her yoga pants. He shifted so he was on his side and pushed the material down past her hips. She wiggled as she helped him take the pants all the way off.

Tor released her nipple and gazed at her body. She was perfectly made with curves in all the right places. He ran a hand down her ribs to her belly, which quivered under his touch. Continuing his downward trail, he reached the top of her panties, which matched the bra. He ran his finger along the waistband before he dragged his hand down the front of her panties until he reached between her legs. It was his turn to moan when he found the wetness there. She was wet enough to soak through the material.

He lifted his head to look at Kenna. "If I take these off you, I'm going to taste you. Lick you until I get my fill."

"God, yes," she said. "Do it. Make me come with your mouth."

He didn't have to be told twice. With a couple of jerks, the lacy bit of material was pulled off and Kenna was completely naked. Wanting some skin-to-skin contact, Tor quickly undid his button-down shirt with one hand. She helped pull it off. He settled on top of her once again.

After taking her lips until she tugged at his hair, Tor slowly kissed a trail down the side of her neck to her collarbone. He shifted lower on her body and gave each nipple a suck on his way down. The smell of her arousal filled his head, making him feel almost drunk. Down farther he went, swirling his tongue inside her bellybutton before dragging it to her hip.

He shifted even farther down the couch, wedging his shoulders between Kenna's spread thighs. He looked at her pussy. It was pink and swollen, glistening with her juices. Tor lowered his mouth and licked her from bottom to top, swirling his tongue around her clit. She lifted her hips, offering more of herself.

More she wanted, more she'd get. He licked and sucked, lapping up her wetness. She tasted as good as she smelled. He feasted until she ground herself against his mouth, her moans echoing in the room. Tonguing her clit, he pushed one finger inside her pussy, moving it in and out. He soon pushed a second, then a third, into her. Her inner walls clamped around them as she matched his strokes.

Tor sucked on her clit and pumped his fingers faster. From the sounds she made, he figured she had to be close to climaxing. When she did, he continued to pleasure her, pushing her orgasm to go on and on. Once it ended, Kenna went limp under him.

"That was spectacular," she said, still breathing hard. "Now it's my turn to return the favor. Stand."

He rolled off the couch and stood in one smooth movement. Kenna sat up and took hold of his belt loops to pull him closer. Tor looked down at her as she undid the button and zipper on his jeans. His cock jerked with each brush of her fingers. She parted the material and freed his shaft. He bit back a groan when she licked her lips as she stared at him.

She pulled his pants down past his hips and along his legs. Tor stepped out of them and then kicked them aside. If she kept hungrily staring at his dick, he was liable to embarrass himself and come before she even touched him.

Kenna wrapped her hand around his cock and slowly pumped it up and down. "You're going to feel so good inside me, but first I want to have you filling my mouth."

Tor fisted his hands at his sides to stop himself from taking hold of Kenna, pulling her under him on the floor, and sinking his shaft between her legs. When she talked dirty, it just cranked him up even more.

She leaned forward and licked him like a lollipop until her tongue had swept across every inch of his cock. She opened her mouth and sucked him inside. Tor groaned and looked down to watch his shaft sliding in and out between her lips. She sucked on him hard. He rocked his hips, unable to hold still any longer. It felt too damn good.

Kenna kept her hand wrapped around the base of his cock while she pleasured him. She dropped the other and fondled his balls, giving them a gentle tug. Tor lost himself to the sensations swamping him. His whole being centered on the feeling of her sucking him in and out. His shaft grew harder and his balls rose closer to his body as the point of no return crept ever nearer.

"Kenna, you're going to make me come," he half growled.

She only pulled back long enough to say, "I want you to. Give it to me."

This time he couldn't hold back the animalistic-sounding growl that punched out of him as she once again wrapped her lips around his cock. She sucked harder, stroking what she couldn't take with her hand. He couldn't keep his release at bay any longer.

Just before he came, Tor felt a burning sensation in his

gums. He ran his tongue over his eyeteeth to find they had dropped, become sharper, much as they did once he'd shifted into his half-human and half-jackal form. Along with that change came the almost overpowering need to bite Kenna where her shoulder and neck met. He stared at that spot, badly wanting to sink his teeth into it.

She sucked him almost to the back of her throat, and Tor's orgasm rushed up to meet him. He threw back his head and moaned, his hands in her hair as his cock pulsed, giving her everything he had. After it was over, he pulled her to her feet and then picked her up. He kissed her and maneuvered them so he sat on the couch with her across his lap, her head cradled on his shoulder. With his release, his teeth had gone back to normal and the urge to bite had left him.

Tor held her close as he fought to regain his breath. He now knew exactly what Anubis had meant about the change coming over, and the urge that went along with it when it came to Tor's mate. There was no question in Tor's mind that Kenna was his.

CHAPTER FOUR

Kenna liked exactly where she was, cuddled up with Tor while the two of them were completely naked. She breathed in the scent of his aftershave and one that was uniquely his own. She could get used to having his strong arms wrapped around her, holding her close.

She ran a hand along Tor's well-muscled chest, stopping at the tattoo on the left side, right over his heart. It was ancient Egyptian in style and done in black. Inside a cartouche was a picture of Anubis with a jackal's head. In one hand he held an ankh while in the other was a flail. Kenna traced it with a fingertip. Seeing it, and thinking about Tor's dark, good looks, tanned skin, and slight accent, it made her wonder if he was Egyptian.

Lifting her head off his shoulder, Kenna sat up straight. "How much longer do we have before you have to leave for work?"

Tor brought her lips down to his for a thorough kiss before he pulled away. "Only enough time for us to finish our beers. And not enough for me to do what I want to do with you. We could have a quickie, but I want to take my time, savor every minute of it. We'll have to continue this tomorrow."

Kenna sighed with regret but nodded. "It will have to be after I finish my shift again. The next two days after that I'm off for the weekend."

"I can take those days off as well. We'll spend them together."

She smiled. "I like that." Kenna ran her hand over Tor's chest again. "I guess we'd better get dressed. For me, sitting here like this with you, it's only going to make me want you again. And since there isn't any time for that, I'd rather have your delicious body covered before I get any ideas about getting you to change your mind about going into work."

Tor chuckled. "I agree. I find you just as tempting."

Kenna slid off his lap and took one last good look at him, running her gaze over his hard, muscled body and landing on his cock that appeared semi-hard. Oh, all the things *she* wanted to do to him. At least they were off to a good start. The oral sex had been the best she'd ever had. And pleasuring Tor had been just as good. She could foresee herself using the majority of the weekend to explore every inch of him, finding out what really turned his crank.

She gathered up her clothes before she pulled them on. Once they were dressed, they sat on the couch with beers in hand to watch more of the movie that still played on the television. It was nice sitting there with Tor, the heat from his body sinking into hers as he held her against his side.

They finished their beers, and Tor put the empty bottles on the coffee table before he turned to face her and swept her up into his arms once again. He kissed her with enough heat to have her body burning for his. Kenna almost begged him to stay but stopped herself. She didn't want to come across as too needy. They were still too new for that. He had to work, just as she had to the following morning.

Kenna walked Tor to the apartment door. "Do you want to meet here tomorrow after my shift?"

He nodded. "Sure. Then you can come to my place. I'll make you dinner."

She smiled. "I'd like that. I've never had a man cook for me before. Are you any good?"

Tor laughed and shook his head. "I promise you I'm an excellent cook. I like to eat, so I learned a long time ago how to make meals I'd enjoy."

"Then I'll look forward to it."

With one last kiss that made her knees weak, Tor left. Kenna closed and then locked the door behind him. Her social life had definitely taken a turn for the better. Nick would be proud of her.

* * * *

Tor didn't bother to go home to change his clothes before he went out on a night of hunting evildoers. He drove to a section of the city that he'd chosen earlier and then parked his car. He found it was easier to hunt down his prey if he walked the streets. In a seedier section of Las Vegas, there was no shortage of mortals who committed evil acts.

It didn't take long before he felt the familiar pull. Tor followed where it led, catching the unmistakable odor of evil tainting the air. He found his prey hunched over in a dark corner of an alley, counting money he'd taken out of the purse he held. Obviously, it wasn't his.

The change took over Tor as he walked closer. He gritted his teeth as the pain that went along with the shift tore through him. Once it was complete, he growled, drawing the evildoer's attention. The man took one look at Tor's half-human and half-jackal furred form and bolted.

Tor managed to easily catch him before he could get very far.

He flung his prey against a brick wall hard enough for the man to have the wind knocked out of him. Tor moved in and grabbed him by the throat as he looked the evildoer in the eyes, forcing his way into the man's mind. What he saw there, feeling the pain and fear of all his prey's victims, Tor knew without a doubt the man was guilty.

"Time to pay for all the crimes you committed," Tor said in a voice that was gruff and deep.

Willing his gold dagger into his hand, Tor held his prey still. The man babbled, pleading for his life. Tor struck fast and true, slicing the blade across the man's chest through to the skin. His prey uttered one last cry of alarm as he slowly faded out of sight.

Tor willed the dagger away and headed for the entrance to the alley. As he walked, he shifted back to his human form. He could expect to experience that pain at least a couple more times before he called it quits for the night.

Before he reached the street side of the alley, there was a pain inside his head unlike anything he'd felt in the past. It was even worse than what he experienced with a shift. He dropped to his knees, gasping, holding his head as the sensation hit him full force, as if something burrowed its way inside his brain. His eyesight faded to black a couple of times. Tor was pretty sure he was on the verge of passing out when the pain suddenly stopped. He took stock of himself before he stood on legs that shook a little. He seemed okay. His head just throbbed a bit with what felt like a normal headache.

He'd gone two steps when a disembodied male voice said, "You're mine now, warrior of Anubis."

Tor stiffened. Thanks to the god of the underworld's warning, he had a feeling he knew who the voice belonged to. "Show yourself, demon. Let's put an end to this now.

Unless you're too afraid to face me."

Laughter seemed to bounce off the alley's brick walls. "All in due time."

No matter how many times Tor bellowed for the demon, the creature didn't respond. Tor continued on his way. If the demon had tried to use the spell that had been used on the other of Anubis' warriors, it mustn't have worked on Tor. He was still in his human form, not trapped in his other. Maybe this demon wasn't as skilled with spells as the other had been.

Tor walked down the street and rubbed his forehead. All this demon had managed to do was give him one hell of a headache. He snorted. If that was all the creature was capable of, it would take a lot more than that to bring Tor down.

* * * *

Kenna couldn't believe how slow the day seemed to pass. Normally, she didn't mind being at work. That wasn't the case now. All she kept thinking about was that she'd see Tor again once her shift ended. What they'd done the night before had been good, but she craved more of him. Wanted to have his cock buried deep inside her. She figured sex would be good with him. The way he'd touched, stroked, and licked just about every inch of her last night showed he wasn't the selfish type of lover some men could be.

During their lunch break, Nick had barraged her with questions about Tor and how her evening with him had gone. She'd only told her friend that she and Tor had worked out well enough and that she would see Tor after work, then spend the weekend with him. Nick had been very impressed with how fast she'd moved with her new man.

After her shift finally ended, Kenna hurried out of the

hotel and then to the parking lot. Once again, she had that same unsettling feeling she got whenever she came there at the end of her workday. This time she was able to ignore it better as she hurried to her car.

Kenna headed straight for her bedroom to change out of her work clothes once inside her apartment. Figuring eating dinner at Tor's place would be casual, she pulled on a pair of blue jeans and a turquoise T-shirt. Having worn heels all day, she opted for wearing a pair of runners.

She'd just tied the last lace on her shoes when the phone rang with a double ring to let her know someone buzzed up to the apartment from the secured front entrance. Kenna grabbed the cordless phone that sat on the nightstand next to her bed and answered it. Hearing Tor's deep, slightly accented voice on the other end, she pushed the numbers to allow him into the building.

Kenna waited at the door with purse in hand for Tor to arrive. Once he did, she opened it and smiled. "Hi."

"Hi back." He put his arms around her and kissed her as if he hadn't seen her in a year. He had her clutching him when he finally let her up for air. "I've done nothing but think of having you in my embrace again."

Trying to think clearly while arousal heated her blood proved more than a little difficult. Kenna pulled her wits about her and smiled. "I did the same thing. Think about you that is."

Tor released her. "We should go. I have food in the oven."

As if on cue, Kenna's stomach rumbled. She gave him a half smile. "Sorry. I didn't have a very big lunch. I wanted to make sure I was good and hungry. You did promise me a good meal."

He chuckled. "Don't apologize. Let's go."

Kenna locked the door behind them, then placed her hand in Tor's when he held it out to her. They rode the elevator down to the lobby and then went outside to the visitors parking. He helped her into his car before going around to the driver's side.

She wasn't surprised when they drove to the MacDonald Highlands community. Tor had money. He'd of course live where the wealthy did. The house at the end of the drive he finally pulled into was huge. The large two-story edifice looked as if a movie star lived there. The front lawn had been professionally landscaped, just adding to the grandeur of the property.

Tor parked in front of the four-car attached garage and then shut off the engine. "Welcome to my home," he said before he opened his door and got out.

Kenna joined him, still looking at the huge house. "It's beautiful," she said. "And massive. Don't you get lonely living here all by yourself?"

He chuckled. "No. I'm what you'd call a bit of a loner."

Tor took her hand and walked her to the front door. He unlocked it and then stepped aside for her to go in ahead of him. Kenna was pretty sure her eyes popped out of her head and her jaw was on the floor. The inside was just as gorgeous as the outside. It was spotlessly clean from what she could see of it in the huge foyer.

She turned and looked at Tor. "If you tell me you do all the housecleaning here on top of knowing how to cook, don't be surprised if I get down on one knee and ask you to marry me."

He caught her around the waist and pulled her close. "What? You only would want to marry me for my domestic skills? You can't think of anything else I have going for me?"

Kenna lifted her arms and wrapped them around his neck. "Well, now that you mention it, you do have a killer body." She took a deep breath. The smell of something heavy with spices and utterly delicious filled her nose. Her stomach growled again. "Whatever you have cooking in your kitchen smells to die for."

"Come on," Tor said and released her. "I better feed you before you pass out from lack of food."

She followed him past the two curved staircases that led to the upper floor and then to the spacious kitchen. All the appliances were stainless-steel. The oven was gas and looked to be chef quality. Obviously, Tor took his cooking very seriously. And what he had in the oven made her mouth water.

"Take a seat at the island," he directed. "I thought we'd have our first course here. That way I can keep an eye on the other food while we eat."

Kenna took a seat on one of the tall stools at the granite-topped island. Tor placed a plate of pita bread cut into triangles along with another filled with hummus in front of her. She loved the chickpea dip. She picked up a piece of the flat bread and then dipped into the hummus. It made her taste buds sing.

Once she swallowed, she said, "This is really good. Did you make it from scratch?"

Tor nodded. "Of course. I also made the Egyptian-spiced chicken that is in the oven from scratch as well."

She looked at him. "You're Egyptian, aren't you?"

"Yes, but I haven't lived there for a great many years."

"I thought maybe you were, especially after seeing the tattoo on your chest. I wasn't sure of your accent, though."

"My accent has faded a bit the longer I've stayed away from the land of my birth. Plus, I don't speak my native language much."

"Have you ever gone back for a visit?"

"No. I haven't found the time."

"I've always wanted to go to Egypt." She smiled. "I think part of the reason I chose to apply for a job at the Luxor was because of the pyramid and Sphinx, but don't tell anyone that. They'll think I'm just being silly."

Tor leaned toward her. "If you think that's silly, you'll think this is even worse. I have purposely driven by the hotel for that same reason. They remind me of home."

"I guess we have that in common."

"Yes, and our love of beer," he said with a wink. "Eat up. The main course will be done shortly."

Kenna had more hummus than she should have but enjoyed it so much she had a hard time stopping. That course done, Tor led her to a spacious dining room just off the kitchen. It was already set with plates and cutlery. Once he seated her, he returned to the other room and then came back with a platter of chicken and roasted potatoes. In a large serving bowl were steamed mixed vegetables.

The chicken breast tasted as to die for, as it had smelled while cooking. It tasted of lemon, and if she wasn't mistaken, also beer along with a bunch of spices she couldn't single out. As she ate, Kenna had to admit Tor was a better cook than she was.

After they ate their fill, Kenna wiped her mouth on a cloth napkin. "That was really good. If I eat any more, you'll have to roll me out of here."

Tor chuckled. "I'm glad you enjoyed it. I told you I knew how to cook."

"That you did. I'm hoping you'll make us another meal sometime."

"I'd be more than happy to. Let's sit out on the back patio and let our food settle."

Kenna nodded and stood when Tor did. He led her through the French doors at the end of the dining room. It was still light out and not too hot. They each took a seat at the wrought-iron table. He reached for her hand and laced their fingers together. She looked around the backyard, finding it just as professionally manicured as the front. There was an in-ground pool.

"You mustn't have lived here for very long, since this is still a fairly new community," she said as she turned back to look at Tor.

"No, I haven't. When I saw the area, I knew I had to

have a home here. I like the large lots and privacy they afford."

"I can see why. I'd want to live here too."

Tor lifted his free hand and rubbed it across his forehead.

"Have a headache?"

"Yes. It just started. I don't normally get them."

Kenna let go of Tor's hand and motioned him closer. "Here. See if this helps." She reached over and used her fingertips to massage his temples. "Better?"

"A little."

He closed his eyes and moaned. She had a feeling it wasn't a sound of pleasure but of pain, since he furrowed his brows as well. "Not much, though."

"It's not getting any better. Maybe we should move back inside. The sunshine could be making it worse."

"You're probably right. There is one thing we can do that is supposed to help get rid of headaches," she said with a wink.

"Really? What would that be?"

Kenna ran a hand down the side of his face and swept her thumb across Tor's bottom lip. "Sex." She licked her lips. "You want to give it a try?"

He gave her a sexy grin. "Definitely."

Tor stood, then pulled her to her feet. Once they were back inside the house, she walked at his side as he guided her to the foyer and then up one of the curving staircases. She only had a short time to take in the huge master bedroom and king-sized bed before he pulled her into his arms, his lips claiming hers. She wrapped her arms around his waist and held on as he hungrily took her mouth.

An ache built deep inside her pussy at the feel of his hard cock pressing against her. This time she'd have all of Tor. She'd been daydreaming about this all day. Both of them breathing hard, Kenna pulled back and stripped off his T-shirt. With all that naked, male flesh on display, she couldn't hold back from caressing it. Her lips made a wet path across his wide, muscular chest. She even traced the outline of his tattoo.

Tor took off her shirt and bra before he bent her slightly over his arm and sucked a taut nipple into his mouth. Kenna moaned, holding on to his broad shoulders to keep herself upright. Arousal surged through her body as wetness pooled between her legs.

Once he'd showered her other nipple with the same attention as the first, Tor turned her and slowly backed her toward the bed. The back of her legs hit the mattress, but he didn't push her down onto it. He reached for the fasteners on her jeans and undid them. As he pulled the material down past her hips, Kenna toed off her shoes, kicking each one away.

Tor lifted her and placed her on the center of the bed once she was free of her jeans and panties. She lifted onto her elbows to watch him take his pants off. His erection stood out straight from his body and bobbed with his movements. She couldn't wait to have it buried inside her. Wetness leaked onto her thighs as she ran her gaze over every delectable inch of him.

As naked as she, Tor climbed onto the bed next to her and stretched out alongside her. Kenna lowered herself onto the mattress. He ran a finger from the top of her chest, between her breasts, and down her stomach until he reached the mound of her pussy. Everywhere he touched he left a trail of fire and need.

He dipped his hand between her legs and moaned. "You're already wet for me. I thought to take it slow, but I crave you too much."

Kenna took hold of his cock and pumped it, eliciting another moan out of him. "We can do slow another time. Right now, I want you inside me."

Tor settled on top of her, his hips spreading her legs farther apart. The very tip of his cock brushed against her

MARISA CHENERY

slick opening. That small touch sent jolts of pleasure through her. Going slow was definitely not an option for her. Ever since the night before, she'd longed for this. Ached for him.

She wrapped her arms around his shoulders as he pushed the head of his shaft into her. Kenna rocked her hips with Tor, taking more of his length with each thrust until he was sheathed to the hilt. He was big and thick, stretching her to her limits and filling her to capacity. And she loved it. He pulled back and seated himself again, and she loved that even more.

Kenna lifted her legs and put them around Tor's hips as he surged in and out of her. She squeezed her inner walls around his plunging cock, increasing the pleasure she felt.

As he continued to thrust inside her, he whispered gruffly into her ear, "I'm not going to last long."

"I won't either," she quickly whispered back.

He pumped his hips faster, taking her harder. She matched his pace, her breath coming in gasps. Tor pulled almost all the way out before he thrust back in, butting up against her cervix. Kenna's body coiled tighter as an orgasm inched closer.

She teetered on the edge when Tor suddenly stopped pumping. His body grew stiff on top of her, his arms clenching until the veins stuck out. She was about to ask him what was wrong, but he let out an animalistic growl and put his arms around her. In a show of strength, he lifted her as he shifted to a sitting position so she ended up straddling his hips, his cock still buried deep inside her.

Tor dropped his hands to her hips, holding on tight enough that Kenna was sure he'd leave bruises behind. He had her ride him fast and hard. She placed her hands on top of his shoulders, rocking against him, taking his cock as deep as he could go.

Just as Kenna came, Tor fisted the hair at the back of her neck and roughly pulled her head to the side so her ear

144

almost touched her shoulder. He bent his head with a growl that an animal would make and bit her where neck and shoulder met. At first, she felt a sharp pain as his teeth broke the skin, but then a sudden rush of intense pleasure tore through her, making her have back-to-back orgasms. He thrust up into her one final time, then stiffened as his cock pulsed, filling her with his cum. His teeth were still buried in her skin. She gasped as she felt something snap between them, almost as if an invisible bond formed, tying them together.

Tor's hold on her loosened and he slowly pulled his mouth away from her neck. His gaze zeroed in where he'd bitten her, and his eyes widened ever so slightly. She would have missed it if she hadn't watched him so closely. Kenna went to kiss him, floating in the afterglow, but he stiffly lifted her off him and placed her beside him. Without a word, he slid off the bed and then walked into the en suite bathroom, firmly shutting the door behind him.

Kenna stared after him, really not sure what was up. They'd just had what she thought was the best sex of her life. Something had to be bothering Tor for him to just get up and walk away. Maybe it was because he'd gotten a little carried away and had bitten her. She reached up and touched where he'd sunk his teeth into her. She felt nothing there, and after getting off the bed and looking in the mirror attached to the dresser, she saw there wasn't even a mark. She guessed it only felt as if he'd broken through the skin.

With a shrug, Kenna walked back to the bed and then climbed onto it to wait for Tor to come out of the bathroom. If that was his problem, she'd just have to set him straight. As far as she was concerned, he could lose control like that any time. She'd loved every minute of it.

For ran cold water in the sink and splashed some on his face. His hands shook as he reached for a towel to dry off. His head still ached, but not nearly as bad as it had just before he'd lost all control. And it wasn't because of the passion that had flared so hot between him and Kenna.

Right in the middle of making love to her, the headache had become intense and cutting. Tor swore he heard the sound of the demon laughing inside his mind just as Tor seemed to lose control of his body. It was as if someone else had taken over. He'd felt like an observer, feeling everything that had happened, but wasn't in the driver's seat.

He'd fought it, but it had been futile. Even when his eyeteeth dropped and the urge to bite Kenna rose, he'd fought. Whoever, or whatever, had control of him had made him roughly act on the impulse that rode him. Once he'd bitten hard enough to break the skin, he'd regained the ability to control his actions. He'd pulled away from Kenna and watched with shock as the deep bite mark he'd given her healed within seconds, not leaving anything behind.

Tor healed like that. He'd felt something he could only describe as a bond form between him and Kenna right after he'd bitten her. He had the suspicion that she was now as immortal as he was. He now understood why Anubis wanted Tor to bring his mate into his world before he acted on the powerful urge to sink his teeth into her. And because of whatever had used him like a puppet, Tor had broken his promise to the god of the underworld.

He jumped when a knock came at the bathroom door and Kenna asked if he was okay in there. Of course she'd think something wasn't right since he'd practically bolted in there without a word after having great sex with her. Tor stood straighter and sighed. He'd have to talk to Anubis, but he couldn't do that while she was in the house.

Tor opened the door and put on what he hoped was a smile that didn't look like a grimace. "I'm fine. Sorry." He looked at where her neck and shoulder met. "For everything."

She returned his smile and reached up to caress his cheek. "I'm not into the kinky stuff, but I don't mind you losing control and using your teeth on me."

If only she knew how out of control he'd been, she wouldn't tell him that. "I'm usually not a biter. So I doubt it will happen again."

"Stop worrying." Kenna bent her head to the side. "See? Not even a mark." She straightened, took his hand in hers, and slowly walked backward, taking him with her. "Come back to bed. I know you have to work tonight, but there's still time for round two."

Tor had actually planned to take the night off, but now he needed the excuse to take Kenna back to her place early. Having a chat with Anubis was number one on his list of things to do. He gathered her close and claimed her lips in a searing kiss. He reluctantly lifted his head, more than enjoying the feel of her naked and willing in his arms.

"I do have to work. And I just remembered I have to start a little earlier than normal. So to make it up to you, how about we spend the entire weekend together as we'd planned, but you sleep over here, or we can stay at your apartment, starting tomorrow?"

Kenna gazed at his chest, circling Anubis' mark with a fingertip. "All right." She looked at him. "We stay here. Your place is a hell of a lot nicer and bigger than mine. And instead of you having to pick me up, I'll drive myself over tomorrow, say after lunch? That way you'll have enough time to catch up on your sleep since you'll be working all night."

"Deal," he said and swooped in for a quick kiss.

Tor wanted Kenna again, but was a little concerned if he'd lose the ability to control what he did once more. The headache was now gone. He just didn't want to risk it. He'd already done enough damage for one night by biting her.

They dressed and soon were outside in his car as he drove Kenna to her apartment. With this new invisible bond in place between them, Tor found it hard to let her go. He had to force himself to stop kissing her, holding her back from getting out of the car. He waited until she was safely inside the building before he headed to his house.

Once he arrived, he headed up one of the curved staircases and then to the bedroom Anubis' temple occupied. He stood before the small altar, and called, "Anubis, I want a word with you."

What do you need, Tor?

"First of all, I had an encounter with a demon last night, but the bastard refused to show himself."

Did he force the change on you?

"No. I thought all he'd tried to do was give me a really bad headache. I'm not so certain of that anymore. And I've found my mate."

And?

"When I was intimate with her my eyeteeth dropped and I had the urge to bite her."

Which you held back from doing, correct?

"The first time, yes. Today, no. In the middle of being with Kenna, the headache came rushing back and I lost control of my body."

What do you mean by that?

"I mean it was as if I were someone's puppet and he made me do whatever he wanted. I was aware of everything that happened, felt everything too, but I couldn't stop what my body did." Tor paused before he continued. "I bit her. I felt a bond form between us."

Have you told Kenna what you are yet?

"No. I wanted to speak with you first. I think my loss of control was the demon fucking with me. I heard his laughter in my mind just before it happened. Could this be another spell?"

It would sound like it. Let me check to see if you are still under the influence of it. Anubis went silent, but Tor felt the god's presence moving around in his mind. Then a minute later, Anubis said, *It was a spell. Not a long-lasting one, though. It probably only works as long as the demon makes use of your body. Once he relinquishes control, the spell ends.*

Terrific. That was all Tor needed. To lose control whenever a demon decided to have some fun with him. "Is there a way I can lure that demon out into the open? I'm not going to want this hanging over my head for long."

Demons are not known for their patience. I doubt you will have long to wait before he tries a physical attack. He will grow bored with his games soon.

"That might be the case, but he can do a lot of damage before that happens. You want me to ease Kenna into my world. How can I do that if the demon takes control of me again and reveals my true nature to her? He could force me to shift before I get the chance to tell her everything."

Since you have already claimed her as your mate, there's no need to take it slow. I suggest you tell her very soon. She is going to notice there is something different about her since she is now immortal.

"I thought she was when the bite mark healed in seconds. Did you give her immortality as you did me?"

No, you did. With your bite, Kenna is no longer mortal. Her life force is now tied to yours. You die, so does she. It was the only way I could make the women meant for my warriors their true mates. I can only grant immortality to a mortal if he or she is dying on a battlefield and is willing to vow to serve me for eternity.

Tor shuddered at the thought of Kenna having to go through that. He wouldn't wish that on anyone. A millennia later, he still sometimes woke up struggling to breathe, having dreamed of how he'd fought to stay alive, not ready to go into the afterlife, before Anubis had come to him on that battlefield in Egypt Tor had fought on.

"I will. And hopefully when I go hunting prey tonight the demon will make an appearance and I can send him to the underworld to you."

I want you to hold off on hunting evildoers until the demon is taken care of. Since you are now bonded to your mate, you not only risk your life, but hers as well.

"I'm immortal."

Yes, but remember the last demon had a spelled dagger that left my warrior weak and vulnerable. If not for a protection spell I put over his house using the demon's blood, he would have been too easy to kill.

"I'll do as you say."

Anubis' presence left the temple. Tor wasn't exactly pleased with the god's edict of no hunting until Tor had taken down the demon. He was used to taking the initiative rather than sitting around doing nothing, waiting for the bad guys to come to him. And not being able to hunt meant he'd have a long night ahead of him before he could see Kenna again. He couldn't show up at her place after they'd made plans to meet the next day. She'd wonder at the sudden change. Plus, she might think he moved a little too fast if he came across as demanding all of her attention all the time. He knew what she meant to him, but she didn't have a clue.

Tor left the small temple and then headed downstairs to the living room where he had a fifty-five-inch LED television. He'd watch some movies to help the time pass before he was tired enough to go to bed.

As he looked through his collection of DVDs, his thoughts kept straying to Kenna. The more he thought of her, the more he remembered how she tasted, how it felt to sink his body into hers. The sounds she made as she came. He longed to be with her, to have her always at his side. He craved her touch and would for the rest of his very long life. His feelings for her had gone from simple attraction to full-blown love in a matter of days.

Maybe it had a lot to do with the bond that had formed between them, but Tor didn't want to go back to his old life of being alone. Kenna completed him, made him feel things he hadn't felt in thousands of years—longing for someone to share his days and nights with being one of them.

Tomorrow he'd take the steps to bring Kenna into his world and permanently into his life. He wanted her living under his roof where she'd be better protected from the evil he knew all too well lurked outside, just waiting for a chance to strike at the next victim. She'd already experienced it firsthand, not that she remembered. He wanted to shelter her from it so it would never happen again. He would always be one of Anubis' warriors, but he now had a duty to protect her, his mate, as well.

* * * *

Kenna found she didn't know what to do with herself

after Tor had dropped her off at home. She prowled around her apartment, missing him like crazy. No other guy had she obsessed over as much as she did Tor. Some great sex and now she wanted to hang on to him and never let him go. Neither of them had even discussed the future. She didn't even know if he wanted a serious relationship with her. And it was way too early to think about bringing up the topic of marriage.

She went to her bedroom and decided she might as well pack a bag for her weekend at Tor's. The first thing she did was head to her underwear drawer. Though she wasn't one for dressing overtly sexy, she did like to wear slinky undergarments. Nick called her the closet slut, that deep inside she wanted to show off her body. She did, but only to the men she slept with. And right now, that man was Tor.

Kenna pulled out some of her skimpiest lingerie. She had one set in particular she wanted to take. After lifting it out of the drawer, she held it in front of her. It was a red satin baby doll with black lace trim along the hem and a sweetheart neckline. The straps were black and thin with tiny black satin bows partway up. A red satin G-string completed it. It was one of her recent purchases and she hadn't had a chance to wear it yet. She had a feeling Tor would like to see her in it. She knew she'd love it when he stripped the baby doll off her.

Once she finished packing, Kenna took a long, hot shower. She washed her hair, shaved her legs, and lathered herself up with her vanilla-scented body wash. Letting her hair air-dry, she applied lotion to her body. Now she was all set to see Tor the next day.

When the hour grew late enough, Kenna went to bed. She thought she might have a hard time falling asleep, since she was more than looking forward to the weekend starting, but that didn't happen to be the case. Sleep claimed her in a matter of minutes.

She had a dream about Tor, but it wasn't a sexy, fun one. It was a borderline nightmare. One she tried to wake herself up from but couldn't. In it, a strange man threatened her, demanding she give him something. What, she didn't know. All she knew was he frightened her. Tor appeared on the scene. Some of Kenna's fear dissipated, knowing he'd take care of the man who threatened her. Tor would keep her safe.

That soon changed when Tor's body blurred, and he shifted into a creature straight out of a horror movie, something half-human and half-animal. He stood taller than his normal height, was more muscular with his body completely covered in black fur. His tail swished behind him as he curled the upper lip on his muzzle and growled much as he had done while they'd made love. Somehow, she'd even added his Egyptian heritage, because the creature he'd become wore a snow-white kilt as they did in ancient times, complete with gold armbands around his furred biceps.

This new Tor focused on the man and grabbed him by the throat. With a flash of a gold dagger, Tor cut the stranger with it, and the man yelled in fear before he literally disappeared. Tor turned toward Kenna, the dagger still in his hand. Blood marred the gold of the blade, dripping as he walked closer. There was more blood than there should have been. It didn't seem to stop.

Kenna told him to stay back, but he kept coming. His gaze snagged hers, and she couldn't look away, felt trapped, unable to move. In a deep, gravelly voice, he said, "You are mine." He lunged at her.

She screamed, which woke her up. Kenna lay still on the bed, her eyes trying to focus in the darkness as her heart beat at a fast rate. She panted in fear, afraid to move. It was only a dream, she told herself. Tor was not the creature she'd seem him shift into while she'd slept. That was only the stuff of horror films, or her dreams, apparently.

Once she could breathe again without sounding as if she'd just run a marathon, Kenna got out of bed and went to the bathroom. She splashed cool water on her face. She rarely had nightmares. And, of course, it would figure when she did, it would be an exceptionally bad one. She just hoped she'd be able to go back to sleep.

Kenna headed to the bedroom and then climbed into bed. She closed her eyes and once again the creature Tor had become rose in her mind. *It's not real, it's not real.* She could tell herself that, but the fear was still there. Not about to let the nightmare win, she rolled to her side and pulled the extra pillow to her chest, holding it tight. She would not stay awake. She needed to rest. She wasn't going to ruin tomorrow by being tired from lack of sleep.

It took a few hours, but Kenna finally was able to push the memory of her bad dream aside to find the sleep she needed. As she drifted off, she thought of Tor and how good it felt to be held in his arms.

* * * *

Kenna awoke in the morning, grateful her nightmare hadn't returned. She stretched and sat up. The small sliver of sunlight that shone through the crack in her drapes told her the day was already a bright one. She threw back the covers and then got out of bed.

After a stop in the bathroom, she headed for the kitchen. It was a little after ten. She decided to make herself some breakfast, then get dressed and ready for the day. Standing at the open fridge, Kenna saw she had all the ingredients to make a veggie omelet. She took out everything she needed and shut the door with her hip.

As she worked, she thought of Tor's huge kitchen and his chef-quality stove. She might not cook as well as he did, but she wasn't awful, by any means. Maybe he'd let her make their dinner tonight and she could try out his fancy things.

She ran through menu ideas as she chopped some of the vegetables. Her mind really not on the work at hand, Kenna ended up cutting herself. She sucked in a sharp breath and lifted her finger closer to her face to see what kind of damage she'd done. She blinked, not sure if her eyes played tricks on her or not. Had the cut just instantly healed? She ran water over her finger in the sink. Her skin bore no slice mark.

Kenna dried her hand, giving the digit she knew for a fact she'd cut with the knife a closer inspection. Yup, it looked exactly the same. She knew that wasn't possible. She *had* cut herself. She'd felt the sting of it. Maybe she was losing her mind and only thought she had hurt herself.

Deciding she'd better not go there, Kenna went back to preparing her breakfast. She'd almost convinced herself the knife incident really hadn't happened when she touched the hot frying pan with the side of her hand. Her first instinct was to hold it under cold water in the sink, but as she turned toward it, the pain ebbed to nothing. Almost afraid to look, she flipped her hand. No burn mark.

She let out a small whimper. Kenna had never healed *that* fast. Before she completely wigged out, she forced herself to continue on with what she was doing. Once her omelet was cooked, she slipped it onto a plate and then sat at the table to eat. With each mouthful, her thoughts became more chaotic, grasping at ludicrous possibilities as to why she'd healed in a matter of seconds.

By the time she'd finished her breakfast, Kenna had worked herself up into quite a state. She entertained the notion of cutting herself to see if she'd still heal at a rapid rate.

Calling herself stupid for even thinking of doing it, Kenna got up from the table and grabbed her sharpest knife out of the block sitting on top of the counter. She sat back down, her hands shaking. Should she? Shouldn't she? What if she cut herself and she didn't heal, and it was bad enough that she'd need stitches? How the hell would she explain why she'd done it without the doctor wanting her to see a shrink?

Then her thoughts strayed to what she would do if she did heal. It wasn't fricking normal. Not by a long shot. And it was something new for her. Before today, she had to wait like everyone else in the world to have a cut disappear. She couldn't think of anything she'd recently done that would be so off the wall as to change her in such a way. The only thing new in her life was Tor and he sure as shit hadn't made her like that.

If she kept that up too much longer, they would have to take her away in a straitjacket and lock her up in the nuthouse. Before she could talk herself out of it, Kenna ran the knife she held across her left palm. It hurt more than when she'd accidently done it since she made sure she went deep enough to make herself bleed more than a little.

She did, but only for a few seconds. The wound healed, not even leaving a scar. The blood that had been spilled absorbed back into her skin. No trace of it remained. Kenna laughed, on the verge of being hysterical, then cried. Then laughed and cried at the same time. She barely managed to pull herself together before she totally lost it.

Kenna dropped the knife onto the table as if it were a poisonous snake. She took deep, even breaths. She looked at the clock on the stove. There was a little less than an hour before she had to leave to go to Tor's place. She could not show up at his door looking like an absolute mess. For one thing, she didn't know if she'd be able to tell him why she was so upset. It was bad enough she thought she was crazy, but it would be even worse if he did too. And she sure as hell didn't want whatever this was to push him away.

She stood and went to the sink to do the washing up as she would any other Saturday morning. That finished, she left the kitchen to head for her bedroom. Dressing helped her get more on an even keel. Kenna would not think about anything that would be considered off in woo-woo land. She'd be herself, not give Tor any reason to think something was wrong.

By the time Kenna had collected the bag she'd packed and then headed out of her apartment, she'd collected herself to the point no one would be able to know she'd somehow acquired a freaky ability. At least in her mind she pulled it off.

CHAPTER SIX

Tor resisted the urge to open the front door and look outside to see if Kenna had arrived. Instead, he went to the living room and turned on the TV. He'd missed her, had even found himself reaching for her while in bed, wanting to have her in his arms.

Since he'd already made them mates, he planned to tell her everything once she'd had a chance to settle in, and after they'd made love once, maybe twice. The sooner he got it over with, the better it would be for both of them. As Anubis had said the night before, sooner or later Kenna was going to notice something was different about her. She needed to understand why before that happened. He could see it freaking her out if she happened to hurt herself and then healed in seconds.

Tor didn't want to risk the demon that had him in his sights finding out what Kenna was to him while she was on her own. Without being under Tor's protection, the demon could hurt her. And if the creature ever found out Tor's and Kenna's life forces were joined, the demon would try to take Kenna out, knowing full well Tor would die right along with her.

Having not spent the night and into the early hours of the morning hunting, Tor had had the chance to go to the grocery store earlier and stock up on what he hoped Kenna would like to eat. Now being immortal, she would be able to eat as much as she wanted—food that was good or bad for her—and not have to worry about gaining a pound. She'd always stay the same. She'd also be able to drink alcohol and never get drunk.

Ten minutes later, Tor heard the sound of a car pulling up his long driveway. He smiled as he hurried out of the living room and then walked through the foyer to the front door. He opened it before he stepped out in time to see Kenna park in front of the garage. He smiled as he headed in her direction. She didn't see him at first, but once she did, she gave him a small wave, then took an athletic bag out of the backseat.

Once he closed the distance between them, Tor cupped her face and kissed her as he'd ached to do since he'd dropped her off at her place the night before. He put his arm around her shoulders and guided her toward the door.

"I missed you," he said as they walked.

She smiled as she angled her head to look at him, her arm snaking around his waist. "I missed you too."

Inside the house, he shut the door behind them. Tor took her bag and placed it on the bottom step of one of the staircases to bring up to his bedroom later. He turned back to her.

"Would you like something to drink or eat?"

Kenna shook her head. "No, I'm fine. Thanks."

Tor looked down and saw she wrung her hands. Gazing at her more closely, he realized her expression was a little on the pinched side, almost as if she appeared anxious about something. He hoped he wasn't the cause of it.

"Are you okay, Kenna?" he asked.

"Of course I am." She wrung her hands harder and spoke faster. "Why wouldn't I be? Everything is perfect. I have nothing to worry about."

"Well, for one thing, you're babbling."

"I'm not babbling. I'm just—" Kenna took a deep breath, then said more slowly, "I'm fine."

"All right." He still wasn't convinced that she was. Something bothered her. "What would you—"

Kenna cut off his words by throwing herself into his arms and covering his mouth with her own. He wrapped his arms around her waist and returned her kiss.

Against his lips, she said huskily, "Take me upstairs and make love to me. I need you inside me."

He groaned as he lifted her off her feet and turned toward the stairs. He'd planned to wait a bit before they got to lovemaking, but he was on board with getting to the good stuff sooner rather than later.

Taking the stairs two at a time, he practically ran to the upper level. All the while, he kissed Kenna passionately. She put her legs around his waist, and her pussy rubbed against his cock with each step he took. By the time he'd reached the top, he was fully erect, aching to sink inside her.

The short trek down the hallway to his bedroom ramped him up even more. Only with Kenna, with his mate, did he feel desperate, wanting to sink his cock into her moist heat. As if he wouldn't survive another minute if he didn't. And she seemed to need him just as badly. She clung to his shoulders, kissing him so hard their teeth knocked together. Tor had a feeling it would always be like that between them.

Setting her on her feet inside his room, Tor pulled away from Kenna's mouth and then lifted her shirt over her head. He dropped his gaze to her breasts and sucked in a sharp breath at what he saw. Her bra was dark pink and so sheer it left nothing to the imagination. Her nipples were taut, just begging for him to suck on them.

That would have to wait. First, he wanted to see if she wore a matching pair of panties. Tor dropped his hands to the top of Kenna's jeans and undid them. He yanked them down her legs to pool at her ankles. She stepped out and then kicked them away with a flick of her foot. Yup, her panties matched the bra. His cock twitched at the sight of her pussy encased in the sheer, shimmering material.

"You're beautiful," he said in a low, raspy voice. "I'm going to take my time stripping you out of that sexy bra and panties."

"You mean thong."

Kenna turned, and Tor groaned. She was indeed wearing a thong instead of panties. She went to face him once more, but he stopped her by placing his hands on her hips. He nudged her hair away from the side of her neck and nuzzled her there with his lips as he ran a hand along the skimpy waistband of her thong. He followed it down the crack of her ass before he skimmed his fingers over the twin globes of flesh not covered by the sheer material.

Tor caressed up her sides, reaching around Kenna's front and cupped her breasts. He tugged her nipples as he ground his cock against her ass. She lifted her hands to cover his and rocked back into him. The smell of her arousal perfumed the air, making him want to taste the wetness that had to be soaking into her thong.

He turned her in his arms. Tor yanked off his shirt, then pulled Kenna against him. He claimed her lips in a heated kiss, unhooking her bra at the same time. She sucked on his tongue, pushing the straps down her arms, and let it drop to the floor.

Kenna's taut nipples brushed against Tor's chest. He released her mouth and licked and kissed his way down to the tight buds. He flicked one with the tip of his tongue, then swirled it around the nipple before he sucked it inside his mouth. She dug her nails into his biceps as she held on to him and let out a throaty moan. He shifted to the other one and suckled on it, her moans increasing in volume.

Leaving her breasts, Tor continued his downward travel. He kissed along her ribs and stomach, ending up on his knees. He slipped a finger under the front of Kenna's thong and dipped it between her legs. The digit came away wet. Meeting and holding her gaze with his own, he slowly brought his finger to his mouth and licked it clean. Her eyes dilated, and her breathing grew more rapid.

Tor's arousal beat at him. He dragged his gaze from Kenna's and hooked the waistband of her thong with his fingers and pulled it down her legs and off. He used a hand to push her thighs farther apart, then went in for the taste he craved.

He licked her pussy, gathering all the wetness there before he swallowed it down. Wanting more, he stiffened his tongue and speared it into Kenna. The grip she had on his shoulders increased as her legs shook with slight tremors. She moaned long and loud.

He pleasured her until he could no longer ignore his need to be inside her. Tor smoothly came to his feet and undid his jeans. He shucked them off, then wrapped his hand around his erection and pumped his fist up and down his full length. Kenna's gaze followed his movements.

"Turn around, bend over, and put your hands on the bed," Tor said huskily.

Kenna didn't hesitate. She did exactly what he'd told her to do. He shifted to stand behind her and took hold of her hips. He positioned her and rubbed his cock against her wet pussy until he was liberally coated with her juices. She was more than ready for him to take her.

He lined up the head of his shaft with her slick opening and pushed inside. Rocking against her, he worked himself deeper until she'd taken all of him. He groaned, loving the way her inner walls closed around him, holding him tight. She fit him like a glove. There was no better sensation than being inside his mate.

Tor took Kenna in long, hard strokes, sinking balls-deep each time. She pushed back to meet him, squeezing her inner muscles tightly around his cock. His shaft grew even harder. He pistoned his hips, an orgasm building.

Pulling out of her, Tor urged Kenna all the way onto the bed, then turned her so she was on her back. He covered her body with his, sinking his cock back inside her pussy. He lifted his upper body on his hands as he continued to thrust into her. He set a fast pace, angling his hips so his shaft rubbed the spot she needed him to send her into climax.

In and out he pumped. His balls rose closer to his body as the point of no return edged nearer. Kenna let out a whimpered moan, her hands clutching his biceps as her pussy rhythmically squeezed his cock as she came. It was all he needed to follow her into release. He growled, filling her with his cum as his shaft pulsed deep inside her.

Once she'd wrung everything out of him, Tor collapsed on top of Kenna. She put her arms around his back and held him close.

He lifted himself onto his bent arms and kissed her tenderly. "I love you," he said, panting to catch his breath.

"What?" she asked softly.

Tor latched his gaze on to hers. "I love you." He did. He could never see himself with another woman. She was it for him, and always would be. It had taken him thousands of years to find her. He wouldn't let his woman go.

Kenna brought his mouth down to hers and kissed him passionately. She pulled away and smiled. "I love you too. And just so you know, I'm not the type of woman to instantly fall in love with a man just because he slept with me." She reached up and caressed his cheek. "I thought I was falling for you too hard and fast. I guess I didn't need to worry."

He kissed the tip of her nose. "I mean it with all my heart. So, when do you want to start moving your stuff here?"

"You want to live together?"

"Of course. I don't plan on ever letting you go. You're mine, as I'm yours. What's the point in waiting?"

Kenna stared up at him, then laughed. Tor scowled. It was a bit of a blow to his ego after he'd professed his undying love for her. He'd wanted to tell her exactly how he felt before he revealed what she was to him. And when she'd said she loved him as well, he'd hoped she'd want everything he wanted — them being together — always.

She stopped laughing, and said, "I'm not laughing at you. Really. I'm laughing at myself, because I'm going to do something so totally out of character for me. I didn't think I had it in me either." She paused, her face becoming serious. "Yes, Tor, I'll move in with you. How does tomorrow sound?"

In way of an answer, Tor kissed her, pushed his tongue between her lips. His cock hardened inside her once again. He pumped in little thrusts until he was fully engorged. Kenna lifted her hips, matching the pace he set.

This time their lovemaking didn't last very long. All too soon they both came, moaning into each other's mouth. Once it was over, Tor rolled to his back, taking Kenna with him. She sprawled on top of him like a contented kitten as he ran his hand up and down her back.

Now that they knew how they felt about each other, and he'd gotten Kenna's agreement to move in with him, Tor had to take the next step and tell her about him being a warrior of Anubis. And that she was his mate. If his luck held, she'd be able to take everything he told her and accept him and what he'd done to her to make her truly his.

* * * *

She and Tor must have fallen asleep for a short while after the last time they'd made love, because Kenna woke up still lying on top of him with her head pillowed on his chest. It rose and fell with his even breaths. She looked at his face. His eyes were closed. God, he was handsome. And from the conversation they'd had, he was hers.

If someone had come up to her last week and told her she'd fall in love with a rich, tall, dark, and very muscular man and move into his fancy mansion with him all in a matter of days, Kenna would have thought that person nuts. There she was, head over heels for the very first time in her life. Nick would have a heyday with it.

Now that her thoughts were no longer distracted, centered on the pleasure Tor gave her, Kenna found herself thinking about her new ability to heal in an instant. She had no idea if it was a temporary thing, or whether she'd have it for the rest of her life. And it wasn't as if it was something she could go to the doctor and get checked out. The idea of getting experimented on wasn't what she'd ever want to experience.

The only person she could think of telling was Tor, mostly because she'd be living with him and there was a very high chance of him noticing she didn't heal like everyone else. It would be hard to live under the same roof and keep that a secret.

Kenna felt eyes watching her and looked to see Tor had awakened. She inched up his body and gave him a quick kiss. "How about we get dressed and go downstairs to find something to eat? I'm a bit hungry. Then I want to talk to you about something."

His brows furrowed. "All right. Nothing too serious, I hope."

"It's hard to say. It depends on how you react to it." She

rolled off Tor and slid from the bed. "I'm going to use the bathroom."

She walked into the en suite and then closed the door behind her. Kenna used the toilet before she washed her hands. She caught her reflection in the mirror above the sink. Was she making a mistake telling Tor? She hoped not.

Back out in the main room, Kenna found Tor standing at the end of the bed with his back toward her. He was just pulling his jeans on over his hips. She sighed to herself. The man had a great ass. He also was someone who didn't like underwear. He hadn't worn any on the days she'd been with him. Not that she complained about it. It was a turn-on to think she just had to open his pants and his cock would be there with nothing else keeping her from it.

Kenna closed the distance between them and placed a kiss on Tor's wide back. He turned his head to look over his shoulder at her. "What would you like to eat?"

She walked around to his side and picked up some of her clothes. Tor turned so he faced her. "I don't know," she said. "Nothing big. Since you cooked for me yesterday, I hoped you'd let me cook for you in your fancy kitchen."

"It's your kitchen now as well. You agreeing to live with me makes it so."

She smiled. "I guess it does. While we're down there I should see what you have in the fridge and pantry to make sure all the ingredients I'll need to make us dinner are there."

"Well, I did some shopping earlier today and stocked up. What are you thinking of making?"

Kenna finished getting dressed. "I haven't quite decided. I'll wait until I see what you have."

"Since you're going to be the chef for tonight, why don't you go downstairs and look around in the fridge? I'm just going to use the bathroom and I'll meet you in the kitchen."

"All right."

She left the bedroom as Tor headed for the en suite. Kenna had just reached the foyer when the doorbell rang. She looked up the stairs, but Tor wouldn't be able to get down there that fast. Since she was already halfway, she decided she'd answer the door.

After pulling it open, she found a large man who looked as if he'd seen better days standing on the other side. "Hi," she said, giving him a leery look.

He grabbed her by the throat and pushed her farther into the foyer as he kicked the door shut. "Hi back. He said you were a pretty thing. I'm going to enjoy this."

Kenna screamed as the man roughly pushed her against the wall and groped her. She tried to fight back, but he was stronger than she. The sound of a loud growl had her looking toward the stairs. What she saw had her heart leaping up into her throat, and a rush of memories she hadn't remembered slamming back into her mind.

CHAPTER SEVEN

Tor felt the pull of evil at the same time he heard Kenna's scream coming from the lower level. Having finished in the bathroom, he ran out of the bedroom to the top of the stairs. Seeing a strange man holding her by the throat, tugging at her clothes, sent Tor into a rage. How dare the evildoer touch his mate?

The stench of evil filled Tor's nose as he rushed down the stairs. For the first time, he looked forward to the pain of a shift as the change took him over. By the time he reached the foyer, he was in his half-human and half-jackal form. He set his sights on his prey and rushed him, pulling him away from Kenna. The man ended up slamming into the front door headfirst.

Tor grabbed the evildoer again. This time the mortal decided to fight. He swung a punch at Tor, which Tor easily deflected. Tor pushed his prey back against the door harder than was necessary before he brutally tore into the man's mind. He saw all the mortal's evil deeds. One memory in particular had Tor growling in outrage. It was one of the demons who hunted him having a conversation with the evildoer. It was the demon who had sent the man to Tor's house to attack Kenna. The creature hadn't revealed himself but kept to the shadows so Tor had no idea what he looked like, but he recognized the voice.

Somehow the demon had to be watching Tor to have learned about Kenna and where Tor lived to be able to send the evildoer there. It was time he and the demon had a face-to-face. Tor wouldn't let the creature use his mate against him.

With a snarl, Tor growled, "Guilty. Time to pay for all your evil deeds."

Tor willed his gold dagger into his hand and shoved it into the man's stomach. The evildoer bellowed in pain before he slowly lost solidity until he completely disappeared.

The sound of a whimper had Tor turning around as he willed the dagger away. Kenna stood with her back pressed against the wall, her face set in a mask of horror and fear. She looked at him the same way she had before he'd wiped her memory of him.

He sucked in a sharp breath at the pain that tore through his body as he shifted back to his human form. He went to take a step toward Kenna, but she held up her hands as if to ward him off, tears spilling down her cheeks. Tor stayed where he was.

"It's all right," he said in a quiet and even tone. "You're safe, Kenna."

She wildly shook her head. "No. I remember everything. I remember what happened in the parking lot at the Luxor, why I feel uneasy there. It was you."

"I would never do anything to hurt you. I saved you that night from an evildoer."

"Yes, but you did something to make me forget. I've had a nightmare about you in that…that other form. Using your gold dagger, making another man disappear after you cut him with it. It scared the crap out of me. I thought it was a figment of my imagination, but now I know it was real. I've been sleeping with a murderer."

This time Tor closed the distance between him and Kenna. He didn't touch her. "No, I'm not. They're alive when I start them on their journey to the underworld. It's my job to send mortals who are full of evil to Anubis to be judged. The god decides what their fate will be."

Kenna took a step to the side so he wasn't directly in front of her. "You talk about Anubis as if he's truly alive. A freaking ancient Egyptian god."

"Because he is. I'm one of his warriors. The first one. When I lay dying on a battlefield in Egypt, having fought for my pharaoh, Djoser, in a military expedition to Sinai Peninsula, Anubis answered my call when I pleaded to one of my gods to save me. In return for restoring my life and giving me immortality, I took a vow to serve as a warrior of Anubis for all eternity."

She rapidly shook her head. "That can't be. If your pharaoh was Djoser that would mean you've been alive since the twenty-seventh-century BC. I did a project in school on the step pyramid he had built in Saqqara for his tomb. I remember it. You'd have to be thousands of years old. It's not possible."

"I am, and it is. I watched the Pyramid of Djoser being built, as I watched the pyramids at Giza. I stayed in the land of my birth for thousands of years before I came to the New World. I eventually ended up here in Las Vegas."

Kenna laughed, the sound borderline hysterical, as her tears continued to flow. "And here I thought I was some kind of freak. Now that I think about it, you had to be the cause of it. I want you to take it back."

Tor furrowed his brow. "I don't understand."

"My ability to heal in seconds," she yelled. "I didn't have it until I met you. You had to have done something to change me. Whatever you did, reverse it."

He sighed, knowing what he had to say next Kenna would not want to hear. "I can't. And it's more than just your ability to heal rapidly."

"What do you mean?"

"You're my mate, Kenna. When I bit you yesterday, I claimed you as mine. You are as immortal as I am. Our life forces are now joined. It can't be undone."

"What the hell are you saying?" Kenna breathed so fast Tor was afraid she would hyperventilate. "Mate? You actually did this to me without giving me a choice? Did I even have any say in it?"

Tor ran a hand through his hair in agitation. "I was to give you the choice. I didn't want to bite you before you knew what I truly was. Somehow a demon who has escaped the underworld managed to work a spell that allowed him to take control of me. I knew you were my mate the first time we were intimate, because my eyeteeth dropped and I had the urge to bite you. I fought it, but when the demon took over, I couldn't stop myself. Anubis wanted me to ease you into my world before I claimed you. The demon took that option from me."

"A demon? Ease me into your world? From what I've seen of it so far, I don't want to be in it. Right now, all I want to do is get as far away from you as I can get."

She sidestepped a few more paces in the direction of the door. Tor stopped her. "You can't leave. You have to stay with me. Only I can protect you from the creature who has set his sights on me. The demon is the one who sent the evildoer to my home to attack you. He must know you're my mate. If he gets the chance again, he will try to use you against me."

Kenna fisted her hands at her sides. "I can't stay here with you. Do you have any idea how afraid I am of you at this moment?"

Unable to not touch her any longer, feeling as if he was losing her by the second, Tor cupped her face. "Look at me, Kenna. Really look at me. Have I ever done anything to hurt you?"

"No."

"And I never will. I love you. I've been alone for centuries. You're my mate, someone I'll always cherish and protect. I don't want to go back to my old life. I know this is all so very hard for you to understand and accept. I might shift into something you're afraid of, but the man is still inside there. It's still my heart that beats in that chest. I'm still the same person. I just look different. And believe me, I didn't want you to find out what I was this way."

Kenna's bottom lip trembled. "I don't know if I can accept all this. And now you're telling me there's no going back. I would have wanted the choice."

Tor pulled her close. She pushed at his chest, but after a few seconds Kenna relaxed against him, her tears wetting his skin. He let her cry herself out before he leaned back and lifted her chin so she looked up at him. Her eyes were red and puffy.

"Stay with me, Kenna. Please. I realize you're going to need time, and I'm willing to give you that. We have an eternity, after all. You said you loved me once. I can make you feel that way again."

"And if I can't?"

"I'm not giving up on you. We'll make this work." He kissed her forehead, and when Kenna didn't pull away, he took that as a good sign. "I need to talk to Anubis. I'd like you to come with me. It might help if you hear his voice."

She stepped out of his embrace and wrapped her arms around her middle. "What exactly would I have to do? I don't have to cut myself, do I?"

Tor could still hear the fear in Kenna's voice, but it wasn't nearly as bad as it'd been a few minutes ago. He smiled to reassure her. "No, you don't have to cut yourself. We just have to go upstairs to the small temple I have set up in one of the spare bedrooms. You should be able to hear Anubis since a bond has formed between us."

"All right, I guess. I don't know how much more freakiness I can take without wanting to huddle in a corner and rock."

"It'll be fine. You'll just hear Anubis in your mind."

Tor held his hand out to Kenna, but she gave a short shake of her head. He dropped it at his side. He wasn't going to push her. He turned and walked toward the stairs. She fell into step beside him. He took her to the bedroom set up as a temple.

Inside, he headed for the altar where he'd already made his offering of food and beer that morning. Tor glanced at Kenna to find her looking around the room, taking it all in.

"Anubis, I have to talk to you," he called to the god of the underworld.

Yes, Tor?

Kenna let out a quiet gasp and took a half step closer so her arm brushed against his. She obviously had heard Anubis as clearly as Tor did.

"The demon who hunts me has made another move. He found out about Kenna being my mate and sent an evildoer to my home to attack her. I need a way to draw him out. I don't want to risk him harming Kenna."

I saw it in the evildoer's memories when he arrived. Challenge the demon. Tonight.

"How should I do that?"

Call to the demon. He will hear you.

"I tried that once. He ignored me."

Play upon the demon's pride. He will not be able to ignore the insult. Just be prepared for him not to fight fair.

"All right. I have Kenna here with me, is there anything you can do to protect her from the demon?"

I know she is there. I can feel her fear. There is no need to be afraid, Kenna. Tor needs you in his life to make it complete. He loves you just as much as you love him, though you cannot see past your fear to believe that you still do. I will fix that. Anubis fell silent, and Kenna stiffened beside Tor. It only lasted a matter of seconds, then the god spoke again. *As for your request to protect Kenna from the demon, I can use a spell that will shield her against an attack from demon-kind, but it will not extend to others with evil intent. As you know, my abilities are not as powerful as some of the other gods.*

"It'll be enough," Tor said. "I just want her protected from the demon."

It is done. Anubis' presence faded.

Tor turned to Kenna, expecting to see her fear still visible on her face. What he wasn't prepared for was for her to throw herself into his arms and cling to him. He closed his eyes and tucked her head under his chin and returned her embrace. He felt as if he could finally take a deep breath since she had seen him in his half-human and half-jackal form.

*

Kenna clung tightly to Tor. Her fear of him was gone, taken away by Anubis. Without it threatening to take her over, she was able to think clearly again. The god had shown her how Tor had lived his life all those millennia, starting with the day he'd taken his vow to become one of Anubis' warriors. That had been particularly hard to see. Tor had been so close to death. Seeing him bloody, barely clinging to life, had been gut-wrenching.

And Tor had been alone for so very long. Living among mortals, keeping his distance since their lifespans were short compared to his. Not once had he tried to form any attachments. That is until he'd stumbled across her. She'd seen the night in the Luxor parking lot through his eyes. Had seen how taken he'd been with her, and how he hadn't wanted to wipe her memory, but had known he hadn't any choice. And also how he hadn't been able to stay away from her in the end.

The love she felt for him was as strong as ever now that

her fear no longer clouded it. She loved this ancient immortal warrior with all her heart. Walking away wasn't an option. Kenna wanted the brief flash of her future with Tor that Anubis had given her.

She pulled back in Tor's arms and stared at him. "I can accept all this now."

"You can?"

"As Anubis said, he fixed me. He took my fear away. If he hadn't, I don't know if I would have been able to get past it." She met his gaze. "Then I would have missed out on the best thing that has ever happened to me — you. I love you as much as I did before I found out what you were."

Tor crushed her in his embrace and kissed her as if there were no tomorrow. She returned it, pouring all the love she had for him into it. He pulled away once he had her pussy wet and aching for him to fill it. His cock was hard, pressed against her stomach.

"I need you again," Tor said huskily. "And I promise you I'll do everything in my power to keep you happy. I'll always love you. You do make me complete."

"And I want you. Make love to me."

He picked her up and carried her to the bedroom. He took his time taking her clothes off, kissing every inch of skin he bared. By the time he'd finished and was as naked as she, Kenna was almost desperate for him, but she stopped him when he would have lifted her onto the bed.

With gentle lips, she kissed where each of the wounds he'd received on that battlefield had been. Last, she explored his chest, especially where Anubis had placed his mark on Tor. Without it and all it stood for, Kenna would never have met the man who now owned her heart.

"Let me love you," she said as she took a step back.

In answer, Tor claimed her lips in a searing kiss before he climbed onto the bed, then lay on his back in the center of it. Kenna followed him and straddled his thighs. She lovingly ran her hands along his chest and down to his six-pack abs. Once she reached his cock, she wrapped her hand around it and pumped. He lifted his hips off the bed, pressing himself tighter into her hold.

Kenna bent her head and licked off the bead of pre-cum that appeared on the very tip of Tor's cock. She moaned at the salty taste of him. Seeing him watching her, she opened her mouth and took him inside. She sucked on him, taking him almost to the back of her throat. His shaft grew harder, and he groaned, his gaze intently following her movements. In and out she took him, increasing the suction as he rocked against her.

"I love how you suck," Tor said on a moan. "You'll make me come, but I want to be inside you when I do that."

And she wanted him deep inside her. Kenna released his cock, then shifted up his body until her pussy hovered over his erection. She lowered herself onto him. He easily slipped inside her. He stretched and filled her. She panted as she took all of him, sheathing him to the base.

Placing her hands on his chest, Kenna rode Tor's cock. She squeezed her inner muscles around him as he slid in and out of her. She took him so deep she couldn't tell where she ended and he began. They perfectly fit each other. And Tor was all hers for eternity. Her eternal warrior. Her mate.

Tor lifted his head and sucked a nipple into his mouth. With each pull on the taut bud, Kenna's body coiled tighter. She increased the pace she set, taking him harder and faster, moaning his name.

Her movements became jerky just as she fell over the edge. Her climax tore through her, intense and seeming to go on forever. Once it was over, Tor took hold of her hips and lifted her on and off him, arching up as he surged into her. His face was set in a mask of male need as he strained for his own release. When he came, he growled and thrust so hard into her, he lifted her knees off the bed.

Out of breath, feeling delicious aftershocks, Kenna collapsed onto Tor's chest. His heart thundered under her ear. He wrapped his arms around her, holding her close.

Once she could breathe normally again, Kenna lifted her head and kissed Tor's chin. "It's a good thing we have an eternity together, because I don't think I'll ever get my fill of you."

He chuckled and tucked her hair behind her ear. "I won't complain about that, considering I feel the same way when it comes to you." Tor sobered. "Are you really sure you're okay with all this?"

She nodded. "I know you didn't have any control. That you tried to fight the demon but lost. Anubis showed me."

"What else did he show you?"

"Your life from the day you gave him your vow to the present. I now feel as if I've known you forever. And probably better than if I'd learned about you in the regular way."

Tor ran the backs of his fingers along her cheek. "Then I guess I'd better thank Anubis the next time I talk to him."

"So, are you really going to try to take on the demon tonight?"

"Yes. The more time that goes by, the more of a threat he'll become. I wouldn't be able to live with myself if something happened to you."

"Just promise me you'll be careful. I don't want to see you hurt, even though you are immortal and heal really fast."

He smiled. "I'll do my best. Don't worry, tonight I'll send the demon back to the underworld to face Anubis. And I promise I'll be careful." Tor rolled and took Kenna to her back with him on top of her. "Enough talk about the demon. It's my turn to love my mate."

Feeling Tor's cock harden inside her pussy, Kenna gave herself over to him and the pleasure she knew he'd give her.

CHAPTER EIGHT

Kenna checked the pots she had cooking on the stove. After their last bout of lovemaking, she and Tor had come downstairs to see what was in the fridge and pantry. As promised, she was going to cook dinner for Tor.

She soon discovered that a trip to the grocery store wouldn't be needed since Tor had picked up a lot of the ingredients she'd use earlier that day. She'd decided to make spaghetti. The sauce came out of a jar, but Kenna added sausage and mushrooms to it.

The pasta done cooking, she drained it and put some on two plates before topping it with sauce. Tor already sat at the island, drinking a beer. She also had one. Kenna had liked the idea that she could drink as much as she wanted and never get drunk. And *really* liked it that she could eat whatever she wanted and not have to worry about getting as big as a house. Immortality did have its advantages.

She placed a plate of spaghetti in front of Tor before she set hers next to him, then came around the island to sit on the stool beside his. "I know it isn't as fancy or exotic like what you made yesterday, but it should taste good. At least I think it does."

Tor picked up his fork, twirled some pasta on it, then put it into his mouth. He chewed and swallowed. "It's good. I like pasta."

While they ate they talked about moving her things out of her apartment to the house. Then the topic of her working at the Luxor came up.

"I'm going to have to quit, aren't I?" she asked, not sure how she felt about that.

"Not right now if you don't wish to, though I'd prefer you did. It's your choice, but keep in mind you will have to eventually. You're immortal now. You won't ever age. At some point, one of your coworkers will notice. It depends on whether or not you want to make the break now or wait until more years have gone by."

Tor did have a point. And if she continued to work during the day, and Tor still had to go out hunting evildoers by night, they wouldn't see each other all that much. And after her recent night shift at the hotel, she didn't want to work those hours again.

"All right," she said. "I'll give them my two weeks' notice. I'm not going to leave them in the lurch. The only person I can see who would be upset by it will be my good friend, Nick. He's a blackjack dealer. And I can't see how I'll be able to cut him out of my life so abruptly without him thinking something is going on. I usually tell him everything."

"Well, you can't tell him about this. If you do, Anubis wouldn't like it at all. He wants mortals to have no knowledge of his warriors' existence."

"I know. I'll just have to think of something when it comes to Nick. I want to keep him as a friend for as long as I can, which means I want to introduce you to him."

Tor nodded. "I'd be more than happy to meet this friend of yours. I don't expect you to cut all ties you have in your life. You do realize you'll eventually have to make a break from your family as well."

Kenna shrugged. "That's not a biggie. My mom died when I was about ten. My dad remarried a few years after that and started a new family. We weren't really close so he was more than happy when I was old enough to move out on my own. I talk to him about once a month and see him only on birthdays and Christmas. I doubt he'd care all that much if I just didn't bother after a while."

"I'm sorry to hear you're not that close."

"Don't be. It doesn't bother me, really. What about your parents? Do you remember them?"

"Of course. I might have been alive for thousands of years, but I remember what it was like growing up in Egypt. My parents were farmers. My brothers and I used to help with the land. I knew farming wasn't going to be for me, so I took up the sword and joined the pharaoh's army."

"You never went back to see them after you became immortal. I saw that."

"No, I didn't. I thought it best if I stayed away, let them go on with the rest of their lives, let them believe I died on that battlefield."

"Do you miss Egypt?"

"Sometimes, but I'm happy here. This is where Anubis wants me so this is where I'll stay. I have no knowledge of the other warriors. He keeps us apart. We each live in different cities from one another. We all work alone."

"That must suck."

Tor chuckled. "I don't mind." He turned his head and looked out the window. "It's starting to get dark. It's almost time."

Kenna understood what he meant. It was almost time for Tor to see if he could lure the demon there to fight him. She wasn't thrilled with the whole idea, but Tor knew what he was doing. He was a skilled warrior and wasn't exactly helpless. He figured he'd shift into his other form at some point once the demon showed up. If evil forced the change on Tor, then the demon would for sure have it happening. There was nothing eviler than that creature.

"I'm coming outside with you," she said as she gathered up their plates and then brought them to the counter.

"No, you'll stay inside."

Kenna turned to face Tor. "Who is to say I'll be any safer in the house? Besides, Anubis used that spell on me that should protect me from any demon attack. So he shouldn't be able to hurt me. I'm going to watch your back."

"I'd feel better knowing you were out of the thick of things."

"And I'd feel better if I was in it. I have to help protect you as much as you want to protect me. Our life forces are tied together. You go, I go. So I kind of have a vested interest in how well you do."

"I don't plan on losing to the demon."

"Then me being outside with you shouldn't be a problem."

Tor stood and walked around the island to stand in front of Kenna. He cupped her face and brushed her lips with his. "Fine. You win, but you will do what I tell you. I don't need to be distracted by worrying about you doing something you shouldn't."

"I promise."

He nodded, then helped her load the dishwasher. By the time they were finished, it was full dark, and Kenna was getting nervous. She just wanted this over and done with so she and Tor could move on with their new life together.

She followed Tor out to the backyard and stayed on the edge of the patio while he picked the ground he wanted to confront the demon on—the nice wide-open space of the expansive lawn away from the in-ground pool, which was as far as he allowed Kenna to stand.

Tor lifted his hand and a sword appeared in it. He shouted, "Demon, show yourself." Nothing happened. "What did you think sending an evildoer to my home would accomplish? If you thought it would throw me off my game, well, you'll have to do better than that. Are you so weak that you must use mortals to do your dirty work?"

Still nothing. Kenna wondered if the demon had actually heard Tor and would show up. The minutes ticked by and she figured the creature was going to be a no-show. She stepped off the patio and walked toward Tor. She had a feeling they'd be going back inside the house.

"I don't think the—" she started to say.

Kenna didn't get a chance to finish her sentence when two men suddenly appeared out of thin air directly across from Tor. The one who held the man who struggled, trying to free himself, had eyes that glowed red. She came to a sudden standstill, knowing full well that had to be the demon. He shoved the man he held into Tor who grimaced.

Tor looked at her, and yelled, "Go inside the house! He brought an evildoer."

She knew what that meant. Tor would be forced to deal with his prey first before he could think about taking out the demon. He wouldn't be able to help himself. Even as Kenna spun around to run, his body took on the change to his other form.

She didn't get very far before the demon appeared right in her path. Kenna came to a halt. Except for his glowing red eyes, the creature would have passed as a normal, not-bad-looking man.

"Where do you think you're going?" he asked as he sidled closer. Kenna took a step back for every one of his forward ones. "I'm going to have some fun with you while your mate is busy."

So that had been the demon's plan. Use the evildoer to distract Tor while the creature went for her. Kenna only had a few seconds to hope like hell Anubis' spell worked. A sword appeared in the demon's hand and he rushed her, moving faster than any mortal could.

The sword swung toward her. Instead of making contact, it bounced off some kind of invisible shield that surrounded her. No matter where the demon tried to strike, his blade couldn't get through. He bellowed in outrage, attacking over and over again.

A streak of black slammed into the demon, pushing him away from Kenna. Tor, still in his half-human and half-jackal form, had come to her rescue. With the evildoer nowhere in sight, obviously taken care of, that left Tor able to focus solely on the demon.

Their swords met with a loud clang. Kenna kept her distance as Tor and the demon hacked at each other, looking for a way to land a strike. Tor handled his sword as if it were an extension of himself. And sadly, she had to admit the demon's skill was pretty damn close to Tor's.

The longer the sword fight dragged on, the more Kenna's nerves tried to get the best of her. Tor and the demon had managed to get in a few good strikes, slicing into skin, but they healed very quickly, not slowing either one down.

Tor growled as he barely avoided a vicious cut that would have landed across his throat. Kenna's heart threatened to beat out of her chest. He was immortal, but if he literally lost his head, it was game over. For both of them.

With a bellow of his own, Tor launched a counterattack on the demon, hitting him faster and harder. The creature lost ground until one of Tor's strikes landed true. His blade sliced across the demon's stomach. It was deep enough to have him leaking like a sieve. The creature yelled in pain, his guard appearing to drop as he lowered his sword. Tor moved in and grabbed him by the throat, looking intently into the demon's eyes. Kenna knew Tor would be pushing inside his mind.

The demon smiled. "That's it, look into *my* eyes." He spoke under his breath in a language Kenna didn't understand.

Tor stiffened before he let go of the demon to grab his head. He growled, the sound full of pain. He panted as he swung around in her direction, his sword raised.

"Run, Kenna," Tor said in his deep, gruff voice. "He has control of me. I can't stop myself."

She stood her ground. "The spell should protect me since he's the one controlling you."

Closer Tor came. "No. It only protects you against an attack from a demon. I'm not one."

Oh shit, Tor was right. An attack the demon launched through Tor would have the desired effect. She was a sitting duck. And she'd waited too long to get a head start on Tor. She'd never make it to the house now, not with how fast he was capable of moving.

Kenna dodged to the left and ran in the demon's direction, trying to lead Tor back to him. The bastard laughed, enjoying the show while he waited for his wound to heal. She had to somehow get Tor to strike at the demon. The creature was still weakened. Plus, he figured he had all the control, making him vulnerable in his conceit.

Tor closed in on her. Kenna ran to stand behind the demon, hoping Tor would take a swing at her and hit the creature in front of her instead. That almost backfired when the demon ducked, and Tor's sword came within inches of her face.

She tried another tactic. She backed up, then took a run at the demon. He couldn't touch her, but she hoped the spell would enable her to touch him. That worked. She slammed into the back of him. Since he hadn't expected her to do something like that, she easily propelled him forward into Tor. All three of them crashed to the ground.

Kenna tenaciously held on to the demon's back as Tor tried to reach for her. The creature ended up sandwiched between them. She felt pain as one of Tor's claws sliced into her forearm, but she ignored it.

Meeting his gaze, she said, "Tor, will the weapon you need to send him to Anubis to appear."

"I can't," he said through gritted teeth. "I can't stop trying to get to you."

The demon shifted under her, almost throwing her off. "I'm a demon," she said.

"What?" Tor growled.

"Picture me as a demon. Make yourself believe I'm one, then try to will a new weapon into your hand."

A black-bladed dagger suddenly appeared as Tor stared at her intently. It headed her way as he went to strike at her. Knowing full well he wouldn't use it on the demon himself, Kenna hit Tor's arm when he struck again, knocking it toward the creature between them.

The dagger sunk into the cap of the demon's arm. He stiffened, then let out a bellow of rage. Slowly, his body became unsubstantial until he completely disappeared. Kenna landed on top of Tor with a grunt. He lay still under her.

"Are you okay?" she asked.

"I have control of myself."

He stiffened as his body blurred, the sound of his bones shifting and realigning loud in the air. Kenna got off him as he took on his human form. Once it was complete, she threw herself back on top of him and held on tight.

"That was too close," she said.

Tor wrapped his arms around her. "I know, but he won't be coming back. The black dagger sent him to the underworld to be judged by Anubis."

Kenna picked up the dagger that lay beside them on the grass. "I guess my idea of getting you to think of me as a demon worked."

Tor took the weapon from her, then willed it away. "That was fast thinking on your part. I wouldn't have been able to do it. I was too busy fighting myself. He would have made me kill you."

"Taking two birds out with one stone." She lifted her head and kissed Tor. "The bastard was overconfident."

"I'm just glad my mate can think fast on her feet." Tor set her aside and rose to stand before he held out his hand and helped Kenna. He bent, picked up his discarded sword, and willed it away. "We need to wash the stench of demon off us, then I'm going to take you to bed. It was too close for me, and I need to be inside you, badly."

She went on tiptoe and threaded her fingers through the sides of Tor's hair as she kissed him with all the love she had for him. They were breathing hard when she pulled away.

"A shower sounds good. And since I'm such a quick thinker, I know what I want to do to you when we're in there." She whispered into his ear what exactly she had in mind.

Kenna let out a squeal as Tor picked her up and put on a preternatural burst of speed, taking them into the house and up the stairs to his bedroom. He stripped them out of their clothes and then had her in the shower in the en suite before she barely had time to register what he did.

She soaped up his muscular body as he did the same to hers. By the time they'd been washed clean, Kenna panted and ached for Tor to fill her. As he kissed her, she pulled at his hair, desperate to get as close to him as she could get. He didn't seem to mind. He picked her up and then put her back against the shower's tiled wall. She wrapped her legs around his waist as he surged inside her.

Kenna pulled away from his mouth and put her head against the wall and moaned. His thick cock thrust in and out of her pussy, pushing the climax that quickly built ever closer to the surface. Tor growled and groaned, his hard ass flexing as he strained against her.

A whimpered cry tore out of her as an intense orgasm took her over. Tor came with her, his cock pulsing deep inside her as her inner walls clutched him in a tight fist. He dug his fingers into her bottom while he held her tightly to him.

Kenna kissed him tenderly, then laughed. "I didn't get to do what I wanted to you."

Tor smiled. "Sorry, I couldn't wait. And we do have the rest of the night."

"Very true. And every night after this one for an eternity."

Once Tor let her down and they rinsed off under the warm spray of water, Kenna led her mate to their bed, then tortured him with her lips and tongue until he flipped her to her back and showed her exactly what she had to look forward to in her future.

The End

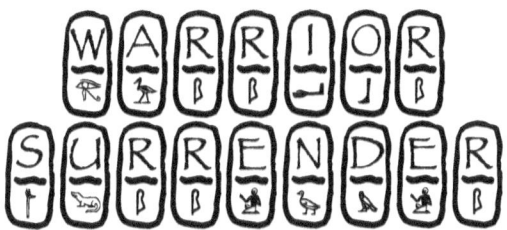

WARRIOR SURRENDER

Jaxon never wanted to tie himself down to a single woman, not even when he was mortal. When a sexy temptress collides with him on the street, dumping her coffee all over his chest, he sees the opportunity for another installment of his *modus operandi*—seduce, bed, and then leave. But this fiery woman sees through his attempts and refuses to be just another notch on his bedpost.

Chyna is prepared to walk away when it becomes clear Jaxon plans to hit it and leave. She has a plan of her own and knows seduction is a two-way street. Once she gets him in bed, he won't want to leave. But she gets more than she bargained for when her lover shows his other, *furry* side and reveals his true nature—as a shifter and warrior to an ancient Egyptian god. She must then decide if she is brave enough to stay...or if she will be the one to walk away.

CHAPTER ONE

Jaxon strolled down the street with no real destination in mind. Even though he'd hunted his prey for most of the night before, he'd taken to the streets of San Diego the following day, midafternoon. Not to hunt. He was just restless. The thought of sitting at home, waiting for the sun to set once again so he could seek out evildoers, as was his job as one of Anubis' warriors, wasn't something he wanted to do. Thus, he was out wandering.

French by birth, he'd been alive since 1772. He'd taken his vow to serve Anubis in 1798 when he'd been a soldier with Napoleon's army. They'd been in Egypt to take the first step against British India to drive the British out of the French Revolutionary War. Taking part in the last battle where the British had defeated the French, Jaxon had almost lost his life, had been pretty near death. He'd been wounded during a naval attack by Nelson in the Aboukir Bay, just off the coast of Egypt. Jaxon had been on the French ship *Orient*. Wounded by British cannon shot, he'd managed to escape the burning ship before it exploded.

Barely reaching the shore, he had called out to any Egyptian god to save him, and Anubis had been the one to answer.

Now he lived in San Diego. For the most part, he was content with his new life. Every once in a while, he'd get restless, but he always managed to get over it. He'd grown accustomed to being alone. And he didn't miss the fact there wasn't a woman at his side to share his life. Even as a mortal he hadn't wanted a wife.

He turned a corner, which took him to the front of a coffee shop. Jaxon grunted, then sucked in a sharp breath as a woman talking on her cell phone, who had come out of the building, crashed into him, spilling her hot coffee on the front of his shirt. Ignoring the stinging burn on his chest, he grabbed her by her arms to right her.

She pulled her cell away from her ear and gave him a look of horror. "Oh, my God. I'm so sorry. Are you okay? Are you scalded by the coffee?"

Luckily for him, being immortal meant whatever burn he'd received had healed in a matter of seconds. The only damage done was to his shirt, which had a big stain across the chest.

"I'm fine," he said. "No harm done."

The woman said a few words into her phone before she ended the call and then put it inside her purse. "Look what I did to your shirt. Here, hold this."

She passed him her cup of coffee before she dabbed at the front of his T-shirt with one of the paper napkins she held. Obviously not satisfied with that, she pushed another up under his shirt and dabbed it from the inside as well as the outside.

Jaxon's cock stirred as the backs of her fingers rubbed against his chest. While she was busy trying to clean him up, he took the time to get a really good look at her. She was pretty with the kind of looks that drew him to a woman. Her long, brown hair fell over her shoulders, looking soft to the touch. He had the sudden urge to sink his fingers into the silken mass and take her mouth with his until she moaned. His dick liked that idea because it went rock hard two heartbeats later.

She must have noticed the state he was in. Her movements stilled just before her brown-eyed gaze lifted to his. Her breath seemed to catch as she stared at his mouth. A pale shade of pink appeared on her cheeks. She pulled her hands away.

"Ah, I'm really sorry," she said. "Let me make it up to you. I'll buy you a drink this evening. And I'm Chyna, by the way."

Jaxon ran his gaze down her body, liking what he saw outlined by her blouse and fitted skirt. The high heels she wore made her legs look long and toned. He wouldn't mind getting her into bed for a night, having them wrapped around his waist as he pounded into her. He could afford to take the night off from hunting. With the crime rate in San Diego low, there weren't as many evildoers around as there had been when he'd first moved to the city over ten years ago.

He nodded. "A drink would be nice. I'm Jaxon."

She smiled. "Great. Meet me at the Waterfront Bar, say around seven? Do you know where it is?"

"Yes. And seven sounds fine."

"I'd stay and talk, but I'm in the middle of my lunch break and I have to get back to the office. So I'll see you later this evening."

After taking her coffee back, Chyna gave him one last smile, then walked away. Jaxon turned to watch her, his gaze landing on her bottom. The restlessness he'd felt earlier had magically disappeared with the prospect of meeting with Chyna again, and the chance of getting to know her a whole lot better while he had her in his bed.

* * * *

Chyna walked to the office where she worked as a receptionist slash secretary with a lighter step than when she'd left it. There had been no chance of her letting a guy as good-looking as Jaxon get away. Bumping into him had made her day, even though she'd spilled her coffee all over his shirt. It had been nice to touch him while she'd mopped up the mess. The man was ripped. He had well-defined abs and a chest she could have stroked for hours, same with the rest of his muscular body.

Everything about Jaxon was gorgeous—his longish dark-brown hair, green eyes that seemed to eat her up, and his sexy, deep voice that had a slight French accent. He was tall. Had to be around six-feet-four. At five-feet-six, she'd perfectly fit under his chin while he held her in his arms.

A delicious shiver went through Chyna at the thought of getting that close to Jaxon. Maybe her recent losing streak when it came to men was finally over. At thirty, she wanted to find a man she could share her life with. The days of her wanting to just have a good time with no strings attached were over for her. Hopefully, Jaxon would be the one to end the string of men who were only interested in getting her into bed and nothing else.

Chyna walked into the office building for the public relations company where she worked. Joy, the girl from the mailroom who covered the front desk while Chyna had her lunch, smiled when she saw Chyna.

"Back already?" Joy asked.

Chyna walked around the large, curved desk and then put her coffee cup on its smooth wood surface. "I just grabbed something to eat at the coffee shop down the street."

"Did you have something good?" Joy asked as she pushed back the steno chair she sat on, then stood.

"You could say that, though it wasn't food, and I

haven't had it yet." Chyna stashed her purse in the bottom desk drawer before she straightened.

"Well, don't keep me waiting in anticipation. What is this something 'good?'"

"It's a gorgeous hunk of a man who is tall, has dark-brown hair, green eyes, and a body with so many muscles he must lift a ton of weights."

"Damn. Now I wish I could have gone to lunch with you. Please tell me you didn't let him walk away without talking to him."

Chyna sat in the chair Joy had vacated and she rolled herself closer to the desk. "I didn't. His name is Jaxon, and I'm meeting him for drinks later this evening."

"I'll keep my fingers crossed that Jaxon will be a good one," Joy said with a smile.

Chyna counted Joy as one of her good friends at work. Only a year younger than her, the other woman and Chyna shared a lot of things about their personal lives. She'd bemoaned about her unluckiness lately when it came to the opposite sex to Joy more than a few times. Joy, who was engaged to be married later that year, had offered quite a few times to set Chyna up with her future brother-in-law. Chyna didn't feel quite that desperate yet to take Joy up on her offer.

"Thanks," Chyna replied. "I'm keeping my fingers crossed as well. I'm due a man I want to keep."

Joy looked at her watch. "I guess I should head to the mailroom. You know I'm going to want details tomorrow."

"I know."

Once Joy left, Chyna settled into the familiar pace of answering phone calls and doing the secretarial work she had to finish before the end of the day. By the time she'd completed everything and could leave, she didn't waste any time forwarding the phone to the answering service for the night. She'd go home, have a quick dinner, then get ready for her date with Jaxon.

* * * *

After Chyna had left him, Jaxon returned to his home in the Santaluz community. He'd bought the place shortly after his move to San Diego. Even though it was well-known for its golf course, he wasn't into the sport. He'd tried it a few times but found it not fast-paced enough for him. He still loved the area, though.

The first thing he did when he stepped through the door was take off his stained T-shirt. There was no saving the light gray garment, so he tossed it right into the garbage in the kitchen. Jaxon ran his fingers over his chest where Chyna had touched him. He could still feel the sensation of it.

He shook his head as he headed to his bedroom of his one-story home. It had been a while since he'd last slept with a woman, but Jaxon hadn't thought he was that hard up that an innocence touch would send his libido soaring. His cock even jerked at the memory of Chyna's attempts to clean him up.

He definitely would have to get her into bed after they had their drinks. A good bout of sex and he'd have her out of his system. That's how it usually worked. Though his reaction to Chyna was stronger than he experienced with other women he was attracted to. It might take more than one round of intense sex to have him stop craving her.

Inside his bedroom, Jaxon swept it with his gaze. There were only a few clothes on the floor he'd have to clean up, and he'd change the sheets on the bed as well. Usually, he didn't let a woman stay overnight, but the idea of having Chyna sleeping in his arms all night wasn't something he found repugnant.

Jaxon shook his head as he moved around the room, picking up dirty clothes. Chyna would *not* be sleeping over. He'd gone for over two hundred years without having that type of relationship with a woman and he wouldn't start now. As a young mortal, he'd come close to it once, but later had found out the woman had played him along with another man for a fool, which had hurt him.

He finished with his bedroom and then did a thorough check of the rest of the house to make sure it was clean. At one of the guestrooms, Jaxon stood in the doorway and looked inside. This was his temple to Anubis. To keep the ties he had to the god of the underworld strong, Jaxon worshipped Anubis every day, setting food and drink out on the small altar each morning. It had taken a huge adjustment for him to feel comfortable doing it since his entire mortal life he'd been a good Catholic. Now he considered only Anubis as his god. The Egyptian god had been the one to answer Jaxon's call for another chance at life. The god he'd followed for so long before that hadn't been there for him when he had needed Him the most.

Jaxon would have to keep the door to the temple shut while Chyna was in the house. She didn't need to see it. Plus, he didn't want to have to explain why he had a room filled with statues, artwork, and other items featuring Anubis. It wasn't as if he'd be seeing her again after tonight. Maybe. He shook his head as he shut the temple's door. He had to stop thinking that way about Chyna. He was a warrior of Anubis. He didn't have time for, or want, a woman in his life. He was a loner, and a loner he'd stay.

* * * *

Jaxon pulled into the parking lot at the Waterfront Bar at exactly seven o'clock. He steered his black sports car into a spot, then turned off the engine. As he got out, he felt the familiar pull of evil nearby.

He cursed under his breath as he followed the

sensation. There would be no ignoring it. Once he felt it, Jaxon couldn't just walk away. He had to see it to its end, which meant he'd now be late for his date with Chyna.

Following the pull, Jaxon smelled the scent of evil in the air, something only he as a warrior of Anubis could smell. The closer he came to the back of the building next door to the bar, the stronger it became.

The change took Jaxon over as he reached the source of evil. He shifted to his half-human and half-jackal form, which no matter how many times he went through it hurt like hell. The shift wasn't voluntary. Being in the presence of an evildoer brought it on every time. It felt as if someone took a grater to his insides. The sound of his bones realigning sounded loud in the air. Once the change was complete, his body was covered in black fur from head to toe and he was much taller, his muscles larger. His hips were covered by a snow-white Egyptian-styled kilt, and around each of his thick biceps was a gold armband.

His tail swished behind him as he turned his large, lupine head toward his prey. A man stood in the shadows while he held another by the throat, pointing a gun at his victim's head. Neither one of them had noticed Jaxon.

A loud growl rumbled out of Jaxon's chest as he approached the pair. A lot stronger than any mortal, he grabbed his prey by the back of the neck and wrenched away the gun he held pointed at the other man. Jaxon heard the evildoer's bones break at the same time his prey yelled in pain. With a quick look in the other male's eyes, Jaxon put him in a trance to keep him from running while he dealt with the evildoer.

Jerking the struggling evildoer around to face him, Jaxon gave him a few hard shakes until the fight left him. His prey's grip loosened on the gun and it dropped to the ground. Jaxon growled again, curling his upper lip, and was rewarded with the sight of his prey crying, begging to be released. Jaxon sighed. It figured. The mortal was tough until someone bigger and stronger came along.

Not wanting to be any later than he already was, Jaxon snared the evildoer's gaze with his and tore into the mortal's mind. His prey whimpered at the pain Jaxon knew he caused, but he didn't care. All the evil deeds the mortal had done in his life filled Jaxon's head, causing him to relive every one as if he'd been on the receiving end. The many victims' cries echoed through his mind.

Jaxon snarled his lip again and sniffed the air. The scent of evil oozed out of every pore of his prey. "Evil," he said in a voice much deeper and gravelly than his normal one. "Time for you to face judgment."

He held up his free hand and willed his hardened gold dagger into it. Along the blade were hieroglyphs, which was a spell embedded in it that would send the evildoer to the underworld to be judged by Anubis. One cut was all it took to invoke it.

With a quick sweep of his hand, Jaxon sliced the dagger across the man's chest, cutting through the material of the shirt he wore and into skin. His prey let out a strangled cry as his body slowly lost substance and faded out of existence. Once in the underworld, Anubis would weigh the man's heart on the Scales of Justice. If he was deemed evil, his heart would be fed to Ammit to be consumed.

The evildoer taken care of, Jaxon still had to handle the victim. He willed the dagger away and crossed to where the mortal stood, looking off into space. He took hold of the man's chin and forced him to look at him. Jaxon erased every memory of himself from the man's mind. He planted the suggestion that the mortal didn't see Jaxon before sending him on his way none the worse for the wear.

Jaxon turned and walked in the direction of the bar. He ground his teeth as the change tore through him, his body shifting back to his human form. Once it was complete, he was again dressed in the black jeans and dark blue, button-down shirt he'd worn before the shift.

He hurried toward the bar's entrance and through the doors. He was now about twenty minutes late. Jaxon hoped Chyna hadn't thought he'd stood her up. His gaze landed on her, and he breathed a sigh of relief. She hadn't left, though it looked as if she was getting ready to do just that. She stood at one of the tables in the center of the room, putting her purse strap over her shoulder.

With long strides, Jaxon crossed to Chyna. "Sorry I'm late," he said.

She turned to face him. "I thought you weren't coming."

"I got a little tied up with something or I would have been on time."

"All right, I'll forgive you this time."

They sat at the table. Jaxon caught the attention of a waitress, and she came over and took their drink orders. She returned a short while later with his beer and Chyna's rum and Coke.

To get the conversation started between him and Chyna, Jaxon asked, "So, do you spill coffee on a lot of guys, then ask them out for a drink?"

She chuckled. "No, I'm not normally that much of a klutz. You're the first."

"I guess that makes me special."

Chyna chuckled again, then ran her gaze over his face and licked her lips. "Oh, I have to agree with that."

The sight of her tongue coming out, sweeping along her bottom lip, had Jaxon wishing they were some place private. His cock hardened as he pictured what he wanted her to do with that mouth of hers.

Tearing his gaze off her lips, Jaxon said, "Tell me something about yourself."

She took a sip of her drink before she answered. "There's really not too much. I work the reception desk at a public relations company. Nothing special. What about you?"

"I wouldn't say my job is regular, but I spend my nights searching for individuals who think they don't have to follow the rules of society."

"So you're like a cop?"

"Not exactly, but I guess it could be considered something along those lines."

"Okay, that sounds interesting, I think."

Jaxon smiled. "It isn't boring." He reached across the table and took Chyna's hand. He was pleased when she didn't pull away.

"I can't help noticing you have a bit of an accent," she said. "It sounds French."

"It is. I was born in France, but I've lived in the States for many years now."

"What part of France?"

"Dijon."

"Do you still have family there?"

"I would think, but not immediate family."

"Sorry to hear that."

He shook his head. "I've been on my own for a long time. I'm used to it. And you? Have you always lived in San Diego?"

"Yup, born and raised. My family is still here as well."

The sounds in the bar grew louder as a large group of males sat at a table close to Jaxon and Chyna's. The men wore matching baseball jerseys. Their voices increased in volume as they talked about a game they'd just played.

Jaxon turned from them and looked at Chyna. "I have a feeling they're only going to get louder."

She nodded. "I have to agree with you."

"How about we finish our drinks, then go to my place? I promise you it will be a lot quieter and we can continue our conversation in peace."

Chyna appeared to think it over before she nodded again. "All right. It's too early to call it a night, but you can't keep me out too late. I have to work in the morning."

"I promise."

They finished their drinks, then stood. Jaxon put his hand on the small of Chyna's back and guided her to the bar's entrance. He'd get her to his place and see how far she'd let him go.

CHAPTER TWO

The heat from Jaxon's hand sank through the material of Chyna's silk blouse and into her skin. Her nipples grew taut and an ache built deep inside her pussy. Just being this close to him turned her on. She definitely wanted him, and he seemed interested in getting to know her better.

Jaxon guided her out of the bar and then to the parking lot. "Which car is yours?" he asked.

"Oh, I didn't drive here. I took a cab. I wanted to be able to have more than one drink. I never drink and drive." She hesitated. "You had a drink. Maybe we should try this another night."

"You don't have to worry about me. I never get drunk so I'm fine. And I promise to stay on my best behavior."

She figured one drink wouldn't put him over, but she never took the chance. Given his large size, Chyna thought it would take a lot of alcohol to get Jaxon in an inebriated state.

The sports car he stopped at and opened the passenger

door of was one of the sleek, expensive-looking ones. It had to be worth a bundle of money. Obviously, whatever it was that Jaxon did for a living — that involved going after bad guys — paid really well. Once she sat on the seat, he pushed the door closed and then came around to the driver's side and got in.

The sun was just starting to set as Jaxon drove into the Santaluz community. A short while later, he pulled onto a long drive on the property of a very large house. He parked the car on the circular part of it, close to the front door. Chyna stepped out of the car the same time he did from his side. She waited for him to come around to her.

Once they stood on the front stoop, Jaxon unlocked the door and then went inside. Chyna followed him in. The interior of the house was just as impressive as the outside. His hand landed on her back as it had in the bar, and he guided her to his large living room. Her shoes sank into the thick, teal-blue carpeting as they headed for the black, thick-cushioned couch. She took a seat while he remained standing.

"What would you like to drink? I have many different kinds of wines, or I can make you a rum and Coke if you prefer."

"I'd love a glass of wine. You can pick for me. I like most types."

"All right. One glass of wine coming right up."

Jaxon walked to where a large, dark-wood liquor cabinet had been set up in one corner of the room. He took out two wineglasses from a shelf under the main part of the cabinet. He opened the wine fridge beside it and then selected a bottle.

She watched how his wide shoulders pulled at his shirt as he moved. Her gaze drifted down his back to his tapered waist. Going even lower, she stared at his muscled ass. Jaxon's jeans fit him just right, giving her a good view of it. She wouldn't mind getting ahold of it as he ground his cock against her.

After Jaxon poured their drinks, he came back to the couch and sat beside her. He handed her a wineglass filled with white wine. Chyna took a sip, enjoying the flavor on her tongue. As she watched Jaxon drink from his glass, she thought there was something else she wanted to taste — him.

Chyna lifted her gaze to Jaxon's, then sucked in a sharp breath. He watched her as intently as she did him. Her pussy clenched at the harsh look of need he wore on his face. Her blood heated as a surge of arousal shot through her, causing her heart to beat faster. She wanted him, but she wasn't going to sleep with him until she was sure he wanted more than a fling. Lately, she'd been burned one too many times.

She put her wineglass on the table before she shifted closer to Jaxon and turned to face him. He did the same, then reached up and trailed his fingertips across her cheek. His thumb traced her bottom lip. Chyna opened her mouth and took it inside, gently sucking on it. The heated look in his eyes increased as his pupils dilated.

He pulled his thumb out of her mouth and leaned in to brush his lips across hers. Chyna pushed forward, forcing their mouths to come together in a tighter fit. With what sounded like a quiet animalistic growl, Jaxon kissed her as she wanted him to. His tongue swept along the seam of her lips, seeking entrance. She opened for him, a moan escaping her when he tasted her, exploring, pushing her arousal to higher heights.

As their kiss became more carnal, their teeth hitting together in their attempts to get closer, Chyna found herself lifted and positioned to straddle Jaxon's hips. He turned and sat back against the couch cushion, his mouth never leaving hers. He pushed her firmer against him, his hard cock coming in delicious contact with her jean-clad pussy. She ground herself along his erection, wetness pooling deep inside her.

Jaxon lifted a hand to one of her breasts and brushed his thumb back and forth across her taut nipple. She moaned into his mouth. His fingers went to work on unbuttoning her blouse enough for him to reach inside and tug a bra cup aside. Breaking their kiss, he lowered his head to what he had exposed. His tongue flicked out, and he licked the tip before he laved it. Chyna sank her fingers into his dark brown hair and squirmed on his lap as her pussy clenched with the need to be filled.

Chyna gasped as Jaxon's warm mouth closed over her nipple and sucked. She felt each pull deep inside her pussy. Wetness leaked into her panties, and she ground against his cock harder. He felt thick and long. If he kept this up, she'd come.

Jaxon released her nipple and rubbed his cheek against it. "You make me so hard," he said in a husky voice. "I have to have you."

She moaned. "I want you too. " Chyna cupped Jaxon's face and forced him to look at her. "Before we go any further, please don't tell me you only want a one-night stand. I don't do those."

Jaxon stiffened under her, and Chyna's high hopes of seeing him again plummeted. It didn't help that he only stared up at her without saying anything. God, why did she have to attract the men who weren't interested in her beyond a night of sex?

Disappointed, Chyna yanked her bra and blouse back into place and slid off Jaxon's lap to stand in front of him. She buttoned her top without looking at him. "I guess I read the signals you gave me wrong," she said. "I thought...never mind. I should go home. I'll call a cab." She turned to walk out of the room, but Jaxon stopped her by taking hold of her arm and turning her back around to face him.

He invaded most of her personal space. "I'm sorry," he

said with his deep, accented voice. "I should have said something before we came here. I don't do serious relationships. Ever."

Chyna jerked out of Jaxon's grasp. "And that's exactly what I want from a man I date. I'll be blunt. I'm thirty years old, not some twenty-something who is out looking for a good time. I thought we were off to a great start."

"We were. So good, in fact, I'll probably end up with blue balls if we don't finish what we started."

She looked him in the eye. She really didn't want to walk away from Jaxon. He was the best-looking man she'd ever had a chance to be with. In the beginning, he hadn't acted as if he was only after one thing. That had to mean there was a glimmer of a chance, at least she wanted to believe that. "Then give us a chance. A couple of months, at least. If you want out then, I'll let you go without a backward glance." Chyna placed her hand on his chest. "I promise I'll make it worth your while to try."

Jaxon stared at her, not saying anything in return, but the heat had come back into his eyes. Chyna wasn't about ready to give up just yet. He hadn't been fast to outright turn her down. Maybe he only needed a little more convincing of what he'd miss out on.

Chyna took a step closer and nibbled Jaxon's chin as she drifted her hand from his chest to the large bulge in his pants. She cupped it, then stroked it up and down. He thrust his hips forward, pushing his cock harder. A low, animalistic growl rumbled out of him when she squeezed his shaft.

"Okay," he said in a gruff voice. "I'll give you your two months, but don't expect anything more from me." He dropped his hands to her ass and hauled her closer, grinding his erection against her belly.

Jaxon went to take her mouth, but Chyna pushed out of his embrace. "Then I'll see you tomorrow evening. You can come to my place and I'll cook us dinner. Can you drive me home now?"

"What?" he asked as his brows drew together. "I promised you two months. I thought that meant you'd stay and we'd seal the deal in bed."

Chyna gave a half laugh. "What do you take me for? If I was to sleep with you now, who is to say you wouldn't go back on your promise? You would have gotten what you wanted — sex on the first, and possibly only, date."

Jaxon took a deep breath, his wide chest lifting, before he blew it out. "Fine, I'll take you home. I'll come for dinner, but I have to work tomorrow night afterward."

"Then we'll eat on the early side. I get off work at five so you can show up around five thirty."

He nodded. "I'll be there."

Chyna sensed Jaxon was out of sorts with her, but she was going to stand her ground. Either he would do as she asked or she'd walk. At least having a couple of months would make her feel less like she'd been used then thrown away. And who knew, maybe he would end up wanting to stick around longer than that.

Jaxon didn't say much to her after that. He brought her out to his car and then drove her to her place once Chyna gave him her address. Judging by his silence, she wasn't sure if she'd actually see him again.

Once they arrived at her apartment building, he stopped the car in front of it. Chyna took off her seat belt and turned to face Jaxon. "I hope to see you tomorrow. Sorry if I upset you."

Jaxon let out a low curse, then leaned across the seat and wrapped his arms around her. He kissed her thoroughly, causing her arousal to flare to life once more. They were breathing hard when he pulled away.

"Don't apologize," he said. "You *will* see me tomorrow. I've just never attempted to have a relationship with a woman before. I'm feeling a little lost. I've been alone for so long, I tend to be a bit selfish at times."

She smiled. "As long as you try, I'll be happy."

Chyna gave Jaxon a quick kiss, then got out of the car. She watched him drive away before she went into her building. She'd have to play it slow with him. Hopefully, he wouldn't lose interest in her too quickly. She wanted them to work. All she'd have to do was convince him his life would be better off with her in it rather than not.

* * * *

Back at his house, Jaxon went to the living room and sat on the couch. He stared at the two wineglasses still sitting on the coffee table. Neither he nor Chyna had finished their drinks. He leaned forward, grabbed his, and drank it down in two large swallows. He didn't have to worry about getting drunk. He couldn't. Ever since he'd made his vow to Anubis and had become immortal, alcohol had absolutely no effect on him. He also could eat whatever he wanted, and as much as he wanted, without gaining an ounce. Basically, he was frozen in time. He would forever look as he had at twenty-six—the age he'd become one of Anubis' warriors.

Staring at Chyna's glass again, he shook his head. He couldn't believe he'd actually agreed to stay with her for the next two months. He didn't do "girlfriends." Up to the point where she was going to walk away, Jaxon had figured she'd just be one of the many women he'd only slept with over the many years he'd lived. Her saying she'd leave if that was all he wanted, he'd had the sudden urge to beg her to stay.

She'd convinced him to give her two months. She had no idea how long that would feel to him. He had no experience in forming a relationship with the opposite sex. Even as a child he hadn't had that opportunity. His mother had died giving birth to him, and he'd been raised by his father who had deemed at an early age that Jaxon would go into the army. He'd grown up to be tough, not to depend on anyone but himself. There certainly had been no feminine softness to counterbalance it.

Now that he thought about seeing Chyna tomorrow, Jaxon had to admit he looked forward to it. They did get along well. And he actually enjoyed talking to her. Maybe the two months wouldn't be as bad as he thought. There really wasn't any chance he'd fall in love with her. He didn't think he was capable of feeling that emotion, considering what had happened to him with the girl in France. The only one who had a chance of getting hurt at the end of this was Chyna, though the thought of it didn't sit too well with him.

He picked up Chyna's wineglass and downed its contents before he grabbed his empty one and stood. Jaxon headed for the kitchen to put both glasses into the dishwasher. That chore done, he walked to the wing where his bedroom was. He'd change into a T-shirt and then head out for a bit of hunting. He might as well since he was used to staying up most of the night anyway. And with Chyna gone early, there were too many hours to kill before he'd be tired enough to go to bed.

* * * *

Chyna blindly reached for her alarm clock as it went off the next morning. She hated getting woken up by the damn thing. In fact, she hated to have to get up early, period. She groaned when she hit the button that silenced the vile thing.

She stretched, then rubbed the sleep out of her eyes. It was going to be another mundane day of work and coming home to an empty apartment to watch TV until she had to go to bed.

As Chyna sat up, she remembered it *wasn't* going to be more of the same old, same old. Jaxon would be coming over for dinner. She threw back the covers as a smile spread across her face. There was actually something to look forward to.

Instead of dragging her ass as she normally did on a work morning, Chyna had a shower, dressed, and ate a quick breakfast of toast and tea in record time. Before leaving, she put the roast beef she'd put into the fridge to thaw overnight into the oven and set the timer to have it come on while she was at work. When she arrived home at the end of the day, it should be done.

Chyna arrived at work, her steps still light, and saw Joy standing at the reception desk. She smiled at the other woman as she drew closer. "Waiting for me, are you?" she asked with a chuckle.

"Of course," Joy said in return. "You know I want to hear how your hot date went last night."

Chyna came around the desk, stowed her purse, and sat in her chair, turning in Joy's direction. "It was good."

"So Jaxon didn't turn out to be a loser who was only after one thing?"

"Well, he's definitely not a loser. The man is rich. As for the last thing, he *was* only after one thing."

"Crap. I'm sorry he ended up being a dud."

"It's not as bad as it sounds. He might have originally only planned on a one-night stand, but I managed to change his mind about it. I got him to promise he'd stay with me for two months."

Joy eyed her. "And after they're up, what then? You're going to just let him walk away?"

"If it looks as if he's the one for me, no."

"Does he know that?"

"Of course not. I wouldn't have gotten two months if I told him. The man has never done a relationship. I'll have to convince him that he'll be happier in one, with me. There's something about him that draws me. I think about not fighting to keep him and I feel as if I'd be giving up something really good. I know, it's weird."

Joy shook her head. "I don't know, Chyna. I think you might be setting yourself up for some major heartache. A lot of guys don't like women trying to change them. It could blow up in your face."

Chyna blew out a breath. "The logical side of me knows that, but the rest of me doesn't want to listen. I really like Jaxon. I had to try something. At first, I planned to leave him and never see him again, but then I came up with the idea of giving him a time limit. Two months should give me plenty of opportunities to get him to come around."

"And what exactly do you have in mind?"

"I haven't quite figured it all out yet, but I plan to show him what he'll be missing if he ends things. I'm seeing him for dinner tonight, which I'll be cooking."

Joy nodded. "Food is a good start. Couple that with some great sex and you could have him eating out of your hand. I know that works with my Kevin."

Chyna laughed. "I'll have to remember that." She hit the button to turn on the computer that sat on top of the desk. "I'd better take the phone off the answering service."

"Yeah, I should get started as well. I'll see you when it's your lunch hour."

Chyna went through the steps to have the phone ringing at the reception desk, then looked at the work she had to have completed before the end of the work day. Now that she'd spoken to Joy about Jaxon, she wasn't feeling as confident about her ability to change his mind as she had before. What if he did walk away at the end of the two months? Yes, they would give her plenty of time to persuade him not to, but they would also give her plenty of time to fall for him.

She gave herself a mental shake and a kick in the butt. She wasn't going to think like that. It would only doom her before she'd even begun. Only positive thinking about Jaxon would be allowed from here on out.

CHAPTER THREE

Chyna rushed home at the end of her day. After she arrived at her apartment, the first thing she did was check on the roast beef. The oven had turned off at the right time, and the meat looked done to perfection. She practically ran to her bedroom to change out of her work clothes so she could get started on the rest of the meal before Jaxon arrived.

She hated to admit it, but she'd thought about him all day. She'd ached to be in his arms again. It had been a while since she'd last been with a man, and now her body craved Jaxon's touch.

Back in the kitchen, she peeled some potatoes and then put them on to boil. She left the roast to rest in the oven for now. She'd have to take it out later to make gravy from the drippings. For a vegetable, she had some fresh green beans she'd bought the other day. It didn't take very long for her to have them ready to be steamed.

Once the potatoes came to a boil and she'd turned down the burner, Chyna went into the living room to wait for Jaxon to arrive. She sat on the couch, her hands coming to rest on her lap. When she realized she wrung them, she forced herself to stop. It was ridiculous, but she had a case of the nerves. In the back of her mind, a little voice said there was still a chance he wouldn't show up. He'd told her more than once he didn't do relationships. There was more than a slim chance he'd changed his mind overnight. And it wasn't as if she could have talked to him about it during the day. They hadn't exchanged phone numbers last night.

The minutes ticked by, coming closer to five thirty. To distract herself, she checked on the food. The potatoes were just about done when someone buzzed up to her apartment. A quick look at the clock on the stove showed it was a couple of minutes before half past five.

She left the kitchen and went the entrance door where there was a panel on the wall. She pushed the button to talk. "Hello?"

"It's me, Jaxon."

"Come on in." Chyna pushed the button that would allow Jaxon through the secured door and into the lobby.

She hurried back to the kitchen to turn off the burners, then returned to the apartment door. A knock sounded not long afterward. Chyna opened it and smiled at Jaxon. He looked good enough to eat in a black T-shirt that outlined his strong upper body. His blue jeans hugged him in just the right places.

He held out a bottle of wine. "For you. I brought white since I wasn't sure what we were having. I figured it would be safer than a red."

Chyna took the bottle and stepped back to allow Jaxon inside. "Thanks. Dinner will be ready shortly."

Once he walked into the entranceway, Chyna closed the door behind him and then locked it. She went to head for the living room but found herself caught in Jaxon's strong arms and turned toward him with his lips claiming hers.

He kissed her thoroughly, his tongue pushing inside her mouth to duel with hers. Desire bloomed deep within her, making her ache for him.

Chyna took a deep breath through her nose, inhaling Jaxon's masculine scent, as well as the smell of the roast beef. With great reluctance, she ended the kiss. "It's not as if I want to end this. I don't want to ruin the food."

Jaxon gave her a crooked smile. "We can't have that. It smells too good to waste. We can wait to take this kiss further."

She could wait, but her body yelled "hell no." Chyna ignored it and led Jaxon into the living room. "Take a seat. I just have a few things I have to finish, then we can eat."

"I can sit in the kitchen."

"All right. I'll put you to work setting the table if you do."

"I can do that. I'd rather be with you than sitting out here while you're in there."

Jaxon followed Chyna into the kitchen. She set him to work setting the table as she finished preparing the meal. He even offered to slice the roast beef, which she took him up on.

It felt kind of homey, sitting at her small kitchen table, eating with Jaxon. Chyna took a few bites of her food before she had a sip of the wine he had brought. "The wine is good," she said.

"As is the food," he replied. "I haven't had a home-cooked meal like this in a very long time." He gave her a sexy smile that just about melted her into a pile of goo. "I could get used to this."

And she could get used to having him sharing meals and her life with her. Chyna immediately tamped down that thought. She would not set herself up to have her heart broken.

"Well, I'll have to cook for you again then. It's nice cooking for someone other than myself." Chyna took another bite of food, chewed, then swallowed. "So, do you still have to work tonight?"

Jaxon nodded. "Yes, but I don't have to leave here until it gets dark."

"You don't have any set time that you start? Only when it's night out?"

"I know it sounds funny. The hours are just part of the job."

"At least that gives us more time together before you have to leave."

He turned a heated gaze on her. "And lots of time to do everything I've been thinking of doing to you." He reached across the table and captured her hand. "Ever since last night, I haven't been able to get the taste of you off my tongue. All day I've craved more of you."

A shiver of arousal shot through Chyna. Her pussy clenched, wetness pooling deep inside it. Her need to have Jaxon shot through the roof. She licked her suddenly dry lips, and his gaze followed the movement.

"I'm done eating. What about you?" she asked in a husky voice.

"Yes."

They stood at the same time. Jaxon met her halfway as she closed the distance between them. His arms came around her and his lips took hers in a searing kiss. It was so hot Chyna was surprised they didn't set the room on fire.

Jaxon picked her up off her feet, and Chyna wrapped her legs around his waist. He carried her out of the room. The thick bulge in his jeans rubbed against her pussy with each of his steps.

It took longer than it should for Jaxon to reach her bedroom. He kept stopping every few paces to put her back against the wall to drive her wild. His lips never left hers, and he ground his hard cock between her legs. A couple of times, Chyna was about ready to beg him to forget the bed and just take her right there and then. Tear off her clothes and his and give her what her body desperately ached for.

When Jaxon finally made it to her bedroom, Chyna kept her stranglehold on him as he lowered her to the center of the mattress. She only let him go long enough for him to strip off her shirt and bra.

He skimmed his hands lower over her body while he shifted down and took a nipple inside his mouth. Chyna moaned and squirmed beneath him. His erection brushed against her inner thigh. The night before when they'd been together, he hadn't let her explore him. This time she wouldn't miss out on the opportunity.

Jaxon released her nipple and kissed his way to the other. Chyna threaded her fingers through his hair and brought his head up so he looked at her. "I want to touch you. Roll onto your back."

In a smooth motion, Jaxon did as she'd asked and then yanked his T-shirt up and over his head. With his gaze locked on hers, he threw the shirt over the side of the bed. Chyna shifted so she kneeled at his side and looked at his bared upper body. His chest and shoulders were wide and thickly padded with muscle. Even his abs were a well-defined six-pack.

Before Chyna focused on the part of Jaxon that was still clothed, her gaze snagged on the tattoo he had on the left side of his chest directly over his heart. It was black and the style was ancient Egyptian-looking. Inside a cartouche was the jackal-headed god, Anubis. In one hand he held an ankh and in the other a flail. She reached out and gently traced it with her fingertips. He made a low, rumbling noise that sounded pretty damn close to a growl.

Chyna skimmed her hand lower over his warm skin. She stopped at the waistband of his jeans. The bulge inside his pants was large. She knew Jaxon was big from when she'd cupped him. This time she'd get to feel him without anything coming between his cock and her hand.

She undid the button and then pulled down the zipper. Parting the material, she encountered a pair of black silk boxers. Jaxon was so aroused the head of his cock stuck out the top of them. She licked her lips in anticipation of getting up close and personal with it.

"If you don't touch me soon, I'm going to explode," Jaxon said in a strained voice.

Chyna lifted her gaze to his. "Then take off your jeans and boxers and I'll do just that."

Jaxon's hands landed on the top of his jeans, and he tugged them and his boxers down and off with quick, hard pulls. Wetness leaked into Chyna's panties at the sight of him naked. The man had a killer body. Having him once wouldn't be enough.

She shifted to straddle his thighs. Her gaze landed on his cock. It was thick and long. He would completely fill her up. Stretch her pussy in the most delicious of ways. The thought of it plunging deep inside her sent a shiver of anticipation through her. He'd more than feel good.

Chyna reached out and wrapped her hand around Jaxon's cock. He groaned, his hips lifting a small increment off the bed. She squeezed him and pumped her fist up and down. He matched her rhythm, pushing his shaft harder into her grip.

"Just like that," he moaned.

A bead of pre-cum appeared on the very tip of his cock. Her pussy clenched and more of her wetness soaked her panties. Unable to hold back from tasting him anymore, Chyna bent and first licked off the liquid before she took him inside her mouth. She sucked on him hard, sliding him in and out. His cock grew even harder as Jaxon's breaths left him in groans and moans.

She kept a firm grip on the base of his shaft as she took him almost to the back of her throat. Each stroke out, she paid extra attention to the spot underneath the flared head.

With her other hand, she reached down and gently fondled his balls.

All too soon, Jaxon pulled her away. He flipped her to her back before he worked on undoing her pants. "I loved having you suck my cock, but I'm not coming that way."

Jaxon tore her jeans down her legs and off, then snagged her panties with his fingers and took those off too. That done, he came down on top of her with his hips wedged between her spread legs. The head of his cock came to rest against the opening of her body. They took sharp breaths.

He reached between them, grabbed hold of his cock, and rubbed the very tip of it into her wetness. With shallow strokes, he slowly entered her. He pulled his hand away and deepened his thrusts until she'd taken every inch of him. She felt as full and stretched as she'd thought she'd be with him buried to the hilt inside her pussy.

He moved in earnest. Chyna squeezed her inner muscles around him and lifted her hips to match his strokes. He almost pulled all the way out of her before he rammed back in. He pistoned between her thighs, taking her with hard thrusts. Her release built, her body coiling tighter.

Jaxon wrapped an arm around her waist and rose to sit upright with her straddling him. She put her hands on the tops of his shoulders and rode him, taking him deeper than she had in the other position. He rubbed in just the right spot, his cock stimulating her clit with each long stroke in.

With his hands on her hips, he urged her to ride him faster, harder. Chyna panted and moaned. She was so damn close to coming. She strained against Jaxon, loving how he hit every nerve ending. Two more thrusts and she fell into an intense orgasm.

Her inner muscles rhythmically clutched Jaxon's plunging cock. He grew harder as he bent his head and nuzzled where her neck and shoulder met. Chyna felt the scrape of his teeth against her skin. He thrust one final time into her and stiffened, a ragged moan leaving him as his shaft pulsed deep inside her pussy with his climax.

Chyna wrapped her arms around Jaxon's shoulders and fought to catch her breath. He rested his forehead against her collarbone, breathing equally as hard. She reached up and ran her fingers through the hair at the back of his head. She'd been right. One time wouldn't be near enough. Even if they made love all night, she'd still crave more of him.

Jaxon took a deep, shuddering breath, then lifted his head. He kissed her gently. "That was definitely worth waiting for."

She smiled. "That's what I was thinking." Her stomach rumbled. Chyna gave him a sheepish grin. "I guess I'm still hungry. How about you?"

He chuckled. "My belly is feeling a little hollow at the moment."

"You stay right here. I'll reheat our dinner and we can eat on the bed."

Chyna gave Jaxon a quick kiss before she slid off his lap, then the bed. She snagged his T-shirt off the floor before she pulled it on. She headed out of the room and toward the kitchen to get the food.

*

After Chyna left, Jaxon stretched out on the bed and rolled onto his back. Making love to her was...different. Not in a bad way. If anything, it was the best sex he could remember ever having. So good, in fact, he was glad she'd convinced him to stay with her longer than a night. If she hadn't, he would have made a liar out of himself. Once had in no way allayed his appetite for her. He wasn't even sure if two months would be sufficient. Just thinking about having her again had his cock twitching with renewed interest.

No, it wasn't because the sex was bad. It was the sensation he'd felt just before he'd come that made it unlike any sexual experience he'd had in the past. Those few seconds before he'd been thrown into an intense orgasm, a change had come over him. His eyeteeth had grown longer, sharper, turning into fangs, as they did when he was in his half-human and half-jackal form. That was strange in itself, but the almost overriding need to bite Chyna where her shoulder and neck met had him more than a little concerned. He'd barely been able to stop himself, but as soon as he'd started to come, the urge had disappeared, and his teeth had gone back to normal.

Jaxon figured he'd better have a chat with Anubis once he was done hunting for the night and had returned home. If there was something wrong with Jaxon, the god of the underworld would be able to fix whatever it was. Anubis had been the one to give Jaxon his shape-shifting ability in the first place.

A few minutes later, Chyna returned, carrying two plates of food. Jaxon sat up as she approached the bed. He had to admit he liked the fact she wore his T-shirt. It was too big for her — the bottom of it reached her mid-thigh and the sleeves ended at her elbows — but he thought she looked better in it than he did.

"Here you go," she said as she placed one of the plates on the bed next to him. A knife and fork were on it as well as the food.

"Thanks," he said and shifted over so she could sit beside him.

Chyna sat on the mattress cross-legged. Before she could start to eat, Jaxon reached over and tugged his shirt up her body and off. She gave him a questioning look.

He smiled. "You look better with it off. Plus, I don't want to be the only one eating while bare assed."

She returned his smile with one of her own. "I don't think I've ever had a naked picnic on my bed before."

"Well, now you can say you have."

They ate in companionable silence until they'd eaten everything. Once Chyna put her utensils down, Jaxon snagged their plates and put them on the floor. He turned to face her.

"That was delicious, but now I'm ready for my second course," he said as he crawled closer.

Chyna leaned back on her hands. Her head fell toward her shoulder blades as he kissed the side of her neck. "And what would you like for this second course?"

"You," he replied huskily. "I want you spread out on the bed while I feast on every inch of you."

She shivered, and the scent of her arousal perfumed the air around them. He loved the smell of it. He breathed deeply, taking as much as he could into his lungs. His cock hardened, more than ready to sink deep inside Chyna's pussy and take her hard and fast.

Jaxon snaked an arm around Chyna's waist and kissed her with all the passion that blazed inside him. Once he had her groaning into his mouth, he pulled away before he positioned her on her hands and knees. He ran a hand over her bottom, then dipped it between her spread thighs to stroke her pussy. His fingers came away wet. She was ready for him.

He shifted so he kneeled behind her and took hold of her hips. Jaxon had thought to take his time with Chyna, but he wanted her too much. He stroked his cock against her wet opening. Once he was liberally coated, he brought the head of his shaft to her pussy and pushed home. Her inner walls closed around him, making him groan. She fit him perfectly.

He took her in hard, deep thrusts. Chyna pushed back, matching the pace he set. Jaxon could already tell he wasn't going to last long, even though they'd already made love once before. She felt too damn good. Already his balls drew close to his body. His cock grew even harder as her pussy gripped it tight.

In and out he surged. A low growl he couldn't hold back rumbled out of him. Chyna let out a keening moan and her pussy squeezed and released his cock as she came. Jaxon's release inched closer. As he kept thrusting, on the very precipice of his climax, his gums burned, heralding the change in them.

His gaze became fixated on Chyna's back where her shoulder and neck met. Still sliding his shaft in and out of her wet passage, he bent over her. He opened his mouth, his upper lip peeling back. The urge to bite, to sink his teeth into her soft skin, battered him. Jaxon lowered his head, intending to act on what instinct screamed at him to finish.

At the last minute, he realized what he'd been about to do. Jaxon straightened and pumped his hips faster. With a loud moan, he came, his cock pulsing, filling Chyna with his cum.

Jaxon gathered her into his arms and took them to their sides. She spooned against him, nestling deeper into his embrace. It had happened again. This unnatural urge to bite Chyna like an animal had reared its ugly head just before he'd come. It didn't make any sense to him. He'd never wanted to go all animal on any of the other women he'd slept with. Only Chyna. The sooner he talked to Anubis about it, the better.

CHAPTER FOUR

Jaxon was on the hunt for evildoers. He'd left Chyna at her apartment with a promise they'd get together sometime the next day. He'd actually had a hard time forcing himself to leave her. The idea of holding her through the night as she slept had been a temptation he'd wanted to act on. And it was a first. He never wanted to spend a night in a woman's bed unless it involved a marathon of sex.

He walked down the sidewalk, waiting for the familiar pulling sensation that meant his prey was nearby. Most nights he never experienced it. It was a good and bad thing that San Diego's crime rate had become so low. It was great for the mortals, but not so much for him. He'd been created to send evildoers to the underworld to be judged. Without them, he didn't have a real purpose.

Jaxon had thought of talking to Anubis about being given another city to watch over, one that would keep him busy, but Jaxon liked San Diego and didn't want to leave it. And now that he'd met Chyna, there was no appeal in leaving it at all. He shook his head and snorted to himself. Two days. That was all it had taken to have him feeling closer to her than he'd ever had with another woman. He just had to wonder if it would last.

The sudden strong pull of evil had Jaxon coming to a standstill as he tried to focus on where it came from. It was so intense, if he didn't get out of sight right now, he'd shift in the open.

Following the pulling sensation, he all but ran into the dead-end alley it led him to. The change tore through him the instant he was no longer so exposed. Jaxon gritted his teeth at the pain of his bones and muscles shifting and realigning. Once it was over and he was in his half-human and half-jackal form, it didn't take him long to spot his prey.

A man stood at the very end of the alley, appearing as if he only waited for Jaxon. His prey didn't have any kind of reaction to seeing the creature Jaxon had turned into as he came closer to the male. When dealing with mortals and prey alike, it was normal to have them almost pissing themselves in fear once they saw him. This man was different. The scent of fear didn't emanate off him. All Jaxon smelled was the rank scent of evil. It was so thick he almost had a hard time breathing past it.

Jaxon walked toward his prey in long strides, determined to "see" the evil within the man. He'd come within a yard of the evildoer when the man spoke some words in a language Jaxon did not know, and Jaxon found himself slamming into an invisible barrier. He took a step to the side and ran into the same obstacle. Same with the other side and at the back of him. It was as if he'd been trapped inside some kind of invisible force field.

The evildoer laughed, the sound full of malice. His prey's eyes glowed red as he approached Jaxon. Whatever that man was, he wasn't human. Jaxon beat at the invisible wall, but it held, keeping him in place.

"I have you right where I want you, warrior of Anubis. There's no escape. So you might as well stop trying to get free."

"What are you?" Jaxon asked.

"I've become your hunter, warrior." He circled Jaxon. "My brethren and I have been hunting down each one of your kind, those of you who vowed to serve the god of the underworld. We escaped to the mortal realm to put an end to Anubis' warriors so the souls you send to him end up with us, where they belong."

Jaxon now knew exactly what that creature was. Anubis had told him to be on the lookout for one since a couple of the other warriors had had attempts made on them recently.

"You're a demon," Jaxon said with a growl.

The demon stopped in front of Jaxon. "Very good. Knowing what I am isn't going to save you now."

The creature lunged through the invisible barrier that kept Jaxon trapped. The demon took hold of Jaxon's lupine head with his hands coming to rest on either side of it. Jaxon let out a howl of pain as something shot from the demon's fingers and into his skull. It felt as if daggers sank into his brain. Even though he was stronger in his half-human and half-jackal form, he couldn't break free of the creature who held him. The pain increased, then the world went black and Jaxon lost all awareness.

※ ※ ※ ※

The sound of waves breaking against shore brought Jaxon awake. His eyes snapped open, and he stiffened when he realized he was outside. Gazing around, he sat up and saw he was under one of the city's docks. The sand was cool beneath him. He looked out toward the water. The sun was just about ready to set.

It couldn't be. He had no memory of how he'd gotten

there, but the last thing he did remember was when the demon had trapped him during his night of hunting. Had he lost an entire day?

Jaxon looked down at himself. He breathed a small sigh of relief that he was at least in his human form. He noticed several large patches of blood on his shirt and jeans. Lifting the T-shirt, he found he'd been hurt. The wound between his ribs looked as if a knife had been plunged into his side. Another on the right part of his chest appeared to be a gunshot wound. He had no memory of being hurt or in a situation that would have caused it to happen.

He rose to his feet, wincing at the aches and pains that accompanied the action. Jaxon looked around. There were only a few mortals about, and they were far enough away they really wouldn't be able to see him in too much detail.

He walked up the beach toward the street. Getting to his place was a priority. Talking with Anubis had become crucial. The god would hopefully be able to shed some light onto what had happened to Jaxon.

At the street, he pulled out his cell phone and called for a taxi. He was nowhere near where he'd left his car parked at the start of his night of hunting. And walking to it would take way too long.

The cab arrived, and Jaxon got into the backseat. The driver didn't even bother to turn around to look at him, which suited Jaxon since he was in no mood to think up some kind of excuse to explain his bloodstained clothes.

After the taxi driver let him out and Jaxon had paid the fare, Jaxon walked the short distance to his car. The first things he noticed were the parking tickets on the windshield tucked under one of the wiper blades. There were two of them. He'd only expected one. He snatched them up and looked at them. His heart skipped a beat when he saw the dates. He hadn't lost a day—he'd lost two. *What the hell?*

Jaxon fished his car keys out of his jean front pocket,

then unlocked the driver's door. He got in before he started the engine. As he drove to his house, he racked his brain to see if anything of the last two days would rise to the surface. Nothing did. It was a bit scary to think he'd blacked out for that length of time. What the fuck had the demon done to him?

At his home, Jaxon parked his car in the garage and then entered the house through the connecting door. He headed straight for the mini-temple dedicated to Anubis. He felt each of his wounds, but he ignored them. He was immortal, and they wouldn't kill him. Plus, they'd eventually heal on their own. Deep wounds such as those took longer than superficial ones.

Jaxon opened the door to the temple room and then walked inside. He went to the altar. "Anubis. Anubis, I need to speak with you."

It didn't take long for the god of the underworld to answer him. *Jaxon? What happened? I lost my connection to you for the last two days.*

"I don't know. I just woke up under one of the docks with no knowledge of how I got there or what had caused the wounds I have."

What is the last thing you remember?

"I was out hunting when I felt a strong pull of evil. I followed it and shifted to my other form. It was a demon. He trapped me in some kind of invisible shield. He told me how he and his brethren are hunting down all of us who serve you to take us out. He grabbed my head, and I blacked out. I don't remember anything else."

This demon must be a lot stronger than the other two who went after my warriors. Anubis paused before he spoke again. *I need to see what he did to you, and what happened during the days you were missing. It is not going to be fun for you. I might have to push past a block to get at the memories. It will more than likely be painful.*

It wasn't as if Jaxon had any choice. He needed to know

what had happened to him. "Do it. Can you at least heal my wounds first?"

Of course. No need to make you suffer any more than you have to.

Jaxon sucked in a sharp breath as a hot, burning sensation zapped through his wounds. The one from the gunshot burned the worst as the bullet worked its way to the surface. Once out, it fell to the floor.

Now for the not-so-fun part, Anubis said.

There was a sensation of someone ruffling through his mind, but it wasn't as unpleasant as Anubis had said it would be. "This isn't so bad," Jaxon said.

That is because I was just seeing if those memories had been blocked from you first, which they have. Plus, whatever the demon did to you, must be buried with them.

"Terrific."

Here we go.

That was all the warning the god of the underworld gave Jaxon before he went to work, plowing through the block. Now this felt as if someone took an icepick to his brain. He held his head and groaned. He closed his eyes and concentrated on not collapsing on the floor. He breathed at a fast rate through gritted teeth. That must be what evildoers felt when he pushed into their mind to see all the evil they had done in their lives. He knew it was painful, but he hadn't known how bad it actually was.

After a long-ass minute, the pain stopped as abruptly as it had started. And that was when his lost memories slammed into him. The demon had fucked him over royally. He'd taken away Jaxon's humanity, so while in his half-human and half-jackal form, he was more beast than man. The reverse of what it normally was. And while in such a state, Jaxon had killed. Not with a sword or dagger but as a jackal would with his sharp teeth and claws. The only good thing about it was that the mortals he'd killed had been evil. The bad thing was that in killing them, he'd sent them to the underworld where the demons dwelled. No wonder Anubis had lost his connection with Jaxon. With no humanity left in him, he'd been working for the demon.

"Fuck," Jaxon said in a harsh tone. "He forced me to break my vow to you."

No, he did not. You were not cognizant of what you did. You never would have done those things if you had been. He used a spell on you to bring out your beast side.

"Will it happen again? Was this a one-time thing?"

Sadly, no, it is not. The demon's spell was used in such a way that it can be triggered again without it having to be cast each time.

Jaxon did *not* like the sound of that. "Isn't there any way for you to remove it?"

No. It is buried so deep in your mind I risk doing permanent damage. It also has a fail-safe. Any tampering of the spell will trigger it, which will destroy your humanity – forever.

"So I'm supposed to walk around for eternity like a ticking time bomb just waiting for the demon to set the spell off whenever he wants?"

It will not be for all eternity, Jaxon. To get rid of the spell, you have to send the demon to me. Once he has been judged, he will no longer have any hold over you.

That just kept getting better and better. "So I guess my number-one priority will be finding this demon and taking him out. Hopefully, he'll reveal himself to me again or I'll be screwed."

You will not have to worry about him hiding from you forever. He is a demon. He will not be able to resist coming to you to gloat.

Now Jaxon had two things to worry about happening when he was with Chyna. At the thought of her, he remembered he was supposed to have seen her two days ago. She probably thought he'd stood her up. That he'd gotten her into bed and now he was finished with her. He remembered he had wanted to talk to Anubis about the biting urge he had while with Chyna.

"There is one other thing I have to talk to you about."

You are worried about what happens when you sleep with Chyna. Anubis said it as a fact, not as a question.

"Yeah. How did you know?"

I saw it in your memories. There is nothing to worry about. You are supposed to want to bite her.

Jaxon scratched his head. "Ah, why would I want to do that? It's never happened with another woman."

Of course it has not. Those females were not your mate. Chyna is. Once you bite her, you will give her the immortality I cannot grant her. I could only do that if she was dying on a battlefield and called out to me to save her life, as you did. Your life forces will be tied together.

He stiffened as a wave of denial surged through him. "No. No, no, no. Chyna is not my mate."

Why not? I never intended for my warriors to remain alone forever.

Jaxon shook his head. "That's not what I mean. It isn't that she can't be my mate. It's the fact that I never want one. I will never tie myself to a woman like that, especially for all eternity."

Regardless, Chyna is your mate. You cannot turn your back on her. The urge to bite her, to claim her as yours, will become harder and harder to ignore each time you sleep with her. At one point, instinct will take over and you will do what needs to be done, but I do not want you to let it get that far. She must be given the choice. I will not be denied on this, Jaxon. You will make her your mate.

Jaxon felt Anubis' presence leave. The god might have told him there would be no escaping the fate that loomed over his head, but that didn't make Jaxon feel any better about it. If anything, it made him want to put as much space between him and Chyna as he could. He'd planned on calling her to smooth things over, but the thought of doing that made his heart race, and not in a good way.

He walked out of the temple room and then headed for

his bedroom. His immortal life had just turned into a huge, steaming pile of dog doo-doo. He had a demon capable of turning him into a beast and something he considered worse than death hanging over him. Jaxon had no idea what he'd do about it all.

* * * *

Chyna had yet to get over her anger at Jaxon. He'd turned around and done exactly what he'd said he wouldn't. He'd slept with her, and even though he'd planned to see her again the next day, he'd stood her up. So much for the two months he'd said he would give her. He'd used her for sex, then tossed her away. And lying to her face, setting her hopes up, that burned her even more.

She had tried to call him early the next afternoon, but his cell phone had gone to his voice mail. At first, Chyna had thought maybe she'd caught him in the shower or something so he couldn't get to his phone. She'd left a message and waited for him to call her back. The wait turned into an hour. That's when she tried calling one last time. With the same result as the previous call, she hung up, her doubts rising to the surface.

Now there it was the morning of the third day and still no word from Jaxon. And being a Monday, Chyna had to work. She was in a foul mood and would have to watch herself or she'd be snapping at everyone who called today. All it would take would be for her to be rude one too many times and she could lose her job. Or at the very least be reprimanded. Unlike certain jerks, she wasn't rich. She had to work for her money.

Chyna had just taken a seat behind the reception desk when Joy arrived. The other woman waved, then walked to where Chyna sat. She didn't feel like talking, but it would be rude to snub Joy for no reason.

"Hi, Joy," Chyna said once the other woman reached

the desk.

"Hi. How did your weekend go?"

Chyna harrumphed. "Let's just say it was the worst one I've suffered through in a while."

A look of concern formed on Joy's features. "Oh no. What happened? I thought you saw Jaxon on Friday. I figured you'd spend the weekend with him."

"That's what I thought as well. It didn't work out that way."

Joy cringed. "Really?"

"Afraid so. I'll give you the short version without all the ranting and swearing that was in the original. I slept with Jaxon on Friday. He asked to see me again on Saturday. On said day, he neither called nor answered any of my calls. All I got was his voice mail. And as of now, the last time I spoke to him was on Friday night. So it looks as if he managed to get his one-night stand, after all."

This time Joy winced. "That has to hurt. I'm sorry, Chyna. I guess he lied about giving you those two months."

"It would seem so. Now my blood boils every time I think about him. I should have walked away when I found out he only wanted one night of sex. That's what I get for being stupid and expecting a man to actually hold up his end of a bargain."

"Try not to let it get to you too much. I know for a fact all men aren't like that. Kevin isn't. You just haven't met the right guy yet."

"Well, hopefully he comes around soon. I'm not getting any younger."

"As I've told you before, there's always Kevin's brother. He's a super nice guy."

"I'll keep him in mind. I'm not ready to try again, though."

"Of course not." Joy looked at her watch. "I've got to run. Try to forget about the jerk."

"That's easier said than done."

Once Joy walked away, Chyna took the phone lines off the answering service. She'd just finished doing that when her cell phone rang. She always took it out of her purse and put it on the desk while she worked. She picked it up and looked at the number on the screen. Chyna scowled. *Now* he called. A little too late. She hit the answer button, then hung up on Jaxon. She didn't even want a voice message from him. It rang twice more and she did the same thing both times.

When it didn't ring again, Chyna figured Jaxon had finally gotten the hint she didn't want to talk to him. The phone at the reception desk rang. She took a deep breath in an attempt to tamp down her anger before she answered it.

"Good morning, Blackstar Public Relations. How can I help you?" Chyna thought she sounded polite and professional.

"You can start by telling me why you keep hanging up on me, Chyna," Jaxon said on the other end.

"You know perfectly well why I am. And how did you get this number?"

"On Friday, you told me where you worked. It was easy enough to look up the phone number. I want to see you again."

Now *that* almost made her see red. It so wasn't going to happen. "No."

"Chyna, you have to—"

"I'm sorry, but I'm not allowed to take personal calls on this phone."

With great satisfaction, Chyna disconnected the call. Jaxon could go to hell for all she cared. If he wanted sex, he was barking up the wrong tree.

CHAPTER FIVE

axon pulled his cell phone away from his ear and stared at it in disbelief. Chyna had hung up on him. Again. *Son of a bitch.* He was in deeper shit than he'd thought.

He'd ended staying up most of the night, thinking over everything Anubis had told him about Chyna being his mate. One part of him still wanted to scream in denial, but there was a small, very small, part that liked the notion that she was meant to be his. Jaxon had tried to stamp it out, but it wouldn't die. It actually battled the side of him that outright refused to be tied to her.

It was just before dawn when that little bitty part of him gained enough ground to have Jaxon longing to see Chyna again. The more he thought about her, the more he wanted her in his arms. It scared the shit out of him. And the thought of never seeing her again made his gut twist.

Was that what it felt like to start to fall for someone? He didn't have a fucking clue. All Jaxon knew was that no matter how much he didn't want Chyna as his mate, he couldn't walk away. He was pathetic. As a mortal, he'd made fun of other men who had become so obsessed with a woman they acted as if they couldn't live without them. Now Jaxon was in danger of becoming obsessed with Chyna.

He pocketed his phone. So Chyna wouldn't talk to him that way. Well, he wasn't about to let her get away with that. She had to give him a chance to explain what happened, why he hadn't been in contact with her. Not that he'd tell her the truth, but he would come up with something else that sounded legit.

Jaxon showered and then got ready for the day as he decided what he wanted to do about Chyna. He fought this whole mate thing tooth and nail, but he still craved her touch and longed to sink his cock deep inside her pussy. And it wasn't just for mere sex. No, he wanted the closeness to her it gave him. Even now he was semi-hard from thinking about being with her again, of taking her.

Once the right time rolled around, Jaxon got into his car and then drove to the part of the city where Chyna worked. He parked before he walked with long, determined strides to the office building where the public relations company was located. If he timed it correctly, she would still be there. She wouldn't have left for lunch yet.

He walked through the door and breathed a silent sigh of relief when he saw Chyna standing behind the reception desk at the opposite end of the room. Another woman was with her. Chyna had her back toward him.

The other woman jerked her head in Jaxon's direction the closer he came and said in a low voice that his sensitive hearing easily picked up, "Some eye candy just walked through the door and he's headed this way."

Chyna turned around. When she saw him, she scowled and crossed her arms over her chest. "What are you doing here, Jaxon?"

He stopped at the other side of the desk. "You won't

talk to me on the phone so you didn't leave me any other option than coming here to see you face-to-face."

"Well, you can just walk right back out the door. I'm not interested."

That was the wrong thing to say. Jaxon had smelled the slight scent of Chyna's arousal as soon as she'd seen him, no matter how ticked off she appeared. She still wanted him. She could tell him until she was blue in the face that she was through with him, but that luscious scent of hers proved her to be a liar.

He walked around the desk to Chyna, cupped her face in both his hands, and kissed her. Jaxon didn't care where they were. The thought of letting another minute go by without tasting her seemed like a crime. And after the shit the demon had put him through, being this close to her made him feel as if his world had righted itself just enough for him to forget for a little while and think his life had gone back to normal.

At first, Chyna didn't kiss him back, but Jaxon didn't give up. He fitted his lips tighter against hers, pushing his tongue inside her mouth. He licked and sucked, tasting her, until a shiver went through her and she brought up her hands to rest against his chest. She kissed him then, her tongue dueling with his.

Jaxon pulled away, satisfied with the dazed look that had come over Chyna's face. Seeing her purse sitting on the desk, he snatched it up before he grabbed her hand. He turned his attention on the other woman, and said, "Chyna is going for lunch."

She smiled and nodded. "Okay."

He tugged on Chyna's hand and got her walking. He'd managed to guide her all the way outside before she seemed to gather her wits about her and dug in her heels. She tried to pull her hand free of his, but he didn't release her and kept towing her along with him.

"Where are you taking me?" she asked in a pissed-off

tone. "You can't just come into my work and drag me away whenever you feel like it."

"I just did. We're going someplace private to talk."

"I only have an hour for lunch."

"I'll have you back on time." At his car, he opened the passenger door for Chyna. "Get in."

Her scowl was back in place, but she did as he'd told her and slipped onto the passenger seat. He closed the door for her and then went around to the driver's side. It was a short drive to the US Grant hotel. Out of the corner of his eye, Jaxon saw Chyna turn in her seat to look at him as he parked the car.

"Why are we at a hotel?"

He shut off the engine and pulled the key out of the ignition. "I booked a room here. We can order room service."

"What? You spent that kind of money on a room for one hour?"

Jaxon didn't answer her. He got out of the car and then walked around to her side. Once she stood beside him, he guided her into the luxury hotel. At the desk, he gave the girl his name, then she handed him a paper to sign before sliding two keycards over to him.

Inside the suite, he took out the room service menu and told Chyna to pick what she liked. After she did, he called in the order, telling them he needed the food as soon as possible.

That done, he turned to face Chyna. She sat on the couch in the small sitting area. "They said the food will be delivered in fifteen minutes."

Chyna gave him a hard look. "You can't expect all this" — she waved at the room in general — "will make me forget about you standing me up on Saturday, then not even calling me back until today."

Jaxon crossed to Chyna and took a seat next to her. "I didn't intentionally try to stand you up."

She rolled her eyes. "Sure, you didn't. It just so happens I slept with you the night before and then you were a no-show. You can't tell me that doesn't look like a one-night stand. You got what you wanted out of me and decided not to bother with the two-month thing."

"No, it wasn't like that. It might seem that way, but it wasn't. If I only wanted that one night of sex, why would I have gone to this much trouble to see you again?"

"All right. If that is true, then tell me why you haven't been around the last couple of days."

"It had to do with my job. The night I left you, something came up that I had no control over. I didn't get back to my place until last night."

"Couldn't you have at least called to tell me?"

"Yeah, I could have, but when I finally had the chance, my cell's battery was dead, and I had no way to charge it. I didn't purposely stay away."

There was a knock on the door. Jaxon got up and answered it. He stepped back and allowed the room service waiter to roll the trolley with their food inside. After tipping the man, Jaxon followed him to the door.

Jaxon returned to the trolley and took the covers off the plates before he brought them to the sitting area where Chyna sat. He placed each one on the glass coffee table in front of the couch. They ate in silence. He figured he'd let her mull over what he'd said.

As soon as they'd finished, he gathered up the empty plates, put them on the trolley, then pushed it out into the hall. He set his gaze on Chyna and walked back to her. He stood over her, feeling his blood heat the longer he stared at her. He wanted her. Now. He needed to connect with her in a way that would let him know she'd stay with him. His cock throbbed as it hardened.

Chyna gazed up at him. "I still haven't decided that I should take you back."

He took her hand and pulled her to her feet. "I can

make you." Jaxon lowered his mouth until it hovered over Chyna's.

"How?" she asked a bit breathless.

"Like this."

He closed the scant distance between their lips and kissed her. The same feeling of his world coming to rights rushed through him as it had back at Chyna's work when he'd kissed her there. This time she didn't hesitate in kissing him back. She pressed herself closer so their bodies touched from chest to knee. The scent of her arousal filled his head.

Jaxon reached up and palmed one of her breasts. He stroked his thumb back and forth across her taut nipple through the material of her blouse and bra. He left her mouth and made a trail of wet kisses across her jaw and down the side of her neck. Chyna tilted her head to the side to give him better access to the soft skin there.

"I can't go back to work late," she said huskily.

"I'll make sure you don't. We just won't be able to take our time. Later, when you're off work, then we can."

Jaxon didn't even bother thinking about the bed. He crowded her against the closest wall. He took her mouth again as he undid most of the buttons on her blouse. With a brush of his hand, he spread the material, then yanked a bra cup aside. He released her lips and bent his head to suck the nipple he'd bared into his mouth.

Chyna moaned, pushing her hips against him. "Hurry, Jaxon."

He didn't have to be told twice. Jaxon continued to suck at her breast as he reached for the sides of Chyna's skirt and hiked it up to her waist. Her panties, he pushed down her long, toned legs. She kicked off her high heels and then stepped out of her underwear.

He let go of her nipple and lifted her off her feet. Chyna wrapped her legs around his waist. He reached between them and stroked her pussy. A groan of pleasure rose out of him. She was wet. He pressed her closer to the wall as he worked on releasing his cock from his jeans.

Jaxon angled his hips, then slowly sank his erection into Chyna. Once he was to the hilt, he pulled back before he pushed home again. In and out he pumped. It felt so good to be inside her. Her pussy gripped his cock with enough pressure to drive him crazy in a good way.

His thrusts became more forceful, and he sank deep with each stroke. Chyna's moans filled the room, ramping up his arousal. Being inside her showed him how much he actually craved her. She satisfied him sexually unlike any other woman had in his past.

Chyna locked her ankles at the small of his back and used her leg muscles to match the pace he'd set. She dug her nails into his back where she held him tight. At the first flutter of her pussy around his plunging cock, heralding her release, Jaxon's balls drew up closer to his body. He wouldn't be too far behind her.

And with his pending release, his eyeteeth shifted to fangs. He lowered his mouth to the side of Chyna's neck. He sucked on her skin as the urge to bite her where her shoulder and neck met built. This time, knowing what it meant, Jaxon tried to shove it away. Not wanting what the end result would be if he did sink his fangs into her.

The harder he shoved, the more intense the urge became. Desperate to avoid disaster, Jaxon pistoned his hips faster, not holding back as his climax rushed to the surface. He bit his bottom lip to stop himself from biting Chyna when his mouth came too close to the place he had to stay away from at all costs.

His cock pulsed deep inside Chyna's pussy as she gripped him in a tight fist, milking every last drop out of him. After the last wave of release hit him, Jaxon slowly pulled out of her and then let her legs down. She leaned into him for support, snuggling against his chest.

"I don't think my legs will hold me up on their own,"

Chyna said, sounding out of breath. "That was intense, and I guess you win. I'll take you back."

"Good," he said as he kissed the top of her head. He put a finger under her chin and forced her to look at him. "I won't make you regret it."

"So, are we back on for the two months?"

"Yes."

"And if I want more than that? What then?"

"We'll take it as is goes."

She gave him a small smile. "I guess that's better than an outright no." Chyna sighed. "I have to get back to work. Joy fills in at the reception desk while I'm on lunch and doesn't get to take hers until I return. So I shouldn't be late."

Jaxon brushed a soft kiss across Chyna's lips before he let her go. "We can leave whenever you're ready."

"Let me use the bathroom, then we can go. I still can't believe you booked this room just for an hour."

"Actually, I had to book it for a night. We might as well use it. After work, go back to your place and pack a change of clothes, then meet me here. I'll give you one of the keycards just in case you arrive before I do. It will make your drive to work shorter in the morning."

Chyna nodded. "That sounds really good. I've never stayed here before."

"We'll make a night of it then."

"Don't you have to work?"

"No, not tonight. After what I went through the last couple of days, I figure I can miss one night."

"Perfect. I'll be right out."

Jaxon stepped back so Chyna could walk around him. He followed her with his gaze as she yanked down her skirt, then went to the bathroom. Once she disappeared inside, he stuffed his now softened cock into his jeans and then did them up.

He ran his hand through his hair. The battle of what to

do about Chyna as his mate still waged deep inside him, but the side that wanted to keep her, let himself fall in love with her, steadily won more ground. He'd have to make a decision soon. If the urge to bite Chyna grew any worse, he had a feeling his choice, along with hers, would be taken away.

CHAPTER SIX

At quitting time, Chyna rushed through the routine of forwarding the phone lines to the answering service and shutting down her computer. She drove to her apartment to pack an overnight bag.

Even though she'd been dead set against taking Jaxon back, the time she'd spent at the hotel with him had told her she wasn't ready to let him go. She just hoped she hadn't made a mistake. She was already addicted to his touch. It would hurt if he decided to break things off.

Inside her apartment, Chyna practically tore her clothes off as she changed out of what she'd worn to work. It took her no time at all to pull on a pair of jeans and a T-shirt, then pack another set of clothes she'd need for the next day into the small suitcase she had open on her bed.

She smiled as she thought of spending the night with Jaxon at a luxury hotel. Chyna had told Joy about it when Chyna had arrived back at work to relieve the other woman. Joy had said Chyna had done the right thing by giving Jaxon a second chance. The trouble he'd gone to at lunch hadn't been an act of a man who wanted only a one-night stand. Joy had also said with a man as gorgeous as Jaxon, it would be a crime not to fight to keep him. Chyna had to agree with that.

Finished packing, she collected the suitcase and her purse, then headed for the apartment door. As he'd promised, Jaxon had given her the second keycard before they'd left the hotel earlier.

It turned out she wasn't the first to arrive. Jaxon was already in the room. He sat on the couch in the sitting room, watching the large LED TV. He rose to his feet and crossed to her once she'd stepped inside.

Jaxon gave her a kiss, then took her suitcase into the bedroom area and placed it on the floor near the end of the bed before he returned. "How did the rest of your day go?" he asked.

"Fine. How about yours?"

"It went all right, but I missed you."

He took her into his arms and pulled her against him. Chyna put her head on his chest and listened to his heart beat beneath her ear. She wished she could come home every day like that from work, to the waiting embrace of the man she had strong feelings for. After being with Jaxon during her lunch hour, she really hadn't been able to stop thinking about him.

No matter how many times she told herself there wasn't any guarantee she could keep Jaxon, it didn't change how attached she'd become to him. Chyna realized she set herself up for some major emotional pain if things went sour, but there was no reasoning with her heart. It refused to listen.

Chyna pulled slightly back and turned her head to look at Jaxon. "So, what are your plans for the night?"

He smiled and kissed the tip of her nose. "First on the list is to get some dinner. Then I thought we could try out the shower together."

She licked her lips at the thought of running her hands all over Jaxon's wet body. She was definitely on board with those plans.

"I'd say that'll be an enjoyable evening for both of us. Where do you want to eat? Here in the room or should we go out?"

"Would you mind getting room service again?"

"I'm fine with that."

They sat on the couch as they looked over the room service menu. Once Jaxon phoned in their order, Chyna settled closer to him as they watched some TV. She felt pampered, sitting in a luxury hotel with room service on the way. The elegance of the place outdid her apartment any day. Though she had to admit Jaxon's home was even nicer than the hotel.

Their meal of beef tenderloin with bordelaise sauce and grilled, fresh-market vegetables was perfectly done. And the bottle of merlot Jaxon had picked to go with it was a great pairing. By the time they finished, they'd eaten everything on their plates and the bottle of wine was empty.

Chyna sat back on the couch and sighed. "That was really good. I wish I could eat like that every night."

"Why don't you?"

She chuckled. "For one thing, I wouldn't be able to afford it, and another, I'm sure the rich food would end up giving me a huge butt."

Jaxon ran his heated gaze over her. "I doubt you'd have to worry about that. Since you mentioned it, I'd better make sure your bottom hasn't increased in size because of the meal."

Chyna sucked in a long breath. "And maybe I should check you out to make sure you haven't gotten...larger...where you shouldn't."

"There is one part of me that is growing as it should. I'd be more than happy to show you."

She glanced at the crotch of Jaxon's jeans and saw the noticeable bulge. "Yes, I definitely think I should check that out." Chyna leaned in and brought her lips to his. She kissed him and dropped her hand to the front of his pants. His cock jerked under her touch.

Once she released his mouth, Jaxon asked, "Shall we continue this in the shower?"

"Yes. I think that would be best."

Jaxon helped her to her feet, then guided her to the bathroom. Inside, her gaze landed on the large marble shower with glass doors. She and Jaxon would have plenty of room to move around in there.

They wasted no time in stripping each other. Now naked, Jaxon stepped into the shower first and turned it on. Chyna waited until he had the temperature adjusted, then joined him, shutting them inside.

The water was warm where it hit her skin, but Jaxon was warmer. He took her mouth in a possessive kiss that left her breathless. She rubbed herself against him, glorying in the feel of his hard cock pressing against her stomach. At lunchtime, they'd been in a rush. Now she intended to take her time, to explore him how she wanted.

Chyna glided her fingers down Jaxon's hard body until she reached his erection. She wrapped her hand around it and pumped. He moaned into her mouth, causing more wetness to pool in her pussy.

Breaking free of his kiss, she nibbled her way down to his chin before she pressed her lips to the hollow of his throat. His pulse beat there at a rapid pace. Chyna continued to stroke Jaxon's cock as she worked her way lower to his chest. She licked each of his flat nipples.

She continued to explore him, learning every part of him as she went. On her knees before him, Chyna set her sights on what she held. Jaxon was fully engorged, his shaft standing straight out from his body. She licked every inch of his cock, then took him inside her mouth, sucking him hard. He rocked his hips, sliding himself in and out. She bobbed her head, matching his strokes, taking him as far back as she could manage.

Jaxon's harsh breathing filled the enclosed space. He gently pulled away. "I think you've done enough checking for now. I need to have a turn."

Chyna stood and smiled. "Should I turn around? You did say you wanted to look at my bottom."

He nodded. "Yes, and put your hands on the wall."

She turned to the marble wall closest to her and placed her palms on its smooth, cool surface. Chyna looked over her shoulder at Jaxon. "Like this?"

His gaze seemed to eat her up. "Perfect. Don't move."

Jaxon shifted until he stood directly behind her. Chyna turned her face back to the wall. A shiver of anticipation went through her as he ran a finger down her spine in a soft touch. It stopped at her tailbone. Two large hands squeezed her bottom.

"No," Jaxon said in her ear, "it didn't get any bigger. Your ass is still perfect. Now to check out the rest of you."

He lifted his hands and covered her breasts as he used one of his legs to spread her feet farther apart. He pinched and pulled the taut nipples. Jaxon's cock slid along her pussy, making her wetter for him. She pushed back, trying to take him inside, but he kept tormenting her, pushing her arousal to higher heights.

Jaxon continued to caress her, leaving her breasts and skimming down to her stomach, which quivered at his touch. He didn't stop there. He trailed his fingers along her skin and placed his hands on her hips. With a small tug, he pulled her a little away from the wall so she was slightly bent over. Her palms on the wall kept her balanced.

The tip of his cock entering her had Chyna pushing back to take more of him. He pulled back, then thrust again. With each stroke, he sank deeper. She moaned once he'd sheathed himself completely. He filled her to capacity, the head of his shaft butting up against her cervix.

Still keeping hold of her hips, Jaxon took her in long, powerful thrusts. Chyna met each of his strokes, her pussy squeezing his cock, increasing the pleasure for both of them. He let out a groan that was close to an animalistic growl. The sound did delicious things to her insides.

Jaxon's cock grew even harder as he pumped his hips. Chyna felt an orgasm steadily build, coiling tighter. She panted, knowing it wouldn't take much to have her going over the edge.

He thrust in and out. Jaxon let go of her hips and leaned over her, his chest covering her back. He placed his hands over top of hers. Chyna felt completely surrounded by him. She turned her head and took his lips. His kiss was hot and carnal, his tongue mimicking his cock plunging into her pussy.

Chyna broke contact with Jaxon's lips just as the first wave of her release hit her. With a keening moan, she dropped her head forward, riding out the intense pleasure that tore through her. Her inner walls clutched his cock.

He stroked faster and trailed his lips down the side of her neck to the place where it met her shoulder. Jaxon sucked on her skin before she felt the scrape of his teeth across it. That soon turned into a nip. Chyna turned her head to the side to give him better access as he bit her a little harder, an animal-like growl rumbling out of him.

Jaxon's movements became jerky as he held her in place with his teeth at her shoulder. His grip on her hands tightened just before he bit her hard enough he'd surely broken through the skin. Usually, Chyna wasn't into the kinky stuff, but he biting her threw her into another intense orgasm. He pumped his hips twice more, then came as well. His cock pulsed deep inside her, filling her with his cum.

With his teeth still holding her, Chyna felt what she

could only describe as something snapping into place between them. Almost like a bond. The feelings she had for Jaxon instantly intensified. It was as if she'd stepped off a cliff and fell into love. There was nothing logical about it. It just was.

Trying her best not to show that anything had happened, she leaned back against Jaxon and fought to catch her breath. He released her completely, allowing her to straighten. Chyna turned to face him. He stared at her with no emotion showing on his face. She opened her mouth to say something, but Jaxon spoke before she could.

"I'll wash up first, then you can have it," he said in an even tone.

Silently, Chyna watched him run the bar of soap over his body in short, jerky motions. He didn't meet her gaze. Not even once. After he rinsed off, Jaxon walked out of the shower and then shut the glass door behind him. She stood under the water as he toweled off before he left the bathroom.

Had she done something wrong? She didn't think so. As far as she was concerned, that last bout of lovemaking had been the best they'd had. Whatever she'd felt had to be only one-sided. The way Jaxon acted, Chyna had to wonder if he'd had the opposite happen to him.

* * * *

Jaxon pulled on the pair of sleep pants he'd packed before he sat on the bed and put his head in his hands. He'd done it. He'd bitten Chyna. His eyeteeth had grown longer and sharper, and he'd sunk them into where her shoulder and neck met. He'd felt a bond form between them. He had tried to fight the urge. Had fought it to the bitter end, which he had a feeling had been his undoing. The harder he'd tried to push it away, the harder it had ridden him until he'd lost all control.

And the bite had the end result Anubis had told him about. Chyna was as immortal as he. Jaxon had watched as the bite mark he'd given her healed in a matter of seconds. A sense of horror had washed through him, but with that emotion had come others he'd never wanted to feel for a woman — love and the need to always have her at his side.

Unable to handle what coursed through him, Jaxon had shut down emotionally. He'd seen the hurt in Chyna's eyes when he'd distanced himself from her, but he couldn't snap out of it. That was the only way he could cope with it right now.

The shower turned off. He lifted his head and scrubbed his face with his hands. No matter how much he hadn't wanted it, Chyna was now his mate. It wasn't her fault. She had no idea what had happened between them. He supposed he had to tell her the truth about everything, but not today. He was already having a hard enough time of it and didn't need to throw that into the mix.

Chyna stepped into the bedroom area dressed in the clothes he'd stripped off her in the bathroom. It looked as if she'd finger-combed her damp hair. She stopped just inside the entrance to the room and stared at him. Her features were guarded.

"This isn't going to work, is it?" she asked in a quiet voice.

"I never said that."

"No, but you don't have to. What happened in the bathroom, I got the message loud and clear. You're not comfortable with us."

Jaxon stood and walked to Chyna. "No, I'm not, but that doesn't mean I want to end what I have with you."

"I don't know if I can handle too much more of your roller coaster emotions. You're obviously still having issues with having a relationship. Maybe it would be better for both of us if I let you go."

Something that felt an awful lot like fear shot through

Jaxon as Chyna had spoken. She couldn't leave him. He took hold of her upper arms and bent his head to look directly in her eyes. "No. You're not letting me go. I can work through this."

"And how long with that take? Days? Months? Years? I'm going to be blunt here. I'm getting to the stage in my life where if I don't find a man to settle down with soon, it'll be harder and harder to do so. Sorry to say, I'm not going to waste valuable time on you if you can't give me what I want. I'll find someone else who will."

The thought of Chyna in the arms of another man had Jaxon fighting back a growl. She was his mate. He'd claimed her as his. There would be no one else for her. Neither one of them could back out now.

He pulled her stiff body against him. It was time for him to be a little truthful with Chyna. "While making love in the shower with you, I felt something pass between us. I don't know if you felt it too. It brought you closer to me. I'll admit it scared the crap out of me, but I'm not going to run away. I know I hurt you when I put some emotional distance between us. I didn't mean to. That was my first gut instinct."

Chyna put her hands on his chest. "I felt it as well. And now? How do you feel?"

He took a deep breath. "The thought of losing you scares me more than my feelings for you."

She lifted a hand and placed it on his cheek. "I've fallen for you, Jaxon. Please don't break my heart."

"I'll do my best to keep it in one piece."

Jaxon took Chyna's lips in a kiss that he poured how he felt about her into. He couldn't say those three little words yet, but the emotion that would allow him to was slowly taking over the part of him that was scared shitless.

He lifted Chyna off her feet and carried her to the king-sized bed. He took his time stripping her out of her clothes, then proceeded to make love to her, letting his actions show her what he couldn't say in words.

CHAPTER SEVEN

It had been incredibly hard for Chyna to drag herself out of Jaxon's arms and go to work the following morning. After the fiasco in the shower, he'd done everything he could to show her he wanted her to stay with him. He'd made love to her, not holding anything back. Even though he hadn't said the words, she'd felt loved.

Now she was stuck at work, waiting for the day to be over so she could see Jaxon again. They made plans before they'd left the hotel to see each other after it was her quitting time. He would pick her up at her apartment, then take her to his place. He didn't know it yet, but Chyna had booked the rest of the week off, using some of her vacation time. Joy would work at the reception desk while Chyna was away. Her friend was more than happy to get out of the mailroom, which wasn't her favorite job.

Chyna had figured her days away from the office would give her more time to see Jaxon since he had to work nights. Spending the days together should help him get over his commitment phobia. At least in theory, that was what she hoped would happen.

Once her work day ended, Chyna hurried to her place to change. She'd just finished when Jaxon buzzed up to her apartment. After telling him she'd be right down, she went to meet him in the lobby.

During the drive to his house, she told him what she'd done when he asked her how work had gone. "I decided to use some of my vacation days and took the rest of the week off. That way we can spend more time together."

"I still have to work tonight, but I want you to sleep over."

"I didn't bring a change of clothes."

"That doesn't matter. I want to come home to you in my bed."

"All right, I'll stay."

For dinner, they ordered pizza. Jaxon ate almost an entire extra-large all by himself. She had no idea where he put it all. There wasn't an inch of fat on him anywhere. If she ate the way he did, she'd be four hundred pounds. Along with the pizza, they had beer. Usually when she drank it, two would have her feeling good. This time that wasn't the case. She was already on her fourth and felt completely sober. He had already had six and he was in the same condition as she.

Once it grew dark, Jaxon prepared to leave, telling Chyna she had the run of the house. He kissed her as if it would have to last him for days instead of hours. She'd noticed a difference in him. Ever since the night before when she'd told him she thought they weren't going to work out, he seemed to want to know more about her. After they'd finished eating, they'd done nothing but talk.

Since Jaxon had given her run of the house, Chyna decided to check all the rooms she hadn't seen. She loved his sprawling bungalow. Living there would be no hardship, not that she was getting ahead of herself. It was just if they ever reached that stage where they wanted to live together, she would be more than happy to give up her apartment.

Chyna went to the wing that had the bedrooms. Two of the three spare rooms had their doors wide open. Inside each one was only a queen-sized bed and a dresser. No personal items were to be seen.

The third guestroom's door was shut. Her curiosity getting the better of her, Chyna tested the knob and found it unlocked. She turned it and pushed open the door. She stepped into the room, her gaze taking in all the pieces of what appeared to be ancient Egyptian art. Everywhere she looked there was a depiction of the jackal-headed god, Anubis. There were paintings of scenes from what looked to be from tomb walls, even a few pieces carved in stone.

Chyna walked to one of the smaller statues that sat on a shelf along a wall. It looked as if it could be the real deal, a piece from Egypt's past, but she had her doubts. She didn't think Egypt would allow any of their antiquities out of the country, no matter how much the buyer was willing to pay. All of the items in the room had to be well-made replicas. They also tied in with the tattoo of Anubis that Jaxon had on his chest.

The sight of what appeared to be a small altar at the end of the room caught Chyna's eye. She walked to it and frowned when she found a couple of slices of bread and a glass of beer sitting on it. They almost looked like offerings. She couldn't see Jaxon coming in there and leaving them because he was too lazy to get rid of them. She'd yet to see him leave any kind of food sitting around once he was done with it.

Chyna touched the bread and found it not too dried out, so it couldn't have been sitting there for longer than a day. Thinking she'd take it and the beer to the kitchen just in case Jaxon had mistakenly left it in the room, she reached for them.

Chyna.

The sound of a male voice saying her name inside her mind caused her to jump. She pulled her hands back and put one over her rapidly beating heart. She turned, half expecting to find Jaxon standing behind her. That he'd been the one to call her by name. The only person in the room was her. She had to be hearing things.

With a shake of her head, Chyna walked out of the room and then shut the door behind her, deciding to leave the bread and beer where they were. She'd have to remember to ask Jaxon about that particular guestroom. No place else in the house had anything ancient Egyptian in it. Maybe he was a closet collector and didn't want anyone to know.

Chyna headed for the living room and then sat on the couch before she turned on the large LED television. She soon became caught up in a movie that played on one of the movie channels. It was a psychological thriller that kept her guessing who the bad guy was. At one point, she heard some creepy laughter. She gazed around, swearing the sound had come from somewhere in the room, but in the end she figured it had to have been from the home theatre system Jaxon had hooked up to the TV.

Blown away by the end of the movie, Chyna switched the channel to something else. It was starting to get late. Her eyes felt heavy. She stretched out on the couch with her head resting on the thickly padded armrest and turned on her side toward the TV screen. It didn't take long for her eyes to drift shut a few times. Eventually, she lost the battle and they stayed closed and she fell asleep.

* * * *

Jaxon returned home after an uneventful night of hunting. He hadn't found one evildoer. Though he hadn't encountered any prey, he'd put the time to good use. He'd thought about Chyna and what she was to him. Now that he'd spent more time with her, he no longer felt he needed to run away screaming when he referred to her as his mate to himself. He enjoyed being with her. And the whole idea that she would never be anyone else's but his gave him a warm feeling.

Thinking about Chyna in his bed, sleeping, waiting for him to return, had his thoughts shifting to all the things he wanted to do to her once he was with her again. He'd wake her up with his lips and tongue, make love to her. His cock ached with the need to be inside her.

He unlocked the front door and walked inside, closing it behind him. Jaxon turned the lock before he headed for the living room where he heard the TV playing. It was so late he'd figured Chyna would have gone to bed already, especially since she'd gotten up early that morning to go into work.

Jaxon stepped into the room and smiled when he found Chyna fast asleep on the couch. He crossed to her, picked up the remote from the coffee table, and turned off the television. She didn't stir. He went on his knees in front of her and ran his gaze over her beautiful face. She wormed her way deeper inside him. Since the bond had formed between them, his feelings for her were only growing stronger, no matter how much he tried to slow it down.

He leaned in and brushed his lips against hers. "Chyna," he said quietly. "Wake up."

She blinked open her eyes, then smiled when her gaze met his. "You're home. I guess I fell asleep on the couch."

"Then I better take you to bed."

Chyna sat up, then shifted as he kneeled between her legs. She put her arms around his neck. "You can take me to bed but not to sleep. Not yet, anyway."

Jaxon pulled her closer until she sat on the very edge of the couch. "You missed me, huh?"

"Of course."

Their mouths met in a heated kiss. Jaxon had missed Chyna as well. The feel of her against him as he held her tight felt right. As if she were the piece he'd been missing in his life and hadn't even known she needed to fill it.

An evil-sounding laugh came from somewhere behind Jaxon. He only had enough time to release Chyna's lips before he was thrown into the change. He groaned as his body shifted to his half-human and half-jackal form. Her eyes grew wide and the smell of fear radiated off her in huge waves. Her gaze shifted to a spot over his shoulder, her mouth opening and closing but no sound came out.

Jaxon rose to his feet, tugging Chyna to hers at the same time, and turned to face the being who had dared to set foot in his home. The demon was on the other side of the coffee table, his eyes glowing red. Jaxon positioned himself so she stood at his back.

"Get out of my house, demon," he said with a growl.

"I don't think so, warrior of Anubis. I've been watching your mate while you were away doing your duty to the god of the underworld. I think she'd be fun to play with."

"You won't touch her."

"Oh, but I will. I can smell her terror." The demon took a deep breath. "It smells delicious."

Jaxon knocked Chyna back onto the couch, then kicked the coffee table out of the way as the demon launched himself at Jaxon with a sword in his hand. Jaxon willed his own into his and blocked the strike that would have cut into the top of his shoulder. With the blades locked together, he gave the creature a hard shove, pushing him away.

He tried to beat the demon back, but the creature's strength was almost an even match for Jaxon's. Even in that form, Jaxon didn't have that great of an advantage. What ground Jaxon gained, the demon slowly took back, getting in a few good hits that left shallow slices across one of Jaxon's biceps and his chest. Jaxon ignored his wounds, making a few of his own, as he fought to keep the creature away from Chyna.

That strategy soon changed when Chyna jumped from the couch and tried to make a run for it. The demon lunged after her, his sword raised to strike her in the back. She must have sensed she was in danger. She spun around and held her hands up in front of her face as the creature's sword descended.

Jaxon reached them in time to block the worst of the strike with his sword. The tip of the demon's weapon sliced across Chyna's forearm. Seeing the blood that welled from the wound sent Jaxon into a rage. Growling and snarling, he went on the attack, pulling on reserves of strength he hadn't known he had.

Just as he thought he'd get a chance to take the demon out, the creature disappeared, then reappeared out of striking range. He bled from a number of wounds.

"Play time is over for now, warrior of Anubis, but you're still mine. Remember that." The demon disappeared.

Jaxon turned to face Chyna. She held a hand over her wound as she stared wide-eyed at him. As he willed his sword away and closed the distance between them, the shift tore through him until he was once again in his human form. His wounds healed with the change.

Even though fear still radiated off her, Chyna held her ground. "What the fuck are you?"

"I'm what the demon called me. I'm a warrior of Anubis."

"So you're telling me that changing into that beast thing is normal for you?"

"Yes. Let me look at your wound, then I'll explain everything." He reached for Chyna's arm, but she yanked it away.

"I already looked at it. I'm probably going to need stitches."

He shook his head. "No, you won't." Not allowing her to pull away from him this time, he captured her wrist in one hand as he wiped away the blood with his other. "It's already starting to heal. It'll be completely gone in less than a minute."

Jaxon held her arm where Chyna could see it. As he'd said, the slice wound disappeared in the amount of time he'd predicted without leaving a mark, not even a scar. He let go of her wrist. She twisted her arm this way and that, staring at it as she shook her head.

"What the hell was that?" she practically yelled. "That is not possible. I'm not supposed to heal like that."

"It's all right, Chyna. Calm down."

Chyna backed up, breathing at too fast a rate. Her face was white. Jaxon felt a little worried that she was about to pass out on him.

"Calm down! How the frick do you expect me to do that? After what I just saw?"

"I know that was a lot for you to take in at once. Let's sit down and I'll tell you everything."

She shook her head. "Not on your life. I'm not getting anywhere near you."

Jaxon looked Chyna in the eye. "You have my word I won't hurt you. I only shift into my half-human and half-jackal form when I'm in the presence of evil. It's not something I do when I choose to. And even if I were to shift in front of you again, I'd not harm you. It's still me, able to talk and think the way I do now."

"Except it's a you who is covered in black fur and has a jackal head and a tail," she shot back.

"Yes, but on the inside, where it counts, I'm no different."

"I can't do this." Chyna slowly backed up a few more steps. "I really can't."

"I didn't take you for a quitter, Chyna. You wouldn't let me give up on you. Well, it's my turn to not let you give up on me. And for better or worse, we're tied to each other for all eternity."

She came to a dead standstill. "What are you saying?"

"The demon was right when he called you my mate. You are. When I bit you in the hotel shower, I claimed you as the one meant for me. A bond formed between us. Now you're as immortal as I am, and we share the same life force. There's no breaking it."

If it were possible, Chyna's face grew even whiter. "You made me immortal and tied us together with an invisible bond that can never be broken?"

He nodded. "Yes."

"What the hell, Jaxon? First, you can barely stand the idea of seeing me past a night, then you begrudgingly gave me two months. Now you tell me you've made sure we'll be together for eternity. How can a commitment phobe go from never wanting to settle down with one woman to that? What really pisses me off is that you didn't give me the choice. You got to make the final decision when I asked you to stay with me longer than a one-night stand. And why do you have to shift into that creature?"

He ran a hand through his hair. "It wasn't as if I decided to do it without talking to you first. You don't understand. Every time we made love, just before I came, I had the urge to bite you, to sink my fangs into you. The harder I fought against doing it, the harder it pushed back until I lost control. Anubis warned me something like that would happen if I kept denying what you are to me. I even told him I didn't want a mate, ever, but there was no getting out of it. I am the warrior of a jackal-headed god. Shifting makes me bigger, gives me more strength over evildoers so I can send them to Anubis to be judged in the underworld."

Chyna stiffened as if he'd slapped her. And Jaxon knew that instant he'd just fucked everything up. Royally. He took a step toward her, then came up short when she flipped him the bird with each hand.

"Screw you, Jaxon," she shouted. "Here I was falling in love with you and all you could think about was trying to get out of having to stay with me. Well, I don't need you. You can stay away from me or I'll kick your furry, kilt-wearing ass into next week. And congratulations, you just made me so furious I'm no longer afraid of seeing you in your other form. Have a nice immortal life without me. Jerk."

She spun on her heel and headed toward the room's entrance. It was Jaxon's turn to be afraid. With the real threat of losing Chyna forever, all the feelings and emotions he'd fought to extinguish when it came to his mate bubbled to the surface and spilled over.

"I love you, Chyna," he said before she left. "Please don't leave me." She stopped but didn't turn around. "I might have wanted to get out of claiming you as a mate in the beginning, but that's no longer the case. My feelings for you grew stronger the longer I was with you. When I saw the demon go for you, and I realized how vulnerable you truly would have been if I hadn't made you my mate, I knew what I felt for you was love. The thought of losing you makes my heart ache."

Slowly, Chyna turned in his direction. The anger that had tinged her cheeks pink had faded. "I really want to believe that is how you truly feel about me."

Jaxon crossed the room and cupped her face. "It's the truth. I swear it on Anubis. You're the first and only woman I'll ever love. Let me explain everything to you. Give me another chance."

She took a deep breath and nodded. Jaxon brought his lips down to hers and kissed her. He shook with the need to make love to her, but that would have to wait. He took her hand, guided her to the couch, and prepared to tell her the story of how he'd become a warrior to the god of the underworld. Something he'd never told to anyone else.

CHAPTER EIGHT

Chyna settled onto the couch as Jaxon took the spot next to her. Her anger at him had burned down to ash. The fear she'd initially felt was gone as well. In some ways, she was a little numb. She had no idea what Jaxon was about to tell her, but she was more than willing to listen. When he'd said he loved her, she hadn't been able to keep walking. It had been the last thing she'd expected him to say, especially in the heartfelt way he'd said it.

"All right. I'm listening," she said.

Jaxon surged to his feet and paced in front of her. The coffee table still sat where he had pushed it out of the way earlier. It was a full minute of Chyna watching him walk back and forth before he spoke.

"I really was born in Dijon, France, but not in the year you originally thought. It was 1772."

"So, you're two hundred and forty years old?" To look at him, Chyna would never have known he'd lived that long. Even though she hadn't asked, she'd kind of figured he was a little younger than her. He didn't look thirty.

"Correct. I'm that old, but I basically became frozen in time when I was twenty-six. That's when I took my vow to become one of Anubis' warriors."

She'd been right. That was why he looked younger than her. Chyna realized she would forever remain looking like her thirty-year-old self. She'd never get any older. Not yet ready to dwell on that for too long, she pushed it away.

Chyna cleared her throat as she stopped herself from trying to freak out again. A little bit of the numbness had worn off. She needed to keep her head to pay attention and understand everything Jaxon said. "How did you become a warrior to an ancient Egyptian god when you're French?"

"I was on the verge of death."

"What happened?"

"I was a soldier fighting with Napoleon in Egypt. We were there to take the first step against British India, to drive the British out of the French Revolutionary War. On August 1, 1798, during a battle, which would become known as the Battle of the Nile, I was on a ship called the *Orient*. The British and French fought in the Aboukir Bay just off the coast of Egypt. Nelson led the naval attack on the French, with the British ending up the victors. My ship took a lot of cannon shot. I was badly wounded but managed to jump overboard before the *Orient* exploded. I barely made it to shore."

Jaxon stopped pacing and stared down at Chyna. From the look in his eyes, she could see he relived what he'd gone through during that battle, and it wasn't a pleasant memory for him.

"Then what happened?" she prompted.

"Once I'd dragged myself to shore and a little away from the water's edge, I realized I was in pretty bad shape. There was no one around to call for help. After fighting my way to the bank, I was too weak to look for it. I was bleeding out from several deep wounds, the blood pooling around me. I wasn't ready to die. I called out to God, but He didn't answer. I grew weaker. I knew I'd pass out and that would be the end of me. Being in Egypt, I'd taken an interest in the ancient gods that had once been worshipped there. Desperate to try anything, I called out to them, promising I'd do anything if they would just spare my life. That's when Anubis answered."

"What did he say?"

"He said he'd save me, but in return, I had to vow to serve him as one of his warriors for eternity. I didn't even think twice about it. I was already a soldier. It was the only life I'd known. Being a warrior to an ancient Egyptian god wouldn't be a hardship for me. So I gave him my vow, and he healed my wounds, granted me immortality, and put his mark on the left side of my chest. Now each night since then I've hunted evildoers and have sent them to the underworld to be judged by Anubis. When I shift, I'm able to see every evil thing my prey has done, to make sure they truly need to stand before the god."

Chyna looked up at the man whom she'd fallen in love with in a matter of days. If not for Anubis, she'd have never met Jaxon. He would have died at a very young age. Even if he had survived his wounds, he wouldn't have been around for her to love. Old age would have claimed him a long time ago. Now that she'd met Jaxon, she couldn't picture him not being in her life. And thanks to that same god, she would have Jaxon forever.

She stood and met his gaze. "If I could, I'd thank Anubis for saving you. If he hadn't, I wouldn't have had the chance to fall in love with you."

Jaxon pulled her into his arms and claimed her lips.

She held on to him, giving back as good as she got. Once he pulled away, she said, "Being one of Anubis' warriors, is that why you didn't want something long-term with me?"

Jaxon kissed the tip of her nose. "I hate to say it, but no.

That had to do with me. Even as a mortal I didn't want a woman in my life. My mother died giving birth to me, and my father decided when I was quite young that I'd go into the army. He raised me to be tough and independent. I'd figured loving a woman would make me appear weak, but I think that opinion really formed when I was younger. I'd gotten close to a woman, thinking I could have that type of relationship with her. I ended up finding out she not only had me but another man and played us both. When I confronted her about it, told her what I was feeling, she laughed and said she'd never want a boy like me on a permanent basis, that I was just an amusement."

"Do you still think that way?"

"No. My life wouldn't be complete without you. Finding you showed me how much I'd been missing." He brushed a lock of hair out of her eyes. "Are you done being angry at me?"

Chyna nodded. "I now understand where you were coming from."

"Good, because you're one tough woman when riled. I don't need you to threaten to kick my furry, kilt-wearing ass again."

She felt herself blush. "Yeah, I can say I have a bit of a temper. And it's not as if I could ever kick your ass while you're in that form anyway. You're twice your normal size."

"Are you okay with what I am?"

"Yes. I think. It's still so weird." Some of the numbness was still with her. Once it wore completely off, she'd have to look at this more clearly, but for now it could wait. "So that was a demon, huh? Have you had to deal with many of them?"

"No, I haven't. This is the first time. They usually are trapped down in another part of the underworld. That one and a few others escaped. So far, two others of Anubis' warriors have sent the demons to the god for final judgment. I'm going to have to do the same for this one or we'll never be free of him."

She should have been scared to think about the demon, but Chyna suddenly felt very tired as the last of the adrenaline left her body. She was too tired to even feel the fear she should. A quick look out the living room window showed the sky was lightening.

She covered a large yawn with her hand. "Do you think the demon will come back soon? We need some sleep."

"I doubt it. He'll want to lick his wounds. Let's go to bed."

Chyna placed her hand in Jaxon's when he held it out to her. Maybe she was accepting all of this too easily, but right now she didn't care. Later when she wasn't so tired, she'd think about it.

Once inside his bedroom, Jaxon stripped Chyna and then put her to bed before he climbed in naked beside her. She turned to him and cuddled close. With the sound of his heartbeat in her ear, she closed her eyes and fell into a deep sleep.

* * * *

Chyna sat outside in Jaxon's backyard at the glass patio table. He was inside, leaving his morning offering to Anubis. He'd explained that the spare room she'd found with all the artwork of Anubis was a mini-temple Jaxon had set up for the god of the underworld. He'd also told her that was the only place he could actually speak with Anubis. Jaxon had asked if she wanted to come with him and talk to the god, but she'd declined. She had everything that had happened earlier to get used to before she spoke with a real ancient Egyptian god.

Along with talking about the temple, she and Jaxon had discussed their future together. She, of course, would be moving in with him. He'd suggested she quit her job, which she was more than happy to do. Joy would be the first one the company would go to as a replacement for Chyna.

With her face lifted to the sun, Chyna closed her eyes and took a deep breath. She was immortal. She still found it hard to even comprehend. And having her life force bound to Jaxon's was so much more permanent than any marriage license. She'd been a little worried when he'd told her that if he ever lost his head, literally, that she'd die right along with him. He'd quickly calmed her fears, saying San Diego was the last place he ever expected it to happen. The number of evildoers was minimal compared to other cities.

"Do you have any idea how beautiful you look sitting there in the sun?" Jaxon asked.

Chyna opened her eyes and smiled up at him. He stood at her side. "And you're looking pretty hunky yourself. All done with the offerings?"

He pulled out the chair next to her and then sat. "Yes. I also spoke to Anubis and told him what happened last night. He's happy that I claimed you, but wished I'd gotten your permission first. He warned me to stay alert when it comes to the demon. After my first encounter with the creature, we're not sure when he'll try to take control."

"Take control? What do you mean?"

"Oh yeah, I forgot you don't know what really happened to me the day I was supposed to see you."

"The demon did something to you?"

"Yes. He appeared before me, forcing me to shift. He used a spell that took away my humanity, leaving nothing but the jackal part in control. It lasted two days. I didn't remember anything. Anubis was able to bring the memories through the block in my mind." Jaxon paused. "I went on the hunt for evildoers, but I didn't send them to Anubis to be judged. I killed them, which sent them to the demon part of the underworld."

Chyna swallowed. "And he can still use that spell on you?"

"He wouldn't have to cast it again. It remains a part of me. The demon just has to trigger it."

That didn't sound good at all. "Can't Anubis get rid of it?"

"He has tried. He even tried again a few minutes ago, but the demon put a failsafe on it. Too much tampering and I lose my humanity forever. The only way to break it is for me to send him to Anubis. Until then, I'm a bomb waiting to go off."

"Shit, Jaxon. We have to get rid of this demon."

"You mean I have to get rid of him. You're going to do your best to stay clear of him." She opened her mouth to protest, but Jaxon spoke before she could. "You're not to put yourself at risk. Remember, with our life forces joined, the demon can take me out by taking you out. It works both ways."

"All right. I'll let you handle him, but..." Chyna's words trailed off as Jaxon shot to his feet. "What's the matter?"

He didn't answer. The sound of his bones realigning filled the air as he grew larger to stand at almost seven feet tall. His body shifted to his half-human and half-jackal form, his muscles becoming bigger. Black fur sprouted from his skin until he was completely covered from head to toe. Gold armbands appeared around each of his thick biceps, and last, a snow-white Egyptian-styled kilt formed around his hips to fall to the middle of his thighs.

The shift complete, Jaxon growled in a gravelly voice, "Run, Chyna. He's here."

"Not so fast," the demon said as he appeared behind Chyna and grabbed hold of her, preventing her from escaping. "Intermission is over. Now it's time to get to the end game, for both of you."

The demon whispered a word she didn't understand.

An instant later, Jaxon growled and clutched his head as if he were in great pain. Once it seemed to pass, Jaxon straightened, and his gaze latched on to Chyna. Her heart tried to beat out of her chest. Looking into his eyes, there was no human intelligence staring back at her. It had been replaced with something feral. It was like looking a wild animal in the eye.

"He thinks you're his prey," the creature who held her said with a laugh. "Now you can run." He released her with a shove.

Chyna took off, not even looking back to see what Jaxon would do. She barely made it into the house and locked the door before he caught up to her. The lock slowed him down some, but the sound of the door being ripped from its hinges rent the air. A low, angry sounding growl followed it.

The only place Chyna could think of where she had maybe a chance of being protected was inside Anubis' temple. She ran faster than she'd ever run in her life. She heard Jaxon hot on her trail. Inside the room, she slammed the door, but there was no lock so she put all her weight behind it, knowing full well it wouldn't keep him out.

"Anubis!" she yelled. "If you can hear me, I could really use your help."

Chyna felt something ruffling through her mind before a voice answered her inside it. *Let Jaxon into the temple. Once he is, I will be able to hold him in place with a shield.*

She whimpered as Jaxon pushed at the door, almost throwing her off balance. "And the demon?"

You will have to be the one to send him to me. One cut is all you need to send him to the underworld.

A black-bladed dagger appeared in her hand. There went her promise to Jaxon to let him handle the demon. She was going to have to save them both. Chyna just hoped she could cut the demon before he managed to take her head.

Jaxon gave a shove at the door that pushed her almost halfway across the room. Chyna recovered and stood her ground. He barreled into the temple, his upper lip snarled, showing off an impressive set of fangs. He growled and ran toward her. He only managed a few running steps before he ran into an invisible barrier. He pushed all around him, meeting with the same results. He gnashed his teeth, then let out a long howl.

The demon stepped into the room. He scowled when he saw Jaxon fighting to free himself from the invisible barrier. "Running to Anubis' temple isn't exactly fair. The god might have control over his warrior, but the same can't be said about me. I guess I'll have to take care of you myself. It won't be as much fun as having your mate do it, though."

Chyna held up the dagger Anubis had given her. "Stay away from me."

The creature laughed. "You think a dagger will be enough to save you? Don't count on it." A sword appeared in the demon's hand. "It's no match for this."

Chyna tuned out Jaxon's snarls and growls and focused on the demon as he came closer. He circled her, a taunting smile on his face. She turned with him, not letting him out of her sights. She needed only one chance to cut him with the dagger, and doubted she'd get very many of them.

The demon lunged, then pulled back his sword at the last minute. He laughed. The bastard toyed with her. He did that three more times, moving so fast Chyna never had a chance to strike back. On the fourth strike, instead of backing up, she stepped closer. His sword cut across the cap of her shoulder, but she managed to get under his guard and slice him deep along his stomach.

He bellowed in anger, lunged to give what Chyna thought would be a killing blow, but it never came. The demon's body lost substance until he just disappeared. She stared at the spot where he'd been for a few seconds as she fought to catch her breath.

Remembering Jaxon, Chyna turned to see him shifting back to his human form. He looked around the room as if he couldn't remember getting there. Once his gaze landed on her, he rushed to her and yanked her into his arms.

"Are you all right?" he asked as he held her tight.

She nodded against his chest. "I'm fine. I just have a cut on my shoulder, which I'm sure is healing as we speak."

Jaxon released her and pushed up her short sleeve to look at her wound. Chyna watched it seal itself and disappear. She was pretty damn glad she was immortal.

"The demon?" Jaxon asked.

"Gone. I sent him to the underworld with this." She held up the black dagger. "Anubis gave it to me, but I think you should have it."

Jaxon took the dagger from her, then must have willed it away since it disappeared. He'd told her about his ability to will weapons in and out of his hand when he needed to. He yanked her close again and kissed her. Their embrace turned desperate. It had been too close a call for Chyna. She needed the closeness only lovemaking would bring.

As if sensing what she wanted, Jaxon took her down to the floor and worked on removing her top and bra. His hard cock rubbed against her thigh. Wetness pooled in Chyna's pussy.

Cradling his head as he sucked on one of her nipples, she asked on a moan, "Shouldn't we do this in the bedroom? Won't Anubis get pissed at us for doing this in his temple?"

Jaxon released her nipple and lifted his head to look at her. "I'm sure he'll understand. I'm desperate to be inside my mate and I don't intend to wait."

Chyna soon forgot about Anubis as Jaxon sheathed his cock inside her pussy and took her in long, hard strokes. All that mattered was showing the man she loved how much he meant to her, and that she'd always be at his side.

MARISA CHENERY

The End

A WARRIOR TO LOVE

After a disastrous blind date leaves Alexis stranded, she hits up a handsome stranger in the restaurant for his cell phone. She connects to more than the cab company. One look from him has her pulse racing and other notable body parts standing at attention. Their instant chemistry has her night making a turn for the better.

A Warrior of Anubis since 1920, Konner finds the loneliness of his life getting to him. And being celibate for the last five years certainly isn't helping matters any. But the sexy damsel in distress stirs passions long buried. He has to have her—in his life and in his bed. She's everything he's ever wanted in his long existence. But the nature of who he is could end this love affair before he has a chance at forever.

CHAPTER ONE

The familiar pull of evil had Konner changing direction and following it. His steps quickened as the sensation became stronger. He picked up the stench of evil in the air—a scent only he, as one of Anubis' warriors, could smell.

He found his prey at the back of a warehouse, attempting to break into it. Konner bit back a groan of pain as the change ripped through him. It only took a matter of seconds for him to shift into his half-human and half-jackal form, but it was pure agony while it lasted. His bones grew larger and realigned, the sound loud in his ears. His muscles became bigger and he stood taller at almost seven feet. Once the shift was complete, his entire body was covered in black fur and he had the head and tail of a jackal. Two gold armbands circled his biceps and a snow-white ancient-Egyptian-styled kilt covered his hips and fell to mid-thigh.

Konner dragged in a deep breath once the change was complete. Not only did his prey reek of evil, he also smelled of some kind of drug he'd recently taken. The man was more than likely stoned out of his mind, which meant he'd be unpredictable.

Once he was directly behind his prey, Konner let out a low growl, loud enough for the man to hear. The evildoer whipped around. His eyes widened when he saw Konner. The man pulled out a gun that had been shoved into the front waistband of his jeans and then fired.

Luckily Konner had faster reflexes than a mortal. He managed to knock the firearm away, changing the trajectory just before the bullet was fired. It ended up grazing the cap of his shoulder instead of lodging in his chest. A wound there wouldn't have killed him since he was immortal, but it would have hurt like hell.

He grabbed the prey's wrist and squeezed until the man let the gun drop to the ground. Konner shook his lupine head. "Now that wasn't smart, mate," he said in a voice that was much deeper and gravellier than his own, still retaining his Australian accent.

The evildoer reached his free hand around to his back and whipped out a knife. "Let go of me, freak of nature, or I'll gut you."

Konner laughed. It took him only a few seconds to remove the knife from his prey's possession and have him slammed up against the building in a grip the man wouldn't be able to break free from. "As I said before, not very smart."

Capturing the evildoer's gaze with his own, Konner pushed into the man's mind. His prey bellowed with the pain Konner knew he caused. Not that Konner cared. As he tapped into the mortal's memories, he saw every evil deed the man had committed. He experienced them as one of the victims, living it as if it had happened to him.

"Evil," Konner said as the last of the memories played out. "Time to face your judgment."

Konner willed a gold dagger into his hand. The blade

had hieroglyphs carved on it—the spell Anubis had infused into it to send evildoers to the underworld. All it took was one cut to do its job. And once his prey stood before Anubis, the god would weigh the man's heart on the Scales of Justice. If he was found evil, his heart would be fed to Ammit.

After a quick slice of the dagger across the man's chest, Konner released the evildoer. The magic of the blade already working, his prey slowly lost solidity until he completely disappeared.

Konner willed his weapon away just before the change tore through him once again. Now that the evildoer had been taken care of, he shifted into his human form. He had no control over his shape-shifting ability—being in the presence of evil set it off.

Once again himself, Konner walked from the warehouse and continued on his way down Chicago's waterfront. He still had some of the night left to hunt evildoers. The farther he went, the more the warehouses changed to restaurants that were open for late-night dining.

The city had changed a lot over the years since Konner came to reside there in the 1920s during the prohibition. He had seen many changes in his immortal life. He'd taken his vow to become one of Anubis' warriors in 1915. He'd fought in the First World War as a soldier in the Australian and New Zealand Army. Shot in the leg at Gallipoli, he'd been taken back to Egypt as the troops had retreated. That was where they'd all been originally stationed to train. Before he could be sent to a better hospital, his wound had become infected and Konner had ended up on the verge of death. He'd called out to any being who would save him, and Anubis had answered.

Konner hadn't gone back to Australia. He hadn't wanted to. It wasn't as if he could tell his family what he'd become. So he'd come to Chicago where there had been plenty of evildoers to keep him busy. Only the last couple of years he hadn't felt fulfilled by performing his duty to the god of the underworld. The loneliness was starting to get to him. He still remembered what it was like to have family around him, and at times, he missed it.

Deciding he could use a drink and a little break, Konner went to one of the restaurants. He walked in and stood at the hostess stand, waiting in line as he stared in the direction of the bar to see what spaces were available. As he stood there, a woman brushed by him to stand by the door. There was something about her that had him watching. She was all dressed up and wearing high heels. She reached inside her purse and pulled out her cell phone. She swore a blue streak under her breath. With his sensitive hearing he was able to make out every word.

She returned her phone and headed toward him to stand behind him in line. He heard her sigh as she leaned around to see how many people were ahead of her. She settled her gaze directly on him.

Konner was instantly attracted to her. In a matter of seconds, he'd taken in her long, reddish-blonde hair, blue eyes, and pretty face. His cock hardened with interest as he ran his gaze down her shapely figure, then up to her face again. She stared back at him with interest showing clearly in her eyes.

*

Alexis didn't normally make it a practice to ask a favor of a stranger, but in this case, she felt desperate enough to try. She turned her gaze to look at the man fully, which caused her lungs to seize. He was gorgeous to the extreme. His light-brown hair just brushed the tops of his shoulders. His eyes were hazel. Doing a quick sweep of his body, she saw it was well-padded with muscle. He also had to stand at around six-feet-three, which had her feeling even shorter than she normally felt.

For a few seconds, Alexis forgot what she was going to ask. She realized she stared as intently as he. After a quick check to make sure her tongue wasn't hanging out, she pulled her wits about her and smiled.

"Ah, excuse me," she said.

He smiled. "Yes?" His gaze locked on to hers.

The way he looked at her had Alexis' body heating in a way she found hard to ignore. After the crappy blind date she'd just been on, the night had definitely taken a turn for the better.

"I don't normally do this, but could I use your cell phone? I need to call a cab. The battery in my cell is dead, and I don't feel like waiting in this long line to ask to use the phone here."

He pulled his phone out of his front jeans pocket and held it out to her. "Sure. Go ahead."

As if he wasn't already attractive enough, the sound of his voice did naughty things to her. An Aussie accent was one she didn't think she'd ever get sick of hearing.

She took the cell from him. "Thanks. I promise I won't take too long." Alexis quickly dialed the number of a cab company. Once she was finished, she gave him back his cell. "Thanks again." She went to walk away, but he stopped her.

"It's kind of late, and who knows how long it will take the cab to get here. Would you mind if I stayed with you until it arrives? I'd feel a lot better if I didn't leave you outside alone."

It wasn't too hard of a decision for her to make. He was a hunk, and so far, he hadn't acted like an axe murder. And if it looked as if he were turning into someone she wanted to stay clear of, there was still the restaurant where she could escape to.

She nodded. "Sure. I'd like that." She held out her hand. "I'm Alexis."

He wrapped his much larger one around hers. "And I'm Konner."

Konner shook her hand, holding it longer than was necessary. Not that Alexis was complaining. His touch sent a tingling awareness through her straight to her pussy.

Once Konner had let go of her, they walked outside. Alexis said, "I hope I'm not keeping you from something."

"You're not." He paused, then said, "I couldn't help hearing you were upset about something."

Alexis grimaced. "Yeah, just a bit. I was on what had to be the worst blind date ever. And to top it all off, the asshole up and left, stranding me at the restaurant. Now I have to somehow think of what I'm going to tell my best friend when she asks what I thought of her cousin. I'm not looking forward to that."

Konner smiled, then chuckled. The two dimples that appeared on either side of his mouth drove his hunkiness factor up even more. They also had Alexis wishing she could check them out. With her tongue. She pulled her mind back to the conversation as he spoke.

"It sounds as if you've had a bad night," he said. "Now I can understand all the swearing."

It was Alexis' turn to chuckle. "I don't normally go around cursing like that. If I get angry enough, I just can't seem to hold the swear words back."

"Then I guess I don't have to worry about you cussing me out since I'm not the one you're angry at."

"Nope. There isn't any chance of that happening. To be honest, you're better company than the jerk I was just with."

At that moment, the taxi pulled up to the curb. Alexis wished it had taken longer. She wasn't ready to say goodbye to Konner just yet, but she couldn't think of a reason to prolong her departure.

"There's my ride," she said. "Thanks for letting me use

your cell and staying with me until the cab arrived."

She stepped toward the taxi, but Konner took hold of her hand and pulled her toward him. Alexis let out a surprised gasp as his lips claimed hers in a slow, heated kiss. It was over far too soon.

Konner pulled back. "Go out with me, Alexis. I promise I'll be a much better date."

Still feeling the imprint of his lips on hers, she nodded. "Sure. I'd like that."

"I'll call you tomorrow so we can decide on a time."

"All right." Alexis rattled off her number after Konner let go of her hand. He took out his cell to put it into his contacts list. "See you tomorrow."

"Since it'll be Saturday, I won't call too early in the morning."

"Sounds good."

After taking one last look at Konner, Alexis turned and got into the waiting cab. She gazed out the window at him as the taxi pulled away. He waved from where he stood on the sidewalk. She had a feeling he would turn out to be a way better date than tonight's disaster.

* * * *

Konner continued on his way after Alexis' cab drove out of sight. He resisted the urge to adjust the front of his jeans to make room for the raging hard-on he sported. That one kiss had brought his cock to full arousal in a split second. He hadn't meant to kiss Alexis. He'd only wanted to take her hand to stop her from getting into the taxi. Seeing her turn away, a feeling of wrongness had swept through him. He hadn't been able to let that be all they had together. So he'd taken her hand. As she'd turned to face him, he'd had an inexplicable need to taste her lips.

The feeling of them against his was forever imprinted in his mind. Same with the sensation of having her slim, curvy body pressed against his much harder one. Her scent and the smell of her arousal had filled his nose.

Even though it had been no easy task, Konner had forced himself to let her go only after a few seconds. He'd craved more of her. Oh, how he'd craved another taste, but he'd reined himself back.

Konner kept walking as he played his time spent with Alexis over in his mind. He didn't know what he was going to do with her. Strike that. He knew exactly what he *wanted* to do with her. It involved both of them naked and some very hot sex. He just didn't know how he'd progress with her after that.

He hadn't tried to form attachments with any mortals, women or men, since he'd become one of Anubis' warriors. And with the disinterest in his life he'd been experiencing, it had to have been at least five years since he'd last had sex. He hadn't felt the need in a long time. Until he'd met Alexis, that is.

* * * *

After paying the cab driver the fare, Alexis got out of the taxi and then walked toward the front door of the small bungalow she called home. She'd actually grown up in it. When her parents had decided the year before that they wanted to move to Florida, they'd given her the house. There was no mortgage on it since her parents had paid it off a few years ago. She hadn't turned them down when they'd come to her with the offer.

She unlocked the front door and then stepped inside. Once closed, she locked it. She kicked out of her pumps before turning on some lights. It was late, but not too late to call her best friend. Sabrina was a night owl, as was Alexis, to some extent. She and Sabrina jointly owned a web design company, which meant they could work out of their homes and make their own hours. It was nothing for her friend to stay up until five in the morning, working. Alexis tended to get more work done by breaking her work hours up during the day. The afternoons and evenings were taken up with her job with some mornings thrown in if she was meeting a deadline.

Deciding to give Sabrina a call before going to her bedroom to change out of her dress, Alexis headed to the living room. She picked up the cordless phone on one of the end tables, then sank onto the plush couch. She figured it would be better to tell Sabrina her cousin was an asshole now instead of waiting until the next day. She didn't trust the jerk not to go to Sabrina with some dumbass story about Alexis being the one to cause the date to fall apart.

Sabrina picked up after the third ring. "Hey, chicky. How did your date with Travis go?"

"I have to thank you *so* much for setting up that blind date with your cousin. Travis was *such* a sweetheart."

"I'm glad…wait a minute. You were being sarcastic, weren't you?"

"How could you tell?" Alexis asked drolly.

"So, you two didn't hit it off?"

Alexis let out a deep sigh. "I know Travis is part of your family, but the man is an asshole."

"Really?"

"Yes, really. When he realized I wasn't going to—now these are his words—put out, the shithead abandoned me at the restaurant with no way to get home. And on top of it all, my cell phone battery died so I couldn't even use that "

"Travis actually said that to you?"

"Yes. I would never make up something like that. I know you thought Travis was a great guy, but if I ever see him again, I'm going to nail him in the balls."

"I'm so sorry, Alexis. I had no idea he was such a jerk. He's always talking about the girls he dates and how he'd like to meet that special woman he could settle down with. If I'd known he only wanted a quick tumble in bed, I never would have suggested the blind date. How did you get home?"

"I know you wouldn't have. And Travis must have been feeding you bullshit. I can't see any woman wanting to be anywhere near him once she got to know him. He's good-looking and knows it. As for how I got home, I asked to borrow a stranger's phone and called a cab."

"You asked a stranger for help? Alexis, do you know how risky that is?"

Alexis shook her head. Sabrina didn't trust anyone she didn't know. "I was desperate. I had no working cell, and I wasn't in the mood to stand in a really long line at the restaurant and ask politely to use their phone. I decided to take the chance."

"Please tell me you asked a woman and not a man."

"Sorry. I asked a man, and his name is Konner. He was a real gentleman, and even stayed with me until the cab arrived to make sure I'd be all right. We're going out on a date tomorrow. He's also Australian and has a great accent."

"Are you sure you should be going out with him? You just met him."

Alexis couldn't stop herself from rolling her eyes, glad Sabrina wasn't able to see it. "Sabrina, you set me up on a date with your cousin, gave him my address to pick me up, and I'd never laid eyes on him until he came knocking at my door."

"That's different. Travis is my cousin. I know him."

"Except you didn't know how much of an asshole he was," Alexis said with a laugh. "Quit your worrying. Konner is a nice guy. He didn't give off any icky vibes like your cousin did, sorry to say."

Sabrina sighed loudly. "All right, I'll stop harping on you. So, when are you going to see this Konner again?"

"I'm not sure yet. He's going to call me tomorrow to set up a time."

"I guess that means you won't be working on a Saturday for a change, which is a good thing. You've been working too much lately."

It was true. Alexis had started working through the weekends when before she'd taken them off. It mostly stemmed from the fact she really had nothing else to do. With her parents in Florida, she couldn't go visit them very often. And as an only child, she had no siblings to take their place. Then there was the whole no-boyfriend thing.

"That's just something else for you to bug me about," Alexis said. "I think you like to nag me."

Sabrina laughed. "So true. If I didn't nag you, who would?"

"Whatever," she said with a chuckle. "I'm going to go. I don't want to stay up too late tonight. I want to be well-rested for my date with Konner."

"Call me after it's over so I'll know he didn't murder you and dump your body in an alley somewhere."

"God, Sabrina. Do you have to be so dramatic? I'll be fine. And I'll call you."

"Don't forget. Talk to you later."

Alexis hung up and shook her head. Her best friend might have some strange ways about her, but Alexis loved Sabrina anyway. And depending on how well her date went with Konner, Sabrina may or may not get a call until the following day.

The next morning Konner woke up a little earlier than his normal time, even though he'd continued to hunt for evildoers until the wee hours after Alexis had gone. He'd sent two more of his prey to Anubis to be judged before he'd called it a night.

Konner got out of bed and pulled on a pair of pajama bottoms before he headed downstairs to the kitchen. There, he put a couple of slices of bread onto a plate and poured some beer into a small glass. The rest of it he drank out of the bottle in a few gulps. Since becoming immortal, alcohol didn't affect Konner the way it had before he'd given his vow to the god of the underworld. To this very day, he could no longer get drunk, no matter how much he drank. Not long after he'd been given his immortality, he'd spent two days doing nothing but drinking. He'd stayed stone-cold sober the entire time.

Once he picked up the plate and glass, Konner left the kitchen and went to the room that had originally been intended for a den. He'd designated it as a small temple, which he'd set up for Anubis right after he'd moved in. Inside the room, he'd displayed all the artifacts that depicted the god of the underworld, which Konner had gotten during his time in Egypt. Back in 1915, it hadn't been too hard to find the real pieces from antiquity for sale.

Konner crossed the room to where the altar sat. He placed the plate and glass he carried on it before he picked up the ones he'd put there yesterday morning. Every day he made an offering to Anubis. It helped keep the connection between him and the god strong. And only in this temple could Konner actually communicate with Anubis.

That duty done, he left the temple and returned to the kitchen to dispose of the old food and drink. Konner left the room and went upstairs to his bedroom to get his cell phone. It was late morning, and he'd promised to call Alexis to make arrangements for their date.

He sat on his bed and brought up his contacts list on his phone. He touched the screen to bring up Alexis' entry, then hit "call." It only rang a few times before she answered.

"Hi, Alexis. It's Konner."

"Hi."

"Are we still on for today?"

"Yes. What did you have in mind?"

"I was thinking about taking you to Millennium Park to one of those free concerts they have going on all summer. I'm not sure what type of music they'll be playing, but I thought it would be something fun to do. Then we can grab something to eat afterward."

"I'd like that. It's been ages since I've gone to one of those. The weather is perfect for an outdoor concert."

"Great. I can pick you up in a couple of hours."

"I'll be ready." She gave him her address, and Konner repeated it to make sure he had it right.

"See you then. And, Alexis, I'm looking forward to seeing you again."

"And I you. See you soon, Konner."

"Bye."

He disconnected the call and smiled. Konner really was looking forward to being with Alexis. It had been a very long time since he'd courted a woman. That's what they called dating back in his day, but it was all pretty innocent compared to how men and women acted with one another today when they were interested in getting to know each other better. There had been a girl back in Australia he'd thought of maybe marrying. That had been just before the war had started and he'd joined the Army.

Konner put his phone on the nightstand, then took off his pajama pants before he walked into the en suite bathroom to take a shower. When he'd eventually modernized the house, he'd made sure this bathroom was done how he'd wanted it. One thing had been the marble-and-glass shower stall with an overhead showerhead and three other heads that ran down one wall. There was also a Jacuzzi tub deep enough to accommodate his large frame.

Showered and teeth brushed, Konner went back into the bedroom area to dress in a black T-shirt and blue jeans. He headed downstairs to make himself a late breakfast of eggs and toast.

He had some time to kill after that, so Konner decided to go down to the finished basement where he had a fully equipped media room. A few years ago, he'd gotten hooked on playing video games. He now had the latest systems. Playing the games on his fifty-two-inch LED television made it even more enjoyable. He'd lost count of the number of hours he'd spent down there lost in a game. This time he'd make sure that didn't happen.

That was exactly what happened. An hour and a half later, Konner realized what he'd done, and that he was going to be late picking Alexis up. That would make a *great* first impression.

Taking the stairs two at a time and moving at a speed no mortal could, he rushed up to the main level. He grabbed his car keys and then ran out the door to the two-car garage. The tires on his expensive silver sedan squawked as he peeled out of his driveway and onto the street.

Having hunted in Chicago since 1920, Konner knew all of the city's streets so he had no problem finding Alexis' house. It was a cute little bungalow not too far from the city center. He pulled into the driveway and parked. As he got out of the car, he hoped she wouldn't be too pissed off with his lateness.

He rang the doorbell and waited for her to answer the door. A few seconds later, he heard Alexis' footsteps on the other side. He gave her a sheepish smile after she opened it.

"Sorry I'm late," he said before she could say anything. "I didn't mean to be. I got a little caught up in something and didn't pay attention to the time as I should have."

Alexis took a few steps back. "Come on in." Once he had, she shut the door. "Don't worry about it. You said you'd be a couple of hours with no set time. You're only a half over that. So, what had you so distracted?"

He gave her the truth. "A video game. I'll admit it. I'm addicted to playing them."

"Which game?" Alexis named off a couple of the newer ones that had recently come out.

The one Konner had been playing was one of them. He told her which one. "Do you play as well?" he asked.

Alexis smiled and nodded. "You could call me an avid gamer."

"Which system do you have?"

"Oh, no systems for me. I'm a computer gamer. I'm a web designer and have my own company that I share with my best friend. I prefer to play on my desktop since I spend so much time on it."

"I'm not as into computers. To be honest, I'm not computer literate. I don't even own one."

Alexis shook her head. "We can't have that, especially in this day and age. I'll have to teach you."

The idea of having Alexis as a teacher gave Konner a sudden interest in computers. "I'd like that."

She smiled. "I'll just grab my purse, then we can leave. I looked on the Internet to see who would be playing at the concert. It's a rock band, and it will be starting soon. We should go if we want to get there before the band takes to the stage." Alexis walked farther into the bungalow and out of sight.

Konner looked around what he could see of her house while he waited for her to return. The bungalow wasn't a newer one, but it had a homey feel about it.

"Nice place," he said as Alexis stepped back into the entranceway.

"Thanks. I actually grew up here. When my parents decided to move to Florida, they gave me the house."

"That was nice of them."

"Yeah, it was, especially since they left me with no mortgage to worry about. It suits me for now. If I ever strike it rich, I'd probably buy a bigger house." She took a step away, then came up short. "Sorry. I should make one quick phone call to my best friend. She's a bit of a worrywart and likes to look out for me. I'm just going to tell her where we're going." Alexis pulled out her cell phone from her purse and made her call.

Konner followed Alexis out the front door after that and waited as she locked it behind them. He walked her to his car. He held open the passenger door for her. Once she was inside, he shut it before coming around to the driver's side.

He backed out onto the street and then turned the car in the direction of the park. As Alexis had said over the phone, the day was perfect for an outdoor concert. It wasn't too hot, and the sun shone brightly. The only thing Konner had to worry about with being in a crowd of people was evildoers. If one happened to be there at the same time as him and he felt the pull, Konner wouldn't be able to ignore it. He'd be compelled to confront his prey and send him to Anubis. He'd also involuntarily shift into his half-human and half-jackal form, which was something he wanted to avoid while with Alexis.

Konner managed to find a parking spot when they arrived at the park. He hurried to get out of the car so he could help Alexis, then put his hand on the small of her back to guide her to where the concert was being held. There were quite a few people already there, but it wasn't a crush, which suited him. The less of a crowd, the less chance one of them would set him off.

He and Alexis took seats in the middle of the rows of chairs that faced the stage. It was only a matter of minutes before the band came out and the concert started. The music blared out of the sound system. Konner clenched his jaw as the music echoed painfully in his ears. It played havoc with his sensitive hearing. Having never been to a rock concert before, he hadn't thought it would be played that loud. He was sure the mortals around him would even find it harsh on their ears, not that they showed that it was. A look at Alexis and Konner saw she didn't seem to mind it either.

The one bonus that came from it was every time he spoke to Alexis or her to him, they had to lean in close and speak into each other's ear. Her scent and nearness had his cock jerking inside his jeans. At one point, when she placed her hand on his thigh and shifted closer, Konner's blood heated as it pounded through his body, his dick hardening.

The longer the concert went on, the harder his cock seemed to get. Konner couldn't focus on the music. All he could center his thoughts on was Alexis. Her scent was the only one he could smell, even though there were so many more around him. He watched her more than he did the band performing. And the sound of her heartbeat seemed to block out most of the music.

Once the concert ended, Konner was more than ready to leave. This hadn't exactly been a great idea. It was something different to do with Alexis, but he hadn't been able to converse with her enough to get to know her better and vice versa.

Konner guided Alexis through the crowd of departing people to his car, then helped her inside. Alone with her, and able to talk without having to raise his voice for her to hear him, some of the tension left his body.

He put the key into the ignition, then turned his head to look at Alexis. "I know it's still fairly early, but if you want, we can go get something to eat now."

Alexis nodded. "I don't mind. I skipped lunch so I'm hungry."

"All right. Then we'll have an early dinner. What kind of food do you like?"

"I'm not picky so just about anything."

"Okay. Do you like sushi?"

"I've actually never tried it. I've been a little leery about the whole eating raw fish thing, but I'm willing to go."

"I felt the same way, but after trying it, I loved it. The Coast Sushi Bar is really good. Plus, they have a relaxed atmosphere. It's BYOB so we'll have to stop to pick up a bottle of wine on the way."

"Sounds good. And since you're the expert, you'll have to teach me all things sushi."

Konner drove to the nearest grocery store. Alexis stayed in the car as he ran in to get the bottle of wine. He picked one he knew would pair really well with the sushi, then hurried back to her.

At the restaurant, Konner and Alexis were taken to a

table and given menus. A waitress came and took their bottle of wine to open before returning with it and two glasses.

Once she left them, Konner asked, "Do you see anything you'd really like to try?"

Alexis lifted her head from reading the menu and looked at him. "I'm not sure. The only sushi I'm familiar with is the California roll, and I know that doesn't have any raw fish in it." She pointed to the set of chopsticks at her place setting. "As for those, I doubt I'll be able to use them."

"I can show you. It might seem hard, but once you get the hang of chopsticks, they aren't that difficult. You sort of hold them like a pencil. As for the food, we can order some California rolls. And believe it or not, raw fish doesn't have a fishy taste to it."

Alexis gave him a look that said she didn't quite believe him. "Really?"

"It's true," he said with a smile. "Just try it." Konner picked up the bottle of wine and poured some into each of their glasses.

"Okay, I'll try some. I'm feeling in an adventurous mood. You can do the ordering since I don't know what will be good."

When the waitress returned, Konner ordered an assortment of hot appetizers, rolls, handrolls, and tempura seafood. Some of the rolls had raw salmon, red snapper, and tuna in them. One of his favorites was a rainbow roll that had a California roll base and was topped with salmon, red snapper, and avocado.

It didn't take long for some of the appetizers to arrive. Konner picked up his chopsticks and selected one of the crispy spring rolls to put on his plate. He looked at Alexis and found her trying to hold her chopsticks the correct way. She looked at the way he held his, then tried to mimic it, but she kept dropping one of them.

Konner took pity on her and reached across the table to position the chopsticks properly in her grip. "Like this," he said. "You should be able to use your fingers to open and close them." He helped her make the movement. "Now you try on your own."

Alexis did as he'd said. This time the chopsticks crossed, and she didn't drop one. She gave a smile.

"Not great," she said, "but I might be able to manage. If not, I'll just eat with my fingers."

"Whatever is easier for you."

Alexis clumsily selected a spring roll and got it to her plate before she dropped it. "So," she said. "How long have you been in the States?"

"Quite a while now," Konner replied after he took a bite of food.

"What part of Australia are you from?"

"New South Wales. Sydney, to be exact."

"Did you ever go to the opera house there? I've always thought of going to Australia, but it isn't a cheap vacation."

"No, I've never been to the opera house."

Of course Alexis would ask if he'd been to the famous Sydney landmark. Most people thought of it when talking about the city of his birth. Since construction on the building hadn't started until 1961 and wasn't completed until 1973, Konner hadn't been living in Australia during that time.

"What a shame," Alexis said. "You had to have done the bridge climb above Sydney Harbour, at least."

Another landmark that hadn't existed while he'd lived there. The Sydney Harbour Bridge had taken nine years to build with construction started in 1923. At the rate Konner was going, Alexis would think he'd lied to her about living in Sydney. The only thing he could do before she asked him if he'd been to another landmark he should have been to and hadn't was to change the topic of conversation as quickly as he could.

"No, I've never done the bridge climb." He cleared his throat. "You said you owned your own web design business."

Alexis didn't bat an eye at the rapid change of subject. "Yeah, I do. After completing the computer programmer program at the University of Chicago, my best friend, Sabrina, and I decided to go into business for ourselves. It took a few years, but we now have steady, regular clients with new ones coming in." She grinned. "Now don't be calling me a computer nerd, because I'm not nerdy in any way."

Konner had to agree with that. In no way did Alexis look like a nerd. "I would never call you that. I promise. Do you work from home, or do you and your friend have a small office somewhere?"

"From home, but Sabrina and I get together to go out for lunch a couple times a week. They're like our business meetings. Most of the time we just handle things through email and phone conversations."

More of their food arrived. Alexis eyed the rolls with the raw fish. She didn't look too sure about it all. He poured some soy sauce into the small bowl in front of his plate, then used his chopsticks to mix some wasabi into it. She followed his example and did the same. He selected one of the pieces of the rainbow roll and dipped it into the soy sauce mixture before he put the whole thing into his mouth. She heaved a big sigh, wrangled her chopsticks, and did the same without hesitating. A look of surprise crossed her face as she chewed.

"Do you like it?" he asked.

Once she swallowed she answered him. "Wow. That is good. I couldn't tell the fish was raw." She ate another piece, then said, "You've never said what you do for a job."

Konner was about to answer in a roundabout kind of

way when an excruciating pain shot through his head. A few seconds passed, and it didn't abate. He barely managed to bite back a groan. He'd never had a headache that bad or one so intense. Nor had he had one since becoming immortal.

He must have shown in some way that he was hurting, because Alexis asked, "Are you okay, Konner? Your face has gone pale."

"I suddenly just got a really bad headache. I think I'll go to the men's room and splash some cold water on my face and see if that helps."

Before Alexis could reply, Konner put down his chopsticks and stood. He took the most direct way to the restroom. Inside, he went to one of the stalls and shut the door behind him. Something wasn't right. Along with the headache, his bones were now shifting beneath his skin. Claws broke through the tips of his fingers before they receded a second later. Black fur sprouted on his arms, then it too disappeared beneath his skin. His vision had become keener, which meant his eyes had shifted to those of a jackal as well. That didn't last long either. The pain in his head continued to pound, making him wonder if he'd pass out from it.

By slow degrees, the headache went away, leaving Konner a bit on the shaky side. He unlocked the stall and then walked to the sinks. A look in the mirror above them showed he was back to normal. He turned on the water before he splashed some onto his face. He had to get back to Alexis. He'd already been in the men's room far too long.

Konner dried his face with a paper towel. He had no idea what had caused that partial shift or the extreme headache. It had never happened to him before. He only ever did a full shift into his half-human and half-jackal form, nothing in between. And the scary part was there wasn't any presence of evil to set him off. He'd felt no pull.

It didn't make sense to him. He couldn't be coming down with some kind of illness that would affect his shifting ability. He hadn't even gotten a simple cold since vowing to serve Anubis.

Even though what had just happened to him was something to be concerned about, it didn't mean he was going to end his date with Alexis over it. Konner would just have to be ready to think of a reason to get away from her if the headache and the other symptoms came back. For now, whatever it had been seemed to be gone and hopefully it would stay that way.

CHAPTER THREE

lexis looked toward the restrooms. There was still no sign of Konner. He'd been in the men's for a while now, and she was a little worried about him. His headache had seemed to set in awfully fast, and his face had gone really white. If he felt that bad, she was going to suggest he just take her home once they were done eating.

Turning her attention back to the food on the table, Alexis fussed with her chopsticks until she held them in a semblance of the right way, then attempted to pick up one of the rolls. It took her a couple of tries, but she managed it.

She put the food into her mouth and chewed. If she had known sushi, and the raw fish, tasted this good she would have tried it a long time ago. Once she swallowed, a small smile tugged at her lips. She'd have to get Sabrina to come there for lunch sometime with her. Alexis would probably have to trick her into it, though. Her best friend was leery of new foods as she was with new situations and people.

Alexis turned her gaze in the direction of the restrooms

again and breathed a small sigh of relief when she saw Konner walk out into the main part of the restaurant. Even from that distance he looked better. Maybe putting water on his face had helped.

She was glad about that. She really hadn't wanted their date to end early. She liked Konner. He was a great guy. With a terrific personality and good looks, he was everything she could ask for in a man. And being sexy as all hell helped as well. Alexis ached to explore his hard body, to learn what really turned him on.

She pulled her wayward thoughts back to less provocative things as Konner sat in his chair across from her. "Are you feeling better?" she asked.

He nodded. "Yes. The cold water helped. I've never had a headache come and leave so quickly."

"Maybe you're coming down with something. Do you want to end our date early?"

"No. I'm fine." Konner's gaze met hers. "I was going to suggest we do something else after we eat, like going to a nightclub, but how would you feel about going to my place? We can play some video games," he said with a smile. "See who the better gamer is."

Alexis had the distinct impression that if she said yes, playing video games wouldn't be the only thing they would be doing. Not that that bothered her. She'd use any excuse to get someplace alone with Konner.

"All right. You're on," she said. "So, what does the winner get?"

Heat flared in Konner's eyes. "Anything they want. Within reason, of course."

"Of course."

Alexis would try her damnedest to be the winner. The thought of telling Konner to take his clothes off while she watched sent a flood of warmth through her body. Though ending up the loser would more than likely be something she'd enjoy as well. The way his gaze seemed to eat her up as he stared at her, his thoughts could be going down the same road as hers.

"Then we're on?" he asked in a voice that had gone a little husky.

"Definitely. Just be prepared to get your ass beat."

"You're pretty confident you'll win. You've never played against me before. I might be the one beating your cute ass."

She gave him a smile. "We shall see." Even though it was an offhanded remark about her ass, a thrill still went through Alexis at knowing Konner thought it was cute.

They finished the rest of the food. To speed things up a bit, Alexis packed in the chopsticks and picked up the rolls with her fingers. Konner paid their bill, and they were soon outside getting into his car.

When they reached the Southport Corridor neighborhood, Alexis realized Konner had never said what he did for a living. Whatever it was, she had a feeling it paid really well. That was proven correct when he pulled into the driveway of a majestic-looking Queen Anne house that sat on a large corner lot. The property had black wrought-iron fencing all around it. It also looked to be worth a fortune. He parked in front of a two-car detached garage and then shut the engine off.

Alexis waited for him to come around and open the door for her. Konner seemed to be a gentleman that way, always opening and closing it. With a hand on the small of her back, he guided her to the double doors at the front of the house. Inside, they stepped into an entranceway that had mosaic floors.

"How big is this place?" she asked as Konner shut the door they'd come through.

"It's sixty-four hundred square feet."

"That's huge. I guess you don't have to worry about feeling you're running out of space."

Konner chuckled. "No, I don't. Come on. I'll show my

media room. That's where I have my systems set up."

He led her to a door that had a flight of stairs going down to what turned out to be a finished basement. Her eyes widened when she took in the catering kitchen.

"Someone could use this basement as an apartment with the kitchen and all."

"I like my privacy too much for that, and I don't need renters to pay for the place. Besides the kitchen and media room, I have a thousand-bottle wine cellar down here as well."

She blinked. "A thousand bottles? You can't have that many down here."

Konner chuckled. "No, I don't. The cellar is more for a wine collector, which I'm not."

He led her to his media room. There was a large LED television hanging on one wall with a thick-cushioned couch facing it. The entertainment unit sitting under the TV had two gaming systems set up on it and the shelves inside were filled with games.

Alexis sat on the couch as Konner walked to the entertainment unit. "So, what game do you have in mind for us to play?" she asked.

He selected one off the shelf and held it up. "This. It's a shooter. Whoever gets the most kills during a match wins."

"You're on. Just to give you fair warning, I'm pretty good at games like this."

Konner turned on one of the systems, then put in the game disc. "So am I," he said as he took a seat next to her before he handed her a wireless controller.

As they played, Alexis soon found out Konner was as good as he'd said. He was definitely giving her a run for her money. She even wondered if she'd be able to beat him. Plus, it didn't help that he sat so close their thighs touched. His body heat sank into hers, making her very aware of him. With each breath she took, she pulled in the scent of his aftershave and the one that was totally his own. She found it hard to keep her full attention on the game, which caused her to make some silly mistakes that worked out in his favor. If he was as affected by her nearness as she was by his, he didn't show it. And it sure didn't seem to hinder his playing abilities either.

Somehow Alexis managed to pull off the win in the last few seconds of the match. She let out a whoop as their scores appeared on the TV screen. The difference was only by one kill, but she'd take it.

"I guess that makes me the better gamer," she said as she turned to look at Konner.

"Or you just were lucky," he replied.

"Either way, I still won."

Konner took the controller from her, then stood and returned hers and his to the entertainment unit. He took out the game disc and shut off the system before he once again sat beside her.

"All right, winner. You can have anything you want. So, what will it be?"

Alexis didn't even hesitate. "You."

Konner moved so fast he had her under him on the couch with his lips fused to hers as he kissed her hungrily before Alexis knew what happened. She moaned into his mouth, returning his kiss, opening her own when he pushed his tongue inside.

She clutched his shoulders as she lifted her legs to put them around his waist. His hard cock pressed against her pussy. She rubbed herself along it, growing wetter by the second. Konner thrust his hips, which increased the pleasurable friction. Alexis had no doubt in her mind if he kept it up, she'd come that way.

A large hand landed on one of her breasts, the fingers tweaking her nipple. Alexis sucked on Konner's tongue as her arousal grew. Her body craved more, but she didn't want this to be over too fast. She wanted to savor every touch, every kiss. Plus, she wanted to do some touching of her own.

She broke the kiss and looked up into Konner's eyes. His pupils were dilated with desire. "I want to watch you take your clothes off," she said with a nip to his chin.

He rocked his hard cock against her pussy, which had her sucking in a breath. "Will I get to watch you take yours off as well?"

She shook her head. "No." She paused, then said, "You'll be the one stripping me."

Konner pushed off her and stood facing the couch. Alexis sat up to watch him. He grabbed the bottom of his T-shirt and started to pull it toward his head in a quick yank. She stopped him.

"Not like that," she said. "Slower." He let the hem of the shirt drop back into place, then took hold of it once more. This time he lifted it at a snail's pace. "A little faster than that," Alexis demanded.

"Do you want me to turn on some music so I can dance to it while I strip? Put on a real show for you?" Konner asked with a smile. "I have to warn you, I can't dance worth shit and I'll look like a nong."

"A what?" Alexis asked with a laugh.

"An idiot. Sorry, Australian slang."

"Oh. Well, we can't have that. It would ruin the sexy vibe you've got going on."

"Then I'll continue."

This time Konner pulled up his T-shirt at just the right speed. Alexis had time to savor every inch of bared flesh as he went. She licked her lips once he'd tossed his shirt aside. His chest was wide and defined with large muscles, same with his shoulders and arms. She noticed the black tattoo he had on the left side of his chest directly over his heart. The style was ancient Egyptian. It was a depiction of Anubis. He had a jackal's head. In one hand he held an ankh while in the other was a flail. The whole thing was inside a cartouche.

Alexis' attention was snagged downward as Konner reached for the button on his jeans. She heard the thudding of her quickened pulse pounding in her ears and she breathed at a faster rate. He slowly undid it, then yanked open his zipper. He took hold of the waistband and pushed the pants down before he stepped out of them and kicked them out of the way. Konner now wore only a pair of black boxer-briefs.

She ran her gaze up and down Konner's body. His legs were as muscular as his chest, shoulders, and arms. And she couldn't help noticing how his cock tented the front of his underwear. There was no mistaking he was a large man there as well.

The anticipation built as Konner placed a hand on the top of his boxer-briefs. He finally pushed them down, bending at the waist a bit as he did so. He stepped out of them and then sent the underwear in the same direction as his jeans.

Alexis swallowed at the sight of a nude Konner. He took her breath away. His cock stuck out straight from his body and was as thick and long as she'd pictured he'd be. She couldn't tear her gaze off him. No longer able to just sit there and not touch, she reached out and ran a hand down the side of his hip. His shaft jerked and a bead of pre-cum appeared on the very tip.

"I've stripped, now what do you want me to do?" Konner asked in a husky voice.

"Let me touch you however I wish." Alexis dragged her fingertips from his hip to his cock, trailing them down its length to the flared head, and rubbed the drop of moisture there into his skin.

Konner groaned. "I don't know how long I'll be able to let you continue to do that before I'll want you back under me—naked."

She looked up. He watched her intently. "Don't worry. I

won't be able to explore you for too long before I'll crave more than that."

Alexis shifted forward so she sat on the edge of the couch cushion and was closer to Konner. She reached up and smoothed her hands down the center of his chest to his washboard abs. It was kind of erotic to have a naked man in front of her while she was fully dressed.

She continued her downward journey until she came to his erection. This time she didn't just trail her fingers along it. She wrapped them around his cock in a tight fist and pumped. Konner let out a deep groan as he thrust his hips to match her strokes.

The sudden urge to taste settled inside her. Alexis had no intention of ignoring it. The thought of what she was about to do had wetness leaking into her panties and her pussy clenching with the need to be filled.

With a firm grip around the base of his cock, she opened her mouth and sucked him inside until he just about touched the back of her throat. She slid him almost all the way out before taking him back in. Konner's harsh breathing filled her ears as he rocked his hips. Alexis sucked harder, swirling her tongue around the head of his shaft with each stroke out.

All too soon, he pulled her away. "It's been a while for me," he said in a strained voice. "I don't want to push my luck." Konner took a step back, then helped Alexis to her feet. "Time for you to get naked so I can do some of the things I'm aching to do to you."

While he slowly undressed her, he whispered some of those things to her. Once he had her down to her panties and bra, Alexis was so turned-on her legs shook, and she didn't think they'd hold her up for much longer. Everywhere Konner's fingers brushed against her skin, he caused her to shiver with delight. Her nipples were taut beneath her bra. They ached to be sucked on as much as her pussy ached to have his cock inside it.

Konner kissed her, nibbling on her lips, before he pushed his tongue inside to duel with hers. While he did that, he unhooked her bra at her back. He pushed the straps down her arms, then gathered the material and threw it away. He left her mouth and sucked on her neck. His covered her breasts with his hands and brushed his thumbs across her nipples.

He pushed her panties down her hips until they fell around her ankles. Alexis stepped out of them and then kicked them aside. Now as naked as Konner, she pressed against him, glorying in the feel of being skin-to-skin with nothing between them. His cock nestled against her belly.

Konner wrapped an arm around her waist, then bent her slightly over it. His lips left her neck and made a trail to the tip of one of her breasts. He flicked her taut nipple with his tongue before he sucked it into his mouth. With each hard pull, Alexis felt a corresponding one deep inside her pussy.

After paying the same attention to her other breast, he lifted his head to look her in the eyes as he slid his free hand down her body to her slick opening. He moaned. "You're so wet." Konner pushed a finger inside her, then another, plunging them in and out. "And you're more than ready for me, but I have to taste you first."

He picked her up, then deposited her onto the couch. Konner kneeled before he pulled her closer so her butt was off the cushion. He held her in place as he bent his head between her spread thighs and licked her pussy. A low animal-like growl rumbled out of him, the sound vibrating against her sensitive skin. Alexis whimpered, wanting a deeper touch.

Konner licked and sucked, paying attention to her clit as he did so. Alexis' body coiled tighter, readying itself to orgasm. She arched her back, lifting her hips. He stiffened his tongue and speared it in and out of her. She panted, almost begged him to make her come.

Instead of pushing her over the edge into release, Konner lifted his head before he took her down to the carpeted floor. He settled between her legs, the head of his cock pressed to the opening of her body. With a couple of thrusts, he seated himself to the hilt. Alexis felt completely filled. She held on to his biceps as he lifted his upper body off her and plunged in and out of her pussy.

The only sounds in the room were their harsh breathing and their bodies coming together. Alexis lifted her hips to meet each of Konner's strokes. His cock grew harder as he strained against her.

Her body coiled tighter again. With him filling her, stretching her, it wasn't going to take much to make her come. He felt way too good. A half a dozen more thrusts and she was there. Alexis stiffened under Konner as her pussy rhythmically clutched his plunging cock. She moaned, intense pleasure flooding her entire body.

Konner rode her faster, harder. Alexis looked up at his face. He had his eyes closed as he strove for his own release. The large vein in his neck stood out, throbbing with his quickened heartbeat. He gritted his teeth, his upper lip curling only a tiny amount. She thought she saw what looked like a fang but forgot about it as he thrust one final time into her. He groaned as his cock pulsed deep inside her, giving her everything he had.

Once it was over, Konner collapsed on top of her, but he kept most of his weight on his bent arms. He nuzzled the side of her neck. They gasped for air. Alexis held him close. Sex with Konner had lived up to her expectations and then some.

Conner fought to catch his breath as his mind whirled. Sex with Alexis was spectacular, but something had been a little off. With him. Just before he'd reached his release, he'd had an almost overwhelming urge to bite her where her shoulder and neck met. His gums had burned, and his eyeteeth had become longer and sharper, like fangs, as they did when he was shifted in his half-human and half-jackal form. Granted, it had been a few years since the last time he'd been with a woman, but that had never happened before. He would have remembered it.

Figuring he must be getting heavy for Alexis, he rolled onto his back, taking her with him so she ended up sprawled on top of him. He pushed some of her hair behind her ear before he brought her lips down to his and kissed her tenderly. He wanted to make love to her again, but he was leery. After what had happened in the restaurant, and now this urge to bite, Konner needed whatever was going on figured out. Which meant he'd have to have a talk with Anubis.

Alexis lifted her head and smiled down at him. "I enjoyed that. I think I have to beat your ass at video games more often, especially if this is what I get for winning every time."

He chuckled. "Losing to you was no hardship. I think I got the reward as much as you did."

"Then maybe we should do it again."

"I'd like that, but I have to go hunting soon."

Alexis' brows drew together. "Hunting? What do you mean by that?"

Konner mentally kicked himself at his slip. He was so used to not having to guard what he thought and said, basically because he usually kept himself secluded. "I didn't mean hunting, hunting. It's sort of what I think my job is all about. I hunt down individuals who need to face up to their crimes."

"You're a police officer?"

"No. I work for myself."

"So, you're a bounty hunter?"

"I guess that would be the closest thing to describe what I do."

"It's a Saturday. Can't you take the night off?" Alexis drew circles around Anubis' mark on his chest with the tip of her finger. "I want to spend the night with you."

Konner bit back a groan. He wanted nothing more than to carry Alexis upstairs to his bedroom and make love to her for the rest of the night, but he didn't think that would be wise. Not until he'd talked to Anubis.

"Sorry, I can't get out of it. I want to see you tomorrow, though. You can spend the night then. I won't be working." Konner was sure once he had his chat with the god of the underworld he'd be all fixed up. Anubis would have to know what was up with Konner, and how to fix it.

Alexis sighed dramatically. "If I have to wait until then to have you again, I think I can manage it. What time do you have to start work?"

"In a few hours."

She rolled off him before she stood to gather her clothes. "In that case, there's enough time for us to have another match or two on that video game we played. Just let me freshen up in the washroom, then I'll come back and see if I can beat you again."

Konner sat up and chuckled. "All right. And the washroom is over there." He pointed to one of the closed doors.

"I won't be too long," Alexis said as she turned away and headed in the direction he'd indicated.

He watched her go, his gaze lingering on her backside. Once she disappeared into the washroom, he smiled as he stood to get dressed. At least dating Alexis, he wouldn't have to worry about her complaining about him playing video games too much. He realized he was thinking of her in the long-term. It wasn't all that surprising. They did get along and seemed to have a lot of the same interests. Plus, he wanted her in his life. The sense of not being happy, feeling alone mostly, that had plagued him more times than he liked to think about had seemed to have disappeared while he was around her.

Once she returned, they spent a little over an hour playing a video game. Having only ever played single player, it was nice to go against someone else. And Alexis turned out to be just as competitive as he. When he got ahead of her at one point in the game by using a sneaky tactic, she actually smacked him in the arm a few times for it.

Konner drove Alexis home shortly before it was dark. He parked in her driveway and then kissed her as if it would have to last him hours, which it did. It had to tide him over until the next day. He waited until she'd unlocked her front door and turned back to wave at him before he backed out of the drive and onto the street. She waved again as he drove away.

Back at his house, Konner headed straight for Anubis' temple. He'd get whatever was wrong with him sorted, then he'd go hunting evildoers for the rest of the night. He opened the door to the room and walked to the altar.

"Anubis?"

Yes, Konner.

The god's voice filled his mind. "I'm about to go hunting, but I need you to fix me first."

Fix you? How?

"Well, it's two things, actually. The first one is a little more personal than the other." He paused as he tried to think of the best way to tell Anubis. "I found a woman I'm going to date. Don't worry, I won't tell her what I am. Now here is the problem. While I was intimate with her, just before I reached completion, I had this need to bite her where her shoulder and neck meet. I didn't give in to it, but if it happens again, it'll be problematic. I don't want Alexis to think I make a habit of sinking my teeth into women while I have them in bed."

Anubis chuckled. *No, you wouldn't want that. You have nothing to worry about. The urge to bite her is the sign that she's your mate. Once you do, she'll be as immortal as you. A bond will form between you. She'll be tied to your life force.*

"My mate?" His lips spread into a large smile. "So I'll no longer have to be alone. Alexis will be mine forever?"

Yes. You aren't the first of my warriors to find his mate.

"I just have to give in to the urge and bite her and she'll be my mate?"

Correct, but before you do, you should give her the chance to accept you as hers. You'll have to tell her what you are, what it means to be one of my warriors.

"That could prove to be a tad difficult. I've never told a mortal what I am. I know I don't want to scare Alexis off."

She might have a hard time accepting it at first, but she should come around. She has to have feelings for you as you do for her or she wouldn't be the one meant for you. Now what is the second thing you need me to fix?

"Something strange happened to me while I was out with Alexis. I was just sitting there eating my meal when I got a sudden headache. It was unlike any I've ever had. It didn't last very long, but while I had it, my eyes shifted to that of a jackal's. I also had claws and fur surface, then disappear. Luckily, I managed to get to the men's room before that happened."

Now that concerns me, Anubis said. *Something like that happened to another of my warriors. It eventually had him completely shifting without an evildoer nearby, and he didn't return to his human form until the next morning.*

"You mean I could shift at any time, any place?"

Afraid so. And it's caused by a spell used by one of the demons who has escaped the underworld. I think one of them has found you. The only way for me to be sure is to search for it inside you or for signs of it having been active.

Konner remembered Anubis telling him about the demons a little while ago. He'd hoped he wouldn't become a target for one of them, but obviously that wasn't the case, it would seem.

"Go ahead and do it," he said.

He felt Anubis' presence moving inside him. It wasn't uncomfortable. It just was a little strange. A few seconds later, the sensation stopped, and Anubis spoke again.

I found a small trace of that spell. It was definitely used by a demon. It was created with dark magic. Right now, you're fine, but the demon can use it at any time and you won't know about it until it's too late. This is just the first step of the demon acting against you. He doesn't have to be in your presence to cast it.

Konner let out a frustrated sigh. Great. He now had a demon to deal with and a mate to win over so he could have his happily ever after. "How do I take care of the demon?"

You must send him to me in the underworld to be judged. Then he won't be able to return to the mortal realm.

"Will my gold dagger work on him?"

No, but you'll be able to will the weapon to you that can

when the time comes.

"Maybe I shouldn't see Alexis again until I've sent the demon to the underworld."

The creature could use her to get to you if he finds out about her, but there's only a slim chance that he will. He'll be more focused on you now that he's found you. You can stay with your mate.

"Then I'd better find the demon."

He'll only reveal himself to you once he feels he has the upper hand. He might play with you a bit before he goes on the strike.

"Terrific. It sounds as if I'm going to be in store for a lot of fun when it comes to this demon."

I have full confidence you'll defeat the creature and keep your mate safe. You are one of my warriors. You have all you need to send a demon back to the underworld.

With that, Konner felt Anubis' presence fade away. Konner left the temple and headed out for a night of hunting evildoers. He had a lot to think about when it came to Alexis now that he knew what she was to him. He couldn't just spring what he was on her, especially not this early in their relationship. He needed her to get to know him as a man first before he told her he was an immortal warrior to an ancient Egyptian god. He'd have to act the part of a normal boyfriend, go out on dates with her, and when he thought she was ready for it, he'd take her out for a romantic meal, bring her back to his place, and tell her everything.

* * * *

Considering it wasn't as late as she'd thought it'd be when she came home, Alexis decided she'd better call Sabrina and tell her friend she was fine. And that Konner hadn't turned out to be an axe murderer and killed her in a gutter somewhere.

Sabrina didn't even say hi after she picked up. She just

started talking. "Thank God you're okay. I was worried."

"I told you Konner was a great guy. He even brought me home early. Well, he had to go to work or I would have stayed at his place longer, if not the whole night."

"You slept with him, didn't you?"

A smile played across Alexis' lips. "Yes, I sure did."

"And from the way you sound so satisfied, I take it he rocked your world."

Alexis laughed. "You could say that. Not only is Konner handsome, a gentleman, and a god in bed, he's also well-to-do. You should see his place. It's huge. He has a media room down in his basement set up for gaming."

Sabrina groaned. "God, he must be perfect for you if he's a gamer too. And I'm sure the two of you played some games while on your date."

"Yes, we did, after we got back from seeing a concert at Millennium Park. And the prize I got for beating him the first time we played was the best one I've ever received. That's when Konner rocked my world."

"So, when do I get to meet this sex god?"

"Soon, I guess. I'm seeing him again tomorrow. He doesn't have to work that night so we should be able to spend more time together."

"What does he do?"

"He's some kind of bounty hunter."

"He must be pretty tough to do a job like that. It can't be an easy one."

"Konner is definitely built for it. And he comes across as being able to handle himself in any situation, but he isn't overbearing or anything. He's perfect to be with. So far, I haven't found anything wrong with him."

Sabrina sighed. "You sound as if you've already started to fall for him."

Alexis had to think about that. Was she starting to have strong feelings for Konner? After their date, she had high hopes she'd be able to have an ongoing relationship with him that maybe would turn into something serious and permanent. He not only rocked her world, she felt as if she was meant to be with him. She already missed him, which was a new one for her when it came to the early days of a relationship. He was the first man she'd ever dated from whom she didn't have to hide her computer geekiness. Even though she'd told him she wasn't a computer geek, she knew she was. She spent way too much time on one not to be.

"Maybe I am," she said.

"Just don't fall too fast or too hard. You still have to get to know him better."

"You know me. I'm not the type to fall in love at first sight. I might take more chances with guys than you do, but that doesn't mean I give my heart to just anyone."

"I know. Sometimes I wish I wasn't so unsure of myself when it comes to men."

"You'll find the right guy one day who'll be able to look past that and get you to come out of your shell. Maybe I should ask Konner if he can set you up on a blind date with one of his bounty hunter friends."

"Don't you dare," Sabrina said in an anxious voice.

"Why not? You were the one who set me up on that disastrous date with your cousin. You owe me one."

"You're never going to let me live that one down, are you?"

Alexis chuckled. "Maybe and maybe not. Anyway, I'm going to go here. I just thought I'd call so you'd stop worrying."

"I'll talk to you later. I hope you have a good time with Konner tomorrow."

"I'm sure I will. Bye."

Alexis ended the call and then put the cordless back on its base. She went upstairs to her bedroom and put on her pajamas. She'd pop a big bowl of popcorn, watch one of her DVDs, and drink one of the beers she had in her fridge.

Usually, she'd do some work, but not this time. She'd only end up daydreaming about Konner and remembering what it was like to be in his arms.

CHAPTER FIVE

Alexis had been all set to take the entire weekend off from doing any work when she'd awoken the next morning. Fate, or should she say a client, figured differently. After turning on her computer, she'd found a frantic email from one of her best customers. Her client had thought to make some minor changes to her business' website herself. When she couldn't get them to work, she'd only ended up making an even bigger mess. Now she wanted Alexis to fix what she'd done, then do the changes she'd tried to do in the first place.

The fixing was the easy part. The changes ended up not being as minor as the client had first said. They were something that would take most of a day since they would end up changing the layout of the entire website and adding new content.

Alexis couldn't tell her client to wait until Monday. The woman would lose a lot of business, and she was one of Alexis' best-paying customers. In the end, she promised she'd have everything done by late afternoon. Now she had no idea what to do about Konner. She didn't want to cancel their date.

She'd just sat to get to work when the phone rang. Alexis had a feeling it was Konner calling. And once she looked at the call display, she saw she was correct. She dreaded having to tell him she couldn't go to his place.

"Hey, Konner," she said after she answered the call.

"How's it going?"

Alexis let out a little sigh. "Not good, I'm afraid."

"I hope you aren't canceling our date."

"I don't want to, but something came up with one of my clients and I have to finish the work by late this afternoon. I probably won't even have time for lunch."

"What if I come to your place? I can bring you something to eat. I'll even feed it to you so you can continue working."

Having Konner feed her would give her naughty ideas. "Are you sure? I'm going to be busy for hours, and you'll be stuck here doing nothing. You'll probably get bored. I'd feel bad."

"Alexis, I wouldn't have asked to come over if I thought I couldn't handle you working. I want to see you again. If it'll make you happy, I'll bring one of my systems with me and some games to keep me occupied. When you're done, we can spend what's left of the day together."

It seemed as if Konner was as anxious to see her as she was to see him. What he'd suggested just put him on a higher ranking than any other guy she'd dated. None of her other boyfriends would have even thought of coming over to sit and wait for her to be done working. They would have just canceled their date.

"Okay, you can come over, and bring your system with you. I'll try to be as quick as I can."

"Take as much time as you need. I'll be over in a half hour."

"See you then."

Alexis hung up and turned her attention to her desktop monitor. She soon got caught up in her work and jumped when the doorbell rang. She looked at the time on her computer and was surprised to see the half hour had already gone by.

She hurried out of the bedroom she'd set up as her office and rushed to the front door. Alexis opened it to find Konner on the other side. He held out a bag of something that smelled really good.

"Here, take this," he said. "I have to get my system out of the car."

She took the bag, then waited for him to return. Once he did, Konner stepped inside. Alexis closed the door behind him. "You can set your system up in the living room. I don't have as huge a television as you, but it's LED."

"That's fine."

She went to lead him to the living room when he stopped her.

"Hold on a minute. I forgot to do something."

Konner came closer and tucked the box he carried under one arm. With his other, he pulled her close and took her lips in a kiss that had Alexis curling her toes. Her whole body seemed to go up in flames as he claimed her mouth. He was the first one to pull away.

"I needed that," he said with a crooked grin.

"So did I. Now I'm going to be distracted by it while I'm trying to work."

"Then I won't do it again until you're done."

She groaned. "Sure, torture me. Come on. You can put your system in the living room, then I'll get back to work."

"Do you need me to feed you?"

She shook her head. "No, I'd better do it. If I let you, I know for sure I'll get nothing done. What did you get? It smells good."

"I picked up some English-style fish and chips. Is that all right?"

"I love fish and chips, and it will be easy to eat while I'm in front of the computer."

After Konner had hooked up his system to the TV and had made himself comfortable on the couch, Alexis took one of the Styrofoam containers of food to her office. She ate the fish and chips while she worked one-handed on the keyboard of her computer.

Twenty minutes later, Konner came into the room and took the empty food container from her. He only gave her a kiss on the top of her head before he left her alone again.

As she continued to work, from time to time, Alexis could hear the game Konner played. Also, him swearing at it when he ended up getting killed. She chuckled at that. She had to admit she'd done enough swearing of her own over a game.

The hours seemed to pass quickly as Alexis immersed herself in her work, getting lost in computer codes. She'd just finished coding one last section of the website and had tested it to make sure it worked when Konner called out to her from the living room.

"Are you almost done?" he asked.

"Yes," she called back. "I have to email the client to tell her everything is up and running again, then I'm all yours." Alexis typed up a short email and then sent it off to the customer. "Done," she said quietly.

"Good. Now I can really distract you."

She spun around on her steno chair and found Konner standing just inside the room without a stitch of clothes on. He was fully aroused, his cock sticking out straight from his body. Alexis ate him up with her gaze as her pussy went instantly wet.

*

Konner breathed in Alexis' arousal as it reached his sensitive nose, which made his dick grow even harder.

While he'd waited for her to finish her work, he'd had a hard time giving the game he played his full attention. He'd kept thinking of all the things he wanted to do to her once she came out of her office, which caused an erection that refused to go away. He'd died in the game more than a few times from inattention.

By the time Alexis had said she was almost done when he'd asked, Konner decided he had to have her. He'd waited long enough to make love to her again, and he desperately craved her touch now that he knew she was his mate. So he'd stripped out of his clothes to show her exactly what he intended to do to her once he reached her office.

Alexis continued to run her hot gaze over his body, seeming to take in every inch of him, lingering longer on his hard cock. It jerked in anticipation of her touch. He walked toward her, letting his hunger and need fill his eyes when she met his gaze.

She licked her lips as if they'd suddenly gone dry. Konner remembered what they felt like wrapped around his cock. Alexis stood once he was in front of her. "You can most definitely distract me now," she said in a voice gone husky with desire.

"I thought you wouldn't have any complaints."

"Nope, I have none, but I just have one small suggestion to make."

"Which is?"

"There's no bed in here. Let's move to my bedroom. It's just at the end of the hall."

"An excellent suggestion."

Konner claimed her mouth before he picked Alexis up off her feet. He turned and walked with her out of the room, heading for her bedroom. His dick rubbed against her jean-clad pussy with every step he took since she'd put her legs around his waist. She really drove him wild when she ground against him. Small mewling sounds left her as she kissed him hungrily. She had him wound so tight he almost bumped her head on the doorframe as he entered her room.

He practically stumbled to her bed. He climbed onto the mattress and shifted until he kneeled in the center of it with Alexis still in his arms. He tried to release her, but she clung to him. He had to pry her legs from around his waist and position her so she was on her knees as he was. He needed to get her naked, to have her luscious body against his with no barriers. He tugged at her clothes.

Once Alexis realized what he tried to do, she broke their kiss and helped him undress her. Now that she was as naked as he, Konner ran his gaze over her shapely curves, his hands following in the same path. Her breathing quickened as a slight blush appeared on her cheeks and upper chest. Her nipples were taut, just begging for his mouth.

Konner put his arm around Alexis' waist and took her down to the bed. He settled at her side and shifted lower until he was even with one of her breasts. He used the tip of his finger to circle the nipple, causing it to tighten even more. He cupped the mound and lifted it to his mouth to brush his lips back and forth across it. She moaned and arched her back, demanding more.

He bit gently on the tight peak before he sucked it inside his mouth. Alexis shoved her hands into his hair to hold him to her. Her hips lifted and retreated as she squirmed on the bed. He took his time, keeping his focus on her breasts and nothing else. Konner released the nipple to suck on the other.

"Konner," Alexis panted. "Touch more of me."

He gave one last suck before he let it go. "Oh, I will," he said against her skin. "I'm in no hurry here."

She yanked on his hair. "You might not be, but I don't want to wait."

He chuckled as he shifted lower on her body, licking

the underside of each breast. Konner kissed a path down the center of her stomach to her bellybutton. As he swirled his tongue inside it, he used his thigh to push her legs farther apart before he settled between them.

He spread her pussy lips and licked her from bottom to top. Konner set to work feasting on her, licking and sucking. Alexis moaned as she rode his mouth. He switched his attention to her clit. He sucked on it as he pushed two fingers inside her and stroked them in and out. Her inner walls closed around them, squeezing. She panted his name, her hands once again fisting in his hair to hold him exactly where she wanted him.

Konner continued to work Alexis, pushing her closer and closer to her release. He added a third finger and plunged it, along with the others, harder and faster into her pussy as he stimulated her clit using his mouth. She arched her hips and let out a whimpered moan. Her inner walls grasped his fingers as she came.

After the last flutter, Konner rose from between her legs and sheathed his cock balls-deep inside her with one thrust. He felt an aftershock ripple through her pussy along his shaft. He pumped his hips, taking her in long, hard strokes. Waves of pleasure surged through him as he sank into her.

His balls drew up closer to his body. Afraid he wouldn't be able to resist the urge to bite Alexis as the need to come built, Konner held her close and rolled, taking her with him. His cock stayed buried inside her pussy.

She sat up on him and placed her hands on his chest. Alexis rose onto her knees until he was almost free of her body before she sank on him. She continued to ride him with long, slow strokes. He was seated deeper than he'd been in the other position. He palmed her breasts, tugging on the nipples. She sat higher and placed her hands over top his. She moaned, riding him fast, her inner muscles gripping his cock.

As Konner's release edged nearer, his eyeteeth shifted to fangs and the urge to bite Alexis rose inside him. This time it felt stronger than the last. He clenched his jaw against it and forced himself to stay on his back instead of lifting to a seated position so he could get at the spot where her shoulder and neck met. He thrust up into her as she pushed down on him, matching each of his strokes.

Her motions became jerky, then Alexis let out a groan with her orgasm. It rippled along Konner's cock, clutching him in a tight fist, which was all he needed to send him into his own climax. As soon as he came, his teeth returned to normal and the urge to sink them into Alexis passed. He groaned out a low growl as his dick pulsed inside her pussy, filling her with his cum.

Alexis bent at the waist and settled against Konner's chest. Her hot breath caressed his skin. He put an arm around her back as he waited for his heart to beat at a slower rate and he was able to breathe without panting. His cock softened and slipped free of her body.

"That was pretty intense," Alexis said once she breathed normally.

"Yeah, it was," he said with a smile before he kissed her forehead.

She rearranged her legs so they ended up tangled with his and looked at him. "I could get addicted to this. To you."

He brushed a lock of hair behind her ear. "The feeling is mutual. It has been a long time since I've wanted a relationship. I want more than a few dates with you, Alexis."

She gave him a smile that lit up her face. "I'd hoped you'd want something a little more permanent. I want this to work."

"That's what I want as well. So let's put it on record that from here on out we don't date other people."

"It's a deal," she said with a small laugh. "I guess that means we're going steady now."

"Or I'm courting you with the hopes of marriage down the road." He wiggled his brows.

Alexis chuckled. "Now that sounds really old-fashioned. I thought 'going steady' was bad enough since it makes me think of us as a pair of teenagers."

"Well, we most definitely aren't that. I can assure you, you come across as an adult woman, in all ways." He reached down and grabbed her ass.

"I'm glad you think so. I know you're no teenage boy. If you had been, the sex would have been over before it had even started."

Konner laughed. "No, I promise you I haven't had that happen to me in a very long time."

Alexis propped herself up on her bent elbow and looked down at him. "Lunchtime was a while ago and it's getting close to dinner. Why don't I make us something to eat since you already brought me food?"

"Okay. I'm not exactly a good cook so having someone else make a meal for me is a treat."

"Then I'd better get started."

Alexis pushed away before she slid off the bed. Konner followed her with his gaze as she picked up her clothes and then headed out of the room. He heard a door shut down the hall and figured she'd gone to use the bathroom.

Shortly after the toilet flushed, Alexis returned to the room and threw his clothes onto the bed. "I thought you'd want these from the living room," she said with a wink. She left again.

Konner took his time getting dressed as he listened to Alexis clanging around in the kitchen. He was going to have to tell her very soon what she meant to him. At least he didn't have to worry about her thinking about dating other men.

* * * *

The next morning, Alexis woke up before Konner. He lay on his side, facing her with an arm under his pillow and the other around her waist. He quietly snored into her ear. She smiled. It hadn't taken much to get him to stay overnight. And she really liked waking up next to him.

After she'd made them an easy dinner of barbequed steaks done on the gas grill outside on her back deck and French fries cooked in the oven, they'd gone into the living room to watch some TV. They'd also talked. She'd told him a lot about her life. He'd kept much of the conversation on her by asking questions. He'd told her some of his life in Australia but not in a whole lot of detail. She got the sense he really didn't want to talk much about it. Thinking he must have a good reason, she didn't push.

They'd eventually ended up in bed again. Each time she made love to Konner, Alexis fell for him harder. And now that they were going to date exclusively, she really did hope their relationship would progress to the point where marriage could be a good possibility.

Alexis slowly turned onto her side so she faced Konner. He didn't awaken. She reached out and touched the tattoo on his chest. It was so very ancient-Egyptian-looking. She shifted her gaze to the rest of his upper body. She could spend hours learning it with her lips and tongue, along with every inch of him.

She lifted the sheets a little and stared at the lower half of him. Yup, Konner was definitely drool-worthy. Alexis dropped her gaze to his cock and took her bottom lip between her teeth when she saw it twitch and harden a bit. She raised her gaze to find him awake and watching her.

He took hold of the sheets and flung them off them. "No need to have these in the way," he said with a crooked grin.

Alexis titled her head up as he gave her a kiss. Once he

pulled away, she said, "Good morning. Did you have a good sleep?"

"Yes, I did."

Konner leaned against her until she rolled onto her back. He settled on top of her with his hips between her spread thighs. His fully engorged cock pressed against her pussy. She lifted a leg and rubbed her foot up and down the back of one of his thighs. She grew wet, wanting his erection deep inside her.

She wrapped a hand around the back of his neck and exerted some pressure to have him bring his lips to hers. He kissed her thoroughly, his tongue dueling with hers. It didn't take long to have passion flaring hotly between them. She had a feeling it would always be like this. She craved his touch, needed it almost as much as the air she breathed.

"Oh, my goodness."

Alexis stiffened, and her eyes snapped open at the sound of the feminine voice filled with surprised shock. It couldn't be. Not now. Not while she was in such an intimate embrace. She pushed at Konner until he rolled off her. She quickly yanked the covers over them.

"Mother?" Alexis asked as she sat up with a sheet held to her breasts. "What are you doing here?"

Her mom stood in the open doorway, a hand partially covering her eyes. "Your father and I thought we'd surprise you for your birthday."

"It isn't until next week."

"I know. We're staying in Chicago for two weeks. As I said, we wanted to surprise you. When we found the door locked, we let ourselves in since we still have a key. I thought you might be sleeping so I left your father in the living room and came here to wake you. I wouldn't have done it if I hadn't thought you'd be alone or that I'd find you in the middle of…" Her mom's words trailed away. "Every time we've talked you said you weren't seeing anyone."

"What's taking so long in here?" her father asked as he came to stand next to her mother. Once he took in the scene, he said, "Oh."

Alexis groaned. "Dad, can you please take Mom and go back to the living room?"

"Ah, sure. I guess this whole surprise thing wasn't such a great idea, after all." He looked at her mom. "Let's go." He tugged his wife away from the doorway as he backed up.

"You could at least shut the door," Alexis called.

Her father returned and did as she'd requested. Once they were safely closed inside the room, Alexis turned to Konner. "I'm sorry. I had no idea they were coming."

Konner grinned. "No need to apologize. I know you weren't expecting them. Your mom said it was supposed to be a surprise."

Alexis put her head in her hand and shook it. "God, it's embarrassing." Never in a million years did she think something like that would happen.

Konner sat up and laughed. "At least we weren't close to the end and had to stop."

She smacked his arm. "I'm glad you find this amusing because I don't. I know my mom got a good eyeful, especially of you. She might have had her hand covering her eyes a little, but I know for a fact she looked. And I really wanted my mother to see my boyfriend's bare ass." She said the last part in a sarcastic tone.

"Being married and all, I'm sure she has seen a male backside many times."

Alexis hit him again. "I don't need the reminder that my parents have sex, thank you very much. We'd better get dressed and go to them before my mom comes back to see what's taking so long." She let the sheet go and slid off the bed before she went to her dresser to get some clothes.

Konner stayed on the bed. "So, it's your birthday next

week?"

"Yes. A week from this Wednesday I'll turn twenty-seven," she said absentmindedly as she put on a pair of panties and a bra. "Konner, please get out of bed."

He chuckled. "All right, I'm moving."

Konner slid off the mattress and stood in all his naked glory. Alexis had a hard time keeping her gaze off him as she finished dressing. She could understand why her mom would look—he had a body any woman would dream about—but the idea of her mother checking him out just made Alexis feel weirded out.

"I'd better do something special for your birthday then," Konner continued as he gathered his clothes.

"If you do, it'll have to be before or after the actual day. My mom claims my birthday as her right to be with me since it's a milestone for her as much as me, her having to go through the birthing process to bring me into the world. And believe me, there will be no budging her from any plans she has then."

"Okay, I'll keep that in mind."

Seeing Konner was now dressed, Alexis sighed. "Time to face my parents. This should be fun," she said with sarcasm in her voice.

CHAPTER SIX

Konner followed Alexis out of the bedroom. Having her mother walking in on them wasn't as big a deal to him as it was to Alexis. In some ways, he thought it was kind of funny, especially how she had reacted. She'd acted like a teenager getting caught having sex for the first time. And it really didn't bother him if her mother had looked at him. Considering his age, he *was* the elder of the two of them so it wasn't an older woman checking out a much younger man.

Alexis' parents weren't in the living room but in the kitchen. Her mother moved around the room, making what looked like breakfast. Her father stood at the coffeemaker getting it ready to brew. It made sense that they'd make themselves at home since the house had been theirs for so many years before they'd moved to Florida. Konner looked at Alexis to see what her reaction was to her parents taking over her kitchen. She seemed to take in the scene and sighed. He followed her to the round table when she sat on one of the chairs.

Her mom turned from the stove and smiled at them. "Good, you're here. I'm going to make pancakes from scratch, not that awful stuff in a box." She came to stand next to the table, closer to Konner. "As you probably already figured out, we're Alexis' parents. I'm Claudia and my husband is Dean."

"I'm Konner," he said in return.

"Oh, you're Australian. It's nice to meet you, Konner. Alexis never told us she was seeing someone."

He heard Alexis quietly groan beside him. "Yes, I am. We recently started dating," he replied.

"So, I guess that expensive-looking car outside in the driveway is yours?"

Alexis broke into the conversation before he could answer. "Yes, it is, Mom. I would have thought seeing it would have clued you in to the fact that I wasn't alone."

Claudia shrugged. "I thought maybe you had it as a loaner or something. I never would have guessed it belonged to your new boyfriend. That would be the last thing I thought of."

"Gee, thanks. Make me sound as if I'm a loser when it comes to men."

Her mother shook her head. "I didn't mean it that way. It's just been a while since you've really dated."

"Don't forget about the pancakes," Dean said as he joined them at the table.

"Oh yes," Claudia said as she went back to the stove.

"Konner." Alexis' dad held out his hand.

Konner shook it. "Dean."

Dean sat on the chair on the other side of Alexis. He looked at his daughter. "I promise no more surprises like this. I wasn't thrilled with the idea, but your mother insisted. You know what she can be like when it comes to your birthday."

"It's okay, Dad," Alexis said.

"I heard that," Claudia said. "And I'm not *that* bad

when it comes to Alexis' birthday."

Alexis and her father shared a look that said otherwise. Konner smiled. That was what he'd been missing since he'd become one of Anubis' warriors, having a family to share inside jokes with. To have a mother to fuss over him when it was his birthday. His parents and two siblings were a long time in their graves. They'd all been very close. It had hit his mother the hardest when he had made the decision to sign up to fight in the war. She'd been so afraid she'd lose him. In the end, she had, but not to death as she would have figured. He sometimes still wondered what his family had thought had happened to him. To them, it would have seemed as if he had just dropped off the face of the earth to never be heard from again.

Now he had Alexis to consider as his family since she was his mate. Each time they'd made love the night before, he'd found it more than a struggle not to bite her. The urge rode him hard, but it was his conscience he had to fight with more. He *wanted* to take that step that would permanently tie her to him. In some ways, he wanted to take the choice from her and just make her his, but he wouldn't do that. He was a man of his word and he'd promised Anubis he wouldn't force her to accept Konner as her mate.

It wasn't long before Claudia had what looked close to a mountain of pancakes piled on a serving plate set in the middle of the table. She sat next to her husband, and they all helped themselves to the food. The conversation flowed easily as they ate. There was no mistaking that Alexis was close to her parents. Konner found he liked the couple. They reminded him a lot of his parents.

Once breakfast was over, Alexis helped her mom with the washing up while Konner went into the living room with her father. They sat on the couch. Dean picked up the TV's remote and turned it on. He switched channels until he stopped on a documentary that compared the First to the Second World War. Konner stiffened as memories of his time during the First World War rose to the surface of his mind. For the first couple of years after becoming a warrior of Anubis, he'd woken up every night with nightmares of what he'd gone through. They now called it post-traumatic stress disorder and soldiers were treated for it, but back in his day, men like him had no name for it and suffered through it alone.

The documentary came to a section about Gallipoli. Konner couldn't hold back a little growl as they showed pictures of the men in the trenches. He remembered all too well what it was like living in them. The filth, the stench of disease, and the wounded and dying, who weren't cleared away as they should have been.

Dean turned to look at him. "Are you all right?"

"Yeah. It's the subject matter that bothers me," he said, barely holding back another growl as he motioned to the television. "Gallipoli was a bloody useless eight months. It turned out to be a disaster. A lot of Australian and New Zealand troops either lost their lives or were wounded. Their British officers were the ones to send most of them out of the trenches against the Turks to their deaths. It was a complete waste of time and men. The officers were incompetent and had disregard for the wounded from poorly planned attacks." Konner's lip snarled as he said the last words.

"You're pretty passionate about it. Someone would think you were there and lived through it."

Konner reined back the emotions that surged through him. He had to remember Dean didn't know Konner *had* barely survived it. He cleared his throat. "More than quite a few of my countrymen lost their lives there. I've done a lot of research into Gallipoli and the First World War."

"So you're a bit of a history buff, huh?"

"In some ways. It can be a touchy subject for me."

"Then I'll turn the channel," Dean said with a smile.

"No point getting you all worked up. Besides, I think the girls will be finished in the kitchen soon."

No longer confronted with the images from his past, the tension drained from his body. Alexis' father had settled on a sports channel and watched all the updated scores for various teams. Konner barely paid it any attention. He wasn't a sports fan.

Alexis and her mother came into the living room shortly after. Claudia sat in the armchair kitty-corner to the couch while Alexis took a seat on the sofa beside Konner. He had hoped to see her again in the latter part of the day after she finished working and before he had to go out on a night of hunting, but he didn't think that would happen with her parents there.

Making the decision that it would be the best thing to leave so Alexis could visit with her parents without him hanging around, Konner stood. "I should go," he said, then looked at Claudia. "Thanks for making me breakfast. And it was nice meeting you both." He turned to Alexis. "Will you walk me out?"

"Sure," she said.

Once they were out of sight of her parents, Konner tugged Alexis into his arms and kissed her. They were breathing hard when he pulled away. "I guess I won't be seeing you later."

She gave him a look that confirmed it. "Sorry. It's not as if I don't want to. My mom will expect me to stick around."

"I know," he said, enjoying the feel of Alexis still pressed against him as she played with the back of his hair.

"It might be a couple of days."

"I understand. I'll miss you, though."

"And I'll miss you." Alexis brushed her lips across his. "I promise I'll be able to get away from them in a few days. I know I'll need a break by then. You can still call me, and you have my cell phone number so you can text too."

He grinned. "I'll call and text."

Konner gave Alexis one last kiss, then let himself out of the house. He had to walk by the living room window to get to his car. He looked at it and found Claudia standing there, waving at him. He waved back with a chuckle. He kind of had his doubts that Alexis would be able to get away from her mom anytime soon.

* * * *

Her mother was driving Alexis nuts. She hadn't lived under the same roof with her parents for quite some time. In the two days since they'd arrived from Florida, her mom had cleaned the house from top to bottom, rearranged all the things in the kitchen cupboards so Alexis could no longer find anything, and had gone food shopping for her. Alexis was starting to feel like a little kid again and didn't like it at all.

Then there was the fact that she missed Konner dreadfully. He was never far from her mind. If absence made the heart grow fonder, it sure as hell was the case with her. She felt as if she were a girl with her first crush. Or a woman who'd fallen in love for the very first time.

Alexis had the feeling it was the latter of the two. Her feelings had never been this strong for a guy before. Already she couldn't picture what her life would be like without Konner in it. And she was pretty sure he felt the same way about her. He called her at least three times a day and texted her about ten. Some of those texts were so naughty she had to go to her bedroom to read them so her mother wouldn't look over her shoulder, asking her what he had said.

He even called her when he was doing his job. Once he cut the conversation short to go after one of the bad guys. Alexis had been worried he'd gotten hurt since he'd hissed in what sounded like pain before he'd said he had to go. Konner had put her mind to rest an hour later when he'd called back and assured her he was fine.

Alexis blinked and realized she'd been lost in thought again when she was supposed to be doing work on her computer. She'd been working on the same line of code for at least a half hour and really hadn't done much of anything at that. God, she had it bad for Konner.

At the sound of her mother clearing her throat, Alexis spun her steno chair around to see she stood in the open doorway of her office. "Is there something you wanted, Mom?"

Her mother nodded and walked to Alexis. "Yes, there is. I want you to pack an overnight bag and leave."

She scowled. "What?"

"You heard me. It hasn't escaped my notice that you've been walking around here moping. I can tell you miss Konner, and that it's your father and I who are keeping you from him. So I want you to pack a change of clothes and sleep at his place. I know he works nights, but it's not quite lunchtime now so you should have plenty of time to be with him before he does have to go."

"Are you sure?" Alexis asked. "You and Dad came here to visit me. I feel as if I should spend my free time with the both of you. And I really should get some work done."

Her mom arched a brow. "Each time I've walked by this room this morning, I've seen you staring off into space. I doubt you're getting much accomplished."

Alexis grinned. "I guess I'm a little distracted. I can't seem to stop thinking about Konner." Her mother stepped closer and kissed Alexis on the forehead. "What was that for?" she asked.

"My little girl has finally fallen in love."

"I don't know, Mom. It's still so soon."

"Nonsense. Your father and I knew we loved each other very early on in our relationship. We hadn't been dating a year when we were married. When it's right, it's right. There's no point in fighting it. And the way I saw Konner when he was with you, he feels it too. Plus, the man has a very fine ass. Don't tell your father I said that," her mom said with a wink.

"Mom!" Alexis said as she laughed. "You weren't supposed to be checking out my boyfriend's butt."

"I only looked a little. It was just out there. What do you expect?"

Alexis laughed even harder. Once she brought herself back under control, she said, "I really shouldn't find this funny. I should be embarrassed as all hell."

Her mom smiled. "It's not as if you're a child. We're adults. Now go to Konner. I'm officially kicking you out of the house until tomorrow."

Alexis stood, then kissed her mother on the cheek. "Thanks, Mom. I love you."

"I know you do. And I love you. Tell Konner I expect him to come over for the day of your birthday to celebrate with us."

"I will."

Alexis saved what she'd been trying to work on before she shut down her computer. Not wanting to take the time to call Konner to tell him she was on her way, she quickly threw a change of clothes into an athletic bag. Before she left, she gave her dad and mom a kiss and told them she'd see them tomorrow.

During the drive to Konner's place, Alexis hoped he'd be at home. She hadn't spoken to him yet today. Given how late he worked at night, she'd made it a habit not to call before noontime in case he was still sleeping. By the time she'd reach his house, it would be close to that.

Her heart beat faster as she pulled into his driveway, then parked in front of the detached garage. She hauled the athletic bag out of the passenger seat before she walked at a fast clip to Konner's front door. Alexis rang the bell and impatiently waited for him to answer.

She was about to ring it a second time when she heard the sound of someone approaching the door from the other side. Konner swung it open and gave her a look of surprise. Having missed being in his arms, Alexis rushed him. He caught her to him as he took a step back to balance them. She put her arms around his waist and clung to him.

"Alexis," he said. "What are you doing here? I thought you had to stay with your parents."

She pulled back enough to smile as she looked him in the face. "My mom kicked me out of the house and I'm not allowed to come back until tomorrow. I was told I would have to spend the night with you."

Konner's grin was sexy, and his heated gaze roamed over her features. "Did she now? Well, I'll have to thank her when I see her again. And having you spend the night has just made my day."

He lowered his lips to hers, taking them as if he'd been dying for a taste of her and wouldn't last another minute without it. She kissed him back with just as much desperation. Alexis pressed even closer to Konner and moaned when she felt the hard length of his cock against her belly. An ache built inside her pussy. It had only been two days, but her body desperately craved his. Her nipples grew taut where they brushed along his hard chest.

"I don't think I can wait another minute to have you inside me," Alexis said against his mouth.

"These two days without you have been hell," Konner replied in a husky voice.

He picked her off her feet, carried her to the stairs that led to the upper floor, and took them two at a time. Even though Alexis hadn't been to this part of his house before, she didn't stop kissing him to look around. All that mattered was Konner getting to his bedroom.

Alexis dropped her athletic bag and purse to the floor

once he had them inside his room. He let her slide down his body until her feet touched the carpet. She quickly toed off her shoes and kicked each one away. She put her hands under the back of Konner's T-shirt and shoved them as high as she could reach before she ran her nails down his skin. He groaned, his kiss becoming more erotic, his tongue sweeping inside her mouth to duel with her own.

"Clothes off," Konner said with a groan that was mixed in with an animalistic growl once he'd released her lips. "I have to have you naked against me."

"Yes," she said in return. "God, yes."

They only broke apart long enough to help each other frantically strip out of their clothes. Once they stood naked facing each other, Konner pulled her against him and once more devoured her mouth. Alexis whimpered with need. Wetness leaked from her pussy and onto her inner thighs. She wasn't going to feel complete until she had his long, thick cock buried deep inside her, taking her in hard thrusts.

Alexis reached between them and wrapped her hand around Konner's erection. It jerked in her grip as she pumped it up and down. He made that animal-like growl again, which had her libido skyrocketing. She squeezed his cock harder and stroked him faster.

Konner soon pulled her hand off him and walked her backward toward the bed. He lifted her onto it and followed her down. He didn't settle between her spread legs and thrust into her as she wanted. Instead, he lay half on and half off her and shifted lower until he was level with her breasts.

He supported his upper body on one bent arm as he sucked a nipple into his mouth. Konner gently bit it before he sucked it once more. Alexis grew wetter, her need for him growing stronger with each passing minute. She shifted under him, lifting her hips in invitation.

"Konner, please," she begged.

He gave her other breast the same attention before he shifted until his body covered hers with his hips wedged between her thighs. Konner pushed the head of his cock into her slick pussy, sinking deeper with each thrust until he was balls-deep. Alexis clutched his shoulders as he slid in and out of her. Pleasure exploded along all her nerve endings, and she whimpered, getting caught up in the sensations.

Konner's cock grew harder, stretching her, making her pant. She squeezed her inner muscles around it, increasing what she felt. The way her body coiled tighter, it wasn't going to take much to have her coming. He pumped his hips faster, harder.

Lost in the moment, on the verge of what she was sure would be an intense orgasm, Alexis cried out, "I love you, Konner. Don't ever leave me."

He growled that animal-like growl he did and buried his face in the crook of her neck. She felt the drag of a sharp tooth where her shoulder and neck met just before Konner bit her there — hard. It didn't hurt. If anything, it gave her a jolt of pleasure that threw her into an orgasm that seemed never to end. As he continued to piston between her legs, he held on to her with his teeth. Alexis felt as if something snapped into place, like some kind of invisible bond. Her feelings for him already strong, seemed to solidify even more.

Konner pulled his teeth away, then lifted his upper body off her, holding his weight on his hands. As he continued to thrust, his gaze drifted to her neck where he'd bitten her. He let out a groan of male satisfaction.

"I love you too," he said on a moan. He moaned even louder as he pushed inside her pussy one final time, his cock pulsing as he came.

He collapsed on top of her, and Alexis wrapped her arms around his back to keep him there. With her emotions running high, she didn't want to let him go.

MARISA CHENERY

She'd blurted how she felt about Konner. She'd taken a big risk, but at least he returned her feelings. He loved her too. Feeling as if all her bones had turned to jelly, she held her lover close and waited for her body to settle.

*

Konner knew he had to be too heavy for Alexis, but her grip told him he was exactly where she wanted him. Not that he minded. He didn't think he could move very far even if he wanted to. What he'd done had left him a bit shaky. He'd bitten her, made her his mate, and tied their life forces together. She was now as immortal as he. The deep bite mark his fangs had left behind had healed within seconds with no trace of it ever marring her soft skin.

He'd promised Anubis he would give Alexis the choice to accept him as her mate after Konner told her what he was, but he'd lost control of himself. Hearing her say she loved him, and that she didn't want him to ever leave her, had pushed him over the fine line he'd walked. He'd acted on the deep feelings he had for her and didn't think of the consequences. He just wanted her as his. The sensation of the bond forming between them had felt so right.

Konner kissed the spot where he'd bitten Alexis. He'd have to tell her about his being a warrior of Anubis and that they were now mated, but he'd wait until he took her out for her birthday meal this coming weekend. It would give him some more days of having her think he was nothing more than a normal man she'd come to love. Hopefully, that wouldn't change once he told her the truth.

#

Alexis had to bite the inside of her cheek to stop herself from laughing. If she gave in, she could offend Konner, and she didn't want to do that since he tried so hard.

He looked at her. "You're laughing at me, aren't you?"

She shook her head. "No, really I'm not."

"Yes, you are. I can see it in your eyes."

A small giggle escaped Alexis before she could hold it back. The way Konner looked at her with a combination of frustration and exasperation she couldn't help it. They sat on his bed, after making love twice more, as she tried to teach him how to use the new laptop he'd bought the other day. The router had already been set up when he'd had one of the service guys from his Internet provider come in and do it for him so getting WiFi wasn't the problem.

No, the problem wasn't the Internet. It was Konner. She had already showed him twice how to get into his email and how to send one, but it just didn't seem to click. And watching him type painfully slow with one finger, it made her want to push him aside and do it for him.

"Fuck, I did it again," Konner said with a growl. "Why do I keep clicking on the wrong things? And this built-in mouse pad is driving me up the goddamn wall. The arrow wants to shoot off on its own or I can't get it where I want it."

"You just need to practice, and you'll get used to it. If you can't, we'll just have to get you a wireless mouse to use instead." She undid what he'd done. "Try again," Alexis said.

"I think I'm too fricking old to learn this."

She didn't hold back the laughter this time. "Come on. You sound like an old grandpa who grew up before computers were invented. You're what? Twenty-eight? Twenty-nine? I hardly think that qualifies you for a senior-citizen discount."

Konner gave her a look she couldn't read before he let out a sigh. "I'm serious. I doubt I'm going to be able to learn this."

"Nonsense. You're an expert when it comes to gaming systems. You should be able to handle this." She took the laptop off Konner's lap and put it on hers, then shifted so he could only see the back of the screen. "Here, I'll give you an incentive to learn."

Alexis signed into her web-based email and typed up a message for Konner. The few sentences were highly erotic. She hit send and looked up to find him staring at her. She clicked to his home page before she handed him back the laptop.

"You took me out of my email," Konner said as he gave her a look that said he wasn't too happy about it.

"Yes, I did. You need to get used to going into it yourself. Now go read what I sent you."

After a few choice swear words when he couldn't get the mouse to cooperate, Konner finally was once again in his inbox. Alexis watched as he clicked open her email. His gaze quickly moved back and forth over the screen. Once he finished reading, he put a hand on the back of her neck and pulled her closer until their lips met. He gave her a kiss that took her breath away.

After he broke contact with her, Konner said, "All right, you convinced me. I'll practice until I can do this with my eyes closed. I definitely don't want to miss out on any emails like the one you just sent me."

Alexis smiled. "I thought you'd think that way."

The rest of the day pretty much went by with computer lessons, cooking food together, and another bout of lovemaking. Alexis couldn't have been happier. The longer she spent with Konner, the more right he seemed for her. And she couldn't find anything about him that would cause her to think she'd made a mistake by rushing into a serious relationship with him.

Now that it had grown dark, Konner stood at the door about to leave for work. Alexis stood with him and gave him a kiss and a hug before he left. She'd miss him, but at least he'd join her in his bed once he came home.

"Are you sure you're okay with me leaving you here alone?" Konner asked.

"Of course I am. Since you have a laptop and Internet now, I'll work on some of my web design projects I have going. I use an online backup site so I can access any files I need from there."

"Okay. I have my cell with me, but if I'm caught up in something, I might not be able to answer right away."

"I'll be fine, Konner. Go. And I'll be in bed when you get back."

He gave her one last kiss, then walked out the door. After she turned the deadbolt, Alexis headed upstairs to get the laptop where they'd left it in Konner's bedroom. Having decided she'd work in the living room with the TV on, she went to that room and made herself comfortable on the couch.

Alexis launched the browser and typed in the website address for the online storage site she used. She opened one of the files she wanted to work on. She went to minimize the browser, then jerked when it went to another website on its own. Alexis hit the back button to return to the website she'd been at. Two seconds later, it changed once again to the other page.

Afraid Konner's brand-new laptop had somehow picked up something it shouldn't have, she closely looked at the page. It didn't appear to be something that would cause a virus. Her brows drew together once she started to read. It was about the Egyptian god Anubis and a group of men he'd chosen to be his immortal warriors to help protect mortals from evildoers. It went on to say each man had been at the point of death on a battlefield and had called out to be saved. And that the god of the Egyptian underworld had done so after they'd given their vow to serve as one of his warriors for all eternity.

Alexis shook her head. Even though it was written as if it was fact, she doubted it was. It had to be a legend or myth from ancient Egypt. Her opinion didn't change about that as she read further and saw that the warriors of Anubis all shape-shifted into a half-human and half-jackal form while in the presence of evil. And while in that form, they could snare an evildoer's gaze, push into his or her mind, and see all the evil their prey had done, experiencing it as if it had happened to them. She pulled the laptop closer to look at what appeared to be a hand-drawn picture of what the warrior would look like shifted. The creature even wore an ancient Egyptian-styled kilt and gold armbands around large, furry biceps.

She looked at the bottom of the page to see who might be the designer or author of it, but there weren't any names. Alexis shook her head. She never knew what she'd find on the Internet.

Alexis minimized the window and clicked to open the

antivirus program to run it just in case there was a virus. Once it started scanning, she opened the window again. Now she really didn't know what to think. The page was gone. Literally. Just a blank page with nothing on it. She refreshed it a couple of times and it came up with the same result.

She'd never seen a computer act like that. And she'd never heard of a virus that would take someone to a page about an ancient Egyptian myth. She couldn't see what a hacker would be trying to do with it either.

Pushing thoughts of the weird website aside, Alexis got down to the business of doing some work. That didn't last very long, though. She found herself fidgeting, her thoughts drifting from what she was doing and straying to what she'd read on the strange page. It eventually got so bad she decided to get up for some water, hoping that would help her to once again find her focus.

Alexis left the living room and went to head to the kitchen but found herself stopping in front of a closed door. She reached for the doorknob as an overwhelming urge to go inside that particular room washed over her. It was so strong, she'd opened the door before she could even guess at what was on the other side or decide if Konner would mind if she did go in there.

A quiet gasp escaped her once she walked into what would have been a den, but it wasn't. Her gaze took in all the statues, big and small, paintings, and carvings that depicted the Egyptian god Anubis. Some of them portrayed him as having the body of a human and the head of a jackal, much like the creature she'd seen on the website. It clicked in that it matched the tattoo of Anubis that Konner had on his chest. This had to be the weirdest coincidence. A small voice inside her mind asked if it really was one.

Alexis shook her head and told it to shut up. It had to be. There was no other explanation. It wasn't as if Konner was one of Anubis' warriors. Now that would be plain ridiculous, considering the story she read about them was just that, a story.

Looking around the room, she noticed at one end there was what appeared to be an altar. There was a plate with some slices of bread on it and a small glass that held some kind of amber liquid. Konner had to have put those items on it, but for the life of her, Alexis didn't know why. Obviously, he was into the god of the underworld. She gazed around the room again. *Really* into Anubis. She guessed there wasn't anything wrong with it, though it might seem a little strange to her. As she'd thought before, it had to be a huge coincidence that he had a room dedicated to Anubis and she'd been taken to a page about the god's warriors.

Deciding she'd already invaded enough of Konner's privacy for one night, Alexis turned, walked out of the room, and shut the door firmly behind her. She wouldn't be telling him about finding his little collection. If he wanted to tell her about it, that was fine. She didn't need him to think she snooped through his whole house while he was away at work.

Alexis went to the kitchen, grabbed a bottle of water out of the fridge, and returned to the living room, determined to get some work done herself. In a few hours, she'd call it a night and climb into her lover's bed to hopefully be awakened in the most erotic of ways when he returned home.

* * * *

After the night Alexis had slept over, Konner had seen her only once before the Saturday he planned on taking her out for her birthday. He'd gone to her place and had dinner with her and her parents the other day. He'd stayed until he had to leave to hunt evildoers. He and Alexis didn't have any time alone, and making love had been out of the question, but he'd enjoyed his visit. Claudia and Drew had seemed to take to him as much as he'd taken to them.

Konner still hadn't told Alexis anything about what he was or about him claiming her. So far, she hadn't noticed any changes in her, but it wouldn't stay that way the first time she hurt herself in any way. The speed with which she'd heal would be a dead giveaway that something had changed.

Now it was Saturday in the early evening and he was on his way to pick Alexis up for their date. He'd decided to take the night off from hunting, to devote it entirely to his mate. At some point during it, he'd tell her everything. Konner still had no idea how she would react to it all. They loved each other. He hoped it would be enough to help her accept it. And she had to since he couldn't undo his making her his mate and tying her life force to his.

He hadn't told Alexis where he was taking her, only that she should get dressed up. Konner had picked a fancy, and he hoped romantic, restaurant. After they had their meal, he'd take her to his place and make love to her before he let the cat out of the bag.

Arriving at Alexis' house, Konner pulled into the driveway and parked in front of the garage. He got out of the car and gave the sleeves of his sport jacket a tug. He'd gone out and bought it along with a pair of slacks, dress shirt, dress shoes, and a tie. He hadn't had to dress up like this since he'd been a mortal.

Konner rang the doorbell. Claudia opened the door and waved him inside. "Don't you look nice," she said as she closed it behind him.

"Thanks. Is Alexis ready?"

"Just about. You must be taking her someplace fancy."

"Well, this outing is for her birthday."

"Quit bugging Konner, Mom," Alexis said with a smile

as she came to stand at the end of the hallway that led to the bedrooms.

"I'm not," Claudia said in return. "I just asked him if he was taking you to a fancy restaurant since the pair of you are all dressed up."

"I was only joking. Tell Dad I said goodbye, and Mom, don't expect me back tonight."

Alexis' mother laughed. "I figured that much out on my own. Enjoy your meal."

Konner took Alexis' hand and threaded his fingers with hers before he guided her out the door and then into his car. Once they were closed inside, he leaned across the seat and kissed her, letting out some of his hunger for her.

After he pulled away, Alexis said, "Mmm, that was good. I've missed your kiss" — she gave a pointed look at his crotch — "along with other things."

He shook his head and grinned. "Enough of that now. We're going out to eat. I've had this planned for days, and we're going to stick with it."

Alexis gave him a playful smile. "All right. I promise to behave since this is for my birthday and all. I guess I can wait a little longer for my present."

"Who says I'm giving you your present tonight? The actual day of your birthday isn't until four days from now."

She placed her hand on his thigh and stroked her fingers up it, not stopping until she reached his cock. It twitched as she gave it a tug through his pants

"Oh, I think I'll get one of my presents tonight."

Konner took her hand off him and placed it on her lap. "No more of that or I'll be walking around embarrassing myself."

He put the key into the ignition and started the engine. He backed out onto the street and then drove in the direction of the restaurant. Konner glanced at Alexis before he focused back on the road.

"You look gorgeous, by the way," he said. "I should have told you that before we left." Alexis wore a light cotton skirt that fell to the middle of her thighs and matching blouse. On her feet were high-heeled sandals.

"Thanks. You clean up pretty good yourself. So, where are you taking me?"

"I have reservations at the Everest."

"French food. You really are going all out."

"Well, you'll be proud of me. I did a search online for a list of Chicago's most romantic restaurants and the Everest was on it."

"Way to go, Konner. You'll be an old hand at the Internet in no time."

He chuckled. "I doubt that. I am ashamed to say it took me three tries and a half hour just to find it."

"At least you did it."

Having reached their destination, Konner parked the car in a parking lot not too far from the building of the Chicago Stock Exchange where the restaurant was located on the fortieth floor. The Everest had complimentary valet parking in their underground garage, but he didn't want to use it. He didn't like the idea of someone he didn't know driving his car.

He took Alexis' hand once he helped her out of the car. "You don't mind the little walk to the restaurant, do you?"

"No, it's okay. It's not that far."

"Good. I prefer to park where I can do it myself."

"If I had a car as expensive as yours, I'd probably feel the same way."

After the elevator ride up to the fortieth floor, the hostess seated them at a table near a window that had a spectacular view of Chicago. The food was delicious, and Konner made a mental note to bring Alexis there again sometime since she enjoyed it so much.

As they finished their meal, Konner lifted the bottle of wine he'd ordered with the food and held it over Alexis' glass to fill. She quickly placed her hand over the top to stop him before he could pour any of the liquid.

"That's enough for me," she said. "I don't need to be feeling it."

"No more wine for both of us then. If you're done, I'll pay the bill."

Konner knew for a fact Alexis wouldn't have to worry about getting drunk ever again. Being as immortal as he, she'd be able to drink and eat however much she wanted and not have it affect her in any way.

"I'm done," she said with a smile. "Thanks for taking me. It was a really nice meal."

Once the waitress brought their bill and he paid it, Konner guided Alexis to the elevator, already looking forward to getting her to his place and having her all to himself.

Alexis walked at Konner's side as they headed for the parking lot where he'd left his car. The meal had been perfect. She'd never eaten in such a fancy restaurant before and had thoroughly enjoyed it.

When they arrived at the lot, there were only a couple of other cars there along with Konner's. It was also a bit on the dark side since one of the lights had burned out. It didn't bother Alexis. With him at her side, she really didn't think she'd have to worry about anything. He was a big enough presence to scare any would-be muggers off, but that didn't look as if it would be a problem. No one else was there, except them.

Just as they neared his car, Konner jerked to a stop and let out a moan of pain. Alexis turned to ask him what was wrong but found herself unable to form the words as she watched with horror as his body began to change shape. The sound of his bones shifting and realigning was loud. Her eyes widened as he grew taller, standing at almost seven feet, his body heavier with muscle. At the end, he was the creature she'd seen in the picture on that website about the warriors of Anubis, right down to the jackal's head, black fur, kilt, and armbands.

Alexis wanted to scream when he turned his gaze on her, but her throat had gone so dry she wasn't even capable of that. She stumbled back, not wanting to be close to him.

Konner reached for her but jerked around at the sound of male laughter coming from nearby. "Demon," he said in a voice that was deeper and gravelly compared to his normal one.

A man stepped out of the shadows. His glowing red eyes gave it away that he couldn't be human. She tried to sidestep away in the hopes that she could make a getaway, but Konner backed up until she was directly behind him. Each step she took, he matched to keep even with her.

"Who is that you're trying to keep from me, warrior of Anubis?" the man, demon, asked as he sauntered closer.

"Keep away from her," Konner said on a growl.

The demon cocked his head to the side to peer at her. "It looks as if she's scared of you. She mustn't like the form your god has you shift into whenever you're around evil. That's too bad since my spell is going to keep you like this until morning."

The demon shifted a little closer, angling himself so Alexis had a better view of him. The smile he gave her and the way he looked at her gave her the chills. A sense of wrongness seemed to roll off him in waves.

Never so scared in her life, she reached inside her purse and wrapped her hands around the one thing that might give her a chance to escape the thing Konner had turned into and the demon—a small can of pepper spray. Sabrina had given it to Alexis for Christmas. At the time, she'd laughed at the gift, but now she was thankful her friend was so paranoid all the time and had convinced her to keep it in her purse.

The opportunity to use it came seconds later. The demon disappeared, then reappeared right next to her. Konner let out a growl and turned, but that didn't stop Alexis from pulling out the pepper spray and spraying it directly into the demon's eyes. He bellowed as he wiped at them. He disappeared again. She frantically searched for him as she kept the can held out at the ready.

"I don't think he's coming back," Konner said. "The pepper spray took care of him for now."

Alexis didn't give herself time to think. She turned, took aim, and sprayed Konner in his jackal's eyes. He bellowed a lot like the demon had, but she wasn't about to stick around. Shoving the spray back into her purse, she took off at a run, not once looking back to see if he followed her.

* * * *

Konner couldn't see and found it hard to breathe. He coughed as his nose ran. Alexis had actually sprayed him with pepper spray. And now he was in agony. Basically blinded since his eyes had immediately swollen shut after getting hit, he felt his way to the car. He tried to open the door, but then remembered he'd dropped his keys just as the shift had torn through him. Returning to the spot where he thought they'd be, he felt around on the ground until he found them. One push of a button and he had the car unlocked.

Inside, he felt a little more protected then being out in the open. Stuck in his half-human and half-jackal form, he didn't need any mortals to see him like that. He wanted to leave, but until he could see again, that wasn't going to be possible.

Luckily for him, his immortality took care of the pepper spray. It only was a matter of minutes rather than the thirty to forty-five minutes a mortal would have to suffer through during the full effect.

Once his vision was clear enough, Konner drove out of the parking lot and headed for home. He took the less-busy streets, which added time to his trip, but he didn't need to be seen by too many mortals looking as he did. His thoughts turned to Alexis. Was she safe? Would she make it home by herself all right? All he could feel was the dread that this would doom their budding relationship.

At his house, Konner went straight to Anubis' temple and called for the god. "Anubis."

Yes, Konner.

"The demon finally made his move. He used the spell you told me about. I'm stuck in my other form."

Did he appear before you?

"Yes, but he didn't stick around long enough for me to send him to you. I think he would have tried to take me out right then, but he had a weapon used on him that I doubt he was expecting."

What happened?

"Alexis hit him with pepper spray." Konner paused. "Then she turned it on me."

Where is she now?

"She's more than likely back at her place. She ran from me. I hadn't had a chance to tell her what I was before the demon used the spell." He cleared his throat. "It's too late to give her the choice, anyway. I lost control of myself and couldn't fight the urge anymore."

Anubis sighed. *It is all right, Konner. I had hoped Alexis would have reacted better at seeing you in this form.*

"Why would you think that? She didn't know what I was."

The other night when she slept over, I took what I thought were steps to help ease her into your world. When she was working on your laptop, I had it go to a page she thought was on the Internet. It gave her plenty of information about my warriors. I even included a sketch of what you look like shifted. After she read that, I drew her to this room. I had hoped she would sort of put everything together and guess on her own what you were, but it obviously did not work like that.

"No, it didn't. She was scared shitless of me. Thus, the pepper spray in the face."

She will come to accept you. The other warriors who have found their mates went through this and did not lose the ones meant for them. Alexis will come around.

"I hope so. For now, I'm stuck at home until I shift back. I wish I had Alexis here. The thought of the demon finding her while I'm not there to protect her haunts me."

Go to her tomorrow. She should be okay for tonight. I do not think the demon will be back that soon, especially after the pepper spray. By morning you will be back in your human form and you can go after your mate.

Konner felt Anubis' presence fade. He looked down at himself, and for the first time, wished he had the ability to shift at will, to undo whatever spell the demon had used. The look of fear on Alexis' face as she'd stared at him in this form would be something he wouldn't be able to forget.

* * * *

Alexis had managed to find a taxi not too far from the restaurant to bring her home. Once she'd arrived, she had ignored the questions her mother and father had asked as to why she'd come back so early. Even when her mom had come to knock on Alexis' bedroom door, she ignored her.

She'd gotten undressed and then put on her pajamas before she'd climbed into bed and curled up into a ball. There she stayed until morning, not able to sleep. Her mind kept replaying Konner shifting into that creature. Along with it, all the information she'd read on that website worked its way in with it. What she thought was just a myth, wasn't. The demon had called Konner a warrior of Anubis, but it couldn't be.

Once dawn lightened the sky, Alexis dragged her

aching body out of bed. Her head pounded from lack of sleep and her muscles protested as she uncurled from her cramped position.

She stretched, then sat on her bed, staring at nothing for the next couple of hours, feeling numb. The need to read that web page took hold and had her rushing to the laptop she kept in her room. Once it booted up, she did a search for the website, but nothing came up. There was absolutely nothing on warriors of Anubis. It was if the page she'd seen that night had never existed.

Hearing her parents moving around, Alexis knew she couldn't stay locked inside her bedroom. Her mom would become too concerned, would demand to know what had happened last night. She couldn't tell her parents the truth. They wouldn't believe her.

After running a brush through her hair, she opened her bedroom door and headed for the kitchen. Her parents sat at the table quietly talking. They grew silent when they saw her.

Her mom stood and came to stand in front of Alexis. "Honey, is everything okay?"

Alexis shook her head. "Not really."

"Did you and Konner have a fight?"

"Sort of."

"I'm sorry to hear that, but if it isn't too serious, you both can still make your relationship work. You love him. Was it bad enough to say goodbye for good?"

Alexis wished she could tell her mom everything, but that wasn't going to happen. Did she still love Konner? During the night, she'd only thought of how scared she'd been of him, didn't remember what it was like before she'd seen him shift. If he really was a warrior of Anubis, then that ability to shift had always been there. And from what she'd read, he was supposed to be one of the good guys. Thinking he was a bounty hunter wasn't too far off from what he truly did each night.

"I'm not sure, Mom."

"Wait until you see him again, then you'll know."

Right at that moment, the doorbell rang. In Alexis' heart of hearts, she knew it was Konner. She didn't know if she was prepared to see him again, but she couldn't avoid him forever.

She hurried out of the kitchen and went to the front door. Alexis heard her parents following her. She unlocked the door and then pulled it open. Konner stood on the porch once again the handsome man she'd fallen in love with. Seeing him, she realized she did still love him.

"Hi, Alexis," he said. "Can I come in?"

She stepped back to allow him into the entranceway. "We need to talk," she told him.

He nodded. "Yes." His gaze skipped to her parents. "Alone."

"We'll go to our bedroom," her mom said.

Before her parents could walk away, the nightmare from last night returned. The demon appeared, and Konner shifted into his half-human and half-jackal form. Her mother screamed, and her father called out to Alexis. She couldn't get to them. She was stuck between a demon and one of Anubis' warriors.

Alexis found herself pushed to the floor by Konner as a sword appeared in the demon's hand. One appeared in Konner's, and then the fight was on. She felt helpless as she watched them do battle. With each blow, the demon managed to slip past Konner's guard, and she became more anxious for the man she loved. The thought of losing him scared her more than what he was.

She looked at her parents and saw her father wasn't about to stand around and do nothing. He must have gone into the closet where he'd put a baseball bat just in case someone ever tried to break in while they were home. With his hand wrapped around it, he worked his way closer until he stood behind the demon. Lifting the bat, he swung, braining the creature.

The demon staggered from the blow, which gave Konner the chance he needed. He rammed the hilt of his sword into the demon's jaw. The creature dropped his weapon as he shook his head. Konner grabbed him by the throat as his sword disappeared to be replaced by a black-bladed dagger. He used it to slice it across the demon's chest. The creature bellowed with rage as he slowly lost substance before disappearing.

"Is he gone for good?" she asked Konner.

He nodded as he fought to catch his breath. "The dagger sent him to the underworld and Anubis who will judge him." He closed the distance between them while still giving her some space and met her gaze with his jackal one. "Are you okay with this, Alexis? This was not how I wanted you to find out."

"Alexis? Is that really Konner?" her mother asked in tears.

Konner walked to her parents, he looked them each in the eyes, and they seemed to fall into some kind of trance.

She went to stand at his side. "What did you do?"

He looked at her. "I put them in a trance. I have to wipe their memory of what happened here. That's why I haven't shifted back yet."

"Do you have to?"

"Anubis decrees that no mortal should know of his warriors."

"What about me? I'm mortal, and you aren't going to wipe my memory. Are you?"

He cupped her face. "No. And you're no longer mortal. You're immortal and my mate, Alexis. That night I bit you, I tied our life forces together."

She looked from Konner to her parents and back to him again. "If I'm immortal, that means I won't age. And if my parents can't know, I'm going to have to give them up at some point."

"Can you handle that? What's done can't be undone. You're mine and will always be."

"I don't know. Everything is happening so fast."

Konner had her mom and dad look him in the eyes. Once he was done, he shifted back to his human form. Her parents stayed where they were, looking at nothing.

"Are they going to be okay?" she asked with concern.

"Yes. I planted a new memory of you having stayed the night at my place and that I've brought you home. Once you're in the shower, they'll snap out of the trance and act as if nothing has happened."

Alexis crossed her arms and took a step back. "Okay."

Konner gave her a questioning look. "Alexis? Are you going to be all right with us?"

She shook her head. "To be honest, I'm not sure. This is so out of the realm of what I would call normal. I don't know if I can handle this." He took a step to close the distance between them, but she held up her hand to stop him. "Konner, don't. I just want you to go right now."

"Maybe if we talked about it."

"No. I can't. Please go."

He gave her a silent nod, turned on his heel, and walked out the front door. Alexis brushed away the single tear that fell as she thought that all her hopes and dreams of a life with him walked out the door with Konner.

* * * *

Two days passed after the episode with the demon, and Alexis was sure her parents thought she'd lost her mind. Every time they brought up the subject of Konner and asked why he hadn't been around, she just about lost it. She had to run to her bedroom to hide the tears that fell. It wasn't as if she could talk to her parents about him. They had absolutely no memory of the demon, or even of Alexis coming home upset that night she'd seen Konner shift for the first time.

No, Alexis was left all alone with her memories and what she had become. She *was* as immortal as Konner had said. She'd tested it out by cutting herself with one of the kitchen knives when her parents had gone shopping. The wound had healed within seconds as if it had never been, which meant she truly was his mate.

The big question was if she could handle him being one of Anubis' warriors. His vow was for eternity so it wasn't as if he could just up and quit like a regular job. She loved him. That hadn't changed. She just had to decide if she loved him enough to give up her parents and everyone else in her life when the time came and she could no longer hide that she wasn't aging.

Once again alone, sitting at her computer, trying to work, Alexis found herself going through the same internal arguments about Konner. This time she really forced herself to think what her life would be like without him. And that she'd live forever alone. There would be no one else to take his place.

That's when it hit her that she couldn't live that way. The thought of never seeing Konner again made her heart skip a beat. He was the only man she could picture herself living her immortal life with. The future looked bleak without him.

Wiping away what she hoped would be the last tears shed over Konner, Alexis stood and walked out of the house with a determined stride. She had to get her man back and do some apologizing while she was at it.

* * * *

Konner was in a worse funk than before he'd met Alexis. He missed her so much he hurt. He roamed his house and Chicago's streets at night like a lost soul. Video games and hunting evildoers wasn't enough to distract him from his heartache.

He'd lost the one woman meant for him—his mate. Even though he wanted nothing more than to go to her house and demand she take him back, he wouldn't do it. She was the one who would make the decision if they were to stay together or not. He'd already taken away one choice from her. He wouldn't do it a second time.

Needing to talk to somebody, Konner headed for his temple dedicated to Anubis. He hadn't spoken to the god in a few days. He just made his offerings, then left to wallow in his misery.

"Anubis."

I am here, Konner.

"I thought I'd check to see if I'd have to worry about any more demons popping up when I least expect them."

That will no longer be a problem. The demon you sent to me was the last who had escaped from the underworld. You and the rest of my warriors will not be bothered by them again.

"Good."

Have you gone to your mate?

"No. I don't think she wants anything to do with me."

Do not give up on her yet, Konner. She will come around. She loves you, as you love her. It was meant to be. She just needs time to realize that.

"I know Alexis loves me, at least I hope she still does, but I don't think that's going to be enough."

Have faith. She will return to you.

"I'd like to, but—"

The doorbell rang right then and kept ringing as if someone wanted to set a world record on the number of times they could press it.

Feeling Anubis' presence leave, Konner rushed to the front door with a scowl. If it turned out to be a kid playing a joke, he'd give him a stern talking to. He yanked open the door before he let out an *oomph* as the last person he expected to find threw herself into his arms.

Konner barely had enough time to step back and slam

the door closed before Alexis pulled down his head and kissed him, seeming to tell him how much she couldn't live without him in between kisses.

Happy to have her in his arms again, he kissed her back with all the longing that had built inside him for the last two days. He cradled her close and ran up the stairs with her to his bedroom.

Clothes went flying every which way as they struggled to get each other naked. Once they were, Konner picked Alexis up again and placed her on the middle of his bed. He followed her down, touching and kissing her soft skin. He cupped her breasts and sucked on each nipple until he had her gasping and squirming beneath him. Wanting to make sure she was ready for him, he caressed a hand down to her pussy and stroked her there. She was wet. He easily pushed one finger and then a second inside her, pumping them in and out.

Alexis reached between them and fisted his cock. "No more foreplay, Konner. I have to have you inside me. Now."

"There's no place I'd rather be," he said on a groan as Alexis slid her hand up and down his shaft.

He pulled his fingers out of her welcoming body and shifted into position. With a few strokes, he sank to the hilt. Being inside his mate again, he knew this wouldn't be a long joining. He wanted her too much. In and out he plunged. Alexis lifted her hips to match each of his strokes, her keening moans loud in his ears, pushing him closer and closer to release.

Alexis' pussy clutched his cock as she climaxed, squeezing him in a tight fist. Konner groaned, thrust into her one final time, then stiffened above her as an intense orgasm tore through him. After it was over, he rolled to his back, taking her with him. She lay on top of him, breathing as heavily as he.

"I'm sorry I pepper sprayed you and sent you away,"

Alexis said once she'd caught her breath.

He chuckled. "I'm sorry I scared you enough that you felt as if you had to do it." Konner locked his gaze on to hers. "All that matters now is that you're here. I do love you, my mate."

"I love you too. I'm going to need some time to adjust to this new world you've brought me into, but in the end, I'll have a warrior to love."

Konner kissed her and poured all the love he had for her into it.

Once he pulled away, she asked, "When did you become a warrior of Anubis?"

"It was during the First World War. I was part of the Australian and New Zealand troops and was wounded at Gallipoli and near death when Anubis answered my call."

She smiled. "I guess you really did grow up before computers were invented, after all."

"I told you I was too old to learn."

With one last kiss, Alexis smiled. "I still have a ton of questions to ask you, my warrior, but they can wait. I now have an eternity to have them answered and a bright future with you at my side."

The End

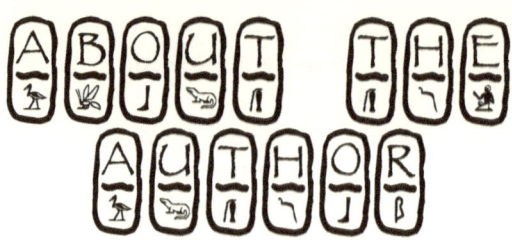

ABOUT THE AUTHOR

Marisa Chenery was always a lover of books, but after reading her first historical romance novel she found herself hooked. Having inherited a love for the written word, she soon started writing her own novels.

She now writes young adult books and erotic romances.

Marisa lives in Ontario, Canada, with her boyfriend, Steve, four children, four grandchildren (she's a young grandma in her fifties) and rabbit and dog.

www.marisachenery.com

www.ingramcontent.com/pod-product-compliance
Lightning Source LLC
Chambersburg PA
CBHW031133260626
47153CB00021B/152